# EMERALD CITY BLUES

I0891655

WESTERN LITERATURE AND FICTION SERIES

Like the iconic physical landscape and diverse cultures that inspire it, the literature of the American West is imbued with power and beauty. The Western Literature and Fiction Series invites scholarship reflecting on the authors and works that define the creative expression of the past and present while championing the literary fiction that propels us forward.

*The Ghost Dancers*
Adrian C. Louis

*This Here Is Devil's Work*
Curtis Bradley Vickers

*The Desert between Us*
Phyllis Barber

*The Saints of Rattlesnake Mountain*
Don Waters

*The Gambler's Apprentice*
H. Lee Barnes

*The Goodbye House*
Lawrence Coates

*Cold Deck*
H. Lee Barnes

*Minimal Damage*
H. Lee Barnes

*Dream City*
Douglas Unger

*Emerald City Blues*
H. Lee Barnes

# Emerald City Blues

*A Novel*

H. LEE BARNES

UNIVERSITY OF NEVADA PRESS | *Reno & Las Vegas*

University of Nevada Press | Reno, Nevada 89557 USA
www.unpress.nevada.edu
Copyright © 2025 by H. Lee Barnes
All rights reserved

Manufactured in the United States of America

First Printing

Cover design by Louise OFarrell
Cover photographs: *Overlooking Hollywood at Night, Hollywood, California*, Tichnor Brothers, publisher, public domain, Wikimedia Commons; "Lunchtime at the Vega aircraft Plant, Burbank, Calif. A quartet of girl workers," War and Conflict number 818, Charles Fenno Jacobs, public domain, Wikimedia Commons.

Library of Congress Cataloging-in-Publication Data
Names: Barnes, H. Lee, 1944– author.
Title: Emerald City blues : a novel / H. Lee Barnes.
Description: Reno : University of Nevada Press, 2025. | Series: Western literature and fiction series | Summary: "Set against the vibrant yet turbulent backdrop of World War II–era California, Emerald City Blues is a heartfelt coming-of-age story. It explores the complexities of love, the power of friendship, and the courage it takes to forge your own path in an uncertain world"—Provided by publisher.
Identifiers: LCCN 2025005660 | ISBN 9781647792206 (cloth) | ISBN 9781647792138 (paperback) | ISBN 9781647792145 (ebook)
Subjects: LCGFT: Bildungsromans. | Novels.
Classification: LCC PS3552.A673854 E44 2025 | DDC 813/.54—dc23/eng/20250307
LC record available at https://lccn.loc.gov/2025005660
N: 9781647792206 (cloth)

The paper used in this book meets the requirements of American National Standard for Information Sciences—Permanence of Paper for Printed Library Materials, ANSI/NISO Z39.48-1992 (R2002).

*To Margaret Dalrymple, editor and friend*

# ACKNOWLEDGMENTS

I would like to express my thanks and appreciation to JoAnne Banducci, director of the University of Nevada Press; Curtis Vickers, its editor; and the support staff at the Press for their efforts on behalf of this novel. I would be remiss if I did not mention my friend Mary Sojourner whose words of encouragement, "I believe her," helped give impetus to my writing the novel. I owe my gratitude as well to Tina Eliopulos, my friend and colleague at the College of Southern Nevada, whose close reading and astute advice were both helpful and encouraging. I will add that this book would not exist as it now does without the efforts of those who have preserved the historical sites in San Pedro, California, where men and women workers contributed such a praiseworthy role in our nation's defeating a fierce and determined enemy. I hope we will forever celebrate "The Greatest Generation."

# EMERALD CITY BLUES

# -1-

When the first flock of geese darkened the autumn sky, I set my bucket beside the pump and watched them fly over our patch of the rolling land called the Palouse. I watched their flight until the sky was silent and they were but a memory on the horizon. I filled the bucket with water and trudged over the near-frozen dark loam to the back door of the house my father built. I lingered at the back step, my hand on the knob, and studied the land to the northwest. A bank of listless clouds, a harbinger of winter, lay upon the hilltops. I saw the clouds and migrating geese as signs. I thought again as I often had how we were at war, how I'd contributed nothing to the cause, and how I was young but wouldn't always be. I measured the torpor that had lately gripped my life and decided the time had come for me to find my worth in the larger world.

Over a three-month period I saved enough in tips from my waitress job to purchase a train ticket, pay for lodging for two weeks, and feed myself if I ate no more than one meal a day. The idea of leaving my childhood home was frightening. I'd never been farther away than Walla Walla and had only a vague notion of what life in the huge cities teeming with people, all of them strangers, might be like.

My assumptions of what that world offered were based

primarily on movies I'd seen at the theater in Pullman where film after film portrayed people in fine dress uncorking champagne or otherwise acting out their roles in a sensual Eden filled with romance and intrigue. Visions of that life fueled my imagination. However, the film that had most captured the child in me was Dorothy casting her gaze on the Emerald City for the first time. I wanted to grasp something as magical as Oz and embrace its hopeful message. I wanted rainbows and all that lay on the far side of them.

I took the bus to Pullman that afternoon and walked to the Oasis where I waited on tables that because of the war were more often than not empty. I pulled Avis, my best friend, aside. We went out into the alley where she could sneak a cigarette. She lit up and began talking about Randy, a boy we'd known since third grade.

"He's coming home from basic training and then he's off. . . ." She stopped and looked at me. "Are you okay?"

"I think I am." I swallowed hard and said, "I'm leaving, Avis."

She flicked an ash off her cigarette. "Oh, not that again."

She was skeptical because I'd told her numerous times, dating back to our freshman year in high school, that I was one day going to leave. "This time I'm serious."

"Sure. Is it because of Jess?"

I recoiled at the question. She knew better. Avis was who first told me about the lie circulating that I'd offered sex to Jess to get pregnant and force him to marry me. "You know what happened. He tried. I fought him off."

"I know. He wouldn't have tried anything if your brothers were here. He's a son-of-a-bitch anyhow and so's his rich dad. I'm sorry." She took a last drag off her cigarette and snuffed it out underfoot. "Let's go see if the lunch bunch has arrived."

At the end of the shift, I cornered her. "I'm dead serious.

I'm going. I'll be nineteen in a few days. Darn it, come with me. We'll go to Los Angeles. No snow. No cold."

She studied me for a moment. "Jesus, you sound serious, but. . . ."

"I am. Let's go together. You're my best friend. You'll miss me if you don't go."

"Eve, I can't go. And what'll you do there?"

"I don't know yet, but I'll find out."

She lowered her gaze. "It sounds a little crazy."

"If you don't want to go, will you at least drive me to the train depot in the morning?"

"Okay, I'll come by just in case."

That evening a nor'wester blew in. I came home from work and found Mother parked in her rocker near the iron stove, a shawl wrapped over her shoulders. A pot of water steamed on the burner. Wedged between the chair's arm and her hip was her Bible. At her ankles sat a bucket of peeled potatoes. I pulled up a chair beside her. Snowflakes swirled past the kitchen window and the walls of the house groaned as they did when the wind blew easterly.

I held my hands nearer the stove and gradually worked up the courage to tell her I'd be leaving in the morning. She stood, moved her bucket to the stove top, and began quartering potatoes.

"Mom," I said tentatively. "I'm leaving, going to Los Angeles."

Her gray eyes sat hard upon me for a moment. She nodded, then went on slicing potatoes and dropping them in the pan. The expression on her face spoke more than words. It said there was no need for explanation, and if there was, she had no desire to hear it. Whatever else sat between us went unsaid for the time being.

"Goodnight, Mom."

"Goodnight, Eve. I'll have breakfast for you."

Alone in my bedroom I looked out the window as snow drifts banked up on the dead bunchgrass along the fence line. I blew on the window, watched my breath condense on the glass, then wiped the window with my sleeve. In the dim light I could barely see the family burial plot on the hillside. It had four headstones, two of them honoring my father's parents, one mother's mother, none of whom I could remember. The fourth headstone was Judy's, the sister who'd held my hand and walked me into my class the first day of school.

I wouldn't be leaving my home so much as I'd be leaving the home as it was since my father left. The other home, the home where his six children grew up, where we once played and argued and gathered around the table to eat, the home where happiness once existed, was only a memory. Like Judy, my sister who'd shared this bedroom with me, that memory was dead. I wondered where my father was, and as I often did, why he'd never returned. Was he in some city having his own adventure? Did he think of us, the wife and children he'd abandoned?

"Your boys are off fighting. Do you care?" I whispered.

I wiped my sleeve across the fog on the window and turned my attention to packing up my effects—four blouses, two skirts, a Sunday dress, underwear, socks, robe, graduation picture, and a dual-bell alarm clock, the sole remnant of my father's being I claimed as mine. I laid out my clothes for the morning, then collapsed on my bed, pulled the quilt up under my chin, and enjoyed the first undisturbed sleep I'd had in days.

In the morning I dressed, slipped on my overcoat, and carried my slop bucket to the outhouse. After I dumped the waste down the hole, I set the bucket on the back steps and returned inside. Mother sat in the kitchen. A Bible lay on her lap. Her wrists resting on the table's edge, she stared at the iron stove. On the table to her right sat the bone china plates and polished flatware that perpetually awaited my father. The unused place setting served not only as a reminder of his absence, but also as a symbol of my mother's sad and misguided optimism.

I shed my coat and went upstairs for my belongings. When I returned, I laid my suitcase inside the kitchen door. Instead of looking up, she stared at the vacant chair reserved for Father.

"Mom, it's true I'm leaving. Look at me."

Her face a stoic mask, she said, "The boys left to fight. Helen didn't leave until she was married."

I took a seat across from her and looked at the plate she'd set for me. "I'm not Helen, Mom. I'm Eve. I'm not leaving because of you or anything you did."

Because pretense was safer than opening volumes of unspoken truths, she responded with a single nod, suggesting that the matter was closed.

We ate our fried potatoes and eggs in silence. When we finished, I gathered up the plates and rinsed them on the spigot outside, then brought them inside and placed them in the bucket of soapy water Mother had set on the stove. Mom had returned to her seat at the table.

She held up her Bible. "I looked for a passage to help me understand."

I crossed the room to her, leaned down, and kissed her cheek. "I love you, Mom. Please believe me. It's not because of you."

Her eyes opened wide for an instant, then she blinked. "You won't come back. You're like him." she said, meaning my father. "And Judith."

"Mom, Judy didn't leave. She died."

"It was God's punishment."

"Mom, it wasn't. She didn't see another choice."

"She killed a baby. It's a sin to do what she did."

"No, Mom. Don't think like that. It was because she went to a midwife who. . . . Mom, let's don't talk about it now."

She watched me slip my arms into the sleeves of the overcoat that once belonged to my dead sister. "That coat's too big for you."

"I know. I'm going now."

"I won't cry," she said.

I knew she wouldn't. Though I'd known for years it was there I'd never fully realized the sorrow that prowled our house. Now I was adding to it.

"You know where the wheat grows best," she said.

"Yes. Where the toe is planted."

I turned to reach for my suitcase, but the photos on the wall caught my eye, especially the one taken of us children the year my father left. There we were in black and white, six blue-eyed children that came from a mingling of Norse, Welsh, and Nez Perce blood, my brothers standing tall in the background, faces sunburned, their pale eyes flat as chalk, their grins daring the world. Clad in checkered dresses we'd sewn ourselves, Judith and I sat in the foreground, our eyes as pale as the boys', our smiles forced. Helen, the eldest at seventeen, kneeled beside us, her arms folded over her white apron, her drawn face and thin body bearing the signs of our meager diet.

I picked up my suitcase and crossed the floor, one more loved one leaving a sad woman to her sadness and her Bible. I slipped on my galoshes and mittens, stepped out into the morning, and looked at the bleak hills and obdurate sky. In the field adjacent to ours Mr. Woolighan's Guernsey stood belly deep in the fresh drifts. She stared at me as I slogged to the road through ankle-deep snow. I waited at the mailbox and faced the chilly wind. I needed to feel the cold to feed my resolve. I wasn't just leaving my home. I was leaving behind the Jess Newsome gossip that had plagued me over the last year and along with that—a long history of being poor.

A few minutes before 8:00 Avis wheeled her family's Dodge pickup around the bend and slowed to a stop. I hefted my suitcase onto the bed and climbed inside the warm cab.

"'Lo," she said. "We can go skatin' instead. You can borrow my sister's."

"Oh, I think I'll go." Though I smiled, I felt like I was accepting a sentence from a court.

"Hoo-kay then." She ground the gearshift into first. "Good."

The tires lost traction as we turned and became wedged in a frozen rut on the shoulder. I held my breath while Avis double-clutched the truck into reverse, then first, again and again until the truck rocked free. I took a final glance at the window that faced the front porch and then set my mind on the road in front of me.

At the terminal Avis sat looking at me as the truck's engine idled.

She said, "I want to go with you, but I don't have that kind of courage."

"I'll write as soon as I have an address. Maybe you'll come."

"Maybe."

I said, "Remember when your parents took us and your sister to see *The Wizard of Oz?*"

"Yes. I loved it."

"I'm going to see what's on the other side."

"Oh, I wish I could see it with you." We hugged and she touched her forehead to mine and said, "Remember, angels don't cry."

I responded as expected. "Yes, angels never cry here."

The train was down to its last minutes before departure. I grabbed my suitcase from the truck bed and hurried inside the terminal to purchase a ticket and check my bag. On the ramp I handed my ticket to the gate agent. He punched it and signaled me through the gate. I scurried over to the steps to the coach car, showed the conductor my ticket, and swung aboard. The coach was warm. I saw an open aisle seat and shed my coat. A soldier sitting on the window seat stood and offered it to me. I thanked him, shed my overcoat, and settled in.

I ran my mittened hand over the glass and looked out to where Avis stood beside her dad's truck. Wrapped in her brother's heavy wool coat, she looked frail and lost, much the way I felt. She waved a white handkerchief. I waved back. The diesel engine hissed to life, the train lurched forward, its wheels grinding on the cold rails. Minutes later the town where I was born and reared faded into a flinty sky along with the rolling hills.

The train rambled through the denuded farmlands of eastern Washington. A skin of shimmering ice clung to the skeletal branches of trees. I watched snow-thatched orchards and fields slide by until the window fogged up and I could no longer see the landscape clearly. I thought about where the wheat grew best. As I sat wavering about my decision to leave, I girded myself with the story. Somewhere in the field where Grandfather Olaf, my mother's father, planted wheat his big toe lay buried. According to family lore he was freeing a plowshare when his mule lurched forward. The steel blade sliced off the tip of his boot and took a big toe with it. Olaf Sorensen tore off his shirt collar, wrapped it around the wound, and finished plowing. He was supposed to have said, "I didn't have any use for that toe anyhow." During the

Depression, after Father left, Mother often told the story of her father's toe to reinforce her children's spirits.

I pulled my coat over my lap and removed my mittens. I dropped the mittens on the floor where I intended to leave them along with my galoshes when I switched trains in Portland. Like my grandfather's toe, I had no use for them anymore.

On the afternoon of the third day of my journey I gripped the rail and stepped down from the train and into the mild air of Southern California. My overcoat hanging from my forearm, I carried my purse to the baggage claim area and handed my claim ticket to a redcap.

He handed me my suitcase and smiled. "Lady, you ain't gonna need a coat like that here."

"Thank you," I said.

I hefted the coat and suitcase inside Union Station. Breathless, I set my load down and turned around, taking in the spectacle. Soldiers and sailors and civilians, at least two hundred in all, packed the terminal. The building itself, with its tall arched windows, polished tile floor, and burnished red ceiling beams, seemed to shimmer like the Emerald City. If this was what Los Angeles had to offer, I had found my place in the world.

"Excuse me," a man in a dark double-breasted suit said. "You're blocking us."

I gathered my wits and looked at my belongings on the floor. In my exuberance I'd stopped and set them down in the middle of a ticket aisle. "I'm sorry," I said and slung my purse strap over my shoulder, then reached down and picked up my coat and suitcase.

I wove my way through the throng. Near the center of the terminal, I asked a pair of women where the telephones were. One shook her head. The second pointed to the far end of the lobby. My immediate concern was to find employment and after that a roof and a bed. On a wall adjacent to the phone booths a cork bulletin board contained a cluster of help-wanted notices. Seeing so many prospects to choose from raised my hopes. I looked first for notices asking for waitresses but reminded myself that I'd come here to contribute to the war effort. Any work that fulfilled that desire, even if it called for me to hoist a shovel, would do. I jotted down several phone numbers, all of which claimed to be serving the war effort.

When I felt I had enough numbers on my list, I fished a nickel out of my coin purse and dropped it in the coin slot. I held the receiver to my ear and dialed the first number. My pulse rose as I waited for someone to answer the line.

On the fourth ring a woman answered, "Lucien's, may I help you."

"I'm calling about a job ad posted on a bulletin board. Are you still looking for help?"

"Yes, we have openings available. Can you sew?"

Can't everyone? I thought. Even my brothers sewed. "Of course," I said. "I helped my mom earn money by sewing. And I've worked as a waitress. Never missed a day."

"Okay. You sound like a prospect. What's your name?"

Thinking sewing suited me far better than shoveling, I said, "Eve. Eve Halvers."

"Where are you calling from?"

"Union Station. It's in Los Angeles."

"Yes, I know," she said. "Hold on." She cupped the mouthpiece. I could hear her muffled voice on the other end of the line.

A tapping sound came over the line. She cleared her throat and said, "Eve?"

"Yes."

"We can probably use you. You'll be manning an assembly line with a crew making boots. Do you think that might be what you're looking for?"

The job didn't fit any romantic notions I'd had, but it was work. "Yes. I can do that."

"Fine. Wait in front of the terminal. A man named Selmo will pick you up within an hour. He'll be wearing glasses with black frames and driving a white Chevrolet convertible."

"Thank you," I said, but the line had gone dead.

Luck was with me. I didn't bother calling other numbers, just toted my belongings to the tall doors leading to the pick-up area. When I stepped out, I saw the edge of Chinatown and the skyline of the city, the tallest building being City Hall. I've seen this view in movies. I'm here, I thought, and I have a job. I deserve to treat myself. I could afford to squander a dollar or more on a meal that included dessert, my first full meal in almost three days.

First impressions, I reminded myself, are important. I needed to freshen my lipstick. I set down my bag and coat and opened my purse and rummaged about for the lipstick. My knees buckled when I realized that my wallet containing the eighty dollars I'd saved was missing. I dug around in the purse pockets, then my coat pockets. The wallet was nowhere in the purse. Someone must have stolen it as I napped on the train or in the terminal in Portland. Left to me was six dollars in quarters in a side pocket and whatever loose change was in my coin purse. I forgot about my appearance and my good fortune at finding a job. I thought to call the police, but they would be as helpless as I was to get my wallet back. What kind of person would do such a thing? I realized it didn't matter who or what kind; I was the victim of circumstances I'd created. I stared at the open purse for a moment, then slung the strap over my shoulder and sat down.

Sometime later a Chevrolet convertible pulled to a stop at the curb. The driver, a short man in his early thirties, wearing a white fedora and a beige double-breasted suit, stepped out and looked about. His glasses fit the description I'd been given. He narrowed his gaze on me and waved. I gave him a feeble wave. The knot on his broad white tie was loosened at the collar. He tightened it, nodded, and opened the trunk of the car, then looked back as if to assure me.

He casually skipped up the steps and stopped an arm's length away. The lenses on his glasses magnified his eyes in such a way that he seemed stupefied. He gazed at me with those curious eyes. "You must be Eve?"

I rose. "Yes, Eve Halvers." I sniffed and wiped my nose with my handkerchief.

"I'm Selmo Stillman. Welcome to L.A. You look tired, must be. If you don't have a place to stay, we'll find you one temporarily."

"Yes, I'm tired."

"Long trips do that." Without asking, he lifted my coat and suitcase and turned toward the car as if everything was settled. His grabbing of my things set me back. After all, who was he? How could I be sure what he had in mind? I reached out and grabbed my coat.

He turned back and looked at me with a baffled expression. "It's okay. You'll be working for me."

I realized then that I'd embarrassed him. I swallowed and feigned a smile. "Someone stole my money." I wondered if my voice sounded as pathetic as I felt.

"Well, don't judge the world by that."

"What should I judge it by?"

"Judge it by the next thing that happens. Come on, I'll put your suitcase in the trunk. You're probably hungry. I know a place that always has meat despite rationing and the cook knows how to cook. That won't get your money back, but it'll be some comfort."

Having no other choice but to trust him, I gathered up my purse and lumbered to the car.

At a roadside diner Selmo ordered a dinner of roast beef and mashed potatoes. He asked if I knew anyone in Los Angeles and had somewhere to stay.

"No, I don't. I'm from Washington."

"D.C.?"

"No, the state. A small town. Palouse."

"Well, there's a hotel near the factory where you can stay until you find something better. That sound okay?"

"I had money for that, but it's gone. I'm sorry. I didn't come here to be a burden. I just wanted . . ."

"It'll be fine. You'll have an income soon enough."

After the meal he drove south down the busy highway. The air began to smell of brine, car exhaust, and coal fumes. A few minutes later I got my first brief glimpse of the Pacific and the Southern California shoreline. I asked where exactly we were heading.

"San Pedro," he said. "That's where the bootery is. Where you'll be working."

Dusk was approaching when he pulled into a parking spot in front of a hotel with a sign that read "Daily and Weekly Rates."

The desk clerk asked if I had identification. All I had left was Judith's birth certificate and I didn't dare show that. "Someone stole my wallet."

She looked at me skeptically.

Selmo stepped around me, crossed my name off the register, and took out his billfold. He showed the clerk his driver's license, then signed his name to the register. "That'll take care of that," he said and slipped a bill out of his wallet. "Take ten day's rent out of that."

The baffled clerk took the bill, counted out his change, and handed me a room key.

Before he left, he said, "We'll take that rent out of your paychecks over time. Get some rest. I'll pick you up in the morning at seven."

The desk clerk said that I'd find towels and washcloths in my room and that there were two bathrooms on the floor, the ladies' being on the right just past the stairs. In the room, as I unpacked for the night, I found a crisp ten-dollar bill on top of my phone numbers' list. How or when he put it in my purse, I had no idea, but Selmo had managed to do it.

I took my robe with me to the women's bathroom where I undressed and stood in the shower until the warm water washed away the strain of the day. I felt refreshed as I toweled off, but the sadness I felt over losing my money was intensified by a sense of anger. In addition to my money, the stolen wallet contained a snapshot of my brothers and sisters and me gathered around our mom and another of Avis and me in our high school graduation gowns. All I had left now of my home was my father's alarm clock and my dead sister's birth certificate and her coat.

# -2-

I WOKE UP BEFORE DAWN and again showered in the ladies' bathroom down the hall. After dressing, I opened the drapes. Sunlight flooded into the room and I got my first glimpse of the harbor. Gulls soared over rows of boats berthed in nearby docks. Farther out on the bay Terminal Island Prison's white walls rose above the outer reach of the island. On the opposite shoreline of the island, hulls of merchant ships in various stages of construction stood ready for the next shift of workers to arrive. A few dozen workers waited on a nearby pier as a ferry turned to dock. Across the bay another ferry took off from the island.

I looked at my watch. It was time for Selmo to arrive, time to start my new life. I took the stairs to the lobby and stood under the sign by the entrance. Selmo pulled his car to a stop. He waved, leaned across the seat, and threw open the passenger door.

"Good morning," he said. "Are you ready for breakfast?"

"Yes, I guess."

We drove to a breakfast café on Miner Street. He opened his door and hurried to my side before I could get out.

"You'll want the avocado breakfast," he said. "Fried eggs with sliced avocado on a bed of toast."

That sounded like a strange combination. "I've never had an avocado."

"It's probably the best breakfast you can get in all this rationing."

I took him at his word and ordered an avocado breakfast along with coffee. He ordered coffee and oatmeal. After the waitress left, an uncomfortable silence hung over the table. He fumbled with something in his coat pocket. My seat gave me a view of Harbor Boulevard busy with morning traffic. A streetcar came to a stop across the street and a dozen or so men and women with lunch pails in hand filed out onto the sidewalks. Across the bay a ferry circled to dock on Terminal Island.

"It's amazing," I said.

Selmo removed his glasses and squinted at me. "What's amazing?"

"All the people up and going to work."

"You'll get used to it." He glanced over his shoulder. "One shift goes out, one returns," he said, sounding indifferent to it all.

I wondered if I would someday feel that way. "What will I be doing?"

"Making boots," he said without elaborating, then began talking about the history of his company. "Lucien's Custom Boots is in a building that dates back to when San Pedro was a port for clipper ships that traded in the Far East."

"That's sounds kind of romantic," I said.

"Not really. The building once warehoused imported goods from East Asia. In 1927 my grandfather bought it and converted it to a bootery. He emigrated from Poland and brought my father with him." He paused and looked off. "My grandfather Lucien learned the trade in the old country. He started the bootery making riding boots first for jockeys and polo players. All handcrafted. When Granddad died, Dad took over."

"The job posting said it was the war industry. I don't know anything about riding boots."

"You don't have to. In time, millionaires and movie stars, as well as polo players, bought our boots. Sadly, those are fewer and fewer. Now our client is the United States Marines."

"Why is that? The riding boots, I mean."

"Little demand and the war took our best cobblers. My best friend too." He sat back and looked off pensively.

After breakfast we drove two blocks north of the harbor. The sign in front of the rustic three-story brick structure read, "Lucien's Custom Boots." From the outside the building fit the impression I had from the history Selmo offered earlier. He circled into the alley and parked in the back. We walked up the stairs to a loading dock and into a time office. He asked the timekeeper for my card, handed it to me, and showed me how to clock in.

"Your shift begins at eight a.m. Punch in no later than five minutes before the hour. You get an hour's lunch break and are paid for that time. Okay?"

"Fine. How'd I get a card so soon?"

"We're efficient. Follow me."

I trailed him up a narrow back staircase to the second floor and into an office where I gave my personal information to Norma, who explained that the thirty-four cents an hour wage Lucien's paid was about five cents higher than what similar workers received nationwide. That was because of a shortage of workers and to compensate for the cost of living in Los Angeles. She added that from time-to-time Selmo handed out production bonuses. She left me with two forms to fill out and sign, went to a side room, and came out with two pairs of work overalls.

She pointed to the side room. "When you're finished with the forms, take these. You can change there. Leave your belongings inside. They'll be safe."

Dressed in overalls, I stepped out. Selmo waited by the door.

"You can move your stuff when Norma gets you a locker. Let's go meet your crew."

"Sir, I have a question."

"Call me Selmo. What's the question?"

I pulled out the ten-dollar bill from my pocket. "Why did you put this in my purse?"

"I don't know what you're talking about, Eve. Let's go to work."

He opened the office door and we walked into a blaze of sound machines whirling, air compressors hissing, and conveyors humming. He stopped at the top rail of the staircase and pointed down.

"Hides are cured and tanned in the back of the factory where they stamp the parts that come out here," Selmo said. "The boot itself is assembled below. Watch."

I stood beside him transfixed. Two rows of sewing machines mounted on workbenches stretched down the sides of conveyor belts. Heads bowed as they joined the leather parts, women sat straddling stools and in fluid motions guided pieces across the machine's plane. A middle-aged man with stooped shoulders, carrying a box under his arm, walked up the line and dropped leather parts into containers beside the sewing machines. The sewn pieces went back on the conveyor and moved on to an area where the conveyors converged. There a team of women mounted boot tops on a cast and connected heels and outsoles to tops with a heat compressor. Another team, two black women and one white, measured boot sizes, matched the right with the left foot, and tied leather laces into eyelets on the throat line. That done, each woman placed the pair in an appropriately marked box.

Selmo pointed to the women tying the leather laces. "Those two are our Black Rosies, Caroline and Bea," he said.

"Black Rosies?"

"That's what they call themselves. I understand that's the case in the entire defense industry. Their mark of pride. Most of the black men you'll see will be working on the docks or in shipyards. We have . . . well, not right now he's . . . never mind. Stay here."

He left me without finishing what he began. For a moment I stood there self-conscious and very aware that the workers on the assembly line were taking notice of me. He returned with a milk box and placed it in front of a lever. He stepped up. Clearing his throat to get everyone's attention, he said, "Ladies. Take your earplugs out."

Some did. Others didn't.

He pointed to me. "This is Eve, our new addition."

My cheeks flamed. I clasped my shaking hands together at my waist to hide them.

"I want you to get to know her and help her." He signaled to a tall brunette seated across from us. "Gretchen, she's yours now. Everyone else, take a fifteen-minute break."

The tall dark-haired woman swung her leg over the stool as if dismounting a horse and walked over. She extended a hand to me. "Hello. Welcome to Boondocker Junction."

I shook her hand. "Boondocker Junction?"

She smiled and dropped her hand to her side.

Selmo picked up the box. "Boondocker's the Marine name for the boots we make. She's saying it affectionately. Isn't that right, Gretchen?"

Gretchen's response was "Selmo, we're low on the hundred-twenty weight thread."

"I'll have some for you this afternoon. Show her the ropes."

We watched Selmo walk away. When he was halfway up the stairs, Gretchen, who appeared to be in her mid-twenties, pulled out her earplugs, and said, "What did he say?"

"He'll get you some this afternoon."

"What's your name?"

"Eve," I said.

She held up the earplugs for me to see. "You'll need these. Not just for the noise, but they come in handy when Selmo's giving speeches. You'll be on our crew. You know how to sew?"

"Yes." I looked at the nearest sewing machine. "But not on any like these."

"You'll pick it up easily. I've trained girls who couldn't sew. What kind of machine?"

"Mom has a Singer treadle. You know, foot operated. We made money sewing during the Depression, my sisters and me and Mom."

"That's good," she said, but seemed skeptical. She began tinkering with the machine.

What I'd said was true. To my memory sewing was always part of our lives. My brothers, all three, mended their own clothes and during the Depression, after my dad abandoned us, Mom's small enterprise as a seamstress kept flour in the pantry and on occasion put meat on the table. Though food was scarce, she still managed to feed hungry rail riders who came knocking at the door. When Helen once told her that we worked too hard for her to give food away, Mom reminded her that those who came knocking were worse off than we were.

Gretchen motioned me over and told me to watch. She straddled the stool. "It's a Consew, made for stitching leather. It gets a little cranky." She moved the wheel and the feet rose. "See how much room there is for moving the leather under the needle. Here, sit and finish sewing the eyelet."

I stitched the eyelet rib on with no problem.

"You sew fine. You'll catch on quick. Be careful though. Go slow and steady. We've had more than one gal stitch her hand going too fast."

Gretchen spent the remaining moments demonstrating how to change a needle and thread the machine. When the crew returned from the break, she called them over. I started to rise.

"Don't stand," a short redhead with a dimpled chin said. "I'm Tiff. Tiffany really."

The second one, a slim brunette, offered her hand. "Hello, I'm Mitzi. Welcome."

I took her hand and said, "I'm Eve."

Tiff said, "We know. Dominique told us."

Gretchen said, "Tiff, Eve doesn't know who Dominique is."

Mitzi said, "Dominique's the rover. She fills in wherever she's needed on the line. If someone's sick or needs a toilet break, she steps in. She somehow knew about you yesterday."

"Let's go to work," Tiff said. She stuffed plugs in her ears. "You'll need some. They help protect us from Selmo's speeches."

She and Mitzi straddled their stools and turned on their machines. A woman, a slim blonde I assumed to be Dominique, took the fourth workbench. I returned to mine and the man who'd distributed insoles and boot tops stepped up to the lever and eased it upright. The women inserted their earplugs as the conveyors came to life. Gretchen handed me an insole from one box and the leather uppers from another. Stitch by stitch my apprenticeship began.

# -3-

GRETCHEN OPENED THE THIRD STORY window and climbed out. Tiff told me to step out. I looked down first. The "balcony," a rickety metal fire escape platform mounted on the outside wall, looked out over the bay and sections of houses and apartments that ran westward to the coastline. Enclosed by an iron rail was a flat mesh surface. Beside it a narrow escape ladder mounted to the outside wall extended down midway to the first level.

Gretchen offered me a hand. "Are you afraid of heights?"

"No, but I might be afraid of fire escapes." I took her hand, lifted a leg over the sill, and cautiously stepped over. Tiff climbed out behind me, followed by Mitzi. The four of us sat cross-legged in a circle on the hard grating. They opened their lunch pails.

"It's a good thing we wear overalls," I said, opening my brown bag.

The girls, as I now understood they called themselves, all nodded. I bit into my bagel. Mitzi stared at it and shook her head.

"What?" I asked.

"You're going to eat a dry bagel? No cheese?"

"It's all I can afford."

"Leave her alone," Gretchen said.

"Here." Tiff pinched a bit of roast beef from her sandwich and handed it to me. "It's got some mustard on it."

Mitzi reached into her lunch pail, uncapped her thermos, and poured some fruit juice in the cap. "Here, you need something to drink with that."

Gretchen said, "I've got an extra lunch pail. You're welcome to it. I'll bring it tomorrow."

"Oh, and I've got these for you," Tiff reached into an overall pocket and came out with a pair of earplugs in her open palm. "I had three pairs."

"Thanks." I took the earplugs and slipped them in my pocket. I felt overwhelmed. They'd barely spoken to me since I started working.

"Let's eat. Then we'll go over the classifieds." Mitzi took a swallow from her thermos.

After we finished, we circled closer. They read through the classifieds, passing them back and forth. Tiff asked how much I could afford.

"A dollar a day. Hopefully, no more than a dollar fifty."

"You'll be stuck with streetcar fare," Gretchen said. "You'll want full use of a bathroom and a kitchen. A closet. Absolutely, you'll need your own. My husband rarely got my goat, but he damn well did when he hung *his* clothes in *my* closet."

Mitzi said, "At least yours hung his. I constantly picked up after mine."

"Guess I've been spared that," Tiff said.

"Okay, time's going by," Gretchen said. "Let's concentrate here for our country girl."

Among several rooms listed, the girls narrowed the prospective rentals down to five, those based on what I could afford and how far I'd have to travel. They agreed that because I would be commuting, the nearness to a streetcar route was paramount.

Once the list was set, Mitzi said, "I can get my uncle to drive us around to addresses. He's one of the lucky ones with a gas rationing stamp, but you'll have to pay for the gas."

"Okay."

By us, I thought she'd meant her and me, but that night when we met at the YMCA for the USO dance, I found out that all the girls were going.

Tiff served fruit punch to the service men while I took a turn handing out cookies on a napkin. I looked up from my seat at the refreshment table at a dark-haired sailor about my age. He, like most of the others so far, hesitated to speak.

"Hello," I said, "would you like some punch and a cookie?"

"No, ma'am," he said and stood smiling at me.

I smiled back and said, "If you want someone to help you with a letter, that's over on the far wall." I pointed to where Gretchen sat at a table with a tablet, a pen, and a small stack of envelopes. "She's not busy."

He ran a hand over his jaw. "No, I'm fine. I wrote a letter already this week."

"Okay, then you want to talk?"

"No, I'd like to dance."

I was hoping not to dance again. I'd danced six trips already and the last time I was on the floor, a soldier stepped on my foot halfway through "We Always Hurt the Ones We Love." He'd apologized and walked me to my seat, but two songs later my foot still hurt.

"I assume you want to dance with me?"

"Yes, if it's okay."

I glanced at Tiff and pointed at the dance floor to indicate I was leaving her in charge. She offered up a nod. I stepped around the table, placed my hand on the forearm he held out for me, and said, "Go easy. My foot's sore."

"Yes, ma'am. Call me Red."

I looked at his dark hair and freckle-less olive skin. "Nice to meet you, Red. I'm Eve."

Artie Shaw's recording of "Stardust" began playing on the turntable. I eased one hand up on his shoulder. He took my hand in his and placed his other hand on the small of my back. We started off slowly and soon settled into a nice rhythm. His moves were easy to follow and it went well for the first few bars of the song. Then, with no hint of what he had in mind, he pulled me close to his chest and bent me backward in a dip. The sudden move struck a raw nerve. I felt as if I were in the Newsome barn being forced backward atop a hay bale. Reflexively, I shoved a fist into his chest.

"Don't," I said loud enough for nearby couples to stop and look at us.

His face stiffened as he stood me upright. "I'm sorry. I didn't mean to scare you. We were dancing so well, I just thought."

I felt foolish. He wasn't taking liberties, merely wanted to perform a dance move.

"It's okay," I whispered and patted his shoulder. "Really. Let's finish the dance, but nothing fancy."

When the song ended, he walked me back to the refreshment table. "Thank you," he said shyly. "You're a good dancer."

"And you're particularly good. Thank you."

He frowned and said, "My name's not Red. My real name's Abner. I hate it."

I watched him back away, turn, and cross the room to where his friends stood in a circle. I felt terrible. He was a lonely kid who wanted to dance. That was all.

Tiff placed a hand on my shoulder and rubbed it. "What happened out there?"

"Nothing. He caught me by surprise is all."

"Don't let them get to you. Some'll try to sneak a feel, but most are nice kids. They don't try anything with me. Maybe 'cause there's too much of me for them to know where to grab." Tiff, in her thirties and single, sometimes made herself the brunt of her jokes, her weight being the primary target of her punch lines.

"It wasn't like that. He hates his real name, Abner, so he calls himself 'Red.' That's sad."

She filled a glass from the punch bowl, set it aside, and picked up an empty glass. She filled that glass, placed it in front of me, and winked as she reached for a cookie. "We can put on masks for others," she said, "but we can't hide who we are from ourselves."

Seeing I'd found not just a friend, but a confidant, I lifted the glass and said, "Here's to cookies and punch. I'm going to go over to the table and help with the letter writing."

Saturday morning, we piled into a Dodge coupe and Mitzi's Uncle Harvey drove us north into Torrance. By midmorning we'd visited and marked off three prospects. The first was too unkempt, the second too far from a streetcar route, and the third had been rented out the night before. After two hours of frustration, we were down to two prospects.

Mitzi's uncle, who'd been patient up to then, said, "How many are left?"

"Two."

"Show me the addresses." Mitzi handed him the paper and pointed to the ads. "This one's five minutes from here," he said and pressed the accelerator.

Gretchen said, "There must be a place that'll work in this track of middle-class banality."

Mitzi, Tiff, and I all stared at her.

"Well, would you call it a Paradise?" she asked.

No, I thought, and I wouldn't call it Oz.

The next house on the list looked fine from the outside, the yard was well kept, and the front porch had a swing seat. We piled out of the car and once all of us were out, walked to the door. I knocked. We heard heavy footsteps lumbering to the door. Then the door cracked open and a middle-aged man, his breath smelling of alcohol, peered out.

"I'm here to see about the room," I said.

The door swung open. He stood at the threshold wearing a red and purple polka-dot robe that gaped open exposing his white underwear and pale legs. He turned sideways, and with a sweep of his arm, motioned us in.

"Wrong address," Gretchen said. She took me by the arm and all of us turned as one in the direction of the waiting car.

"It's a nice room," the man hollered.

As we squeezed ourselves into the car, Mitzi's uncle asked, "What's wrong with that one?"

Tiff said, "The guy was a little lacking in charm, but his robe was oddly fashionable."

Mitzi chortled, Gretchen shook her head, and I laughed.

The man was still calling to us even as Mitzi's Uncle Harvey put the car in gear. The door to the house didn't close until we drove away.

The final house on the list was in south Gardena near the border of Torrance. As were the other houses in the neighborhood, it was a small three-bedroom bungalow painted white. It sat in the middle of the block. The lawn was well trimmed, and colorful flowers grew in pots on the sides of the front steps. All in all, it looked promising.

We spilled out of the car, looked at one another, and lined up on the walkway leading to the door. This, the last chance for the day, was also convenient to a streetcar stop.

"We can do this next Saturday if it doesn't work," Mitzi said. "Go knock."

As I was about to press the doorbell, the door opened and

a slight woman with a pale complexion squinted past me. She wore a floor-length evening dress and black high heels. Her brown hair was drawn into a bun atop her head. Her one concession to wearing makeup was the deep violet lipstick on her thin lips. She squinted past me at the girls. She shook her head and said, "I have only one room. This is not a hotel."

"These are my friends. I'm the only one looking for a room. I'm Eve, who called."

"Oh, yes. Fine. I'm Doris. Uh, Mrs. Sauer, come in." She took my hand and shook it.

One at a time as they entered, the girls introduced themselves. She shook their hands in a formal manner and waved them in. We exchanged grins in the foyer and looked about. The living room, though small, was impeccably clean and wallpapered with a brocade pattern threaded with golden strands. A tall bookshelf filled with volumes covered most of one wall. She walked us to the dining room and invited us to have a seat. She asked me to sit next to her. Lying atop the table were two sheets of paper. She handed me one. On it, written in neat cursive, was a heading that said it was a rental agreement.

"This is just the financial arrangement," she said. "If it suits you, we'll go over the rest."

I read it and handed it to her. "That's fine."

"So, Eve. You'll want to see the room and the kitchen first. If you ladies will excuse us."

I looked at the girls who didn't dare meet my gaze for fear of laughing. "Yes. I'd like to see it."

I followed her past the kitchen and down a narrow hall. She opened the second door on the left. Furnished with a single bed and five-drawer dresser with a mirror, the room was about the size and just about as dreary as James Cagney's cell in *The Public Enemy*. It did have a closet and was impeccably clean. Its window looked out onto the neighboring bungalow some ten feet away. I'd hoped for better, but I was at the mercy of my circumstances.

"What do you think?" she asked.

I hid my disappointment and said, "I think it's fine."

She opened the closet door to show me it was empty. "Let's go see the kitchen."

As soon as we entered the kitchen, she began opening the cabinet doors, then all the drawers and finally the oven door. She pointed out how everything was organized and kept clean. At two dollars a week the price was right. It would have to do for the time being.

"Okay, you convinced me. I'll take it." I smiled at her but didn't get one in return.

We returned to the dining table. I winked at my friends and said, "Yes."

Mrs. Sauer motioned for me to sit. "Besides the money terms in the contract, Eve, there are other conditions. You must clean after you cook. You may use my dishes if you don't have any. If you break a glass or a dish, you must replace it. At least once a week you must wash the sheets and pillowcase on the bed. Are you with me?"

She signed her name on the contract and said, "You purchase your own groceries. Unfortunately, I have just one bathroom. Please clean it up after you've used it. Don't leave a speck of makeup in the sink. And don't use all the hot water if you use the shower instead of bathing."

Even though we didn't have indoor plumbing at home, Mom insisted on cleanliness. "I understand. It's kind of like it was at my home."

"Good. Most important is, no men in my house."

I looked at the girls, who were all grinning, and said, "I don't have a boyfriend."

"Fine. Three dollars a week as I put in the ad and the contract. First week in advance."

"The contract read two dollars," I said.

She looked at it and shook her head. "My mistake." Using the pen, she scratched out the two dollars, replaced it with three dollars and initialed the change. "Here, you need to initial next to mine."

I took a deep breath, scratched down my initials, and signed the rental agreement. "Is there a grocery store nearby?"

"A Safeway, two blocks north, one west. Near the streetcar stop."

She left and returned with a key.

"If it's okay, I'll move in tomorrow."

She slid the key over for me to pick up. "That's Sunday. Make it after I've come home from church. Say, around noon. Also, I go to bed early and I'm a light sleeper. Be quiet if you come in after dark. Ring the bell twice before you unlock the door if it's past nine thirty."

"Yes, ma'am."

"And strictly, no men. The last girl snuck one in, and I sent her packing."

"Yes, ma'am."

"Good then. I look forward to having company. My husband is in the army and my daughter lives elsewhere. We'll see you tomorrow."

As soon as the door closed behind us, the girls broke out in laughter.

"I know," I said. "I can deal with her."

"Who talks like that? She has all the charm of a rabid bat," Gretchen said.

"At least she wore clothes," Tiff said. "Hollywood semi-chic. Not a loose thread and no wrinkles. If that's what she wears at midday on Saturday, I wonder what she wears to church."

Mitzi's uncle, who'd been patient up to then, leaned across the car seat and hollered through the open window, "I've got a wife waiting. You know what that means, Mitzi."

"Yes, Uncle Harvey." She turned to us. "Let's go, girls."

We hurried to the car and crowded into the seats.

"You've been a saint, Uncle Harvey," Mitzi said. "I'll buy you a Coke and a hamburger."

He looked at her in the mirror. "I don't drink Coke. How about a milkshake?"

"Deal."

"Guess the wife can wait a little while longer," he said and fired up the engine.

The car windows rolled down, all of us feeling in high spirits, we headed to San Pedro. Mrs. Sauer, whose name we all agreed fit her, was the topic of conversation and the target of a few one-liners from Tiff, the best being, "If she was a warden, the prison guards would help the prisoners escape and take off with them."

That evening we drove to the pier in Santa Monica and danced to the swing music of Spade Cooley and his band. Tiff was approached by a redheaded sailor who stuttered as he asked her to dance. She smiled and took his hand. He walked her to the dance floor and soon the two of them seemed to be floating along on a cloud. I, too, danced with a couple of sailors, one who smiled and said that I was the prettiest gal in the room. I looked about, then told him he wasn't a very good liar.

That night I was full of the Los Angeles I had imagined when I began my journey. Soon, I would find myself immersed in a different Los Angeles, one I couldn't have imagined.

# -4-

THOUGH ONLY THIRTY-EIGHT, MRS. SAUR acted much older and was easy to anger. She scolded me if I made "too much noise" or came home late from the USO and forgot to ring the doorbell twice before keying the door. In the evening when I went to the living room and wrote in my journal, she'd take a seat nearby and talk. It became obvious that when she'd mentioned welcoming having company around what she really welcomed was having an audience.

After breakfast Saturday mornings, she encouraged me to sit "for a quick chat." At first, I politely listened, nodding occasionally until the "chat" evolved into a tirade about one subject or another, her favorites being undisciplined children and slow mail delivery. When she spoke of her husband, her face tightened. He'd been a major in the National Guard but had been called to active duty to command a combat engineering battalion somewhere in the South Pacific. Since hearing her husband's unit had liberated a leper colony, she was consumed with the idea that he might contract leprosy or some other rare disease. She read literature about exotic tropical ailments. According to her, nothing could cure a certain Asian worm that targeted the intestines. The fear that he would bring some disease home seemed to menace her more than the possibility of his being maimed or killed in action.

In ways she reminded me of Hosanna Lander, the town scold in Palouse, a sad woman who chased us children off when we played near her house. Mrs. Sauer, like my mother, was a Bible Lady. Before dressing in the morning, she knelt at a cross in the living room, her Bible clutched to her breast, and prayed for her husband's safe return and for her daughter to "find some common sense." Her daughter Vanessa, who was my age, had married a soldier and had gotten pregnant in the weeks before he shipped out overseas. I saw her in passing when she dropped her toddler off at the house. Penny, a one-year-old, remained with Mrs. Sauer on weekdays when Vanessa worked. That may have accounted in part for my landlady's crankiness. More than once, she complained she was "too young to be a grandmother."

After three Saturdays of having our chats, I decided to take my journal with me to see the city and record my thoughts. When the clock eased toward eight-thirty, I excused myself, washed and dried the dishes, then walked two blocks to meet a Yellow Car that took me downtown. My first venture alone into the city, I found the energy of the people daunting. Alone in the bustle, I came to appreciate the astonishing nature of the city that seemed built in defiance of good common sense. In the shadows of the tall buildings or on the crowded sidewalks I went unnoticed in the flood of pedestrians. Their faces expressionless, they bobbed past me like pods of dolphins. I felt isolated and questioned my coming to Los Angeles in the first place.

Following my third Saturday venture into the city, I became aware that it wasn't me who was invisible. It was merely that Angelinos, seemingly immersed in self-purpose, paid little attention to one another.

In the evening following workdays, if I didn't attend a USO dance with friends, I lay in the bedroom with a book from Mrs. Sauer's library, or recorded entries in my journal, or wrote to Avis or Mom. Avis, who'd had a crush on Link dating back to sixth grade, forwarded his letter to me. Mom sent only one short letter, mentioning only that Link had written to her, and that August and Richard were at sea and couldn't mail letters, which I already knew.

On Sunday's Mrs. Sauer attended early mass. To avoid her company and enjoy the day I purchased a bathing suit with the intention of going to Newport Beach. After a quick breakfast, I washed the dishes, then slipped into the swimsuit and a robe. With my purse and a towel in hand, I headed to the front door. As I opened the door, I came face to face with my landlady.

"Eve, where are going dressed like that?"

"To Newport Beach."

"It's probably not a good idea to walk the streets in a bathing suit and that's more than a six-mile walk."

Even if I had been up to walking six miles to the beach and back, she had dampened the idea. But anything would be more sufferable than sitting with her as she bemoaned how the war was ruining her life. I changed clothes, randomly picked a book off the shelves, stuffed my journal in my purse, and said goodbye.

"Where are you going?"

I feigned a smile. "Out to enjoy the day."

"You need a bonnet. You'll get sunburned."

"I don't have one."

"Wait." She left the room and returned with a pink bonnet and placed it on my head.

"Thanks," I said. "I'll be back in time to fix my dinner."

For a time, I strolled through the neighborhoods, looking

for anything of interest. I found the new suburbia, houses crammed together, yards with manicured lawns and neatly trimmed shrubs—the landscape Gretchen, who'd attended college, referred to as "middle-class banality." Then amid all the sameness, I saw life. Two elderly women waved at me from a swing seat on their porch. Three young girls played hopscotch on the sidewalk. Cars rolled by unhurriedly with their windows down. All were reminders that life went on despite the war and none of it seemed banal.

Near noon I found a corner café with sign that read, "All We Serve Is You." The waitress sat me at a table for two and asked what I wanted to drink. A scattering of people sat at tables and in booths. Two families had young children and both parents, a sight I had rarely seen since the war broke out.

Sitting alone at a table in a café with only the company of a book about Magellan's voyages left me feeling dejected. I swallowed down a sandwich and left. I walked until I came to a school playground where mothers sat in clusters and watched children play on the swings and a merry-go-round. I found a seat on a bench near a baseball diamond and watched mothers shout encouragements to their kids. One girl was on the field with all the boys, and she played third base. I was reminded of the times I filled in to play ball when my brothers and their friends were short a player. She dared the boy in the batter's box to hit the ball to her. A mother shouted, "Bend your knees!" at the boy who was standing stiffly. Following her advice, he bent his knees and hit the next pitch, a line drive that the girl caught.

I watched the play for a time and left the park feeling restored for having spent a day doing nothing but being free.

That night I lay in bed and reread Avis's letter updating me on life in Palouse. She'd closed the letter with "Angels," meaning may angels look over you. I folded the letter, turned off the light, whispered, "Angels," and let my head sink into the pillow. My good sense told me it was time to accept that this sort of banality was now my life. Still, I yearned for more, not excitement exactly, but something to make me want to spring out of bed in the morning, something to make me laugh, something to make me feel whole and worthy. As I drifted toward sleep, I conjured up a vision of the Emerald City on the far side of a rainbow. Then I reminded myself that rainbows are merely sunlight refracted in a field of moisture. I picked up my journal and wrote a passage about loneliness in a big city and what I missed about home.

# -5-

Thursday the fifth week of my working in the factory I sat before my sewing machine, stitching an eyelet. Working precisely and steadily, I trimmed off excess thread, checked for flaws on the near-finished boot. As had become habit, I jotted down: "We love you, Marine," on a note, signed my name and inserted the note in the toe box. That done, I sent the boot down the conveyor for its heel and picked up the next pieces of leather. I wasn't alone in doing this. Others on the line had husbands, brothers, sons, or friends on the front lines. They wrote messages too.

Selmo walked into the cacophony and pulled his wooden milk box to the center of the room. He stepped atop his milk box and pointed to his ears. "Ladies, take a break."

When we didn't stop, he realized he hadn't shut down the conveyors. He skipped down off the milk box and pulled the main lever. Work and sound came to a halt. He raised his hands and called out, "Ladies, ladies, please." He stepped back atop his box, cleared his throat and said, "The battle on Kwajalein has expanded. Our boys have hit Roi Island, and they have hit it hard."

Just as we'd not heard of Kwajalein when the Marines had begun the amphibious assault, none of us had heard of Roi Island, but we knew the boys he spoke of were Marines. Soon after beginning work at Lucien's, I'd become accustomed to Selmo's occasional battle updates. A little over a week before, American soldiers had parachuted into a place called Anzio, which was equally important news, but on that occasion, Selmo had referred to the soldiers as men. He insisted on the distinction. Out of fondness for Marines, he'd taken to calling them *our* boys. Following suit, the women in the factory referred to them the same way. In another era all this might have seemed theatrical, but not on February 3, 1944, when brothers and husbands were wading to the shore under fire from Japanese machine gunners.

His eyes took in the room until certain he had our attention. "We know what this means. Our boys will need new boots in no time. Put some love into your work. For now, let's join in a moment of prayer, appealing to the God who oversees the affairs of Christians and Jews alike, and the One whom the Japanese pray to as well." He bowed his head. He boomed out a short prayer and finished with "Dear God, have the misguided Japanese accept their fate and surrender before too much blood is shed." Following a moment of silence, he said, "Amen," and switched on the conveyor belt.

He walked to my station and stood across the conveyor from me. "Eve, does your job call for you to write notes and put them in the boots?"

"No, sir."

"Well, why do you do it?"

I thought to say others wrote notes, but some didn't, and it wasn't right to pass on blame. I picked up two pieces of leather from the conveyor. "To help morale, sir."

"I see. And you think it works?"

"I don't know."

"No, you don't. None of us do, and there is a paper shortage. But I like the idea. It's a fine one. We do what we can, don't we?"

I joined the pieces and began stitching them together. "I use my own paper, sir."

He shook his head absentmindedly. "I have uncles and aunts and cousins in Europe. We haven't heard from them since the second year the war broke out. I wish our Marines were in France giving the Nazis a bloody nose." He pushed his glasses up the bridge of his nose and looked about. "I'll have notes printed for every pair of boots."

I glanced up from my machine. "Mr. Stillman, it won't be the same."

He gave me an injured look and said, "How's that?"

"A woman's handwriting makes it personal." I cut the running end of the thread and picked an eyelet from the box.

"You're absolutely right." He reached into his pocket, pulled out a ten-dollar silver certificate and placed it on my sewing machine table. "Don't forget there's a paper shortage. Make those notes small." His face all business, he shuffled down the aisle, glancing from side to side at his workers as he passed by. When he mounted the stairs leading to his office, he turned for a final look as if to lower the curtain on his performance.

Selmo wasn't known to be impulsively generous. It was apparent he wanted others to notice the bill. Tiff, sitting diagonally from me, grinned and wrinkled her nose. I scooped up the bill, unzipped my work overalls, tucked the money in my bra, and stuck my tongue out at her.

When the lunch bell sounded, my crew picked up our lunch pails and ascended the stairs to the third story where we met at the end of the hall. Gretchen opened the window to the fire escape. Each of us helping the one behind her over the sill, we stepped out onto the grill. The grating swayed and the bars creaked as we settled in.

Uncomfortable as the grating was, the view of the bay and the sea air were a respite from the tedium of assembly-line work. Though the air smelled also of exhaust fumes, smoke from refineries, and tannin, we pretended otherwise.

Tiff said, "What a place for fine dining. Where's the man in the tuxedo?"

"How do you fine dine a sardine sandwich?" Gretchen said, looking at hers.

The day was clear. The grumble of vehicles resounded off the brick walls. Out on the bay buoys rolled with the waves. Farther out on the shimmering surface two oil tankers took on ballast. The tip of Santa Catalina rose on the horizon.

Gretchen dangled her legs over the edge, set her sandwich aside, then lit a cigarette and took a long draw. She offered me one. I shook my head and unwrapped my sandwich. She blew smoke in the air and watched it dissipate.

"You going to the dance tonight?" she asked.

At the dances we cast off the tediousness of the day's work. Gretchen, married and living with her mother-in-law, went as a duty to her husband who was serving overseas. I'd overheard some women hinting that more than dancing was on Gretchen's mind. The more I was around her, the more I believed she was the victim of idle gossip.

"No," I said. "I'm giving my feet some R and R. Besides, Mrs. Sauer goes nuts when I come home after ten at night."

"Tiff, are you coming?" Gretchen asked.

"Yep. My feet can take it. What can't take much more is my butt. We sit every minute we're at work."

"Amen to that, sister," Mitzi said. "Eve doesn't have the patriotic spirit yet."

"I do too." The girls knew that with three brothers at war, I was as patriotic as anyone, but after a month of sweaty hands on my back, grinning boys trying to sneak a feel, and too many clumsy feet landing on mine, my patriotism needed a rest. "It's my feet and my landlady."

"The Wicked Witch of Gardena," Tiff said.

"I will have no men in my house," Tiff said. "And if my husband comes home, I'll have him castrated."

We laughed.

I watched a circle of pelicans fishing the waters as Gretchen and the others passed around ideas about what to do if they didn't go to the USO. I bit into my sandwich, tuna between two slices of dry bread. The taste was worse than flat.

"You know about Selmo?" Tiff asked.

I swallowed another dry bite. "Know what?"

"He has a mistress."

"She's supposed to be beautiful," Mitzi said. "Nothing around but longshoremen, all too old to serve. Selmo's young. In his thirties. Come on, think about it. He must have a mistress."

"That's silly," Gretchen said. "Mitzi, I don't see the logic."

Hating gossip as I did, I said, "Gossip has no logic. Its purpose is to entertain and hurt."

The girls all stared at me. "That's wise," Tiff said.

A gust blew in from the harbor and brought with it an odor of diesel and dead fish. Mitzi wrinkled her nose at the smell. "What the hell is that stink?" she said.

I swallowed a bite and said, "It's the smell of gossip."

Gretchen tossed away her cigarette and lit up another.

"No smoking," Mitzi said. "If the fire escape burns down, there's no way to escape."

Gretchen took a deep draw. "Mitzi there's far more chance of the fire escape collapsing from an overload."

Mitzi's sometimes off-the-cuff remarks and Gretchen's world-of-doom pronouncements brought something special to our day.

"Gretchen," Tiff said, "You're a pessimist. If you designed houses they'd look like crypts. Look at the water. Oh, God, I love this city. If only there were a few men."

"Eve says there are," Gretchen said. "She sees them on the streetcar."

Tiff shook her head. "I mean our age who aren't in uniform. First there was the Depression, and we were all poor and couldn't afford shampoo. Now there's the war and shampoo is rationed. On top of that, we're all alone."

The platform shivered as Mitzi rose sharply to her feet. "We're not alone. We've got each other."

"Know what?" Gretchen took a deep drag off her cigarette and said, "We're proving we can do without men. I bet in every war the women left behind had at least a half-hearted hope the men wouldn't return." She said it with such certitude that the rest of us were taken aback. "I heard a woman professor lecture at UCLA. She said the war must be seen as an opportunity, that a new society is being 'forged.' What a great word. What do you think, Eve? Can we make it without men?"

Being the youngest, I was reluctant to enter heady conversations, though I often agreed with Gretchen. Thinking of my mother who'd been deserted, I said, "Some who make it without a husband or a man are maybe better off."

"There." Gretchen flicked ash over the railing. "From the mouth of the country girl. If meat is no longer rationed, why can't we get fresh meat? The answer is men get it first."

"Why do you always blame men? You're married to one," Tiff said.

Mitzi pulled at a strand of her long hair across her face. "Know what I think? They could win this tomorrow or the day after. Men just love war. They don't want to come home."

"That's crazy." Tiff flicked her hand at a fly, then looked for support from the others. "I think Gretchen's pulling our leg. Who's ever heard of a woman professor?"

"Stereotypes, Tiff." Gretchen squinted from the sun's

reflection on the harbor. "It's true about the professor. There are others, but not enough. Think about it. In the future we may not only see women professors and doctors and judges, but we may also even get the meat first."

Silence fell over the landing as we contemplated this new vision. The war had displaced many conventional certainties. Whether we were aware of it or not, ideas, including marriage and a family, that had long conditioned us were fading at that very moment. Women could survive without men, but a world at war was frightening enough without dwelling on that. I took my journal out of the bib of my overalls and jotted down what Gretchen had said.

Gretchen grinned as if thinking about the future she'd described, then her expression went flat. "Don't get me wrong. I love Robert and I miss him. He and I have an unusual marriage. He listens and doesn't judge me. He . . . Oh, never mind. Really, other than the shortages, we don't have it that bad. With or without men."

Tiff said. "I'm sick of washing my hair with soap because I can't find shampoo. Say, I've got an avocado. Who wants half?"

"I do." I set my journal aside and held out a hand.

"What do you write in that?" Mitzi pointed to the journal.

"Stuff. Nothing important."

Tiff said, "I wouldn't mind meeting a man who could make my stomach tingle."

Gretchen shot back, "That's childish. When Robert comes home, we'll be an important part of each other's lives, but not the centers."

A second silence fell over the group as the girls avoided eye contact. Tiff sliced her avocado in two and handed me a half.

Mitzi said, "I'm sick of bologna. Does someone want to trade for half a sandwich?"

I took a bite of avocado. "You know," I said, "I was raised on apples and pears. Loved them, but this green thing tastes like magic."

"Look, here he comes," Tiff announced. "Our favorite male. In formal dress."

A gull rose to the edge of the escape and hovered on a current of air. Tiff broke off a bread crumb and held it in her fingers.

"Hi, Gulliver," Mitzi said.

Gulliver swooped in, grabbed the crumb in his bill, and immediately banked away.

"You're going to lose a finger that way," Gretchen said.

"Wouldn't he look great if he had a tie to go with his tuxedo?" Tiff said.

"Isn't that just like a man?" Mitzi said. "Give 'im what he wants, and off he flies."

We chuckled.

"Selmo must be sweet on you," Tiff said to me.

I laid what was left of my sandwich on my lap and stared at her. "What? No."

Mitzi said, "Remember no one's seen his mistress. He may be looking."

"Or wife," Tiff said. "Who wasn't at last year's company picnic or Christmas party."

I watched the Terminal Island ferry dock. At the rail shipbuilders stood alongside women who worked the tuna canneries. A tugboat pushed a barge laden with material through the channel separating the island from the mainland. On the far side of the island stood a line of tall cranes loading war wares onto boats, to the east were docking bays that housed the skeletons of Liberty Ships under construction, and on the outer reach, the prison stood out as a reminder of the underside of Paradise.

"Well, he called it a party, but it was barely one. Look, Eve's in a mood," Tiff said.

"Yes, she is," Mitzi said. "Thinking about Selmo, are you?"

"I wasn't thinking about Selmo, at least not *that* way, and I'm not in a mood," I said.

"Ten dollars," Tiff said. "And no envelope? He's not done that before."

I laid what was left of my sandwich on my lap and stared at her. I didn't want to be associated with him that way, didn't want rumors floating about us. He'd been kind to me the day he picked me up at the train station. I'd come to like the job mostly because of the girls and didn't want to quit, but I would if Selmo dared make an advance.

The others revived the banter about Selmo and his wife and his supposed mistress. I made a final note in my journal and returned it to my bib.

Gretchen said, "Won't it be nice with the war over?" She flipped her cigarette off the landing and watched it spiral to the alley. She stood. The landing groaned. "You think if we all jumped at once this would break?"

"Don't be morbid," Tiff said. "We need a break. Let's go to the Jade Room."

"Pants and power," Gretchen said. "Let's have us a time tonight. No fruit punch or two-left-footed sailors. A movie, *Casablanca*. I could see it a hundred times. Bogey, there's a man!"

From a window below, the sound of a harmonica drifted up. We listened to the mellow tune and when the playing stopped, I asked, "Who's that?"

"Just H.T.," Tiff said. "He sings, too. He's been gone for two months. Just came back."

"The tall black man who came to work last week?"

"Yeah, that's him," Tiff said. "Actually, he's worked here

for years. I heard his mom had an operation. She's raising her daughter's kids. He had to take care of her and the children. In my opinion, that makes him a good man."

I was impressed with that as well as his harmonica playing.

Dominique stuck her head through the open window and said, "Boss is pacing the floor with his watch in hand." That said, she vanished into the hallway.

"Someone promote her to foreman?" Mitzi asked.

"No, hall monitor and blonde bitch," Tiff said.

I was surprised at Tiff's remark. She was usually kind or funny if she said something about someone. "Maybe she's just trying to help."

"She told me I needed to lose thirty pounds," Tiff said. "But forty would be better."

"Well, up hers," Gretchen said.

Dominique, seemingly too free of convention for the others, wore looped earrings and styled her blonde hair and her clothes to look like Jean Harlow. Her breasts hung loose under her blouse. Scuttlebutt had it she had a son living somewhere and she offered no accounting for the boy's father. Mitzi told me once that she'd heard Dominique had a Latin lover and the father of the boy was in prison. I thought her a bit exotic, as if she were imagined into flesh and bone and on those times when she whisked by to take a seat on the line, I was reminded of pirates and Arabian princesses.

"Ever notice how she flicks her hair as she sits to sew?"

"Tiff," I said, "Maybe you're jealous because she gets all the shampoo she wants."

"And probably rinses with champagne. Maybe I am jealous."

The landing swayed as we climbed through the window. Gretchen held my wrist. Below the dock worker sang in a baritone voice that reminded me of the rumble coming from a distant train. I trailed the others down the stairs. As I turned the corner to the main floor, I saw him limping across the floor with a book in hand.

I watched him pass by and said, "Hello."

He muttered something but didn't look my way.

"What's that you're reading?"

"I'm not reading it. I'm holding it," he said without smiling.

I smiled for both of us and said, "What's its title?"

This time he looked at me, his lips in a lopsided grin. "*Their Eyes Were Watching God.*"

"Is it about religion?"

He turned away and said, "Not so's you'd see it."

Just then Tiff came back through the doors leading to the factory. "You coming?"

I watched him limp away to the loading ramp. "Yeah."

"What were you looking at?" she asked.

"Him, the dock man. How'd he get that limp?"

"Never mind, him. He doesn't talk to us. He'd rather read some book or play the harmonica."

After seeing a movie that night, we all went to the Jade Room on Ventura, a nightclub frequented by military officers, low-ranking government bureaucrats, businessmen, and high-toned women and B movie actors. I kept Judith's birth certificate handy in case the maître d' carded me. Had she not died, she would have been twenty-three. Prepared to show the certificate, I looked the headwaiter in the eye and smiled. He looked me over and motioned us to follow.

He guided us to a table near the bandstand where a three-piece combo was playing. Three older men at an adjacent table looked us over as if appraising merchandise. We ordered drinks, ignored them, and listened to the trumpet player, a black man in his late thirties, as the tune he played rose to a crescendo. When he stopped, he turned to the bass player and wiped his head with a handkerchief to mimic Louis Armstrong.

Tiff said, "He's on marijuana. Most of them smoke it."

"Most? How do you know? I mean, do you know all musicians?" Gretchen asked.

I waved my napkin. "We agreed. No arguing."

"The ones I've slept with smoke it," Tiff said, lying as she often did for shock effect.

"Which adds up to none," Gretchen said. "Oh, shit. Don't look now, but there's Selmo, and I bet that's not his wife." She turned her face to hide her profile.

Having been warned not to, the rest of us naturally looked.

"Good Lord, she's got to be ten years younger," Tiff said.

"Maybe more," Mitzi said.

Gretchen said. "I bet no more than a couple. Women like her have the means to stay young. She probably gets facials every day."

Mitzi said, "Let's pretend we didn't notice. If he sees us, he'll gracefully duck out." She was the oldest among us by five years and worldly by our standards.

It struck me as odd that we should feel guilty when Selmo was the one out on the town with a beautiful young woman, while his wife was at home. We kept our eyes on the band, and when the musicians took a break, we huddled close and talked as if nothing in the room existed other than our conversation. Amid Tiff trying to tell a story, the maître d' arrived with four champagne flutes followed by a waiter with an ice bucket.

"Ladies, the champagne is compliments of the gentleman," he said, pointing to Selmo.

The waiter held the neck of the bottle to the side and uncorked it. We looked at Selmo who held up his own champagne flute, as did the woman with him.

"It's a bribe," Gretchen said. "Now we're his accomplices."

"Pretty nice hush money," Tiff said.

I folded my napkin and stood.

"What are you doing?" Mitzi asked.

"Going to say hello and thank him." I laid my napkin on the table and crossed the room.

Before even seeing a wedding band on the woman's finger, I figured she was Selmo's mysterious wife, and he was likely in love with her and only her.

Selmo stood as I approached the table. "Doreen, this is the young lady I mentioned, the one who writes notes."

Doreen's silk dress was black, as was her hat. A lace veil hung gracefully down one side, forming a shadow over her eye. She smiled warmly and stood. She was taller than me by two inches and slim. The dress with its stylish shoulder pads complimented her trim figure. It made me self-conscious of my cotton dress, unpadded at the shoulders, and my JCPenney heels and clutch bag. She offered me her hand, soft and unused to work, and smiled warmly.

"From what Selmo reported, you're as I'd imagined. Have a seat, will you?"

I looked back at the others who seemed stunned. I wanted to flee, but Selmo had pulled a chair back for me. I was trapped.

# -6-

In late April, Tomea Sandoval, a tanner who worked in the back of the factory, received a telegram saying her husband had been killed in action in a place called Monte Cassino, a muddy, godforsaken hill that meant nothing to Ramon Sandoval, except that Germans occupied it and he'd gone to Europe to kill them for his country. Taking the mountain, a strategic point to Allies and Germans alike, marked the turning point in the Italian campaign. Tomea had never heard of Cassino. Now she was widowed because of it. She had two children.

The sad news buzzed among us as we clocked in. I initialed my time card, placed it in the rack, and headed for my station. At the door leading to the factory floor Selmo intercepted me and walked me aside.

"Can you cook?" he asked.

"Sure. Why?"

He said Tomea would be needing assistance with her children. "It's best that she has some company to comfort her."

"I barely know her," I said.

"That's better. We won't produce any size tens today. You're a sport. You'll stay on the clock." He took my elbow and gently marched me past the women seated to start the shift. They watched us pass by. Gretchen rolled her eyes. Tiff shook her head.

The morning was brisk. We walked to his 1941 Special Deluxe, it's top down. "Hope you don't mind the air," he said. "I'll put the top up if you want."

"It's fine."

"I like the air in my face," he said.

He opened my door, and when I was seated, he closed it and hurried to the driver's door. We drove in silence toward Compton. He was preoccupied and seemed to take no notice of me. I gazed at the manicured lawns and gardens and wondered why, out of all the women, I had been selected, but I didn't ask. When the chill air got to be too much, I slipped on my sweater.

I leaned back, took in the cool air, and wondered what it would be like to own a drop-top Chevy and cruise Highway 1 or drink champagne on a whim instead of riding a streetcar to work and eating dry cornflakes for breakfast and hotdogs for dinner. Perhaps I was jealous, or maybe he was spoiled. Welcome, I thought, to the Golden State where life was more golden for some than others. In that way, it was Palouse and every other place, but the weather was better.

The streets teemed with trucks, cars, jaywalkers, and window gazers. We turned off the main boulevard and into a channel of residential streets. I broke the silence and out of farm-girl innocence asked why he wanted someone to look over Tomea.

"Her husband," he said as if that settled the matter.

"Her husband? Did you know him?"

"He was my employee and his father worked for my father. How can I not do something if something can be done?"

"It's kind," I said.

"Not exactly. My father taught me a sense of obligation for our employees even as he taught me the value of work."

I'd been told his father had made him work every part of

the business—tanner, dyer, cobbler, and dock loader, but he didn't seem like a working man. Those I knew were farmers and lumberjacks, men with calloused hands. My impression of Selmo was that he was spoiled and a bit buffoonish, a belief perhaps promoted by the women I worked with. Now I had a better opinion of him, in part because he denied he was acting out of kindness.

He turned onto a narrow street with no sidewalks and coasted to a stop in front of a set of cracked concrete steps that led to a narrow courtyard planted with snapdragons and pansies. Other than patches of green shrubbery the block was grim—wooden bungalows and one-story apartments painted in gray or white tones, asphalt shingle roofs, yellowed shades half-drawn or blinds cracked just enough to allow in splinters of light.

Before I managed to open the door, Selmo hurried around and opened it. Somewhat awkwardly, he offered his hand. I hesitated. His wife was lovely. Surely, his intentions were harmless. But what if the others were right about him? I looked at his eyes through the thick lenses that shielded them for any signs but saw nothing to hang doubt on. I accepted his hand.

He lifted a box loaded with groceries out of the backseat and told me to come along. I followed him up the walkway. The apartments formed a horseshoe. Tomea's was the third on the left. The blinds were drawn. Selmo asked me to knock. A stout woman in her sixties opened the door. She fanned herself with a Spanish fan.

"We came to see Tomea," he said. "This is Eve. She's going to help."

"*No comprendo, señor.*" The woman guarded the threshold with her robust body and a resolute gaze.

"*Bueno, vimos ayudar a Tomea a salir de su apuro.*"

"*Si. Lo siento. Esparases.*" The woman raised a finger and stepped inside.

"I'm impressed," I said.

"Don't be. If I had to go much beyond that, I'd be lost."

"You're being modest."

"No. The tanners taught me some Spanish. Tomea's husband was one of the best I ever saw. Like my father, he loved leather."

"And you?"

"I'm hard pressed to make boot manufacturing seem romantic."

"But it's important."

He set the box down and looked at the door. "Better than going barefoot."

"You like what you do?"

"Sure. Why not? Do you?"

I shrugged. "I guess. Sure."

The woman returned and motioned us inside. He gathered up the box and set it on a small table in the front room. The room was dark and cramped but impeccably clean.

Selmo and the woman exchanged conversation in Spanish. When she finished speaking, he nodded and looked at me. "Her name's Lucinda. Says the children are with the grandparents. Tomea is in the bedroom. Apparently, she's been crying since the telegram came."

I asked if I might open the blinds to let in some sunlight.

Selmo told me to go ahead, but when I started to open them, Lucinda rushed over. She shook her head and lectured me in an agitated voice.

"She says the room must stay dark," he said. "Wait here."

He followed Lucinda to the back bedroom only to return alone a few minutes later. I stood in the center of the living room. He asked me to sit.

"We've had this happen twice before. The first forty-eight hours are really bad. You stay. Tomea will be grateful for the company." He said that I was to use whatever I needed from the box he'd brought, even if it was only to feed myself.

"Someone will have to call my landlady. She'll worry about me."

"What's her number?"

He copied Mrs. Sauer's number into a pocket notebook. "Tomea has no phone, but there's a pay phone on the corner by the store we passed." He tore a blank page from his notebook and jotted down his home number. He set the note along with some coins on the coffee table and told me to call if I needed anything. He looked toward the back room. "Hope she's better soon. I need both of you at work."

He reached for the doorknob, then turned back and said, "I'll check by tomorrow. Want to know why I picked you?"

I nodded.

"You impressed Doreen. I put a lot of stock in her opinion. She has a great deal of intuition, and I have none."

It began to sprinkle. I cracked the blinds and then went to the back to see if Lucinda and Tomea were hungry. Tomea lay with her back to the bedroom door, sniffling. Beside her, fan in hand, head tilted back, Lucinda snored. The only light in the bedroom came from three candles that burned atop the dresser under a wooden cross and a laminated picture of Madonna. I left the door ajar and tiptoed away.

An hour later Lucinda emerged from the room and handed over her fan, a gesture that suggested it was my turn to watch over her friend. She pointed out her apartment to indicate that was where she was heading. I pulled a chair next to Tomea's bed. She'd cried herself out. The sheets were damp. I said I would change them. She shook her head, rolled on her side, her back to me, and returned to her previous state of silent staring. Light from the flickering candles cast our shadows on the wall. A moment passed and she touched my hand and said, "I will eat now."

I left the door ajar and went to the kitchen and spread the curtains. The sky had darkened. Rain pelted the roof. I opened a can of tomato soup. Selmo had brought fresh bread, a tube of liverwurst, and mustard. While the soup heated, I slapped together two sandwiches. I heard water splashing. It was hard to determine where it came from because the rain was falling hard. I called out to Tomea. When she didn't answer, I dismissed it as rain pouring from the roof or the strangeness of the day playing on my imagination. I poured two bowls of soup and placed them on a tray beside the sandwiches. I hoped the meal would lift her spirits.

"Soup," I said cheerfully and backed through the doorway.

The room was empty. I set the tray on a nightstand and called out to Tomea. She didn't answer. A ribbon of light shone beneath the bathroom door. I knocked and asked if she was all right but got no response. The door was locked. I banged on it and called out. She moaned. I hit the door with my shoulder. It didn't give, so I stepped back, turned sideways, and threw my weight into it. The latch gave way, and I stumbled into the bathroom and nearly fell into the tub on top of her. She lay curled up, her eyes glazed over. The bath water was pink from the blood that oozed from both forearms.

A razor blade lay on the linoleum. I picked it up and slipped it in my pocket. She stirred from her semiconscious state and muttered at me in Spanish. I grabbed two towels and wrapped her arms. She squirmed but didn't otherwise resist. The towels didn't fully stem the bleeding. I needed something better to apply pressure. I scoured through the dresser until I found a drawer with men's belts. Then I hurried back to the bathroom, looped the belts around the towels and tightened them. Lifting her from the tub proved more difficult than I'd imagined, but I managed to get her onto the floor. That was all the farther I could go. She needed an ambulance.

"Stay," I said as if it were in her to move.

On the way out the door I grabbed the coins and the telephone number Selmo had left. The clouds had lifted, and a half-moon lit the way. I banged on Lucinda's door. When she opened her blinds, I pointed to Tomea's apartment and hollered for her to help.

The doctor left the treatment room. An officer in a dark blue uniform entered. He carried a notebook in one hand and a pen in the other.

He said to the nurse. "Is this the slasher?"

The nurse nodded. "She took three pints."

"My nephew's in Europe. He might need blood." He looked at me. "Who are you?"

"I work with her."

He lowered the notebook and propped his pencil atop an ear. "Okay, tell me, was she bored or was it over some guy?"

I felt blood running to my cheeks. "Neither. Her husband was killed in action. In Italy."

That gave the cop pause. He lowered his head and swallowed hard. When he looked up, he cleared his throat and asked, "Where?"

"Italy, and that's all I know."

"Italy," he said pensively and fumbled with his notepad. "I need to write a report. Give me some information. I mean if you can."

He asked his questions politely. I answered those that I could. Finished, he thanked me and said that he would get back to me, if necessary, but it wasn't likely. He smiled sheepishly and turned to go. After taking two steps, he paused.

"Do they think she'll survive?"

"Is that for your report?" the nurse asked.

He lowered his gaze. "For me."

"It looks like it," the nurse said. "But she's going to need support when she leaves here."

"Thank you. I'll check back on her later. I promise to go easy on any questions."

When the nurses wheeled Tomea to a ward, I followed. No one questioned my right to be with her. The nurses lifted her onto the bed and strapped her arms to the side rails. One said that I could do nothing to help and may as well leave and get some sleep. I said that I had come along with the ambulance and was waiting for others to arrive. She located an outdated copy of *Life magazine* for me.

I sat beside Tomea with the magazine opened in my lap. I started to read, but the words soon blurred. I awoke to the sound of voices in the hallway. I closed the magazine and looked at Tomea. She seemed remarkably at peace. The same officer sat in a chair in the corner.

"I didn't want to wake you," he said. "I have a couple of questions."

Just then Selmo nudged the door open and looked in. He glanced back over his shoulder and then held the door open for Doreen.

"How's she doing?" Selmo asked.

The officer asked Selmo who he was. His tone made it obvious he was being protective.

"I'm her employer. Why's she strapped down?"

"So she won't tear out the stitches," I said.

"Guess those questions can wait." The officer stood, let his notebook drop to his side, and walked to the bed. "She'll be up and around in a day or two. I know the staff here. They'll take good care of her. I'm on duty tomorrow. My wife's fudge is the best. I'll bring her some."

"That's nice of you," Selmo said.

"Got a nephew fighting in Italy. Could be in her husband's unit. Well, good night."

After he left, Doreen said, "You must be very tired by now."

I was and was not, but how could I rest? "I'm fine," I said.

"We'll take over." Selmo removed his glasses. His gentle eyes brought a kind of mature dignity to him. "I brought someone along to take you home."

Doreen took my hand. "Yes, go on now. It's nice to see you again."

As I stood, the room swirled. I sat back down.

"Are you okay?" Doreen asked.

"Yes, just dizzy."

"Have you eaten?"

"No. I haven't." I recalled the untouched food on the tray in Tomea's bedroom. Letting food go bad was a sin. Mother hated waste.

Selmo went to the hallway and said, "Come on in."

Holding his fedora, the dock man stepped into the room. He turned the hat around in his hands.

"H.T., you know Eve, right?"

"I've seen her." The dock man nodded to me. His hair seemed sprinkled with a film of dust, which I realized was a smattering of premature gray. He was older than I'd thought.

"Do us a favor," Selmo said. "You know someplace nearby to eat this late?"

"The Kettle. All-night diner."

"Feed her, okay?" Selmo spread open his billfold, gave H.T. a five-dollar bill, and turned to me. "Go with H.T. He'll get you home."

When I stood, my legs held up. I took a last look at Tomea and said, "She probably didn't mean it."

"Probably not." Selmo grimaced. "She'll realize her husband would want her to live."

"You're kind."

Doreen whispered, "Don't say things like that. You'll embarrass him."

"What was that?" Selmo snapped.

"Nothing, dear. You get some sleep, Eve," she said and patted my hand.

H.T. acknowledged me with a nod and said the car was near the front entrance. I followed him out. He had a long stride, and, despite his limp, I couldn't keep up. He looked back twice as if urging me to walk faster, but I intentionally walked no faster.

He opened the passenger door on Selmo's Chevrolet for me. "Where you'll be eatin' at isn't the best, missy, but it'll fill you." He slammed my door.

On the seat lay a thick book that I assumed was Selmo's. I picked it up and tried to read the title, but it was too dark in the interior to see. When H.T. slid in behind the wheel, he looked at the book and seemed to take exception to my holding it.

I laid it down and said, "Thanks for doing this."

"Okay, missy." He removed his hat.

"Eve, call me Eve." Even more so than with Selmo, I felt ill at ease with him. I decided to try to relieve the tension. "Someone told me H.T. stands for Hard Times?"

"Howard Thomas. Last name Elders, missy."

"Eve," I said. "Last name Halvers."

"Halvers? What kind of name is that?"

"It's my father's. My mother is a Sorensen."

"Okay." He started the engine, adjusted the mirror, and pressed the clutch. "Late as it is, probably ought to eat soup."

He shifted the lever into first gear. The car lurched forward before I could speak. The pavement glistened like black glass. The tires hissed over the moist surface. The top was up, but the car was cold. I asked him to turn on the heater. He did but without speaking, then lit a cigarette, leaned back, and looked ahead.

I was content with the silence. The image of Tomea lying in the tub preyed on me. Hers was desperation beyond my understanding. I wondered why I'd failed to see the signs. Would her despair have been obvious to someone more worldly? It occurred to me that in an oblique way I'd saved her life, but would she be glad to have her life back, or resent me for interfering? I cracked the wing window to let air flow in. The moist breeze flowing in softened the night.

H.T. said, "Thought you wanted the heat?"

I looked at his profile. "Hardly Talks. That must be what H.T. stands for."

He smiled painfully and looked in the rearview mirror.

"I like the smell of the air after a rain," I said.

He rolled down his window, flicked the cigarette out, and began humming a tune I didn't recognize. Even when softly humming the sound of his voice was remarkably compelling. He seemed lost in the tune.

"What's that you're humming?" I asked.

"'See That My Grave Is Kept Clean.'"

I thought it an odd answer that further supported my opinion of him. "Never mind." We didn't speak again until he pulled into the diner parking lot.

"We're here."

No light came from the restaurant. "You're sure it's open?"

He shut off the engine and opened his door, grabbed the book off the seat, and walked to the darkened diner. He went through the door without looking back. He seemed determined to make a campaign out of being rude. I considered staying in the car and demanding that he take me straight home, but

I was hungry and felt obligated to honor Selmo for his kind thought. I picked up H.T.'s hat, shoved the door handle down, and leaned a shoulder into the door.

The café, decorated in red and white tables with aluminum moldings and red vinyl chairs with chrome legs, was lit with florescent lights. Blackout shades covered the windows. Red-topped mushroom-shaped stools lined the front of the counter. The café smelled of bacon and burger meat. H.T. sat in a back booth by the window, his large hands holding the book open, his eyes intent on its pages. Against the wall behind him stood a jukebox.

Except for the tinkling of spoons on coffee cups and the muttered conversation of a waitress and a patron, the diner was hushed. A half dozen men and women, apparently shift workers, sat scattered throughout the tables, some reading papers, some sipping coffee. There was something haunting about working late shifts. I was reminded of my many nights working the restaurant in Pullman, the hollowed-out eyes of men sitting with both hands wrapped around their coffee mugs. These men were no different, and the café was much the same, a place of respite for those who couldn't rest.

The eyes of the customers followed me down the aisle, and when I tossed the hat on the table and slid into the seat opposite H.T., they continued to stare. A sense of melancholy crept over me. I didn't belong here. I had seen too much blood and despair today. It was my turn to be rude. I moved the hat beside his elbow.

"You forgot it."

He didn't look up. "No, I didn't."

Murmurings came from nearby tables, and I was suddenly aware of how my being with H.T. might be interpreted by the others. After all that had happened that day, I dared not look at their faces for fear of causing a scene.

"They're staring," I whispered.

H.T. handed me a menu. "I eat here once a week or so. Food won't likely kill you."

"Is that the good news of the day?" I was too hungry to study a menu. I set it aside and said, "Chicken soup and grilled cheese sounds good. Will you order for me?"

He looked up long enough to nod.

Thinking music might help me better pass the next several minutes, I went to the jukebox and read the selections. They were the standards. I dropped in the few coins Selmo had left me, pressed buttons randomly, and returned to the table. A couple of male customers stared at me. This time I stared back until they looked away.

H.T. glanced up, but he didn't speak. I looked at the title of the book he read, *The Grapes of Wrath*. I was struck with curiosity about the man reading it. I wanted to ask about the book, but it was obvious he wasn't open to any questions. "Swinging on a Star" played in the background.

The waitress, who'd not come to take our order, stood with her elbows on the counter talking. A few minutes passed before H.T. looked at the counter and closed the book. He waved to get the waitress's attention. She didn't acknowledge him.

"Miss, we'd like to order." His baritone voice carried across the room.

The waitress looked our way, said she was coming but kept talking. The music drowned out their conversation, but it was apparent that we were now central to it.

H.T. set the book aside. "One too many black men with one too many white women."

I didn't like the idea of her adding to the weight of the day. I walked to the counter and pointed to our booth. "We'd like some service. I don't know what he wants, but I'd like soup and a grilled cheese."

The men she was talking with lowered their heads. She

wrote down the order, and I returned to the table. H.T., his jaw tense, sat sullen. I asked, "Are you okay?"

He kept his eye on the window shade. "Does it matter?"

"Why are you being rude?"

He cut an eye at me. "White bitch won't wait on us, and I'm rude?"

The full day fell on me at once. Too exhausted to argue, especially with someone so mercurial, I said, "Just take me home."

"Selmo wants you to eat."

We sat, H.T. staring at the counter, me looking at pictures of movie stars on the wall while listening to music. The book lay on the table as if holding it down. Several minutes passed before the waitress arrived with a tray. She set my soup and sandwich on the table with a rattle.

"Anything else?" she asked.

"Some courtesy," H.T. said.

Unflappable, she pointed to a sign on the wall. "In case you can't read, it says that we reserve the right to refuse service to anyone."

I pushed my food away. "Let's go, H.T. I don't want to eat here."

"Eat," he said. "Selmo wants you to."

"Honestly, let's go."

The waitress said, "Suit yourself, but you have to pay."

H.T. dug in his pocket and laid two dollars next to the plate. "Keep the change."

It was sprinkling. We drove the boulevard in silence as the wiper blades slapped back and forth on the windshield. The gloom that pervaded the interior of the car reflected the gloom of the night. Although I felt H.T. had every right to brood, his reticence added more vexation to a trying day. I felt some satisfaction in refusing to eat the meal, but that did little to relieve my hunger pangs. Hungry as I was, I was equally tired. I felt a surge of guilt for what had transpired in the café. It almost seemed as if I'd schemed in some way with those in the café, the waitress and even the men who leered at us. I wanted to tell H.T. that I too was angry over the treatment we'd been subjected to and that I admired the way he'd conducted himself in the café. I didn't. Instead, I looked at the storefronts we passed.

He broke out humming, his deep voice almost mournful.

When we came to a stop at the next red light, I said, "The waitress was a bitch."

He glanced at me and said, "Her mother was a bitch."

"Her grandmother was a bitch."

"And her great-grandmother." He smiled. He had a pleasant smile, but it vanished almost at once and he returned to humming.

"What's that tune?"

"You wouldn't know."

I ignored his gruffness. "The other day I heard you singing. You're good."

"What would you know?"

"Stop it."

"Stop what?"

"You're very rude. You were rude when I asked about the book. I don't like rudeness."

"Well, Missy, I'm drivin' miles away from where I should be 'cause of you."

"I didn't say you're Frank Sinatra."

He smiled again. "You like him?"

He was obviously baiting me. "Isn't everyone supposed to?"

"No."

In truth, I wasn't a Sinatra fan. In that way, I was the

exception to the day. "I can't figure out why a woman in her forties would open her blouse in public and ask him to autograph her brassiere."

"This light's forever. So, what should she do?"

The full impact of the day finally hit me. "Just take me home, and please don't talk."

"That's what I've been trying to do," he said.

When the light changed, I was grateful. He pressed the accelerator, and the tires slipped. The car went sideways for an instant before he righted it. "Wet," he said.

I said, "I do like the way you sing. It's the blues, right?"

"Good guess."

"I'm not familiar with the blues. The radio where I lived played big band and Sinatra, that stuff."

He grinned to himself.

"So, what makes your music the blues?"

"When I'm picking cotton, I'm singing. And when I'm singing, I'm picking cotton."

I squinted at him. "What? Is that a riddle?"

"You might say."

"Did you pick cotton?"

He shook his head. "I've got to pay attention to the road."

I remained clammed up for the rest of the drive. As we neared my street, I felt relieved the day would soon be over. Twice a week Mrs. Sauer left a change of sheets, folded and waiting at the base of the bed. It was too late to bathe, but clean sheets would take some of the edge off the day. I let slipping between clean sheets occupy my thoughts for a time. Then as H.T. turned right onto a thoroughfare two blocks from Mrs. Sauer's, he muttered something I couldn't discern. He tapped the brake and brought the car to a stop at the curb.

"Just behave," he said.

A white beam illuminated the car's interior. I looked in his direction. His eyes were trained on the rearview mirror. Sweat glistened on his forehead. I glanced over my shoulder and saw the pulsing red light. "But you didn't do anything," I said.

He opened his window and reached for his billfold. "Yes, I did."

I glanced back at the glaring light. A policeman approached our car from the left side. An inordinate time passed before he shined his flashlight inside the car, first in H.T.'s face, then in mine. He asked for a driver's license. H.T. handed his over to the cop who shined his light on it, and asked H.T. to step out. Then he leaned in the window and said, "Miss, break out some ID."

H.T. opened the door, and the cop stepped back, his hand resting on the stock of his revolver. My temples pounded as I unsnapped my purse. The only identification I carried was my dead sister's birth certificate. A second cop tapped on my window and when I turned my face, he hit it with a flashlight beam. He walked the light over the dash, the floorboard, and the back seat. I rolled down the window and handed him Judith's birth certificate.

"Get out," he said.

I stepped onto the curbside. The patrolman held his flashlight under his armpit and studied the paper in the light, then shined the beam in my face and asked my date of birth. I gave him Judith's birth date. He nodded.

"Where were you born?"

"Whitman County, Washington."

"Where're you headed?"

"Home," I said.

"To Whitman County?"

"No. Where I rent a room." I gave him Mrs. Sauer's address.

"Where you two coming from?"

"Did I do something, officer?"

"You don't ask questions. You answer them."

I glanced at H.T. He glared, telegraphing me to behave.

"A hospital. No, the hospital and then to eat. I hadn't eaten all day. H.T. was taking me home and so. . . ."

"H.T.'s the Negro?"

I nodded.

The other cop walked H.T. away from the car. The officer questioning me looked back toward the cruiser where H.T. was leaning over the hood, legs spread wide. Up to then I'd been only confused. Now I was scared.

"What're you doing to him?" I asked.

The cop pushed back the brim of his hat. "Just answer questions. Whose car is this?"

"Mr. Stillman's. He told H.T. to take me home in it."

"From the hospital?"

"From the hospital. You see Tomea, a woman from work, tried to kill herself because her husband was killed in Italy."

"When?"

"I don't know. Yesterday. The day before. I don't know. I was watching her for Mr. Stillman and . . . What's this all about?"

"You were doing fine. Keep talking."

"H.T. didn't steal the car, if that's what you're thinking."

He grinned. "Who said anything about stealing a car?"

My ears burned. I felt inept and decided under the circumstances volunteering anything further was unwise. He'd have to pry details from me a question at a time.

"Who's Mr. Stillman?"

"He owns Lucien's Bootery off Harbor Street." I could tell the policeman presumed I was lying. Worse, I realized that it sounded like a lie.

The officer told me not to move and went to the squad car.

The cops conferred for some seconds, their eyes on H.T., who stood, dignified and defiant, in the cruiser's headlight beams.

A minute later the cop who'd been questioning me returned. He waved the certificate in my face and said, "Tell me something."

"What's that?"

"A young gal like you, what're doing in the company of a felon?"

"A what?"

"An ex-con."

The question took me aback. Up to then my concern had centered on the birth certificate and what they were doing to H.T. I explained that I worked with H.T., that he seemed like a nice man, and that I knew nothing of his background.

"You make it a habit to ride around at night with Negroes you don't know anything about? A nice man who did time for manslaughter?" the cop asked.

I read the vulgar thought behind his eyes. "I don't make anything a habit. And he *is* nice."

He nodded slowly and said, "And I'm a ballerina." He shined his light on the seat where the book lay. "Hand me that."

I gathered up the book and handed it over. He held the birth certificate in his flashlight hand, opened the book and examined it under the light. He handed it back.

"*The Grapes of Wrath*? Is this your library book?"

"No. His," I said.

The cop shook his head, returned the birth certificate and grinned. "Two more days and we could have booked you for an overdue book."

"An overdue book?" I folded the certificate and slipped it in my purse.

The officer told me to have a seat in the car.

A moment later the first cop peered at me through the driver's window. "Sorry for the inconvenience, Miss, but you'll have to step out and come to the patrol car."

He escorted me to the front of the cruiser and stood me beside H.T. As one watched us, the other cop searched under the seats and in the trunk of Selmo's car. I glanced at H.T. He stared straight ahead, his expression one of detachment.

Cars slowed as they passed by. Drivers gawked. It struck me that at that very moment the world was in disarray, and here in a Los Angeles intersection, H.T. and I, who'd done no harm to anyone, were the center of a petty drama that meant one thing to me and quite another to H.T. The officer slammed the trunk shut, looked toward us, and shook his head as if disappointed.

The one beside us handed over H.T.'s driver's license. "You're free to go."

As I passed the one who'd searched the car, he glared. I held my chin up and walked on by. We didn't speak again until H.T. pulled to a stop at the house. The house was dark, but I wondered whether Mrs. Sauer was waiting up as she sometimes did. H.T. kept the engine idling.

I pressed down on the handle and cracked the door. "Thanks, I'm sorry that happened with the police."

"I got to go."

"You could say you're welcome."

"You wanna talk all night?"

I opened the door and stood beside the car. "I'd like to hear you sing sometime."

He continued to stare straight ahead. "I owe Mr. Stillman favors. This was one."

"You were great company," I said as caustically as I could and slammed the door.

He kept watch until I unlocked the front door, then drove

away. When the taillights rounded the corner, I opened the door and went inside. Glad to at last be out of reach of the day's ugliness, I made the bed with the fresh sheets, brushed my teeth, and undressed. I took my journal to the bed, sank into the mattress, and pulled the bedspread to my chin. I jotted down the day's events under the headings of "Despair" and "Indignant cops." My last thought was that all that happened that evening wasn't because of either him or me, but because of the two of us being together. That awareness didn't remove the effects of the day. In some muddled moment between sleep and consciousness I imagined hearing footsteps crossing the living room but couldn't be sure the sound wasn't just part of a dream.

# -7-

In June, the Allies marched into Rome unopposed, and I received a packet of mail from Mother. My hands shook as I opened the envelope and dumped the contents. I untied the ribbon that bound the letters. One was addressed from Link to me. I smiled. I loved all my brothers but had a special attachment to Link, who despite his easygoing ways had been our fearless protector. At age twelve, he'd challenged three boys who'd bullied August because he stammered. Link got the worst of it, but in the aftermath the boys apologized and never bothered August again.

After Dad left, Link dropped out of school to work odd jobs, sometimes bringing home a pocketful of coins that he and Mother would count out on the kitchen table. He never held back anything for himself. Once a week, winter or summer, he and my other brothers walked the train tracks, sling bags strapped over their shoulders, and gathered coal from the track bed. I was reminded of them at playful moments, their arms strung over each other's shoulders teasing one another. Other times they fought with each other. Occasionally, when they were short a player or two, my brothers invited me to play baseball with them and Link warned the other boys not to go hard on his sister, but not too easy on her either. I pictured Link grinning, somehow seeing humor in our family's dire state.

Link was mature in ways the rest of us weren't, and quick to scold. He'd admonished me to stay away from boys like Jess, a warning I'd heeded until the day I took work at the Newsome farm. Had Link not been off to fight the war, Jess would never have attempted what he did.

I tore open the envelope and read it:

> Dear Little Sis,
>
> I hope this letter finds you well. Your brother is now a paratrooper. I'm with the 101st Division somewhere in England assigned to a glider company, but I can't talk about my duties, etc. I'm having some good times here when we're not training. My buddy Oscar, a kid from Pennsylvania, and I met a fine British family. We're now learning a game called rugby. It resembles football but is rougher. I have bruises to prove it. The English gals are friendly and very brave, but there is a sadness in everyone's determination. They've lost a lot. We're losing loved ones and so are they, but their homes and history have been destroyed by bombs.
>
> Mom wrote that you left some time back. She said Jess had been spreading things about you around town. I wrote to her that it wasn't true, that no matter what he said you wouldn't do what he's claiming. I want you to know he'll pay for it. Anyhow, I understand why you'd leave home. You always were a dreamer, and you can't catch a dream if you don't chase one.
>
> All my love,
>
> Your brother the missing Link.

Comforted by the news that he was safe in England, I placed the letter in my suitcase and forgot about it. It was good news soon followed by news on the radio of more progress on the war front, news that encouraged all of us at Lucien's. The Germans were retreating in Italy, and hopes were they'd soon surrender, so that all efforts could be directed at defeating Japan. Then on Tuesday June 6th came the story that incited both optimism and worry when news of the Normandy invasion broke over the radio waves. British, French, and American soldiers had embarked in bad weather, over high, rough seas and were now ashore, engaging several German divisions. Too many rumors were tacked to the news of the invasion to determine precisely what the truth was, but men were dying in mass.

That day, as the girls smoked on our break, Tiff said my brother was probably involved in the invasion. I fell silent. What if I heard that Link was wounded or worse? *Don't*, I cautioned myself, as if thinking it was the same as willing it. Although I was uncertain what exactly glider companies did, it sounded as if it were safe duty. Besides, he might still be in England. I calmed myself with that thought.

That Thursday, June 8th, Mitzi and I went to the Fox Theater in Hollywood. The show opened with film of the Allies entering Rome. As Romans on the screen waved flags at passing tanks, the audience, mostly women, stood. Some cheered, some hugged each other, some shed tears, and some did all three. I was glad no film of the Normandy invasion was shown. In the row in front of us, a woman stood and began to sing "Happy Days Are Here Again." Then, one or two at a time, the audience joined in. Soon all were standing and singing. Smiling strangers reached out to strangers to hold hands. Mitzi urged me to my feet. The projectionist started to show the cartoon but stopped it in mid-frame. The lights came on. The audience sang until the moment exhausted itself. Finally, we applauded and sat.

Tears streaked the cheeks of the woman who'd started it

all. She wiped her eyes, then looked back and asked us if we had anyone overseas. Mitzi said she had two cousins. I said, "Three brothers, one a Merchant Marine, one a sailor, and a third with the Hundred and First."

"The ones trapped behind German lines," she said.

"No, he's in a glider," I said naively. "He's not . . ."

"Yes, them. The paratroopers. They got scattered. I heard it."

I started to protest, but words wouldn't come.

"Oh, no. What have I said?" She covered her mouth. "I'm sorry."

"Hush up," someone said.

On the big screen Porky Pig stuttered. I bit my lip to hold back the tears. Mitzi asked if I was okay. I squeezed her hand, then let go, and walked unsteadily up the aisle. I stopped halfway to the lobby and removed my heels. It didn't help. In the lobby I found a couch and sat. My hands shook. I tapped a cigarette out of my pack. Like my coworkers, I'd taken up the habit. It took three tries before I could light up. I drew smoke deep in my lungs, leaned back, and exhaled.

Faces of schoolboys from home reeled through my mind. I remembered how Link had praised Dick Neubauer who, even before Pearl Harbor, had joined the Canadian Army. I pictured boys from Palouse and Garfield, flush with excitement as they cheerfully answered the call to duty. In the months following Pearl Harbor a third of the males under age thirty from Palouse, Garfield, and Potlatch, including my brothers, were in uniform. Palouse held farewells for them. The community's first casualty was Truman Hartley, killed when a truck rolled over him as he and others pushed it out of the mud during a training exercise, hardly the heroic act he or the proud citizens of Palouse had imagined. Now Link was likely trapped somewhere behind enemy lines or worse.

If anyone, why not Jess Newsome? No, not Jess. He got a deferral because his brothers had signed up and he was the last son of a wheat baron, the spoiled boy used to having things his way. Yes, but not with me. My thoughts shifted back to Link. *Please, not him.* I felt I was being selfish at the same time. But of course, if one were to die, it would be him. If there wasn't a lion's den to jump in, he would dig a pit and find his own lion to put in it.

I took a last draw on the cigarette, snubbed it out, and lit another. Mitzi stood holding the theater door open. "Eve, you'll miss the movie."

I buried the cigarette in the ashtray, slipped on my heels, then stood, and smoothed my skirt. I walked calmly to the open door. Somehow it seemed that the least I owed my brother was to be dignified.

"Are you okay?" she asked.

"Fine. I'm fine. Let's see the movie."

# -8-

THE DAYS OF SUNLIGHT LENGTHENED and the heat inside the factory became unbearable. Even with windows open the air was stifling, and some days more oppressive than others. Work on the line never slowed. The Marines, now fighting in Saipan beside Army soldiers, needed boots. Boots, Selmo reminded us almost daily, were what kept the Marines advancing. His speeches did nothing to relieve the temperature, but every two hours he shut down our stations and told us to take a break. Come summer, he said, it would worsen.

As the days warmed, I became more and more detached from my surroundings and the daily breaks on the fire escape. Each lunch, every discussion seemed a repetition of one before. I knew by then that Gretchen was right, that we were making it on our own without men. It wasn't that I didn't want men in my life. It was the idea of being on my own that appealed to me. After work I hurried to escape the noise and heat and hiked 10th Street uphill, past South Pacific Street and Grande Avenue to Gaffey Street where I caught my streetcar and wrote down random observations in my journal.

I couldn't sleep. I spent the early night hours sitting with my ear to the radio in Mrs. Sauer's den, after which I retired to my bedroom, jotted nonsense in my journal, and wrote letters to Mother and my brothers or Avis, whose letters in turn updated me in on happenings in Palouse. Lying in bed, I'd find myself restless, dissatisfied with something I couldn't define.

This wasn't the life I'd anticipated, in part because I missed some of my past life and it wasn't what I'd imagined on the other side of any rainbow. It was my first spring away from home seeing the shadowed slopes of Kamiak Butte and smelling the rich earth freshly turned by plowshares and watching the clear evening sky busy with flitting barn swallows. The very things I'd run from I now missed.

Tomea had returned to the factory. She wore a black scarf on her head and dark long-sleeved blouses and went about her new job as a quality inspector. The long-sleeved garments that covered her wrists served as evidence of her act and added to the whispers that trailed her. She avoided people, and especially avoided me. I hadn't told a soul about that evening, but from the way Tomea looked at me I gathered that she thought differently.

I often stumbled upon H.T. I'd turn a corner, and he'd be coming from the opposite direction, humming, or I'd step outside to smoke, and he'd be loading a shipment of boots on the back of a truck, or I'd pass through the warehouse at lunchtime, and he'd be seated on a crate reading a book or playing his harmonica. Several times I said hello, but he avoided eye contact and offered a nod, nothing more. I'd done nothing to merit his rudeness, so I stopped acknowledging him.

In the weeks following the incident with Tomea and the episode with H.T., nothing eventful had occurred at work to break the daily routine. Since midmorning I'd been looking anxiously up at the clock. At the sound of the lunch bell, I bolted from my stool and dashed to the hallway. When I stepped inside the women's room, I heard sniffling. So as not to embarrass either of us, I coughed to announce myself and waited.

I said, "I can come back."

Whoever occupied the stall neither moved nor spoke. She blew her nose. I opened the door to leave. The toilet flushed and the door opened. Dominique stepped out, daubing her eyes with a square of tissue. She said, "It's free now."

I asked, "Are you okay?"

She blew her nose. "I'm fine."

Her tears were none of my business. Still, I spoke up. "You don't look. . . ."

"I said, I'm fine."

"Are you sure?"

"You better go before someone barges in on you too." She ran her fingers through her platinum curls and stormed off.

I was baffled at her behavior. She'd always been polite when we spoke in passing. She didn't invite conversation beyond that and seemed to prefer being alone on breaks. I respected her for being private, but at the moment she seemed in need of a friend. After I finished in the ladies' room, I looked for her and found her sitting on the back steps.

"Mind if I join you?"

She looked up. "Don't ask a bunch of questions."

"Okay." I sat. The concrete was warm. The smell of decay from garbage cans up the street wafted over to us. I pinched my nose, said, "Phew," and opened my lunch pail. "Can't imagine anything less feminine than a lunch bucket," I said.

"How about our overalls?"

I looked at hers. "A necktie."

"Can't even tell we have tits, for Christ's sake," she said.

No one in my family used such language. My Methodist mother forbade it, my brothers had sheltered me from it as best they could, and none of us ever discussed any part of the human anatomy normally covered by under garments.

"Can't tell we have breasts," I corrected.

"That's my experience," Dominique pulled at her bib to emphasize the fact. "Why aren't you with your friends up on the balcony?"

"Everyone needs a change."

She re-wrapped her sandwich and closed it in her lunch box. "You don't need this big of a change." She stood ready to leave.

Just then a truck turned up the alley, negotiated a half-turn and backed up to the dock. H.T. stepped out of the storage room. He glanced at us and quickly went to meet the truck driver, a woman. She handed him a clipboard. He nodded, initialed the invoice, and returned for his dolly. He hummed the same tune I'd heard him hum in the car.

I looked up at Dominique and shook my head. "You don't have to leave. I'll go."

"I appreciate what you're trying to do, but don't."

"No?"

Dominique climbed the steps. She reached the top and opened the door.

"Wait," I said.

She paused and raised her eyebrows.

"Do you have someone to talk to?"

"What kind of question is that?"

"No particular kind. But if you need a friend, try me."

"I don't mix work and friendship."

She passed through the door. On the loading dock H.T. pushed a dolly with a stack of boxed boots to the back of the truck. He stopped so the driver could count the boxes and looked in my direction. I smiled and waved. He smiled back.

When the truck drove away, he came over and sat beside me. "That night it wasn't your doing," he said. "It's people. It's how they are." He looked directly at me, something he'd not done since dropping me off in front of Mrs. Sauer's.

"What about how people are?" I said.

"People see and assume . . . It was just that, but you should'a been angrier."

"I was angry. At the cops and at you," I said.

"I wanted you to know is all." He rubbed his jaw, stood, and walked away.

Dominique waited by the time-card rack. She watched me and the others slip out of our overalls and hang them on a hook. I clocked out and stepped toward the exit. She headed me off.

"I'll buy drinks." She smiled. It seemed sincere, if bashful.

"I've got a streetcar to catch," I said, "and I told the girls I'd go to the USO."

"Oh." She looked toward the door. It was true she looked like Harlow, maybe prettier. At the same time, there was something girlish about her. "Fine, I understand."

I wondered what had brought about the change. "No. I really don't want to go to. . . ."

She said, "It's fine."

Wondering if she had an ulterior motive, I looked at her closely. "There's the trolley."

"There are lots of them, and we call them streetcars," she said.

"You're right. There are lots of streetcars. Wait here. I'll tell them I'm taking a rain check on the dance. Besides, my feet haven't recovered, and it's been a while."

The others were gathered outside on the dock waiting for me. I said, "I can't go tonight. Something unexpected came up. I'll go next time."

Mitzi said. "But we'll miss you."

Gretchen shook her head. "It'll be hard, ladies, but we can have fun without Eve."

Trailing the others as they walked away, Mitzi looked

back and shook her head. My insides churned. I realized as they turned the corner without me that they had become family to me.

Dominique waited inside the back door. "Ever been to Tasco's?"

"No. I never heard of it."

"Well, follow me."

We stepped down from the loading dock. H.T. stood on the platform, arms folded across his chest, sleeves rolled up exposing his lean forearms. I waved. He didn't. "To hell with you," I muttered and right away felt a rush of shame.

I hurried to catch Dominique who was already headed down the alley.

"Who were you talking to?" she asked.

"Myself."

The alley opened onto 4th Street. Gretchen and the others stood at the corner, talking in a circle. They saw us and nodded knowingly, then disappeared down 4th. I knew I would be the topic at lunch the next day.

Tasco's sat a block off the piers, sandwiched between two brick warehouses. A single upstairs window above the entrance faced the harbor and opened to a modest balcony decorated with pots of pansies and daffodils. Dominique pointed to the upstairs and said, "That's where the tavern owner lives with his wife and daughter."

When she opened the front door, a ship's bell announced our entry. The place was empty. A mahogany bar ran the length of the tavern to the kitchen. A sign above the bar read, "No Ship-Deck Language Tolerated on the Ship's Deck." A burly bartender looked up from under his square-shaped eyeglasses and bushy red eyebrows and called Dominique by her name. He wore a white shirt and a red vest with a gold watch chain hanging out of one pocket. He took his pocket watch out and said, "You're early. Go ahead, seat yourselves."

A row of brass kerosene lamps hung from the main support beam. Muted light from them glistened on the bar's polished surface. Like the bar, the tables all reflected the lights. Brass fixtures hung on every wall—ship's bells, anchors, spyglasses, sextants. A bandstand on the far side of the tables was built in the shape of a captain's deck. I felt like Alice must have when she fell into the rabbit's hole or Dorothy waking up in Oz.

Dominique said, "The floor, bar, ceiling, every scrap of wood and most of the brass came from clipper ships that sailed from here and brought tea and spices back to the West Coast. Romantic, huh?"

"Where's Dorothy or the Queen of Hearts?" I asked.

Dominique said, "What?" She gazed at me and nodded. "Okay, Alice. You'll probably not see her, but there's bound to be a few Mad Hatters coming in soon. Any Dorothy will be a hardworking woman."

I knew then that Dominique and I would get along. I'd heard comments from women who snickered at her as she walked past. I'd credited it to jealousy. I wondered what they would have to say if they tried to get to know her. She motioned me to a stool and introduced me to the bartender and owner, Sandy. She ordered two beers and two oyster stews.

Sandy slapped his towel on the bar and shouted, "Special customers. Two Iberian oysters."

A woman gazed out over the pass-through. "Hello, Dominique. Long time, no see. Two pretty ladies. The men will be happy."

The tavern was empty. "What men?" I asked.

Dominique and Sandy grinned. Then Sandy moved down the bar to polish a spot.

"Tell me," Sandy asked, "did you come to San Pedro to make boots?"

Dominique grinned. “Of course she did. Why else would a woman be here?”

“True. Why would anyone want to do anything else? Isn’t that why Dominique came?”

“Actually, I came to Los Angeles chasing a dream.”

“What’s that?”

“To be an actress. It’s a cliché, but it’s true. I got hooked when I played Buttercup in *The H.M.S. Pinafore* and Rosalind in *As You Like It.* I came to L.A., worked, and paid for acting lessons. I even auditioned twice for bit parts.”

“I love movies, even imagined myself as a sultry femme fatale. But I never really considered acting. I refused to take a minor role in a school play because I was too shy. You’re brave.”

Dominique tilted her head and looked at me questioningly. “You’ve got the face.”

“No, I don’t. Tell me what happened. Your dream and all.”

“I guess it’s the same as a lot of girls’ stories. I met a man, got pregnant, and had a son. That doesn’t go well on an acting résumé. I read for the roles, but never got a real screen test.” That said, she fell silent, and her mood darkened.

I didn’t know what to say to lift the gloom. I had my own dark story but bringing that up would only further dampen her mood. The strained silence went on. Minutes passed. Finally, the woman who’d spoken from the pass-through brought out a brass tray and set two steaming bowls in front of us. They smelled of butter and salt and garlic.

“I’m Rosemarie,” the woman said in a booming voice, “cook and sometimes Sandy’s wife.” She looked in Sandy’s direction and they exchanged smiles. She leaned a hand on the back of Dominique’s chair and asked, “Have you heard from Eduardo?”

Dominique shook her head.

Sandy came over to us. He leaned his elbows on the table and looked at me. "Stew's a Danish recipe, but my sometimes wife's Portuguese, so here it's Iberian oysters. Enjoy it."

Rosemarie elbowed him in the ribs. "Let's let them eat in peace."

When they moved away, I asked Dominique who Eduardo was.

"A long story, too complicated. Eat." She picked up her spoon. "One spoonful of stew, one mouthful of beer." She demonstrated this for me.

I dipped my spoon in the bowl. "I've never had oysters."

"Now you will."

I blew on my spoon, then took a mouthful. The broth was good harbor for a hungry mouth. I spooned more into my mouth and took a swallow of beer. Dominique did the same. We ate without talking. Finished, she pushed her bowl aside and ordered two more beers. Her brow knotted as she gazed up at the ceiling seemingly looking through it.

"Are you okay?" I asked.

She nodded and smiled.

"Was Eduardo your husband?"

"How do you know I have one?"

"People talk."

"My son's father." She lit a cigarette and offered me one. "Andy's six. Lives with my parents near Porterville. Here, look." She fumbled in her purse and came out with a pocket album of snapshots. She laid the photos before me on the bar and began thumbing through them one at a time. "This one was as a baby."

"The diaper's a giveaway," I said.

She paused to study me, then said, "That's funny."

"Why didn't you laugh?"

"Because I don't have a sense of humor." She turned over

another snapshot and told its story and then another. I enjoyed the unhurried moment. Looking at children's pictures beat the clumsy dancing of sailors.

She returned the pictures to her purse and called for another beer. "He'll be handsome, don't you think?"

"Very handsome."

I took out money to pay the tab, but Dominique shook her head and said, "Meal's free."

"Where'd that rule come from?"

"Wait. You'll see."

The door opened, and five stevedores entered, all men, ranging in age from the thirties to the sixties. They appeared exhausted as they saddled up on the bar stools. One looked in our direction, smiled, and waved at Dominique. He nudged his friend who said something to Sandy.

"I can't just set them up drinks on you without asking if it's okay," Sandy said in a roaring voice to the longshoreman. He winked at us. "Ladies, you think these gentlemen are worthy to buy you a drink?"

Dominique looked down the bar and smiled at our would-be benefactors. "You been loading boots for Marines?" she asked.

The men exchanged glances. The one who'd offered to buy said, "Ma'am, we've loaded everything there is to imagine the last month, but probably more boots than anything else. For Marines and soldiers and sailors and maybe even the Boy Scouts."

His friends laughed, and we joined in.

When the laughter trailed off, Dominique said, "Well, if that's the case, we'll accept your offered kindness."

Within the hour the bar filled with boisterous fishermen, merchant sailors, tugboat crews, and a few female stevedores and cannery workers. They stood elbow to elbow, three deep behind the bar. The men's eyes roamed the room as men's eyes will. Whenever we caught one looking at us, we smiled. Those fortunate enough to have a stool at the bar acted as helpers, passing beer on to the others and handing the money back to Sandy. The room warmed up with the heat of their combined bodies. They talked of war or nostalgically of the amazing Joe DiMaggio and baseball, spoke as if the summer of 1941 had been the only summer of their lives.

A fresh-faced woman barely twenty-one balanced a tray on her shoulder and scurried up and back from the kitchen, filling orders of crab cakes, oyster stew, and breaded cod, and taking new orders by memory. A man brought out a concertina and began playing it. Another man joined him in singing a ballad I'd never heard before. The second man sang in a melancholy tenor. They performed a second song. The third song the man with the concertina struck up was "Waltzing Matilda" and others at the bar joined in singing it.

Over the next hour a scattering of men and women came and went. Twice we stood to leave, but Dominique and I couldn't get to the door because the other customers pleaded for us to stay. Photos of Dominique's son went around the bar, passed from hand to hand. Fathers and mothers who carried photos of their kids brandished them for others to see, lean youngsters in military uniforms posing bashfully, faces untouched, hands stuffed into the pockets of their starched trousers. The pictures came with stories from proud parents, or expressions of concern because some were in Europe or island hopping in the Pacific.

The chatter went on as the cash register rang up proceeds. Then as quickly as it had filled, the bar emptied as if the tavern had been tilted and its assemblage poured out. Sandy opened a bottle of beer, came from behind the bar, and sat beside us.

"Most of them going back to load and unload, twelve- and

sixteen-hour shifts. It ain't just about money." He looked down the bar. Greenbacks left to pay bills or as tips were scattered down the length. "I don't always know who paid for what or if they did. Probably evens itself out at the end of the day."

I said, "It's like watching . . . I don't know, a play, I guess."

"Sandy, you drinking beer again?" his wife shouted from the pass-through window.

He swallowed the remaining contents in the bottle and set it down. "I just quit, Darlin'. That's the last one I'll ever have." He patted the back of my hand. "Nice to meet you."

"Likewise."

He looked at the bill in front of Dominique. "Someone paid for your food and drinks," he said and stuffed Dominique's money in her hand and closed her fingers over it. "If you hear from Eduardo, tell us what he has to say."

We climbed the hill from Beacon Street to the streetcar stop on Gaffey Street. I was lightheaded from the beer, but the walk steadied me. The night softened the port the way snow softened the Palouse Hills. The moon lit the harbor. Out in the channel a ship was taking on ballast. A tugboat's horn sounded, and a second tugboat echoed the sound of the first like two lovers lamenting their separation. Despite Dominique's being beside me, I felt terribly alone. Perhaps it was the warmth I'd witnessed among those in the bar, the sense of purpose and belonging that seemed to bring them together. I was grateful to Dominique for taking me.

She stood beside me staring out at the black water. She'd been lighthearted in the bar but now seemed on the verge of tears.

"I'd like to know who Eduardo is," I said.

"I told you."

"That's not what I mean."

She frowned. "So's you can tell your gossipy friends?"

"No, so we'll have a secret to ourselves."

She lit a cigarette and thought a moment. "Sandy's nephew, a dock worker. He's tan and handsome and had a wonderful smile that disappeared when I told him I was pregnant. He got drunk and got in car wreck, put two people in the hospital and one in the cemetery, a nine-year-old girl. They sent him to Chico for ten. Manslaughter." She took a draw off the cigarette and held the smoke in her lungs. She blew it out slowly. "He got out a year ago on some deal that allowed convicts like car thieves and embezzlers to enter military service. You'd think they'd want the murderers and robbers instead. Now, he's in the South Pacific somewhere. I get money for my son. I send it to my parents."

"Is Eduardo why you were crying?"

Dominique dropped the cigarette on the walkway and ground it underfoot. "One secret at a time. We had a swell time, didn't we?"

I felt thankful for her inviting me into her world. "Only the swell-est."

"It's beautiful sometimes," she said, "the water."

The moon's reflection shimmered on the water. In daylight it was blue and gold, and at night a silvery black. Gray wasn't the color of life here. When I thought of gray, I pictured Mother trudging up the stairs to undress and comb out her long single braid, appropriately gray now because gray colored her life. Tonight, I didn't want to think of sad things or of home because when I did, I thought of Jess, of how he'd eased the pitchfork away from me and squeezed my hand in what appeared a caring way. For an instant, it had seemed I was no longer the girl whose father had abandoned the family, the girl whose family was on the county dole. But a man's touch can be as big a lie as his words. It occurred to me that, had I not fought him off, I might be like Dominique, a single woman with a child and no father for it and I could have been the one crying in the restroom.

"I'm glad you came after me," she said.

"Yes," I said. "This is the best time I've had since arriving in Los Angeles. Those men treating us like . . . I don't know. Like we were part of their play. No one stepped on my feet. And none of the men tried to pick us up."

Dominique reached over and squeezed my wrist. "Sandy doesn't allow it."

"We'll do it again, won't we? Let's."

"We'll see." She let go of my wrist. She must have noted the dismay in my face because she smiled and said, "Sure, we'll do it again."

That night as I drifted between consciousness and sleep, I thought about the sad soldiers and sailors at the USO who struggled to make small talk. I wondered about the man who'd fathered Dominique's son. Did she love him? Was he off fighting the war? Was she waiting for him? I felt a kinship growing between us and understood Gretchen better now as well. We could have fulfilling lives, or at the least less-troubling lives, without men.

# -9-

Selmo turned off the conveyor, carried his milk box into the aisle, climbed atop it, and announced the news. American pilots had hit Japan. "Japan," he insisted, "can't hold out against American bombs. It's our turn and their Pearl Harbor."

It seemed an odd thing to say about it being "their" Pearl Harbor. After all, it was Pearl Harbor that rallied us. And the bombing, forever etched in our minds, defined much of the purpose in our daily work, and in ways, who we were now as women.

Tiff whispered loud enough for most to hear, "It's like punching Tojo in the nose."

That seemed more appropriate and those of us near her laughed. Selmo rendered his standard speech about the boys needing boots and stepped off his milk box. At lunch, when the others went up to the fire escape, I looked for Dominique. I found her on the steps of the shipping dock. She'd not yet opened her lunch pail.

I said, "Come on. We're eating on the balcony."

"Here's fine with me."

I figured the others might begrudge me for it, but I felt that if they gave her a chance, they'd grow to like her. The world being in the shape it was, it seemed ludicrous that we would squabble among ourselves. If the men could overcome their difference to fight a war, couldn't women unite because we too were needed? Did we all have to be the same to get along? I hoped that kind of sour thinking wasn't a part of Gretchen's society of a sisterhood. I figured bringing Dominique to the balcony would put the sisterhood to the test.

"No, let's go up there."

"I'm afraid of heights, really. We can talk about movies."

We'd talked occasionally the last few days. She was an encyclopedia of movies and actors. Perhaps because her personal life was in disarray, those subjects made for safe talk.

"We're not talking about movies today. And you're scared, but not of heights."

"Fine, Miss Know-it-all. You go on. Besides, you haven't seen *Mrs. Miniver.*"

"That makes no sense. Let's go. We can see the harbor from up there."

She looked down the alley at the drab brick and concrete. "I know where we can see *Mrs. Miniver*. Ten cents. Whadda you say?"

I wasn't giving her a way out. Before she could react, I snatched her lunch box and headed to the door. "Follow me."

She hollered, "Give it back," and scurried after me.

Her lunch box in one hand, mine in the other, I hurried up the steps, taking the stairs two at a time. She trailed behind.

"Damn it, Eve, this isn't funny. Give me my lunch box."

"Keep up," I said.

"That's it. Our friendship's over."

"No, it's not."

At the top landing she overtook me and grabbed the wrist of the hand holding her lunch box. She tried to wrestle it away. I surprised her with the potato-picker strength that belied my hundred and fifteen pounds and pulled her to the ledge of the open window.

"Let go," she said.

"Girls," I said, "Dominique and I are joining you."

"That's what the noise is all about?" Tiff said.

"Come on out," Gretchen said.

"Here," I said and shoved my pail through the open window, then twisted my wrist free from Dominique's hold and took her lunch box.

"Give us a hand," I said.

Tiff glared. Mitzi appeared miffed. Gretchen took my pail and held it for me. She showed no measurable reaction. I set Dominique's on the grating and lifted a leg over the sill.

Dominique grabbed my shoulder strap from behind and said, "Don't."

I dragged my back leg over the sill and swatted at her hand. When she let go, I stumbled forward, banged my head on the guard rail and fell back on my butt. The grating quivered. I gazed down between my knees at the trash cans three stories below.

Gretchen said, "Trying to kill us?"

I took a slow breath, sat up, and reached for my lunch box. It was a glorious day. A breeze blew in and the sun was high overhead. The world seemed without shadows. I grinned. "Nice day and I get to share it with my friends."

"Yeah, nice." Mitzi said resentfully.

"Come on out," I said to Dominique.

She held back. "Heights scare me. Just hand me my lunch. I'll go on."

"No, come on out." I met the looks of my friends with one of my own that showed how determined I was. "It's wonderful out here."

"Don't make her if she doesn't want to," Mitzi said.

"Yeah, she's afraid," Tiff said.

"See, they don't want me out there."

"I do. And so will they." I crossed the grating and stuck my head inside. "It'll be okay."

Dominique shook her head.

"You stay." I faced the others who appeared to take delight in her discomfort. "Do you know how much this hurts? Dominique and I are friends now, and you're my friends too. Don't make me choose. Just all of you try, please. Gretchen, we're sisters. Tiff, you have a big heart. Mitzi, you keep us steady. We depend on each other, right?"

Gretchen gave me a feeble nod. Tiff lowered her head. Mitzi looked away.

"Okay then. I'll leave. From now on don't treat me any different from the way you treat her." I bent to pick up the lunches.

"All right," Dominique said, "I'm coming out." She lifted a leg over the sill and straddled it. Her eyes closed, she stopped halfway out. "Oh, Lord, this is crazy."

Mitzi said, "There's nothing to fear. Come on."

"I'm scared. Honestly." Dominique lips trembled.

"Just don't look down," Gretchen said. "You'll get used to it."

Tiff stood, said, "I've got you," and offered a hand to Dominique.

Her eyes still closed, Dominique set one foot down tenderly, then the next. Once she was on the grating, Tiff and I each took an arm and steadied her.

"You'll be fine," Tiff said. "Take a look. It's beautiful."

Dominique refused to open her eyes. I pinched her arm.

"Ow. Why'd you do that?"

"See, it's not so bad," Mitzi said. "Who wants to trade half a sandwich?"

"Don't trade," Tiff said to Dominique, "not even if she's holding your family hostage."

Dominique looked down and winced. I waved my hand in front of her eyes.

"Sit and don't look down. Look at the bay or us."

She eased herself down and I opened her lunch box and handed her an apple.

She bit into it and looked off. When she swallowed it, she said, "You know, the smell of garbage isn't as bad up here."

Gretchen shifted her weight, and the platform shook.

"Oh, Jesus," Dominique said.

"It's fine," I said. "It does that." I looked at Gretchen, who shrugged.

Someone mentioned a movie and conversation shifted to gossip about movie stars. Gretchen, who loved movies, mentioned *Heaven Can Wait*, starring Gene Tierney and Don Ameche. "Don Ameche," Gretchen said, "could put his shoes under my bed any time. Except if my husband's home. He probably wouldn't approve."

Mitzi said, "What husband would?"

Gretchen said, "Mitzi, you need a sense of humor."

Dominique pointed at me. "Ladies, who do you think Eve looks like?"

Mitzi said, "Gene Tierney. Tiff and I saw the resemblance when she first came to work."

"Stop it. I don't either." I shook my hair and struck a pose for them. They laughed.

"All the same I don't believe movies," Mitzi said. "Femme fatales. Gangsters stalking them. I mean, it's unrealistic. Though I do think James Cagney makes a good gangster."

Dominique said, "*Heaven Can Wait* is not like that. It's a movie about a man who stole the affection of a girl named Martha from someone she was engaged to."

"Well, it's still not believable." Mitzi said.

"Acting is making what's not believable seem believable. Don't have a closed mind."

They stared at one another.

"I hear Clark Gable has halitosis," Gretchen said.

Dominique said, her tone the voice of authority, "Vivian Leigh said the worst part of filming *Gone with the Wind* was kissing him."

Gretchen appeared mortified. "The way they kissed, who'd have guessed?"

"The absolute truth," Dominique said. "See, they convinced us despite his halitosis."

Mitzi said, "I still refuse to believe movies. I mean, gangsters do not chase women and kill them to guard a secret. It's . . ."

"No woman in her right mind would say that about Clark Gable," Tiff said.

"Breath like the garbage in the alley," Dominique said.

"That bad? Really?"

"She's an authority on film," I said.

Dominique nodded. "That's not all true. But I don't know much about anything else. I do know a really good place to have a beer and a meal."

"And where's that?" Mitzi asked.

"I'll take you there. And I'm sorry for saying you have a closed mind. You're mostly right about movies."

"What about telling me I'm overweight?" Tiff asked.

"I've been sorry ever since. What I meant is that you're so pretty, guys wouldn't take their eyes off you if . . . and then I said that. Will you forgive me, please?"

"Yes. You were right. But maybe only twenty-five pounds."

Dominique's apology dissolved any remnants of resentment that lingered between her and the girls. Talk shifted to food we ate at our homes as girls. That evolved into trading stories about our hometowns. Mitzi was reared, as was Dominique, in central California and she also had a daughter living with her parents because her husband was serving with the army overseas. Dominique talked about her son, how she missed him, and how she hoped to see him for a full week over the summer. She traded half a sandwich with Mitzi. We laughed when she bit into it. I wanted to tell Dominique that I was proud of her, but I held back because saying so would break the spell.

As we stood to leave, I my journal slipped out. I grabbed it before it fell and as I did, the fire escape rattled. Dominique gasped and reached for the railing.

Tiff said, "It makes noise, but is actually as safe as the Santa Monica roller coaster."

"Very comforting." Dominique said, "Roller coasters terrify me."

"But you wouldn't be afraid of some underworld figure stalking you?" Mitzi said.

Dominique smiled. "I would if, instead of a gun, he had half of one of your sandwiches in his hand."

We laughed as she mounted the sill to step inside.

# -10-

THE GIRLS WENT WITH US to Tasco's, but Mitzi and Tiff left after eating. Dominique, Gretchen, and I stayed until Sandy closed for the day. I caught the last streetcar home. The porch light was on. It was usually off by ten. I keyed the door and opened it. Mrs. Sauer sat on the couch.

She sat upright when I entered. "Eve, I've been waiting up for you."

"That's nice, but you didn't have to."

"That's not what I mean." She patted the cushion next to hers. "Sit."

I took a seat, folded my hands on my knees, and turned my face away from her in hopes she might not smell alcohol on my breath. She didn't approve of drinking, at least not in a bar. Her expression seemed pained, much the way it did when she mentioned her fears about her husband contracting an incurable disease.

"I rent you a room."

"Yes, ma'am," I said.

"And you keep it up. That should be enough. What business do I have meddling in your affairs?"

"Ma'am?"

"But I've been a mother since I was your age, and I would certainly want, if my daughter lived under your mother's roof, to have her intervene, your mother that is, on my behalf." She took a deep breath, exhaled, and looked at the ceiling. "You've been drinking, haven't you?"

"Yes."

"Well, that may be tolerable. You're young and Los Angeles is a very advanced city. It's nothing like where you come from. There are things a girl . . . a young woman must realize. Are you following me?"

"No, ma'am."

"Well, you see, I can't have you out at all hours. One time, some weeks back, a Negro drove you home. Do you know what's at risk, the dangers of being with one of them? And this is not a neighborhood where you'll see many, or I should say none, except for Mrs. Dolan's housekeeper who, if you knew the truth, is no different from you or me inside."

I didn't share her obvious distaste for other races but didn't care to discuss the matter. I raised an eyebrow and asked, "What's at risk?"

She seemed not to hear. "Is that how you got home tonight? Was it in that Negro's car?"

"Ma'am?"

"I said, is that how you got home?" Her tone was accusatory.

My cheeks flushed, ears ringing, I sat silently and thought who I rode home with was no one's business. I owed her no explanations. I rented a room and abided by all the conditions she'd set forth. I sprang to my feet and stared down at her. "I'll be out at the first of the month. In the meantime, don't speak to me unless it's absolutely necessary."

Mrs. Sauer looked up as if she'd been slapped. She took a moment to compose herself and then said, "I'm just looking out for you. Sorry you feel that way."

"I'm tired," I said. I walked to the hallway and hesitated. I looked back at her. "You know, your husband could get shot."

"My husband has nothing to do with this."

I nodded. "You're right. I just thought you should think about it and not diseases."

"I do think about it. Now it's my turn to say don't talk to me unless it's necessary."

I went to my room and gently closed the door.

I was, in ways, my mother's daughter, a stoic from a family of stoics. A descendant from a half Nez Perce grandmother and a Norwegian grandfather, I'd been conditioned from childhood not to complain. After Dad abandoned the family, Mom wouldn't tolerate even small complaints. Whenever I groused about my scuffed-up shoes or a patched blouse, she'd say, "The wheat grows best where the toe is planted," meaning plow on and don't complain. Maybe that's why I didn't go to the sheriff following what had happened with Jess.

I washed off my makeup, showered, and spread the drapes before I crawled under the clean sheets. I lay gazing out the window into the dark, feeling a growing anger that Mrs. Sauer had ruined a fine evening. I slapped the pillow, pretended it was Mrs. Sauer and hit it again, this time with a closed fist. It was unlike me to want to strike out. Other than my brothers, I'd never struck or harmed another person except to free myself of Jess who pinned me, tore my panties off, and groped me. I looked at the branches of the chinaberry tree outside the window, took several deep breaths and calmed myself. I'd put nastiness behind me before and could do it again. I'd move, yes. But where would I move to in this city of neighborhoods crammed with bungalows and apartments filled to capacity, and mostly unaffordable?

Don't feel sorry for yourself, I thought, *think of your brothers*, two on ships, Link off fighting Germans. Everyone wasn't Mrs. Sauer. There were the dockworkers, pleasant and generous, friendly, hardworking men and women grabbing what good times they could in Tasco's. And my friends at Lucien's. I found my resolve. I could plow that field. I'd find an apartment, one close to work, send Mother and Avis the new address. I had clothes to pack. All would be fine.

I drifted off to sleep. In my dreams I pictured myself lumbering home, my shoes scuffing over the dirt road, summer dust rising up from the surface, my torn panties in my hand and blood running down from my nose, nothing I could do to squelch it. I woke up as I had too often to the memory of that day and again it played out in my head, his shadowed face hovering above as he forced me back on the hay bale, barn smell all around. Relax, he told me, "You'll like it." I struggled against his weight and pushed his hand away. He twisted his wrist away from my sweating hands. Before I realized it the hem of my skirt—the skirt I burned two days later—was pulled up to my waist and his hand was ripping my panties off. He was too strong, too insistent. He tugged at the elastic. "Don't," I said. I cried. I had only three pairs of panties. Mother would know. I stopped struggling for an instant. Was that consent? He thought so because he unbuttoned the front of his bib overalls and dropped them to his ankles. That's when I took off.

I lay awake wondering, as I had too often, if the image would ever leave me.

In the morning I crawled out of bed, dressed, and went to work.

# -11-

Dominique, who'd also been renting a room and commuting, sat beside me and together we read classifieds daily until finally we located a two-bedroom apartment within walking distance from the harbor. It sounded too ideal to still be available. She called the number from a pay phone by the harbor and talked for a time, nodding to me. She hung up the receiver and grinned.

"It's available?"

"Yes," she said, "but the manager said some other people are interested."

"Let's go right away."

It was a steep four-block climb from Gaffey Street to the two-story Spanish colonial-style apartment building. Painted white, it sat high on the hillside overlooking the port. We took in the facade before we ascended the stairs leading to the entrance. We pushed open the wrought-iron gate and entered a courtyard planted with roses and pansies all around. Mimosa shaded the flagstone pathway and the masonry wall that surrounded a fishpond. A bubbling two-tiered fountain sent ripples across the pond where white water lilies floated.

I took in the floral fragrance that lay thick on the damp air and smiled at Dominique, who returned the smile. "Paradise," I said.

"All the flowers. Makes you wish you were a bee," she said. "There's got to be a catch."

Twenty-eight dollars a month divided between us made it affordable. A courtyard with a pond and flowers? Something had to be wrong. We had visited a half dozen apartments, some too expensive, others too small, too distant, or too dank—always too something. This was ideal.

I frowned and said, "We'll take a peek anyhow, okay?"

I knocked on the manager's door. A man cracked open the door and peered out through the slit. "May I help you?"

"We're the ones who called," Dominique said.

"No children," he said. "The ad said, 'No children'."

Dominique cut an eye at me. "This is Eve, and I'm Dominique. Just us."

"Okay, okay. Give me a minute."

He came out still cinching up the belt on his pants. At first glance he seemed innocuous in every way. In his mid-thirties, his skin doughy, he wore glasses, was perhaps an inch taller than I, and paunchy. He bolted his door and secured the bolt with a padlock, then motioned us to follow. We climbed the steps.

Atop the first landing he faced us and said, "My name's Mr. Tinkler. You may not be able to occupy it right away." His right brow strayed up as he talked.

We turned at the top landing and stopped at the first door on the right. He jangled his keys looking for the right one. "There are just too many jobs in Los Angeles, the war and all, and not enough cheap help available for me to have the place cleaned." He slipped a key in the slot.

"It can't be all that bad," Dominique said.

"No," I said, "We can tackle it."

Any doubts we might have had about the extent of cleaning the apartment needed quickly vanished. Soot and ashes spilled out of the fireplace when I opened the screen. The curtains were soiled, a film of dust lay on everything. The cupboards were stained, as were the sinks, the bathtub, the toilets, and the kitchen counter. The hardwood floors needed a good scrub and mopping and waxing, and the walls were desperate for paint.

"It doesn't need cleaning," Dominique muttered. "It needs demolition."

"What was that?" Mr. Tinkler said. He looked us in the face, but it was as if he were studying the size and shape of our heads.

"It's a mess," I said.

He neither agreed nor disagreed and didn't seem to care. "Try soap and water. I'll take two dollars off the deposit." He snorted and rubbed his nose with the back of his hand.

Dominique looked at me and shook her head. I agreed, and had I not gone to the window and spread the curtains, we might have come to a different verdict, but as soon as I spread the curtains and looked out at the harbor, I was entranced. The bay and the tip of Catalina beyond the channel matched the imaginary view of a world I'd left home to find.

Dominique sauntered up and stood beside me. She gazed out a moment and whispered in my ear, "Don't show any enthusiasm." She wheeled about, taking the manager off guard, and said the walls would take a few dollars' worth of paint and the rest would require three days of cleaning just to make it livable.

He backpedaled and stood at the door holding the key ring at his chest as if to ward her off. "Okay, forget the damage deposit."

"We have another place to look at," Dominique said.

I continued to look out the window until she nudged me. I spun about and smiled flatly.

"Twenty off the deposit," he said. "Take it or leave it."

"Twenty-two a month. You supply the cleaning equipment," I said before I realized it.

Dominique turned and whispered, "You want it?"

I raised my brow and said, "I don't know."

He thought a moment and said, "Twenty-two, but you supply your cleaning equipment."

I nodded to Dominique, who said, "We'll clean it and move in the first of the month."

"I can't hold it that long without a deposit," he said. "My aunt owns these, and I have to account to her."

"Let's talk," Dominique said and pulled me aside into one of the bedrooms.

"It's great. I want it."

"It's a mess," she said and shouted, "Mr. Tinkler! Would you come here?"

He stood in the bedroom doorway.

"To hold it we'll give you five dollars toward the first month's rent, and we'll need one key tomorrow to start cleaning."

"I'll unlock it for you when you come to clean. If you have a car, park it in the street and not in the alley."

"No car," Dominique said. "We work in the port and can walk."

"We can pick fresh flowers every day," I said to Dominique as an afterthought.

Mr. Tinkler stomped his foot down on the floor. "Don't touch the flowers. Ever."

The three of us took turns staring at one another.

"Okay, five and a key," Dominique crossed her arms and stared at him.

"Right, five and the key." He handed her the key and held out an open palm.

Dominique and I opened our purses. I fished out two quarters and two ones from my coin purse. He took the money and handed over a key from his brass ring. I walked to the window and spread the curtains. It was more than I'd hoped for, a first home of my own and I'd share it with my good friend. This, I thought, was what I'd come here for.

On the way to the street, we paused at the garden. "You are a tough negotiator," I said.

"We have to be. Men are too used to thinking we'll bend to their will. They see someone to take to bed or, if it's business, they see a skirt and think they're dealing with an idiot."

"That's sad. You sound like Gretchen."

"I probably sound like a lot of women. Anyhow, I like it, especially the garden."

"Too bad he doesn't show the same care with the apartments," I said. "And he's weird, but isn't the view wonderful? Really? Besides, he looks harmless."

She smiled. "Weird is nothing unusual in L.A. When I first came here, I worked changing linen at a hotel with one woman who wore a corset and a collar like she was Queen Victoria and insisted she was cousin to the Kaiser. That's when I understood L.A. stands for Loco Adults."

A bee landed on her shoulder. I brushed it away. We laughed at nothing. Then I noticed the curtains on the manager's apartment pulled aside just enough for him to peek out.

# -12-

Even before we occupied it, ramshackle as it was, the apartment became home in my mind. I refused to stay another day at Mrs. Sauer's, so until we could occupy our new home, I slept in a chair in Dominique's room in a converted garage behind a clink-brick bungalow. With help from Gretchen and Tiff it took two days to paint the walls. We spent the next four evenings getting the place as spotless as possible. The day we had the power turned on, we discovered that we had, as Dominique described it, "The noisiest refrigerator in the western world."

"The only thing louder," Tiff said, "involves using explosives."

Except for a cot and the kitchen table that came with the apartment, we had no furniture. After Tiff and Gretchen left, we went to the liquor store and bought two bottles of cheap Burgundy. We sat cross-legged on the floor and opened one in front of the dormant fireplace. Dominique lay back, looked at the ceiling and said, "I'll tell you something shocking about me."

Little had shocked me since coming to Los Angeles. I smiled and said, "That's not likely."

"You know, the day you saw me crying?" She paused.

"I remember."

"I was crying over Carl."

"Carl?"

"He was my boyfriend . . . I mean, lover. Two years we were together. Two. One day he vanished, no note, no phone call. Gone."

I lay down nearby and said, "Did you call the cops?"

She turned her head away and stifled a laugh. "Not that kind of vanished. And don't be shocked. Some women, especially actresses—I don't mean all—take on lovers. This is Los Angeles." She smiled. "A makeup artist I met from England said that what is considered *common* behavior in good company is commonplace here. Haven't you wondered in these days of rationing where I got my warehouse of makeup and soap and shampoo? Men in the movie industry have connections. They flatter you and give you gifts. You're welcome to use any of it."

I took a sip of wine from my water glass and asked, "You have any idea where he went?"

"Who knows?" She sat up. "You ever had a lover, Eve? No, of course not. You probably haven't got an idea of what a man's body is about."

"I've got brothers."

"Brothers. Oh, boy. Ever see a man's erection?"

Her openness was shocking. Instantly I knew she wanted to appear jaded, as if she were playing a role in a film. At the same time, I remembered her tears. They had been honest, and her pain had been sincere, and she, despite any facades pretending otherwise, was vulnerable.

"Look," she said and stood and posed sideways, then turned to the other side. "I'm Jean Harlow. 'Underwear makes me uncomfortable and besides my parts have to breathe.'"

She started with Harlow and moved on to Betty Grable, "'I have two reasons for my success and I'm standing on both of them'."

I laughed and she laughed along. She recited more lines she'd memorized from various actresses, some from the roles of women scorned or otherwise damaged. She lowered her voice to a husky alto and used hand movements to dramatize her character's pain. She touched a finger to her lips and skipped to the window, where she spread the curtains, stiffened her back, and looked out. Standing in dramatic profile, she delivered her finale. "'With the man the world is his heart, with the woman the heart is her world.'"

I thought she was putting me on, and I laughed.

She frowned, picked up her glass, and swallowed down the contents. "Why'd you laugh? That one was serious."

"If we're going to be serious . . ." I held up my glass, "we need more wine."

"Wait. I'm best at improvisation." She held up an index finger, walked to the kitchen, and set her glass down. She pulled three tomatoes from the crisper. When she returned, she stood above me holding the tomatoes in her palms. "Looks aren't all there is to acting. Watch this."

The first two tomatoes went in the air with no difficulty but inserting the third into the act created a problem. "Out of practice," she said and placed the odd tomato between her knees but continued juggling the first two. She missed catching one and it spattered on the freshly cleaned floor. Distracted, she forgot about the one between her legs and now two split tomatoes lay oozing seed and juice on the tile. She dropped the third, stomped on it, and said, "That's how to make catsup. Now you've seen improvisation."

I stood up and said, "Improvise cleaning it up with a mop."

"Wait," Dominique said, "I'm going to rid myself of Carl once and for all." She aimed an imaginary gun at an imaginary Carl whose blood lay at her feet. "Bang!" she dropped the imaginary pistol and backed into the wall where she slid to the floor.

I was about to applaud when she murmured, "He's nothing but a cheat who found another woman to support him."

I sat beside her and placed an arm over her shoulder. She gave herself over to her tears.

"He's not worth it," I said. "You're too good to suffer for him."

"No, I'm bad. I hate to think it's true. Our hearts shouldn't be our world. We should try for more than that."

We sat for a time, her sobbing, me comforting her. Finally, I said, "I've got a solution," and sprang to my feet. I hurried to my room for my journal. I sat again, crossed my legs under my knees, and began writing on a blank page. Dominique stretched her neck to see what I wrote, but I held the pad away until I finished. I showed her what I'd jotted down—Carl's name. Through it I'd drawn a dagger with blood dripping from the blade.

"What's that?"

"He's wounded and bleeding. Come on with me."

I helped her to her feet and led her into the bathroom where I tore the page out, ripped it up, and tossed it in the toilet bowl. I guided her fingers to the handle and told her to press down. We watched water swirl as the throat of the toilet gurgled and swallowed the shreds.

"Now he's where he should be," I said. "Somewhere at sea sinking to the bottom."

Sitting on the floor, we finished another bottle. Occasionally she sniffled. I wiped tears from her cheeks. When I could no longer bear her sadness, I started laughing.

She asked, "Why are you laughing?"

"Because you aren't. And because I'm sad for you."

"See what I mean about our hearts? He's making you sad and you never met him." She wiped her eyes and said she'd always wanted a little sister when growing up and now she had one. "I'll be the worst possible influence on you. Won't it be wonderful?"

"Yes," I said, "it will."

It all seemed so simple that evening.

# -13-

Dominique and I both wore a size five. She insisted on sharing her wardrobe, which filled a closet. Before we went anywhere, she'd hold a dress on a hanger up to my body and study me critically. "Too neutral," "too solid," "stripes make you taller," "no, not with red"—she made the decisions on what I wore. She showed me how to apply makeup, said I used too little rouge, that my fair skin called for blush. She often called me "Evil," a nickname she'd created the day I first coaxed her to eat with the girls on the fire escape.

We traded stories over time, offering up details of our lives a little at a time. Dominique too had worked as a waitress and occasionally we had laughing fits over anecdotes we passed back and forth about customers or bosses. She also came from a farming community. Her family, still living in Ventura County, had suffered during the Depression similarly to mine. People she described from her hometown of Bardsdale had their counterparts in Palouse. I told her about my father deserting us when I was ten, how my brothers scavenged coal from spillage on the railroad tracks, and that my friend Avis had nearly died from chicken pox.

Since revealing her affair, Dominique guarded her personal past. She was most often cheerful, but sometimes, when her mood darkened, she withdrew into a dense silence, suggesting that she had secrets too painful to speak of. I respected her silence because I too had private matters such as my sister's death and Jess Newsome trying to rape me.

As often as not, we were too fatigued from work and an evening celebrating at Tasco's to stay up and talk. Then one night, as I was about to turn off the lights, she said, "Don't. Not yet. You never talk about a boyfriend."

"Other than Carl you don't either."

She looked at her hands folded on her lap. "Not all scars are visible."

The idea of scars being invisible set me to thinking. I'd done nothing to be ashamed of, still I guarded that piece of my life. In the beginning I'd lied to Mother about the dried blood on my nose and the black eye, telling her I'd fallen from the ladder in the loft of Mr. Newsome's barn. The physical scars were long gone but the event revisited me, sometimes at night and more often in daydreams.

I said, "Come on, I'm tired. How about you?"

"Yeah. Is the chair hurting your back?"

"No. I'm from farm country. I can sleep in a feeding trough."

She flicked off a light. "Goodnight, Evil."

I pulled my knees to my chest and let the darkness close in. I heard her moving about in her bedroom and closed my eyes. Memories drew up around me, old visitors—the slow walk home, my feeling every rock through the thin soles of my work boots, him walking into the barn. He took my hand tenderly, sneered, then grabbed the back of my neck, and pulled me to him. I was nothing, his father's employee, hired to fork hay into the stalls. He thrust his tongue in my mouth. Though I resisted, he forced me on my back atop the hay. He lifted my skirt and ran his hand up between my legs.

I twisted away. He slapped me and pinned me down. I clawed at his face, drawing blood from his cheek. He seemed baffled and ran his palm over the scratch. The message in his eyes was clear—who was I? He was the son of a wealthy farmer. I was nothing, a girl with a slut for a sister, the daughter of a lumberjack who'd abandoned his family. He backhanded me and said, "That's nothing. If you talk about this, it'll be worse. Now, lay there." When he stood and unbuttoned the bib of his overalls, I saw my chance.

I blamed myself, wondering what I'd done to encourage him. Weeks passed. Small-town rumors are quickly embraced when the target of the rumor is a girl wearing threadbare clothes, a girl whose sister died from an abortion. I pretended not to hear the whispers. One day I came home from school and found Mother, Bible in hand, sitting in the dark. "Is it true?" she asked. "Did you give yourself to that Newsome boy?" "No. No," I shouted over and over. My final protest was answered with the spine of her Bible striking me on the side of the head.

The door opened, interrupting my thoughts, and Dominique said, "Are you asleep?"

"No."

She flipped on the light. "Are you okay? I heard you moan like you were in pain."

"I'm fine."

"I wanted to tell you I'm seeing someone."

When did that start? I wondered. "Who?"

"Someone I met months ago when I showed up to audition and didn't get a chance to."

"A director?"

"Sort of. Were you crying?"

"No. I don't cry. I'm okay. Go to sleep."

She shrugged. "You can trust me if you ever want to tell me anything."

"Same here."

She switched off the light and said, "You need a bed. We'll get you one."

# -14-

THE JUNE GLOOM FADED, AND summer bore down on Los Angeles. In other ways the weather was unseasonable. Santa Ana winds, more common in cool weather, blew hot and relentlessly from the leeward side of the mountains. Shifts inside the bootery seemed endless. It felt as if we produced as many pounds of sweat as we did boots. The heat exacerbating the monotony made us temperamental. The confinement, the sweat, the cracked fingernails, the chemical air accumulated geometrically. We became more aware than ever that we were working women wearing overalls and operating machinery. Even news of B-29s dropping bombs on Kyushu did nothing to alleviate the strain of hard work.

Adding to my stress was that Selmo went out of his way to mention that his wife had been asking after me. Some workers had noticed the attention he paid to me and commented on it. When Tiff said Selmo was making a play for me, I snapped back that she was jealous because no one ever made a play for her. Mitzi said that Tiff had it coming, but Gretchen accused me of being cruel. I apologized and blamed it on the heat. Tiff chalked it up to the war.

The only one who wasn't affected by the heat was Dominique. On Thursday that week we cut short our evening at Tasco's and on Friday after work she packed some clothes.

Saturday morning, I heard her humming at dawn as she readied herself in the bathroom.

I knocked on the door. "Are you all right in there?"

She opened the door and stepped out. "Did I wake you?"

"No. What's up with you? Are you going to see someone?"

She smirked and said, "Maybe I am. What's it to you, my lovely?"

"You're not the Wicked Witch. I never should've told you about Oz."

"I'll be back evening time in the marrow, my sweet child?"

"Stop the movie crap. You going to tell me his name?"

She gazed at herself in the mirror and tilted her head to one side. As if talking to herself she said, "Maybe. I . . . I'm finally getting the break I wanted."

"Break?"

She flew past me, picked up the suitcase she'd stored beside the door and said, "We could do with some rain. I'll see you tomorrow. Don't hold up dinner for me."

I suspected that she was seeing Carl again.

As the Fourth neared, a long overdue rain fell on Friday the preceding week and cooled the factory. Selmo brought out his milk box at midafternoon. That week, Russians were battling to retake the city of Minsk from a hundred thousand Germans. We anticipated hearing bad news. Instead, he stopped the conveyor and told us to take the rest of the day off and Monday as well.

"Tuesday, as you know, is the Fourth of July. I've reserved a place on Seal Beach for a party. Bring your kids if you have them but come no matter. All of you."

For a change, his speech got applause. A day at the beach and extra time off would wrest away the grind of work and the ongoing news of war. Our spirits lifted, we filed out of the factory chattering to one another about what we could bring to the party.

That evening I was caught up in the holiday spirit and suggested to Dominique that we go to Tasco's. She'd not gone out with her guy, whoever he was, for more than two weeks and she stayed in the apartment on weekends. Her mood had darkened as the days progressed and the climate in the apartment had become increasingly tense. I decide to coax her into going to Tasco's.

"We need to see Sandy," I said. "And have some Iberian stew."

"I can't," she said.

"Can't. It's a good walk in the evening and Sandy loves having you come in."

"That's why I can't."

She went to her room and closed the door. Her answer was cryptic and left me wondering if what was going on with her was more than a bad breakup. Several times I'd assured her she could confide in me, but she'd kept the man's name and any information about him to herself. Whoever he was, it troubled me that he was making my good friend unhappy. I went to Tasco's on my own, where everyone who'd come to know us asked where Dominique was.

It sprinkled in the early hours on the third of July before the party. Dominique left the apartment without waking me and I awoke to find her gone. Concerned about her and worried about some missing letters from Mother and Avis, I decided to clear up my business with Mrs. Sauer, who'd not forwarded my mail. I knew for a fact that Avis had written letters that never got to me because she'd recently sent letters addressed to the apartment that referenced information from those previous letters. Mrs. Sauer either kept my mail or destroyed it. I knew she was quick to judge and easy to anger, but I hadn't figured her for being mean-spirited.

I ate a bowl of oatmeal standing at the kitchen window. The view overlooked a steep bank and the harbor beyond. Much farther out Santa Catalina rose above the salt waves, a jeweled rock on the horizon. I watched the harbor color up under the rising sun, the sky cloudless, waters a slate green. The day was lovely, but its joys seemed lessened without Dominique. I rinsed my dishes, dressed, and stepped out to catch a streetcar.

The courtyard smelled of roses. Our peculiar manager did little to repair cracks in stucco or leaks in faucets, but he devoted hours to the garden, his stubby fingers weeding or pruning or pinching. He'd break from his task occasionally to unscrew the cap of a pocket flask and take a swallow. I asked once in passing why he didn't grow a victory garden with vegetables like others did. He didn't answer, just stared at a bulb he was about to plant and waited for me to go. The leaves glistened with a light dew. It was against his rules, but I couldn't resist the temptation. I took my scissors from my purse, looked around to see if he was watching, and snipped off a bloom. I held the flower behind my back and scurried down the pathway and out the gate.

I took a streetcar. When I reached the Heights, I walked up San Clemente and knocked on the door to Mrs. Sauer's. I got no response, so I opened the mailbox. Inside were two letters from Mother, three from Avis, and one forwarded to me from England. I knocked on the door again. Mrs. Sauer didn't open the door. I banged on it and told her I knew she was there. This time she cracked the door and peered out.

"What do you want?"

"The rest of my mail. Give it to me."

"That's all there was. I've left it in the mailbox, but the mailman never took it."

"You knew my address. You could have forwarded it. That's cruel."

"I did write your mother, Eve. I told her that you'd taken up with a black man." She smirked and slammed the door shut.

"If you get any more, forward them," I shouted.

I was one of three passengers on the streetcar. I opened the first letter, the one written by Link and forwarded to me by Mother.

He wrote that during the invasion his glider had landed off target, and it had taken four days to reunite with his unit. In the meantime, he'd fought alongside some British paratroopers, who fed him, gave him cigarettes, and said that he was "a good bloke for a Yank." Many of the enemy, he claimed, surrendered happily. Some were older conscripts, and a few were mere boys. He said it seemed strange how men who didn't want to do it were killing each other. Then he stated without elaboration that he'd been wounded while liberating a French village, was recovering in a British hospital, and would probably return to his unit in a month. Getting back with his buddies was mostly what he thought about.

I folded the letter and sniffed the flower bud. I tore open the next envelope. Avis said her father had sprained an ankle, and Jess Newsome was engaged to Holly Rice, a young woman from Colfax. Mother wrote that she was fine. The boys were sending money, she had plenty to take care of her needs and I could stop sending her money, because if five dollars was all I could afford, I probably needed it more than she did. In the next letter, she informed me that Link had been wounded but was fine. She finished with: "I'm disappointed to hear from your landlady you've taken up with a Negro, but I expected something like this when you ran off. I suppose it'll be all over Palouse soon enough. It's not enough that I hide my face because of Judith."

I noticed the driver looking back at me in his mirror.

"Bad news?" he asked.

"No," I said. "Good news."

"Well, we all need some. Tomorrow's the Fourth after all. We need reasons to celebrate more than our independence."

"Yes."

The Fourth, I thought. Christmases had been disappointing after father abandoned us, but the Fourth was bright and happy. I thought of Fourth of Julys spent at the Riverside pavilion across the Idaho line west of Potlatch. At dawn we'd awaken, six of us, and walk the ten-mile stretch, arriving in time to watch the rodeo. Helen and Judith went off on their own. I stuck with my brothers, a bothersome stray they tolerated. I was also a convenient brunt for their jokes, though they would allow no one else to tease me. We'd play baseball, compete in the gunny-sack race and tug of war. At dusk we watched the sky light up. Afterward, exhausted and content, we rode one of the many hay wagons to Palouse.

Back home I opened the door. Dominique stood in the doorway to her room. I said "Hello," and crossed the room to the secondhand couch we'd purchased two days before. Feeling stupid and weak, I grabbed a cushion and slouched down facing the window.

"It's the day of the picnic. No sadness," she said.

Her mood was brighter than it had been for days. I handed over the letter. She read it slowly and said, "Your brother?" When I nodded, she folded it and handed it back.

"He sounds okay. Is that what made you sad?"

"No, I'm happy because he's a stranger I fought with a hundred years ago, and because he teased me and made me go to school. If you had brothers, you'd understand. They belong to you in way a father or a boyfriend can't. I miss them. It's hard to explain."

"Try. They're men. I know a little about *men*. Actually, I know too much about them."

It was the first time in days that we'd talked like this. I set the cushion aside and sat upright. "I know you better than I know my brothers. In some ways they're odd, and I don't understand them, but I also know losing one will be like losing part of me." I shook my head. "I don't cry. I've never seen Mother cry, and she's gone through. . . ." I thought of her remarks in the letter and bit at my lip.

"Remember what we agreed in one conversation? Men aren't worthy of our sadness," Dominique said and asked, "Is Link handsome?"

I shook my head. "Dominique, he is my brother."

"Well, I was just thinking with a name like Link, he should be handsome. A name like that, he should be a movie star. A hero. Link Manly. What do you think?"

"I think you and Hollywood were made for one another."

"True."

"I mean you're both full of it."

"Yes, but I don't pick the manager's flowers. No more. Mr. Tinkler saw you and came up here screaming. Remember how hard it was to get an apartment?"

I was tempted to lash back at her, accuse her of seeing Carl, instead I said, "One bud." I looked in my purse for it and realized I'd left it on the streetcar.

"Well, no more. What's in the other letters?"

"Nothing important. Town gossip."

"The picnic. Let's go be happy tomorrow. Now that you've got reason."

# -15-

A LITTLE AFTER ONE O'CLOCK Mitzi and her cousin Nora picked us up in a fire-engine red 1937 Studebaker pickup. Nora drove, Mitzi rode in the front with her, while Dominique and I rode in the bed. The sun bore down on us, the air was sticky, and Nora seemed to hit every pothole enroute to Seal Beach. When we reached the beach, Dominique and I breathed a sigh of relief and scrambled over the tailgate.

"You think she missed any potholes?"

Dominque grinned. "I think she hit some twice."

"Well, how'd you like the ride?" Mitzi asked, gathering up the lunch basket.

"It's like one of your sandwiches with wheels," Dominique said.

Mitzi looked at me. "What does she mean?"

I elbowed Dominique and said, "Dom means it was great ride."

"Oh."

Coils of glistening seaweed rotted in the sun. Docile waves curled shoreward, fanning out like white lace on the beach leaving bubbles on the sand. Revelers had spread blankets and towels along the beach. Some lay in the shade of umbrellas. Others tanned themselves. A handful of determined surfers, hopeful for some point breaks, paddled about on their boards, but it seemed from the number of surfboards planted upright along the beach that few breakers had come in.

Lucien's ladies had seized a prime plot of sand. Women who worked the night shift seemed content to keep to themselves. We four spread blankets near the volleyball net so we could watch the company game. I took a spot on the blanket. Nora lay down near me, closed her eyes and balanced an open bottle of beer on her abdomen.

Three boys and a girl splashed about in the shallows. The girl held her own in the roughhousing. When a boy dunked her, she came up laughing and buried his head in the surf. I sighed. I was reminded that I'd been a tree climber, a girl who threw snowballs with the boys. I played baseball and football with my brothers and their friends, and I'd once dived off a cliff into the Snake River.

Tiff and Gretchen hadn't yet arrived. Others around me chatted. About what, I didn't care. I didn't come to fill time with idle talk. I wanted to feel weightless in the water. I pointed to a raft bobbing a hundred yards out, and said, "Dom, Mitzi, let's swim out there."

Mitzi looked at the raft. "You crazy?"

"No." I adjusted the bottom of my swimsuit, strapped on my swimming cap, and waded into the water.

Dominique called out, "You need goggles."

I looked back, shook my head, and dove in. The instant I hit the water I felt weightless. Saltwater burned my eyes, but I didn't care. I swam steadily to the raft, climbed atop it, and immediately plunged back in, determined to see what secrets the sandy bottom had to offer.

Turning in fits and starts, a school of blue and yellow fish darted beneath me. I surfaced for air and went back under, but the fish were gone. Disappointed, I returned to raft, removed my cap, shook my hair loose, and lay on my back.

Above me a chalky cloud wandered on a blue canvas. I shut my eyes and drifted off. Mother came to me in a dream. Her face animated, she called me inside to "Come see Mr. Halvers, your father." My father, clean shaven and wearing a plaid flannel shirt, sat on a chair beside the fireplace. He motioned me forward, but I couldn't move. He opened his arms. I told him no and ran outside, slamming the door.

The raft tilted and startled me. I awoke with a start and found I wasn't alone.

H.T. sat on the far side. He glanced over his shoulder at me. "Hello, missy."

I sat up. "I fell asleep."

He pointed toward the shore. "They'll bring out hot dogs pretty soon."

Water beaded down his shoulders and his lean arms. His round shoulders appeared hard as bridge rivets. Scars, two above and one below the knee, several inches long, explained his limp.

"How long have you been here?" I asked.

He shrugged and looked out where a distant ship was following the shoreline northward. Whenever I'd seen him in the weeks since the incident with the cops, he was either working or on a break reading a book. More than once, he'd seen me and looked away.

"You swim out here just to not talk?"

"No." He began humming the tune he often hummed.

"What's the name of that song?"

"I tol' you."

"No, you didn't. Don't make fun of me. It's a proper question. It deserves an answer."

"Well, miss high-and-mighty. The title is 'See That My Grave Is Kept Clean'."

"Really? That's the name?"

"Title, Missy, not name. It's a song by Blind Lemon Jefferson."

"You have good voice. You could make a living singing. I'd like to hear you sing sometime. I mean really sing, not hum."

He thought about that for a moment and grinned. "Lots of people have good voices. Lots of singers go hungry. It ain't much different for artists and writers."

"Okay. And I'm not high and mighty."

"Right."

"The night you drove me home. You talked about picking cotton. What was that about?"

"Cotton? Oh, a bluesman named Big Bottom said that about picking cotton when a bigmouth in the audience asked him about his singing. My people's music comes from workin' in the fields, mostly as sharecroppers. The singer from east Texas I know of the best is Lightnin' Hopkins. Guess you'd call cotton picking a metaphor for a black man's breaking his back in the fields and his heartbreaks and life itself being his blues."

"See, you can talk."

"But I don't when I'm swimmin'. Well, missy, there's shark out here. Come dark, you can see fins. Be gettin' dark in a couple of hours."

Oddly, this time when he called me missy, it made me feel special. "Trying to scare me?"

"Thought you might wanna know. That's all."

"I've been wanting to tell you I'm sorry for all the trouble I was to you that night."

He gazed at the blue horizon, stood, and hooked his toes onto the edge of the raft. He smiled back at me. "Don't think about sharks when you swim back."

When he surfaced, I shouted, "That wasn't funny."

I watched him stroke toward shore, then I dived in. I

looked for sharks on my way to the beach, cussing him as I did. Despite his teasing me, I liked his sense of humor and that he'd shared some history of the blues with me.

The rest of Lucien's employees had arrived and set up tables. Baskets of bread sat on one table next to three large watermelons, several packages of wieners, bags of marshmallows, and a dozen bowls of potato salad. A boy barely in his teens fanned flies away from the food with a towel. A beer barrel stood at each end of another table. On the third table fruit pies lay spread out alongside a tray of candied apples. Because sugar was closely rationed, as was meat of all kinds, I wondered who'd sacrificed to provide all the food.

Two buckets containing crabs stood under a table. Desperate, the crabs tried to claw their way to freedom only to slide back down. I pointed to them and said, "They're alive."

Nearby H.T. stopped stacking firewood and walked over. He looked at the buckets and smiled smugly. "Won't be for long."

Gretchen laughed and said, "Eve, we'll all benefit from their sacrifice."

"Ain't that the truth," H.T. said.

A boy circled the buckets containing the crabs. He plunged his hand into the water and shouted, "Ow" as pulled his hand out. He shook a crab off his thumb, but the claw stayed. He shook his hand and hollered until H.T. hurried over. He latched onto the boy's hand and pried the claw off carefully. He tossed it aside, looked at the boy's thumb and said, "You'll be fine."

The boy ran to his mother who'd been looking for him.

H.T. picked up the claw and blew the sand off. "Couldn't let 'im have the best part."

Selmo, garbed in a white Panama hat, white trousers, and mesh sandals walked up as H.T. laid wood in the oil drum. H.T. placed the grill atop the drum and stepped back. Selmo sprinkled kerosene over the firewood, bent down on a knee, and used a lighter to start the fire. As he stood, he nearly lost his glasses. In his effort to keep them on his nose, his hat fell onto the grill.

He adjusted his glasses, looked at the burning hat, and said, "A worthy sacrifice."

H.T. and a tanner named Domingo placed the crab buckets atop the grill.

Nearby, smiling youngsters splashed about in the surf, making wild noises. I was content to watch. Their happiness silenced the echo of the distant war. A few women joined them in the shallows and splashed water alongside the kids. Selmo tapped the back of my shoulder. He handed me a wiener on a stick. I took my wiener to the fire and joined the group.

As I was roasting my wiener, Selmo came up behind me and said, "You aren't much in the spirit of the day."

The other employees took note of us. I turned away from them. "I'm fine."

"War's tough on us. Even tougher when you're 4-F and your friends are on the front line."

"You make military boots. That's a contribution."

"No one gets killed making boots. Anyhow, there's something I wanted to ask."

"What's that?"

"Doreen would like you to come for dinner. She wants you to meet a cousin of hers."

Unsure how to best decline his invitation, I turned my attention to the flames.

"He attends USC," Selmo said as if it were an incentive for me to accept the invitation.

"I'm not sure I'd fit in."

I pulled my wiener from the flames and blew on it. "I've never heard the name Selmo before. Where'd you get it?"

"Short for Anselmo, the first man my father hired. Quite a guy, Anselmo. He and my father would eat hot peppers with lunch and laugh at how much they sweated. He died. Eight, nine years ago. I'll give you the details about Friday's dinner later. Excuse me."

As he walked away, I realized that he'd committed me to attending the dinner. Angry, I prepped my hotdog, slapped some mustard and relish in the bun, and walked to the blanket where Gretchen and Tiff sat with two New Zealand merchant sailors they'd just met. I sat down. When one sailor said he was hungry, I offered him my hotdog.

He took a bite and said, "This'll be needing some draft."

He and the other men headed for the beer barrels.

I roasted another hot dog and when I returned, Gretchen said, "What was that about?"

"The sailor was hungry."

"No, earlier, you and Selmo."

I bit down on my hotdog.

"Come on, tell us."

Just then a black Packard Patrician pulled up to the beach and drew our attention. The car's headlights flashed, and the driver killed the engine. Selmo rushed to the car and opened the door. Wearing a swimsuit and a chic white robe wrapped over her shoulders, Doreen stepped out gracefully, gave him a hug, and presented him a cheek to kiss.

"Well, well, the queen," Tiffany said.

Doreen walked to the back of the car and opened the trunk. Selmo brought out a big flat box. Their heads bowed in conversation, the two of them walked to the gathering.

As the Doreen show was going on, the sailors returned from the bar with beer bottles in hand. They plopped themselves down beside us ladies. H.T. came over with two plates of crab and laid one in front of me.

"What do I do with it? It's got its shell."

He handed the other plate to Mitzi and said, "If you're hungry, you'll figure it out."

Mitzi slipped close beside me, held up a crab leg, and said, "Don't be bashful." She broke the leg open with her teeth and sucked the meat out. I followed her example and soon a second crab dropped on my plate. I looked up to see H.T. returning to the boiling pots.

At 7:30 a breeze arose. Gretchen and Tiff excused themselves to walk the shoreline with the sailors. Mitzi, Dominique, and I watched the sunset bleed into the water.

Doreen at his side, Selmo shouted. "Cake. Line up, everyone."

Doreen sliced a piece of cake, put it on a plate, and handed it to Selmo without a fork.

"A few words," Selmo said, but before he got a word out, Doreen forked a bite of cake into his mouth.

Our mouths watering, we formed a line. When I stepped up, I asked for a small slice.

"Glad you're coming Friday. I get so tired of majors and colonels and their wives."

"I didn't . . . you know, say I would."

"It's nothing too fancy. Please come."

I looked over my shoulder. "I'm holding up the line."

She smiled warmly and handed me the plate. "You'll enjoy it."

She didn't mean the cake.

Darkness came and the gathering sat, arms wrapped around our knees, as we took in the salt air. Selmo asked H.T. to play a tune on his harmonica, one we could all sing to. H.T. sat cross-legged on the end of a table. He ran the harmonica over his lips and said, "This was one of the first songs I learned." He blew into the instrument and rested it on his hip. "I was five."

He began Woody Guthrie's "This Land Is Your Land." The tune, coming from a mouth organ, sounded melancholic. We locked arms and sang. People nearby joined in. H.T. played three more requests, then Selmo called it a night.

As we shook sand from the blanket, Dominique asked. "Are you okay?"

I looked out at the tumbling waves. "Not really."

Dominique, Mitzi, Nora, and I said our goodbyes to the others and trudged to the pickup. I was astraddle the tailgate when H.T. called my name.

"What's he up to?" Dominique whispered.

"I don't know." I called to Nora to wait.

Dressed in trousers and a shirt now, he stood with his hands buried in his pockets.

"You want something?"

He turned his eyes to the beach.

"I'm waiting."

"Do you really think I'm good at singin'?"

I took a breath and said as patiently as I could, "I wouldn't lie to make you feel good."

"Come Friday and Saturday I'm singin' at a club in Compton called Pork Skins."

"I've heard of pig skins. What kind of name is that?"

He looked at me. "No kind, I guess."

"Are you asking me out?"

"To hear the blues. The blues is to the ear the way crab is to the mouth."

I remembered being angry at the way the cops mistreated him . . . and me. I struggled momentarily to answer. He was black, years older, and a part of a world foreign to me, but I liked that he came to the little boy's rescue and made light of it. He reminded me of my brothers that way.

Dominique hollered, "Eve, we're waiting."

He scraped a line with his foot in the sand. "You can say no. I'll understand."

The way he said it warmed me. Was my imagination painting a picture where there was none? Why not? I thought. I did want to hear him sing. "I'd like to. Yeah, sure. It has to be Saturday." As I said it, I realized that I *was* committed to attending a Friday dinner at Selmo's.

"I'll be drivin' that." He pointed to a cream-colored Plymouth parked beside the Packard. "Can't come 'til past seven. I'll pick you up at the curb."

"You'll need my address."

He looked at the beach again. "I know where you live."

"I moved from there."

"I said I know where you live. Eight o'clock. I'll pick you up on the street."

"Eight o'clock is late to start."

"It's a blues club. That's early."

I flicked a strand of hair off my cheek. "Fine."

When I settled in the bed of the truck, Mitzi stuck her head out the passenger window and looked back. "What's going on between you two? Selmo might get jealous."

Dominique spoke up. "Don't you know? Eve and H.T. fly to Alaska on weekends for secret meetings with Stalin and Roosevelt."

"Very funny, Miss Snooty," Mitzi said.

"Can we go now?" Nora asked.

On the ride home Nora drove slowly, but still managed to hit a brigade of potholes between the beach and Harbor Boulevard. I appreciated that Dominique didn't talk. I had enough to think about—dinner Friday at Selmo's. I would need an evening dress. And there was the coming Saturday to consider.

Mr. Tinkler sat on the retaining wall of the garden, his

legs swinging back and forth as he whistled off key. I said hello. He didn't reply, but his gaze followed us all the way to the steps.

Dominique shut the door to the apartment, bolted the latch, and drew the drapes. "If this weren't such a find, I'd move. He's too . . . I don't know, weird."

She dropped on the couch. "I could sleep right here for a week."

"Wasn't it a day?" I said and collapsed beside her. "I missed having fireworks."

She clasped my hand and squeezed it. "Be careful."

"It's nothing like that." Even as I protested, Mother's words came back. Was I taking up with a black man?

Dominique released my hand, yawned, and went to her room. I sat on the couch, wrote about the day in my journal, and tried not to think about the coming weekend. When I turned off the lamp, I saw a shadow pass on the other side of the drapes. "Who's there?" I asked. The shadow withdrew and footsteps sounded as the intruder crossed the courtyard. I opened the drapes and looked out, but whoever was out there had vanished.

# -16-

I FIDGETED ON THE KITCHEN stool while Dominique bent over and pinned the hem. She'd made the emerald-green gown from raw fabric and imagination, pattern and all. She said that it was a copy of an open-shouldered dress Harlow had worn when playing opposite Cagney in *Public Enemy*. It fit well everywhere but my bust. I stared down at my visible cleavage. I'd never worn anything so revealing.

"I feel a bit naked."

She looked up. "Well, the shoulder padding is. . . . I'll take some out."

"Honestly, I feel exposed."

"Don't be a farm girl. This is L.A. Besides, any girl in her right mind would be happy to look like you."

"Really?"

"You don't know, do you?"

"Know what?"

She shook her head, stood, and told me to raise my arms. When I did, she tickled me, and I nearly fell off the stool. She laughed for the first time in days.

"You laughed," I said.

Her face locked up. "We're finished here."

I stepped down. "Please tell me."

"I've told you. I'm fine. Leave it at that."

"Tell me. If you're my friend, you will. Is it Carl?"

"There is no Carl. Remember, you stabbed him and sent his remains out to sea." She ran her fingers through her hair and shook her locks playfully. "Let's get *you* ready. Take off the dress so I can hem it."

"Dom, I'm just concerned. You're my friend, my good friend."

"Yes, I know." She looked away. "Let's hurry."

Whatever was troubling her would have to wait. We expected Selmo in less than two hours. I slipped out of the gown, handed it to her, and stood in my slip.

Dominique looked at me. "Every man at the party will be drooling over you."

"I don't think so. And that would make me feel very awkward."

"You're so young. Well, we have to make you sophisticated. I'll put your hair up. And I have a green hat to match."

"Why do you think they invited me?"

She shook her head. "Does it matter if you meet a rich guy?"

"That's not why I'm going. I'm not looking for a rich man. And I'm in no hurry to. . . ."

"It's the only reason you should go." She studied me a moment, lifted my hair, and looked at my profile. "I changed my mind. A hat will go best if you wear your hair with bangs."

She insisted I take her black handbag and wear her black heels, said that black went well with anything, provided the woman wearing it was gorgeous. She stitched the hem. I slipped into the dress and sat on the couch. Dominique laid a matching wrap over my shoulders and retired to her bedroom. I heard the radio click on. When the knock came at the door, I shouted that I was leaving. She came out of her room and winked.

"Stunning," Selmo said when I opened the door.

"Careful with him too," Dominique whispered in my ear.

I saw no reason for concern. Selmo was a gentleman, if a chatty one, and not interested in me the way Dominique imagined, though I had no idea what his interest was.

We arrived at Selmo's some forty minutes later. The house, constructed of stone and redwood, sat recessed on an incline east of Laguna Beach. The second story was a framework of beams and glass windows beneath a hip roof. Parked in the horseshoe driveway were two Cadillacs, a Buick, and two dark-green Chevrolets with government plates. He pulled in beside his wife's black Packard and parked under a mimosa. Its feathery leaves rustled in the soft breeze that blew in over the waves. He told me to wait, stepped around to my door, and opened it. I stood beside him and took in the home, thinking this must be what's on the other side of the rainbow.

Selmo cleared his throat and said, "It was built in nineteen sixteen, but we had it remodeled. You know, in Los Angeles anything that becomes old must be made new. That's true especially of Hollywood actresses." He chuckled and added, "That's what my wife says."

He took my elbow and walked me up the stone steps leading to a redwood fence. He opened the gate, gave me an exaggerated bow, and motioned me into the courtyard. From there the house appeared much larger. As impressive as the house was, the twelve-foot copper front door embossed with flower vines seemed a bit of overkill. Selmo saw me staring at it.

"Ah, the door," he said, "It came from a villa in Italy that was destroyed in an earthquake. Only the door remained intact. My father had imported it before the 1929 crash."

He walked me to the stoop and opened the massive door with surprisingly little effort.

Inside, we met a low grumble of human voices coming from a farther room. A thick rug lay in the center of the mahogany floor leading to the back room. My high heels sank in the weave and I nearly tripped. Selmo gripped my arm and saved me from the embarrassment of falling. He called out to Doreen, then removed my wrap, and called out again.

When Doreen didn't answer, he said, "Wait here."

I stood beside a spiraling staircase and gazed up at the bare windows which looked out at the stars. I felt overwhelmed and if I'd had the option of driving myself, I would've turned and left. In a short time Selmo returned, smiling, and said Doreen was coming to introduce me around. He barely got those words out before she entered and kissed his cheek.

"You look exquisite," she said.

"Thank you." I tensed up as she gave me a sisterly hug.

She clasped my hands and stepped back. "Don't be nervous."

Selmo said, "Excuse me. I'll be back in a bit." That said he climbed up the staircase.

I felt ill at ease being left alone with Doreen, who kept holding my hands. When she finally let go, she said, "The others have arrived, except one couple. Come."

She reached over and took one of my wrists in hand, then led me through a hall, down three steps, and into a spacious room furnished with two leather couches and several leather chairs. A six-stool bar with a brass rail ran along a wall on the far side. Seated on the couches were four middle-aged couples and an elderly man. A young man sat by himself on a stool at the bar. The men, dressed in white trousers and navy-blue blazers, stood when we entered.

"Everyone, this is Eve," Doreen said, "our guest of honor."

I wanted to melt into the floor; still, I squared my shoulders and smiled as she led me around the room. She introduced each person by name. The elderly man I'd first noticed had dyed-black hair and moustache and his knobby wrist fit his shirt cuff like a clapper in a bell.

He clasped my free hand and cleared his throat. "I understand you send notes of encouragement to our Marines. Very commendable."

He held my hand longer than I expected or wanted. I blushed and said, "Other women do it too. For the soldiers' morale. Marines, I mean. Their morale."

"That doesn't diminish the fact." He nodded to the others who were intent on him.

I was thinking, if this was the other side of the rainbow, I wanted the next train to Kansas. Thankfully, Doreen gently eased my hand away from his.

"She needs a drink before you start on the war, Andrew." On the way to the bar, she whispered, "He'll talk your leg off, at least up to the knee. He's a World War I veteran."

"Thanks for saving me."

"Saving you?" She looked genuinely puzzled. "You are charming."

At the bar she introduced me to the young man. He presented his hand and said that his name was Thomas. Doreen said that he was a student at USC, majoring in liberal arts with some thought of attending law school. She told him to fix me a drink and left me in his care. He held up his glass and swirled the ice in it. "Scotch and soda on the rocks, my drink. Would you care for one?"

I smiled. "Thanks, but no."

"Are you a champagne girl?"

"No, I stitch boots."

Instead of chuckling as I'd expected, he looked puzzled and quickly took a swallow from his drink. When Selmo came in, all the men but Thomas stepped out on the veranda to smoke.

Out of the blue, Thomas began bemoaning the inconveniences the war was causing as if we'd been discussing it. "We don't go to Catalina," he said, "one of the sacrifices that has to be made to fight a war. The first thing to go was tennis balls. How many tires can you make out of three tennis balls?" He laughed at his remark, a sharp-pitched laugh that was like an icepick in my ear.

"Washington's not doing enough to end the war." He seemed satisfied that he'd made some point and didn't offer what actions they were or weren't taking to stall victory. I listened to be polite but avoided commenting. My silence pleased or impressed him. In either case, he took it as reason to continue. "On the upside, the war's good for the economy, all in all."

I wondered how my brothers would feel about their sacrifice benefitting the economy.

Thomas downed the last of his drink. "I've been talking too much, haven't I?" His cheeks flushed when I didn't disagree with him. "So, you make boots." He swirled the ice in his glass.

"Yes."

He raised his voice so others in the room could hear. "Women do everything now."

Only women were present, and they were now watching us.

"I saw one driving a steamroller the other day," he said. "I mean it. Three women were on a crew fixing one pothole, but a man was swinging the shovel while they watched."

"Thomas," Doreen said, "before the war it would have been a crew of four men, and three men would've been watching one swing a shovel. And I believe the term is operating. One operates a steamroller, whether male or female."

The women laughed. I smiled, thinking I could get to like her.

"This one was driving it, Doreen," he said as if regaining whatever upper hand he imagined he held.

I was hungry and out of my element. A polite smile on my face, I sat silently hoping dinner would come soon. The last guests, Mr. and Mrs. Elkhorn, arrived in the company of a Marine major in dress blues. Doreen swept the men out through the French doors onto the veranda. Selmo and the others stood at the rail smoking cigars and drinking cocktails. I hoped Thomas might step outside as well, but he said cigars bothered him. I smiled and pretended to understand as he advanced some theories of an economic chaos that would follow the war. He didn't notice that I shifted around on my feet as if I had pebbles in my shoes. The housekeeper rang the dinner chime; Thomas stopped a thought in mid-sentence and said, "Well, about time."

"Yes," I said, "about time." I felt as if I hadn't breathed for twenty minutes.

Doreen pointed to the bottles of California Chardonnay that rested in three silver ice buckets. "Folks, I'm sorry for the wine. When the war's over, we'll serve Pouilly-Fuissé."

Mr. Elkhorn said, "Provided the Germans don't drink it all up."

"Don't they drink just beer?" Thomas said.

"Let's eat," Doreen said.

I felt awash with apprehension that I might blunder and draw attention to myself. Beyond using a salad fork first and not slurping soup off a spoon, basics Mother had taught me, I didn't know proper etiquette. Place cards marked each seat. Mine was adjacent to Thomas's.

After holding my chair for me, he sat and continued talking. "A nation dependent on the revenue generated by war will find itself without an enemy or a mission. Many will become unemployed. You'll have to try your hand at something traditionally female. Otherwise, where will all those returning soldiers work?" he said.

I said, "Maybe they'll all become lawyers," and stabbed a slice of cucumber.

Overtaken by a sudden sense of rancor, I stared at the cucumber on my fork. I wanted the war to end, wanted my brothers back safely, but I also wanted what I'd found at Lucien's, not only the sisterhood I shared with my workmates, but also the independence work itself afforded. Aware that others were looking, I sat up straight, ate the slice of cucumber, and watched how the other guests ate.

"So, what did you do before the war?"

I resented his sudden and shallow interest in me. "I was a girl," I said and forked a bite.

"That's a clever answer, but it's my job to be humorous."

"I thought humor was spontaneous," I said. "Never saw it as anyone's job."

His looked past me as if searching for a response. A clumsy moment passed, then he gave me a lukewarm smile, picked up his salad fork, and began eating. Soon he returned to talking about his view of the war's end. I nodded occasionally to be polite. After we finished the soup and salad the housekeeper brought out plates of veal piccata and cauliflower au gratin.

For some reason, I was reminded of the Thanksgiving a week before my father left, the last time the family gathered as a whole, and the room filled with chatter and laughter. I pictured him carving the turkey we knew he'd stolen. He said that Weyerhaeuser had nearly skinned the hills around Potlach of timber and he needed to seek work elsewhere. He left, Helen married, Judith died, and my brothers left for the war. Now I was here, ill at ease among strangers, and Mother had only empty chairs at her table.

Doreen, seated across the table, smiled. "How do you like it?"

I realized my fork was idle in my hand and I'd not picked up my knife. I cut off a bite, bit down, and said, "Wonderful."

I ate slowly, taking dainty bites, and placing my fork down on the plate as I chewed. Except for the polite compliments given to Doreen who credited all to her housekeeper, the table conversation ebbed. Thomas watched me out of the corner of his eye.

The major said, "One benefit of this damn war is no one serves rice."

The diners laughed. I didn't catch his intended meaning, and just as everyone else stopped, I laughed to be polite. The others looked down at their plates.

"Eve has brothers serving overseas," Doreen said, and her guests began eating again.

"Marines?" one man asked.

"One's in the army. Two are on the seas," I said.

"Well, let's toast to their safety," Mr. Elkhorn said.

After the toast, I lowered my head, and thereafter listened closely if someone made a remark. When our plates were empty, Doreen asked if I would help with dessert. I followed her to the kitchen. A dozen bowls were lined up on the countertop. She lifted out three one-gallon containers of chocolate ice cream from the freezer and handed me a pewter scoop.

"Three scoops each," she said. "You can't imagine what I went through to get chocolate ice cream. It's probably easier to get ahold of bombs."

I spooned three scoops in the first bowl. "Thanks for saving me."

"What? Oh, the joke. Forget it. Well, what do you think of him?"

"Thomas?"

"Tommy." She grinned. "We used to call him Tommy, but he won't stand for it now."

"He's. . . . If I were to describe him, it would be smart."

"He does pride himself that way. You don't find him boring?"

"Well, well, how's the belle of the ball?" Selmo said, rescuing me from having to answer.

"You mean Eve of course," Doreen said.

"Tommy put you to sleep yet?" he asked.

"Sel, don't be that way," Doreen said. "She's enjoying herself."

"Your cousin," Selmo said, "should supply pain pills with his conversation."

"Eve, don't pay any attention to him. He likes Thomas. Don't you, dear?"

Selmo spooned himself a bite of ice cream. "Thank God for the black market."

"Guests first," Doreen said and slapped his hand.

After dessert, the women gathered by the fireplace, and except for Thomas, the men stepped outside. I sat on a love seat beside Doreen.

"Would you like to see the beach?" Thomas asked over the women's conversation.

I looked at Doreen, hoping she would disapprove.

Mrs. Elkhorn gazed at my exposed cleavage. "Do you have a shawl?" she said. "In my youth no woman in her right mind would walk the beach at night without a wrap."

"I have one that goes with the dress."

"I brought a wool shawl. You're welcome to it."

"I like really it in here," I said.

Doreen said. "I'll get a shawl. It's a pleasant night, but to be safe. . . ."

There was no graceful way to refuse. Doreen left and returned with a shawl she handed to Thomas to place over my shoulders. Trapped, I stood and pulled the shawl close.

"Thomas, have her back in an hour."

The ocean thundered in. I removed Dominique's heels and held them in one hand. The sand was damp and cool. I stopped and looked at the coursing waves. At night, the ocean was spectacular and frightening. I wondered what it was like for my brothers out on the high seas. Even as a boy August had spoken of sailing, so when war broke out, he chose the Merchant Marines. I wanted to think he was relatively safe, but I couldn't ignore the sea's dark potential.

I turned away from the water and began walking. "I like the beach. This was a good idea."

Thomas reached for my free hand. I pulled it away.

"Too fast for you?"

"Too fast for any girl." I wondered what I'd do tomorrow if H.T. reaches for my hand.

He grinned. "It's the times. Who knows about tomorrow?"

"I've gotten the same line from sailors and soldiers I've danced with. They were going to war or returning from it." My smile was icy. "Let's just walk."

"I sail. My father's boat is a twenty-two-footer." He stepped closer. "You're very pretty."

"It's the darkness," I said. I picked up the pace to stay ahead of him.

He closed the distance. His hip brushed mine and he rested his arm tentatively on my shoulders. "It must be tough on you girls."

I stopped and faced him. "Tommy, if you try anything, I'll slap your spoiled, stupid face."

He dropped his arms to his sides and stepped back. I wheeled about and walked off. He didn't move until I called out, "Better catch up. If I go inside without you, people are going to think the wrong thing."

He slowed as he came to my side. "I guess that would look bad."

I laughed.

"What now?"

"Thomas, you'll probably be a real nice guy in about ten years."

"Would you walk with me on the beach then?"

I placed my hand in the crook of his arm. "No chance."

On the ride home Selmo dropped the top on the Chevrolet and turned the heater on high. He apologized for Thomas, said that he'd advised Doreen against playing cupid. "Doreen can be forceful at times and she's determined to find someone for her cousin. He's not all bad, but women don't see their cousins the way men do."

"He's pretty bad," I said.

"He tried something, didn't he?"

"I told him I'd slap his face if he tried it."

Selmo grinned. "Good."

As we neared the apartment, I gathered up the nerve to ask a question that had troubled me since the night H.T. drove me to Mrs. Sauer's. "Tell me, what favor does H.T. owe you?"

"Did he say that?"

"Not exactly that way."

He looked straight ahead and didn't answer. I thought the matter was closed, but when he pulled to a stop at the apartment, he said, "I can't say what H.T. meant. You'll have to ask him."

"Thanks, I did have a good time and the meal was the best I've had in L.A."

"I'll tell Doreen."

What I didn't know as I walked up the steps to the apartment was that the evening, including Thomas, had been a test.

# -17-

Dominique stopped me as I was about to go down to the entrance and wait for H.T. on the sidewalk. She took my right hand in hers, turned it palm up, and ran her fingers over the lines.

"What are you doing?" I asked.

"Seeing your future."

"Give me my hand." I tried to pull away, but she held onto my wrist.

"You will live to be old," she said. "I see you will also be troubled by a broken heart."

"Stop it."

She let go. "Really, I just wanted to say, don't do anything foolish. You're white and from a hick town. You don't know anything about the kind of life he lives, or his people."

That idea had nagged me the night before as I lay waiting for sleep to come. Not a single black family lived in Palouse. Still, I was versed in all the taboos that went along with being white and crossing "the line." But I was committed to going with H.T., not just to hear him sing, but to know him better. Though I had no idea what might develop from seeing him, dating him, I realized the more I thought about him and our being on this date, that I was attracted to him. And safe with him.

I nodded. "Maybe I am doing something foolish, but I want to. What do you or I know about *his people*? They may be wonderful. I suspect he's wonderful too."

She shrugged. "I'm just worried. And think. Let's say you and him . . . you know, imagine what kind of future you'd have with. . . . H.T.'s nice enough, but he *is* a Negro."

I reached for the doorknob. "Don't be like that. Not with all you've done to mess up your life." As soon as I said the words, I wished I hadn't.

"Fine. I'm trying to help you. You're welcome." She spat the words at me and glared.

I waited for her to compose herself, but she wheeled about and ran to the bathroom.

I descended the stairs and walked through the courtyard out to the curb. For a moment as I waited in a light breeze, I felt I was being watched. I studied the shadowed courtyard but saw nothing out of the ordinary. I looked uphill at the street as H.T.'s crème colored Plymouth turned the corner.

He pulled it to a stop at the curb, and leaving the car idling, he stepped out and opened my door. "You look like a fine lady."

"Thank you. I feel like one." I did. And I felt like I was in the hands of a gentleman.

He settled in behind the wheel, flashed a smile at me, and put the car in gear. We drove west. Troubled by what I'd said to Dominique, I sat in silence. Who was I to judge my friend? She was just concerned about me.

H.T. explained we'd be going to a neighborhood mostly populated by blacks. He asked if that was what was on my mind. Though Dominique had watered the seeds of my apprehension, I said, "I don't think so."

"We'll see. You'll like Pork Skins. It's about food and music and dancing."

"Really, I thought Pork Skins would be about football."

He gave me a baffled look.

"I was joking. Tell me about the singing."

"Oh, pig skins, sorry. Anyhow, it's an old club. I mean, old for Los Angeles." He talked mostly to assure me. He named off a string of singers I'd never heard of who'd played at the club. Oddly, the more he tried to make me feel comfortable, the more he implanted the idea of my being an outsider to his world. I didn't want a repeat of the previous night, feeling self-conscious and out of place as I had, or even worse.

He glanced at me. "You okay? You ain't said much."

"I'm fine. Tell me more."

He adjusted the rearview mirror and said, "The legend of Pork Skins is that during the early days the ground floor was a bakery owned by a woman named Mimi. Then before the Depression, the basement became a mortuary. The dead were buried in a cemetery across the street. When it became overcrowded, the mortician, some white man, stacked the dead ones on top of another in the graves or dug up bodies to make room for new ones. They say families don't know if they're visiting a relative or stranger or both."

He glanced at me and smiled sardonically.

A smile, a second one, I thought. "That's not funny. It's morbid and sad."

"Ah, it's funny too." Without waiting for me to respond, he went on. "During Prohibition Mimi leased the basement to a man who ran a still. It became a speakeasy. She brought in blues singers. Now it's a blues club, legal liquor."

We pulled into a parking lot near a brick-and-mortar building with a metal roof. A sign over the front door read Mimi's French New Orleans Bakery. Beside the door a secondary sign written in bold white lettering said Lorna's Pork Skins, and an unlit neon arrow pointed to a stairwell that led underground.

"Is there still a bakery on the ground floor?" I asked.

"Nah, they store the booze there and it's Lorna's apartment."

"She owns it?"

"She and the boys kind of share owning it."

"Boys? What boys? Hers?"

"What you don't know is a whole lot of not knowin'." He grinned and reached over the seat back to get his guitar case. He came around and opened my door, then slung his guitar case over his back and pointed to the stairwell. At the rail he offered me his arm and said the steps weren't very sturdy. Instinctively, I reached for his hand.

"No, we don't do that. Take my arm."

I didn't know what he meant by "we don't do that." I laid my palm on his forearm and we descended a flight of wooden steps that creaked underfoot. A faint rumbling of human voices funneled up from a room below. The steps dead-ended at a cubicle where a thick-necked man seated on a stool stood and raised his palm. His head seemed too small for his huge body. Beside him was a metal door with a sign that read, "Entrace," which I figured was a misspelling. A bare bulb hung over his head. He bared his teeth in what seemed a painful smile.

"Hard Times," he said, "'bout time you come. Crowd's waitin'."

H.T. turned to me and said, "You wait here."

He set his guitar against the wall and stepped over to the man. They spoke too softly for me to hear. The bouncer nodded when H.T. pointed to me. H.T. motioned me over.

"Antoine needs to see your driver's license."

I took my sister's birth certificate from my handbag. "I don't have a license, just this."

The bouncer shined a flashlight on the certificate, then my face. He stared, his expression flat as a tar shingle, and said, "Hard Times, I ain't lettin' her in. Cop's been around."

H.T. turned to me. "Stay here with Antoine for a minute."

My legs stiffened at the idea of staying alone in a darken cubicle with the huge bouncer. I glanced at Antoine's grenade-shaped head and whispered, "Don't leave me with him."

"I'll be right back." H.T. pointed to the open door and whispered, "Don't worry."

He limped off. Antoine sat back down, folded his arms, and glared at me. The murmur of human voices and tinkling of glasses drifted out of the darkness. I set my eyes on the open door. A hallway led to a room cast in muted light.

Antoine said, "Go ahead, take a peek, curious girl, but don't go in."

I stepped just inside the doorway.

"'At's far enough," he said.

I leaned against the doorjamb and peered into a smoky room packed with people seated at tables or strung out along a bar. Their faces merged with the shadows. I stepped back and waited nervously for H.T. He appeared as a tall shadow threading his way through the crowd, beside him a heavyset woman. As they reached the far end of the hallway, I stepped back and bumped into Antoine who'd come up behind me. Startled, I turned around.

His hard breath enveloping me, he said, "Stand easy, girl."

I could hear the resonant voice of the woman as they entered the narrow corridor. When they stepped out, the woman, flashing a big-toothed smile, hurried to my side. There was something irresistible about her smile and she carried her heft like a fur coat. Dressed in a green silk dress and wearing a wide-brimmed black hat that slanted to one side, she could best be described as grand.

She looked me over. "I've seen matchsticks with more shape, hon. Call me Lorna." She offered me her hand and shot a look at the bouncer. "Antoine, you let this sweet lady in."

"Doin' my job, woman," he snorted.

The woman gave him scornful look. "Watch your manners."

"Missy," H.T. said, "Lorna's the sweetest mean woman in Compton." H.T. snatched up his guitar. "Lorna, she just needs some pork skins to gain a little shape." He turned his attention to me. "She'll take care of you." He slung the guitar case strap over his shoulder and strode into the hall.

Lorna cleared her throat. "No need bein' frightened, little bird. I own a part'a this place, which means you be my guest."

"What makes you think I'm scared?"

"'Cause, hon, you're shakin' like a dog sheddin' water and just pretendin' otherwise."

We measured one another. I blushed. She laughed boisterously and nodded as if she'd entered my thoughts.

She hooked my arm in hers. "We'll pretend you ain't so skinny. What you say your name was, hon? Never mind, I won't get it right no how. Just let's go. And don't be eatin' off my plate. Woman like me needs her nutrients."

"The sign on your door is misspelled," I said, and as soon as the words left my mouth, I wanted to take them back.

"Hon, ain't nothin' misspelled. Entrace is what I serve here. You know, the innards. Them and pork skins."

My cheeks flushed. "I apologize."

"Nothin' to apologize for."

The air inside the room reeked of cigarette smoke and human sweat, alcohol and freshly ironed starch, and pomade and perfume. The smell of meat frying came from another room. The tables were laid out in a tangle so there were no aisles, just narrow spaces between the chairs that some customers slipped through sideways. People in the center of the room sat engulfed in a haze of tobacco smoke. Men moved chairs forward as we neared, and conversations died off as

Lorna sashayed by with me in tow. A man turned, watched us pass by, and muttered something.

Lorna swung about. "Mind your tongue, Daniel Morse. This here hummin' bird's a lady."

Men in military uniform, all of them black, stood at the bar. At USO dances I'd seen the occasional lone black soldier. Until now I'd not considered how many were serving in uniform. That was when I looked around and realized I was the sole white person in the club, a revelation that caught me unprepared. I felt even smaller than Lorna had described me.

"Don't stare, hon," Lorna said to another man. He looked away. She leaned her bulk into me and said softly, "Some people ain't got the good manners to mind they own business."

Another man grumbled something to his party when we rounded his table.

"Ozzie," Lorna said in a booming voice, "Antoine ain't had no entertainment tonight."

The man looked back toward the landing that served as the lair for the sullen bouncer. After that exchange people seemed less interested in me. As we neared the stage, we passed a door painted the same flat black as the walls. A man's voice shouted from the other side, "Come on eight."

We reached a table near the stage. Lorna said, "Cornell, this here's Honey."

He stood. "Well, damn if she isn't."

"You ladies introduce yourselves and be polite." Lorna pointed to a chair for me to sit on.

The two women, both with surly expressions, introduced themselves. Cornell wore the brim of his Panama hat down so that his eyes were barely visible.

He said, "What's your real name, gal?"

"Eve."

"Oh, yeah. The one got all this started. Well, what would the world be without sin?"

"Don't know about the world, but I'd be a lot poorer without it," Lorna said taking a seat.

The women, Sasha and Barbara, laughed as if on cue.

A waitress in a tight skirt and black mesh stockings strolled up and asked what I would like. Although I'd never had one, to appear sophisticated, I ordered a gin and tonic.

"You old enough, honey?" Lorna asked.

"I've got a birth certificate." I unsnapped my purse.

"What kinda answer's that?" Lorna said. She told the waitress to bring some pork skins to the table and said, "A Coke will do the pretty girl just fine." She leaned toward Cornell. "Don't get no ideas about this gal. She's here with Hard Times."

Overhead lights flashed on at each corner of the stage. A black curtain suspended on a wire at the back of the stage opened. H.T., holding a three-legged stool and guitar, stepped out. He placed the stool near the apron of the stage, then sat on it, and strummed his guitar. The audience murmured as he adjusted the tuning pegs. He fidgeted about getting comfortable on the stool. The guitar resting across his lap, he withdrew his harmonica from a shirt pocket, then looked about the darkened room. Conversation in the room slowly died off.

"Anybody out there?" he said.

"Who're you?" a man called.

H.T. shaded his eyes and looked for the man who'd spoken. "Can you hear back there?"

"Said, who the hell are you?"

H.T. tucked the harmonica in his shirt pocket and held the guitar in a position to play. He fingered a riff, then addressed the man. "Hard Times is who I am. Ya'll know me if you don't recognize me. I been followin' you around all your life."

"Oh, yeah, ain't it true," a woman said.

Someone hollered, "You can talk. Can you sing?"

"If my mama told me the truth of it," H.T. answered.

Someone shouted, "We ain't come to hear no comedian. An' you ain't funny."

H.T. played a chord. "This here's 'bout a man lost a mule and a woman same day."

"Ain't no mules in Los Angeles," a man said.

"They's one in this room," another man said. "Let the boy play."

H.T. held the harmonica to his lips and played six bars, then repeated the same six bars, and began. "I seen hard times bustin' rock. Hard time punchin' a clock. Ain' no hard time like an empty room . . . an empty bottle too and an empty tune. That slow mule I set out to ride . . . took me to New Orleans." His eyes closed. He fingered the frets and strummed, leaned his ear to the sound box and listened as the fingers of his left hand danced up the neck, and those of his right plucked the strings. "Found a gypsy girl, fortune-tellin' queen. Sat the night in an empty room, scrapin' hard to find a tune, singin' the blues. Singin' a poor man's blues.?" He opened his eyes and played some riffs on the guitar. "Set the night con-tem-platin' that gypsy's news."

His forehead shone. Sweat beaded down his neck to his collar. He looked in my direction but didn't seem to see me or anyone. Then he clasped the harmonica between his palms, placed it to his lips, and closed his eyes. As he played the mouth organ, the expression on his face suggested he had entered a mysterious place he was guiding us to.

A woman in the back sang a high sad note and held it. A man hollered, "Sing it."

H.T. sang a few lines, then turned his attention back to the harmonica.

A waitress sashayed up to the table, set a basket of pork

skins in the center of the table, a Coke in front of me, and left humming to herself.

H.T. worked the harmonica back and forth across his lips, its mournful sounds evoking thoughts of trains at night, foghorns echoing across the bay, and long sad nights gazing up at the ceiling. I closed my eyes and let the music carry me with it. Lorna brushed my hand and broke the reverie. A woman at a nearby table began to clap. Applause washed over the room. Someone shouted, "Blues Man! Blues Man!"

Lorna pushed the pork skins in my direction. "Well, well. You gonna listen to the blues, you be needin' some nutrients," she said.

"Hard Times is earnin' his money tonight," Barbara said.

"Know any songs by Mr. Robert Johnson?" a man shouted.

H.T. stood from the stool, and without answering, stepped down and approached our table, standing beside Lorna and me. He looked at Barbara and then Cornell, who looked back dispassionately.

"Need a touch," he said and took a quick sip from Lorna's whiskey. He handed the glass back to her. He glanced at me, then mounted the stage.

"Johnson, you say?" He seemed at ease now as he seated himself and looked toward the audience. "You mean a fella got his-self poisoned on account a pickin' the wrong woman? Tall boy packed a gun longer than a man's arm? That man?"

"No, man, the other one," the same man answered.

The room broke out in laughter.

"Never heard'a him either." H.T. said. He strummed several bars as if warming up his fingers. Then he began to play in earnest, fingers jigging over the frets as he plucked the strings with a tortoise shell pick.

He held the guitar aside and addressed the audience. "I heard records is all. I'll do my best." He looked at the ceiling as if reading lyrics and began singing "Hellhound on My Trail."

After that he switched to songs from the Delta Belt, beginning with "I Got the Bluebird Beat." A few couples locked arm in arm shuffled forward. Cornell stood and offered a hand to Barbara, who swayed like a cradle in a breeze as she moved. Already several black soldiers and sailors were dancing with partners, some in the aisles.

The room had warmed up a few degrees. I was no longer the only white in the audience. Two couples, recent arrivals, watched from the back, where they waited for seats. A spattering of women now sat at the bar, which earlier had been occupied only by men.

H.T was singing "It Feels So Good" when a commotion broke out by the staircase. He stopped in the middle of a note. Suddenly an explosion of shouts filled the room. It was too dark to see what caused the disturbance. A man shouted out for everyone to stay calm, then the lights switched on. A woman hollered, "The police is here."

Several men in dark uniforms spilled down the stairs and plowed into the crowd, shoving patrons aside as they advanced. Antoine went down under the weight of three officers. Lorna shot to her feet, and hollering at the cops, pressed her way through the stunned crowd. She demanded to know what this was about, said that she'd have someone's head. Two cops turned her around and handcuffed her.

An officer made his way to the center of the room and hollered, "Don't get excited, folks! There's a paddy wagon outside. Plenty of room for everyone."

Another cop pointed in the general direction of the tables by the stage where I sat. "Just stand up and walk outside in an orderly way."

Two middle-aged cops shoved their way to our table. Both out of fright and because people struggling to leave had blocked my path, I stood next to my chair unable to move. Cornell said something to Barbara who moved to shield him from the view of the cops. He reached inside his jacket, extracted something, and held it behind his back. As the officers neared the table, Barbara stepped into their path. She slapped one when he tried to get by. He twisted her arm behind her and took her to her knees. The second cop came to help. When Cornell turned away, I saw what he'd been hiding from view. He wiped the revolver clean on his trouser leg, dropped it to the floor, and kicked it under a nearby table. He caught me looking and narrowed his eyes.

More cops assailed the room. All during the fracas H.T. remained seated on the stool. I looked at him for reassurance. His face was an impenetrable slate. When a cop stepped onto the stage, H.T. stood and lowered his guitar to his side. The affronts he'd endured the night we'd been stopped by the police had left me confused and indignant. I felt all that again and was terrified as well.

The cops had subdued Barbara. One was handcuffing Cornell, who paid no attention to the cop, just stared at me. I turned my attention from him to the stage. A cop had H.T. in an arm lock. I felt a hand grip my arm and looked at a blonde-haired cop who said, "We got a snowball in this coal bin."

A second officer latched onto my other arm and nudged me into a line behind Cornell. The police now in control of the room hustled everyone toward the entrance, prodding us along with the tips of their nightsticks. No one was overlooked. They even marched the service men in uniform along. I was near the back of the line behind Cornell who looked over his shoulder. Flaring his nostrils again, he narrowed his eyes.

Outside the line moved slowly but steadily toward the waiting paddy wagons, where two cops frisked people before they got into the vehicles. H.T. and Lorna were quickly loaded into a paddy wagon. A cop slammed its rear doors and it drove off.

A patrolman approached a detective in a gray double-breasted suit. He dangled a snub-nosed revolver in one finger for the detective to see. They exchanged words and the patrolman pointed toward the club. The detective nodded, took out a handkerchief, and wrapped the revolver in it.

The line advanced. A cop told me to not to move. He brushed his hand down my sides, over my breasts and ran one under my skirt and up my thigh. I closed my eyes. My insides went cold. His hand lingered at my panty line for a moment. When he finished, I opened my eyes, and the cop took my arm and walked me to the paddy wagon.

"Get in and don't talk," he said.

Cornell was already seated. I stepped over his outstretched feet and sat beside a young woman. "What they do to you, girl?" she asked.

"I'm not supposed to talk," I whispered.

"You still got freedom of speech, girl."

Cornell leaned forward so that I could see him. He shook his head. Then the doors of the paddy wagon slammed shut. A bolt slid across the door, and a padlock snapped closed. It was dark inside the cab, but light enough to see Cornell's gaze laying hard on me.

He said, "You just be smart, girl. Ever'thing'll be fine."

# -18-

My purse sat open atop the table. The cops had rummaged through the contents, some of which were scattered on the table. A broad-faced detective with pronounced jowls and weary brown eyes told me to take a seat across the desk from him. He appeared undecided between being bored or irritated. Pen in hand, he studied me.

"I'm Detective Sharkey," he said.

"Can I have these off?" I showed him my handcuffed wrists.

He shook his head. "While we're making introductions here, I need a name."

"Eve Halvers," I said and immediately knew I'd made a terrible mistake.

"This belong to you?" He pointed to the purse.

I nodded.

"Name on the birth certificate says different. Says Judith."

"Eve's my nickname. My real name is Judith."

He turned the purse upside down and spilled the remaining contents on the table. He held up my lipstick tube. "Eve, or whatever your name is, this isn't a game. You were in a disorderly house, gambling and prostitution. I'm going to give you one chance to come clean."

"Sir."

"When someone lies to me, it makes me think they think I'm dumb. Do I look like a big dumb cop?"

I shook my head.

"Good. I'm guessing this lipstick's yours, but the certificate isn't. Go ahead. Tell me."

I licked my lips. "The birth certificate is my sister's."

"Good. How old are you?"

"Almost twenty-one."

"How almost?"

"Nineteen, almost twenty."

He jotted this down on a pad and looked up at me. "Kind of young to be a whore."

My cheeks flushed and my hands went numb. I started to object, but I thought I might choke if I did. Though I'd done nothing wrong, I felt ashamed. He stared at me with his pain-seasoned eyes.

I swallowed and managed to say meekly, "I'm not."

"No. Of course you wouldn't be. Hell, no. White girls who hang out in that environment with Cornell Jones are never whores."

"I'm not, but I was treated like one. An officer ran his hand between my legs."

"He was probably looking for a gun."

"A gun? I'm not a whore. I'm not." It was as if I were back in Palouse, making silent denials to the accusing eyes of neighbors. I was the sister of Judith who died from an abortion, Eve the girl who rumors claimed had sex with Jess for his dad's money. My eyes watered. I wiped them as best I could with the back of my hand and told myself, don't be weak.

"I work for a living. I make boots for the Marines. I've never been with a man."

"You were in a place owned by the boys."

"I don't know what you're talking about. I met the owner. She's Lorna."

"She's a front, a cover for Dragna and the boys. You know, the mob."

I swallowed and lowered my head. "I came here six months ago from Palouse. That's in Washington. I just met Lorna and I don't know anything about a mob. H.T. works with me. He invited me to come. I just wanted to hear him sing and play the harmonica. I'm a decent woman. Show me some courtesy."

Detective Sharkey looked me over, then offered a kind look. "I'm sorry."

"I didn't do anything."

"You were at the same table as Lorna and the Tomato Man and his girls," he said. "An officer saw you. The Tomato Man doesn't socialize with women just because they're charming."

"I don't know who you're talking about."

"Jones. That help?" He stood, came to my side of the desk, and leaned against it. "Cornell Jones."

"I told you. I just met him. I'm friends with the singer. I work with him."

"He's not your pimp? You're not lying for him? Come on, Eve, did you see something?"

My crime was being nineteen and apparently being female as well. I dared not mention the gun, so I stopped talking. I likely faced some repercussions for being in the club. That scared me, but I was far more afraid of Cornell. For the next few minutes, Detective Sharkey harangued me, citing laws he could charge me with, including prostitution. "I'd believe you under other circumstances. But soldiers go in there to blow their pay on a dice game or spend it on pussy."

"Don't use words like that." I spat back.

His blasé stare sat on me for at least a minute. Then he

inhaled, leaned back, and exhaled. When he looked at me again, his expression was fatherly, as was the tone of his voice. "Let's start over. Tell me how you expect me or anyone to believe you, a young white girl in there with all those Negroes? A place where vice is a good part of the goings on?"

"They were nice to me. A lot nicer than you've been." I looked down at my hands. "And no one used the kind of language you did."

"Okay, that's fair, but look at me," he said, his voice soft. "Tell me, did you see a gun?"

"A gun?"

He un-holstered his revolver and held it up. "Like this, a revolver with a short barrel? It was near the table where Officer Mullin saw you."

"How do you know it was me?"

"White women kind of stand out in a crowd of colored folk."

I shook my head. "I was confused when the police charged in . . . and scared. I didn't know what was going on."

"Is that when you saw it?"

"Saw what? I didn't say I saw anything."

"Okay. I can pretend you didn't, but will the Tomato Man? Know how he got his name? I'll tell you. When he was nineteen, he choked a sap to death and buried him in a tomato farm in the Valley. Sadly, we couldn't prove the case. Now you know."

"What am I under arrest for?"

"We'll start with being a minor in an establishment that serves liquor and move on to frequenting an establishment of gambling and prostitution, then obstruction of justice." He smiled. "You started out to have a good time. How's your night going now?"

My new wallet lay on the table open. I reached for it.

"Leave it." He sat and rested his elbows on the desktop. "Now, about the gun. . . ."

With no explanation for it I suddenly felt emboldened. "I want to call an attorney."

"Everyone wants an attorney and a telephone, but we're going to talk some more. And then you're going to have to be tested for venereal disease before you can make bail."

"What?"

"It's the law. You have to understand we're at war and the government considers prostitution and syphilis a threat to national security."

I was mortified at the idea. "I'm not a prostitute and I don't have any diseases like that. And why would it be anyone's business if I did? No. I won't."

"Then you won't make bail."

"Is this because you want me to say I saw a gun?"

"No. And I believe you're not a prostitute. But it is a law. There were soldiers and sailors in there and prostitutes and pimps. The federal government requires it. If you have a disease, they can put you in a federal detention facility."

I thought, what kind of country do I live in?

Selmo sat in the bail bondsman's office smoking a cigar. As I entered, he lifted the cigar to his lips and drew on it slowly. He didn't address a word to me until after the papers were signed and we were alone on the sidewalk.

"I didn't expect anything like this," he said.

"Neither did I. I'm sorry. I didn't know who to call."

He opened the car door for me. "The night's shot. We may as well grab breakfast and coffee. I have to come back for H.T. It's taking longer for him."

I was thankful H.T. was allowed a phone call or I would have still been across the desk from Detective Sharkey. "Why'd they arrest him? He didn't do anything but sing."

"They arrested everyone," Selmo said. "I took care of the hospital bill. I can't, for the life of me, understand why you had to be tested."

"Apparently it is a federal law. All the women were tested. But none of the men were." I slid inside the car, and he slammed the door. When he was seated, I asked, "Why just us women?"

"I never heard of the law. Let's just go."

As we rode about looking for a café, no mean feat on a Sunday morning before church, he puffed on his cigar and stared straight ahead through his thick glasses. Eventually we came to a place called Fred's Time to Eat. We sat at the counter. I ordered pancakes and coffee. He asked for toast and coffee.

He held up the cup and explained, "Doreen and I have to eat with her parents later."

The raid and the humiliation of a nurse taking a swab from me to test for venereal disease remained in the forefront of my thoughts. As we drank coffee and he made small talk, it became obvious Selmo was uninterested in talking about the night's events. He said that his lawyer would handle things, and for him that seemed to settle matters, but I needed validation. A cop had run his hand between my legs and over my breasts, taking his time as he did. Another cop had called me a prostitute. A middle-aged nurse had me remove my panties and lie down to satisfy some federal law. I'd been labeled a prostitute. I appreciated that Selmo had come to my aid, and I trusted him, but no kindness could ease the anger I felt over the indignities I'd endured, each of them permanently crystallized in my mind. I wanted to tell my side of the events. Maybe even bring up my seeing the gun, but I couldn't draw him or anyone else into what was my problem, so I feigned interest as he spoke about Doreen's plans for the day and a vacation they intended to take in the fall to Mt. Shasta.

The waitress set down our food and said, "It's real butter. The last of it."

I drowned the pancakes in syrup and forked a bite, then another. The food began to restore me. Selmo seemed pleased that I had an appetite.

"You had a rough night," he said. "It should be a lesson. You want to know why it's taking H.T. so long for bail?"

I took a sip of coffee. "Yes."

"His mother Ruth was my father's housekeeper. After my mother died, Ruth looked after my dad and me. H.T. was five years younger. The summer he turned fifteen, his mother asked if my dad would give him a try at the bootery. I had bad eyesight and was a little clumsy. He was athletic and could sing. Dad liked him, and I was jealous. I even told my father I was jealous.

"Funny, my father never let it bother him, me being jealous. He told me 'Just be kind to Howard.' That summer he took H.T. to lunch with him almost every day, bought him a guitar and a harmonica. When I asked about the instruments, my father reminded me how I'd given up the piano to play marbles. One day I asked why he liked a nigger more than me. He'd never struck me before. He slapped me and asked where I'd heard that word. I said it didn't matter. I was his son and when did I get to go to lunch?

"You'd have to know my father to appreciate what he said. He said, and I'll never forget it, 'I fed you every day of your life and now you resent me feeding a boy who never had a father. You go downstairs right now and apologize to Howard. Tell him what you said and apologize.' That was the last thing in the world I wanted to do. But I did it. I've never forgotten the hurt in H.T.'s eyes. He tried to hide it, shook my hand, and asked if I'd go fishing with him on the pier.

"Dad died the next year. I was twenty. I quit college and

took over the business. I had Anselmo, the one I was named after, my father's friend, to help me then. I sort of forgot about H.T. or pretended to. Ruth kept in touch. She was given a trust in my father's will, which I still administer. Anyhow, shortly after H.T. turned eighteen he got into trouble with the law. I heard about it later. A neighborhood fight. Someone was cut. H.T. stepped in to help the one who was cut and the boy with the knife went after him. H.T. hit the knife wielder who fell and hit his head on the curb. The boy died. H.T. went to jail. Ruth knew what was behind it, but never said a word to me. Maybe she was ashamed. I don't know.

"A few months later, I read about a Negro inmate having his leg nearly hacked off. It was H.T. I finally did what my father would have had me do initially—hired an attorney. It took years, but we got him out. He never got in trouble again, but this is the second arrest for hanging out in . . . well, a raw place. He had to take you along. Now you know why the delay. He has a record."

I had plenty to think about, but little to say. I waited as the waitress poured coffee into our cups. When she left, I explained that I'd all but asked to go with H.T.

Selmo looked toward the blacked-out window. "I'm not one to decide people's lives. And maybe, if my business were finance like the men in Doreen's family, I could. . . . Dad was close to his workers, made me work right beside them. So here I am hinting to you that the world isn't ready for a young woman like you to go to a place like that, or to be with a black man."

"No?"

He shook his head. "We'll keep this to us, and you can put it behind you."

"And then?"

"Just be patient and see."

I wished it were that simple. It wasn't. There was the Tomato Man, a gun, cops, Lorna and her warm, fleshy arm, smoke, music, all these considerations. I sensed it would visit me again and I anticipated and wanted that visit and I wanted to seek comfort in H.T.'s arms. He was with me, he experienced the ordeal, and he alone could offer me the kind of understanding I needed. I dared not say all that to Selmo, so I said, "I'll try."

He smiled, sipped his coffee, and said, "Let's finish and go get H.T."

Selmo escorted me to the staircase. I was exhausted and so was he. It showed in his eyes.

"You don't have to walk me up," I said.

He waited until I got my key out and said, "Doreen would like you to have lunch with her. She's picked a place in Hollywood. I don't go there myself, but she likes to see movie stars. Would you like to go?"

"Why?"

"You'll have to take that up with her. You're not obligated. Not with this on your mind."

I said that I would think about it, thanked him for everything, and left him at the base of the stairs. When I looked back from the doorway, he was gone, but I noticed someone standing under the shadowed canopy of a mimosa.

Dominique sat on the floor, her back pressed to the couch. She wore a housecoat and between her legs was a bottle of brandy, beside her a box of tissues. Several more were wadded up on the floor. She sniffled and said hello.

"What're you doing on the floor?"

She saluted me with the bottle. "Celebrating."

I dropped down on the floor and sat facing her. "Celebrating what?" I used a fresh tissue to wipe away the most recent tears.

"Celebrating the next big event of my life. I'm goddamn pregnant."

Hearing that muted all the night's events. I scooted around beside her, wrapped an arm over her, and pulled her close. She began to sob. I rocked her. I knew what she was going through, and I felt at once worldly and wise and helpless. Nonetheless, I said, "Don't worry. We'll make great parents."

# -19-

ON JULY 15 MARINES HAD all but secured Saipan, the Allies engaged Germans in a brutal clash at St. Lô, and the Democratic convention that would nominate the ticket of Franklin Roosevelt and Harry Truman was about to convene. At noon that Saturday, far removed from all those world-shaping events, Doreen and I sat sipping tea in the Musso & Frank Grill in Hollywood. The tables were filled mostly with tourists who came to see celebrities dine. Waiters in formal red waistcoats, ties, and cummerbunds sauntered about taking orders and serving meals.

Ever since receiving her phone call inviting me to have lunch, I'd felt ill at ease. Hanging over the idea of a pleasant meal was the fact that Selmo had bailed me out of jail and that I didn't want to be drawn into their personal lives.

She set down her glass. "Beautiful, isn't it? I could eat here every day. Did you like the fishpond we stopped at earlier?"

"Yes."

"I've heard the Japanese have untold ponds like that. It's an art form to them. You'd think people who create things like that would have something better to do than try to conquer the world." She smiled at her own wisdom. "Shall we order?"

I nodded.

"I remember coming here just before the war and having

an artichoke salad and pasta with my grandmother. Wonderful times." She brushed a string of hair away from her lips. "Oh, who cares. It's now, isn't it? Let's eat."

We studied our menus. She set hers aside. "I know the menu well. Why don't I order for us?" She looked around the room. "I saw Betty Grable here once. She has a figure like yours. Dancer's legs. Did you do dance at all?"

Do dance? I thought. I wasn't used to people who talked that way. I thought about Lorna's booming voice and large presence and wondered what she was going through with the law. In way of an answer, I said, "Mostly I try to keep boys from stepping on my feet."

"No, no. The ballet. You could have. You have the body. I did ballet. It demanded more than I had to give. My way of saying I wasn't a great talent or, at least, not a great student. Well, what are we hungry for? I confess, the heat kills my appetite. Would you have taken lessons?"

"We had no money," I said. "Besides, the nearest place for lessons would be Moscow."

"Russia? Surely there was someplace closer."

"The Moscow in Idaho." I sipped my lemonade, looked off at the wood paneling, and hoped the waiter would hurry.

She cleared her throat. "Oh, we have a Moscow too. Well, I never cared for geography. That's something boys do, like math. Selmo's a whiz at math. You like him, don't you?"

"Yes. Everyone does."

"Isn't that the truth? He does all sorts of things for his workers. More than I would."

"You seem like someone who cares. We all liked the cake you brought on the Fourth."

Doreen picked up her cup and said, "It was a first. I really went because I kind of wanted to get to know you after our introduction at the club."

I wasn't sure what Doreen wanted from me but was certain she had motives other than friendship. I suspected she wasn't going to get to her real purpose any time soon. "Me?"

"You know, many girls your age are married and have babies. This war has made people crazy, rushing into marriages without knowing each other, the husband off to war. It's . . . . What do you suppose will happen to them after the war?"

"I don't know. It's hard to think of it being over. It seems like it's gone on forever."

Despite the heat, my appetite was up, but she seemed in no hurry to order. Food was merely a treasure hunt for her, but hunger and I were old companions.

"I'm probably jealous. You see, I can't have children. The women I know have children and most do not appreciate them. Women all over the world are giving birth to children of men who'll die in the war and there will be all these fatherless children."

She began to detail her ideas about what would happen after the war, the sudden families, and fathers coming home as strangers to their children. My thoughts drifted to Dominique who'd suffered a week of crying and sitting by the phonograph listening to "September Song" over and over. I'd watched as she composed letters one after the other only to rip them up. I'd pleaded with her to call the father or go see him. Finally, after ignoring my pleas, she broke out crying. She said it was impossible, that he was married, and it was all her fault. She'd gone to bed with him because he was an executive at a studio who promised her a chance for a role in a film.

"We'll experience an influx of fatherless children," Doreen said, breaking into my reverie. "Do you understand the problem I'm getting to?"

"Excuse me?"

"Do you understand where this is going?"

The waiter came to take our order. I listened to Doreen calmly order for her and me.

The waiter, a bald man in his forties, seemed impressed with her exactness. "Thank you, Madame," he said. "If you glance at the far corner, you'll see Peter Lorre coming through."

Doreen said, "Well, thank you." She watched the actor walk to a far room and said, "There's where the celebrities dine. The help here know I like to say later who I've seen. See how small my life is? Oh, I do love Sel. He's a dear man who loves me very much." She let the thought die and asked, "More than a week later how do you feel about Thomas?"

"Honestly?"

"Yes."

"I haven't given him a thought."

"I'm not surprised. He was kind of a test."

"Test?"

"Yes. Of character. See, you impressed me at the club that night. Coming directly over and saying hello, very assured."

"The champagne. I didn't want to be rude. The others, they thought you were. . . ."

She stared at me as the unfinished idea hung between us. "Thought what?"

"Well, women gossip. You know."

Just then Spencer Tracy walked in. Every head turned to the entrance where the maître d' held a menu to his chest. Even waiters paused to watch the maître d' walk the actor through the restaurant. I wished Dominique were with me. Seeing him might take her mind off her problem.

"I wonder if he's meeting her," Doreen said.

"Who?"

She stared as if seeing me for the first time. "Katharine Hepburn."

I nodded. "Dominique has talked about her."

"You don't know who she is?" Doreen scooted closer. "I know it's shallow. The bug comes with living in L.A. Sooner or later, you'll be bitten by it. Everyone is. Did you know that Peter Lorre is Hungarian? Technically we're at war with them and the Austrians. Guess that makes him the enemy." She chuckled at her joke, then said, "Famous writers come here too, I hear, but who knows a famous writer well enough to recognize one?" She gave that a further thought and added, "And who cares?"

We ate a casual meal, drank more tea, and she paid the bill. On the drive to the apartment, she talked about her family's mortgage business and said they were not as close to her since she'd married the son of an immigrant. She asked if I ever went to movies.

"Occasionally. After Dad left there wasn't much money. I saw Andy Hardy movies. That's Mickey Rooney. And I loved *The Wizard of Oz*."

"You know Judy Garland's a drunk, don't you?"

"No. That's sad."

"It is. We'll have to go to a movie now that we're getting to know one another."

I liked her but didn't. I was curious about her motive in seeking my friendship. "Doreen, why are you doing all this?"

She smiled and turned off Rodeo Drive. "In time, Eve."

# -20-

CRYING HYSTERICALLY, DOMINIQUE TOLD ME she'd decided to abort the baby in Mexico, but she didn't know where to go and begged me to help. Because I hadn't spoken to Tomea since her attempt at suicide, I felt guilty turning to her for help. I found her at lunch break and asked her where in Tijuana someone would go for an abortion. Her face expressing shock, she crossed herself, mumbled a prayer, then asked, "*¿Es el problemo tuos?*" and crossed herself. I told her it was for a friend. She didn't seem convinced but said she would get information for me.

The following day she came to my station with a note written in both English and Spanish. She laid a palm on my shoulder and said, "*Suerte*, Eva."

"Honestly, Tomea, it's for a friend."

"Well, luck to her then."

Dominique and I sat at the terminal and endured a grueling delay as we waited for the train to San Diego. The day before she'd seemed somewhat ambivalent. She'd barely slept overnight and by morning her mind was made up. While she was committed, my heart wasn't.

"Dom, I want you to listen."

"The damn train's not coming. What else can I do but listen?"

I took her hand. "The day my sister Judith left, the guy who'd convinced her to have an abortion dropped her off at the midwife's house more than a hundred miles away. Neither my mother nor I knew where she had gone or why. She and I shared a bedroom, shared secrets, but not that one. She died. Really, think about it. Please."

"Okay, I'm scared already." Dominique pulled her hand away and touched a finger to her lips. "Shush. People are all around and don't need to hear it."

I said, "But you do need to hear it. Please."

She looked around. "Talk softly and don't preach. It's my mistake, not yours. I'm the one who let him. He said he could make it happen for me. Understand, I want that, want people to see me on the screen. I want my mother and father to. . . ."

I took her hand again and squeezed it. "I'm not judging. It's not a moral question. It's . . . well, there should be some third option, some safe way. I just see it as risky."

She nodded. I let go of her hand.

"Before she left that day, Judith was pale. She went to the outhouse and vomited. When she came in, she went straight up to her bed. Mom took her Bible into the room and started praying. She thought my sister had been drinking."

I looked into her swollen eyes. "Dom, Judith was barely twenty. Please, think about it."

"I love you the way I loved my sister. That's why I. . . . Okay, I'll shut up." I thought about Tomea. What she did for me violated her Catholic belief about the sanctity of life, but it was obvious she felt obligated to me, and I knew I was taking advantage of that obligation.

Dominique gazed at the floor. "I have a son I never see. My mother and father are raising him. It breaks my heart. This breaks my heart. Eve, just be my friend."

The train hissed to a stop. I helped her to her feet. Once

we embarked, she sat on the window side and watched the coastline roll by. At 4:20 p.m. we stepped off the railroad car in downtown San Diego and walked the Embarcadero to the hotel. That evening we ate on the wharf overlooking the harbor. Thinking it might lift her spirits, I told Dominique about lunch with Doreen and Spencer Tracy's surprise arrival. She merely nodded and picked at her plate. Others nearby discussed news that Americans led by Omar Bradley had broken through Nazi lines at St. Lô and the Germans were in retreat.

"Isn't there any other way?" I asked.

She shook her head. I lost my appetite, chewed two more bites, and set my fork down.

By eight o'clock we were tucked in for the night. I awoke several times to her sniffling. A little before three in the morning I heard her retching. I went to her and held her shoulders until her dry heaves ended, then I helped her back to bed and got her a glass of water. She didn't cry after that and the worst of it physically seemed behind her. We propped our pillows behind our heads, sat in the dark, and waited for dawn.

Despite the war, crossing into Tijuana proved easy. It was hot and markedly drier than Los Angeles. I hailed a cab and handed Tomea's note to the driver.

He read it and handed it back. A thin man, who spoke with the intensity of a sparkler, he said in a self-important tone, "You can trust me. I weel get chu there."

His cab, a converted Dodge delivery truck, had canvas flaps covering the windows. The passenger door was held closed by a rope looped around the center post. He untied the rope, opened the door, and stood aside for us. Before we stepped in, I gave Dominique a questioning look. She lowered her head and swung into the seat.

The driver hurried to get behind the wheel and glanced at

us. "My name ees Albino," he said and then the taxi jerked away from the curb. As it accelerated the cab sounded like it had been lubricated with gravel. I lifted the canvas covering my window. Vendors busied themselves setting up carts and displays. The place was colorful, but cheerless because it spoke of poverty and struggle. We passed strings of adobe buildings, some whitewashed, some blue. Still others were yellow and green and red like parrot plumage. Rain slicing down from tin roofs had stained the walls. Flies swarmed a dead cat. A teenage boy urinated on the sidewalk curb.

Albino turned off the boulevard and took a side street. Gradually gaining speed on the back road, the cab rattled as if the doors might at any moment fly off their hinges. Albino apologized for the road and drove on with the sincerity of a spaniel. Occasionally he looked back and smiled reassuringly. He turned the cab east down a narrow street where the air smelled gamy. An ochre dust hung over the road's surface and formed a haze that made the air appear to be rusting. Toddlers ran about in various states of dress. Women toted wares on their backs. Men sat on boxes under torn awnings. Some people cooked their noon meal over open flames. The farther we went the more the air smelled of urine and smoke. The rawness of the poverty struck a chord in me. Even during the peak of the Depression as unemployment hit every other household in Palouse, shirts were starched and dresses were washed and pressed. There was no smell to that poverty. I felt ashamed that I'd never endured the kind of despair I was seeing.

I closed the canvas and glanced at Dominique. She stared straight ahead, her face cast in resignation. I reached over and squeezed her hand. She closed her eyes and bit her lip.

Although I didn't believe my words, I said, "It won't be like my sister. It'll be fine."

Dominique said, "Fine for the guy who got me this way. I didn't tell you, but when I went to him when I knew, he said, 'It's not mine.' Not . . . his? He called me a whore. I'll never say his name, never."

I understood. I said, "It'll be okay," and immediately realized it sounded patronizing.

"No, it won't. When he called me a whore, he opened his wallet and threw these at me." She opened her purse and pulled out a roll of twenty-dollar bills. "And said, 'Here take care of your mess.' Now I'm here with his dirty money." She began trembling and took my hand again.

As the cab rambled on, I began to understand, as I hadn't before, what drove my sister to take the risk. I held my friend's shaking hand and realized I would likely have taken the same risk if Jess had succeeded and I'd ended up pregnant. My friend deserved better, but better wasn't available. We were part of a sisterhood that was universally stuck with taking one of two options left us. I released her hand and looked out the window.

Albino pulled to a stop in front of a two-story office building with a terra-cotta roof and a sign that read *Medico y Farmacia.* He untied the door and pointed upstairs. I paid the fare with American green. He handed me some Mexican bills. I had no idea if I'd lost in the transaction or not, but I trusted the driver. In his broken English he asked if we wanted him to wait. Dominique was making her way up the outside staircase to the doctor's office. I said I wasn't sure.

"No charch," he said. "I stay."

"Okay. I don't know how long we'll be."

"*Un hora, no mas*, maybe less," he said with authority.

I caught Dominique before she opened the door. "How're you doing?"

"Please, don't even talk." She waited for me to push the door open.

A nurse came from around a counter, greeted us in broken English, and asked what we wanted. I showed her the note.

"Ju?" she asked.

"No." I pointed to Dominique.

She motioned for us to be seated and opened a door that led from the office to a white-walled room with one lone bed on the far wall. She closed the door only to open it an instant later, reappearing in a gown. She tied on a mask, gloved her hands, and motioned to Dominique.

Dominique paused at the door and looked inside. "Where's the doctor?"

"No need one," the woman said. "I do all. Bery good."

I grabbed Dominique's hand. "Don't do it. Don't take the risk."

"What kind of choice do I have?"

They went inside and shut the door. I closed my eyes and thought for the hundredth time that week that I'd made a mistake leaving home. I thought of my brother August, Judy's twin. He was out on the seas somewhere when his twin sister died and we had no way of telling him. She was buried for two weeks before the letter I wrote got to him. I told him she'd died of septicemia and gave no mention of the abortion. I looked around the room again, seeking anything to assure me it was clean enough for what needed to be done.

Albino dropped us off as near to the bridge as he could get. When he saw blood on his seat where Dominique had sat, he crossed himself. I helped her out. A line of both Mexicans and Americans strung out a hundred feet ahead of us. The afternoon sun pressed down hard. Every few seconds the line advanced a step or two. Each time it moved, the family in front of us—father, mother, and three teenage girls—stood, gathered all their belongings, and moved three to six feet, again to sit and spread out their baggage.

We'd stuffed our purses with sanitary napkins the nurse had given us, but there was no place to change. Dominique's distress was obvious—a paling of the skin, sweat, and shakes. The girl and boy in front of us stared at her.

"How're you doing," I asked.

She looked down. Blood trickled to her ankle. "Look. Oh, Jesus. I wish I'd die."

"Don't say that." I looked up the line. "Sit. I'll be back."

Disregarding the grumbling and hostile remarks from those I passed, I charged up the line, looking in people's faces and telling them my friend needed help. I was uncertain what I was looking for. Help, yes, someone kind and ready to help, someone like one of my brothers or Gretchen or H.T. Most in line weren't Americans. The few who were looked away when I asked for help. Near the front I saw three men, heads nearly bald, and felt my hopes rise. One was burly. I walked in front of them and looked up at the husky one.

"Will you help me?"

"What?" They looked at one another and seemed reluctant. They were probably on a few hours' leave, I figured, and in a hurry to return to duty.

"My girlfriend is stuck back there." I pointed. "She's bleeding. I need someone to carry her to the front of this line and get us through."

"Ma'am, we. . . ." the big one started.

"Please. She's hemorrhaging. I'm scared."

"I'll help, lady," the one to my left said. His alcohol breath lay on me.

The big one nudged him aside. "He's drunk."

"Please. My friend's extremely sick. She's had a . . . miscarriage. You're soldiers?"

"Marines, ma'am," the big one spoke for them all.

"Marines. We make your boots. Boondockers. At Lucien's we adopted. . . ."

"Boots, huh. What's your name, lady?" the big Marine asked.

"Eve."

"You're kidding. Hey, guys. She's the Eve that signed my note."

"Will you help?"

He grabbed my hand, and hauling me along, threaded his way down the line. Dominique sat slumped forward on the curb. I ran to her and brushed her hair back. The big Marine kneeled, said, "Ma'am, the Marines have landed," and swooped her up.

She blinked. "I'm bleeding."

"No worry, I've had blood on me before." He turned toward the front of the line.

The other two Marines had advanced not far from the gate. The one carrying Dominique shouted, "Come on, guys! Anyone tries to stop us, knock 'em over."

He fell in line behind them, and the others formed in front, nudged people aside, and said politely that they had an injured woman.

"What the hell?" one man protested.

"Who do think you are?" a woman shouted.

"I got an injury here," the big Marine said over and over as we came closer to the gate.

Hearing the commotion, the startled customs agents turned their attention to the line.

The Marine holding Dominique stepped up. Blood stained his shirt. "My wife's having problems, sir. We're all Americans. We need a doctor. Fast."

The agent looked at the Marine's burred hair and at Dominique who was semiconscious and moaning. "Yes, you do." He grabbed a phone and looked us over as he spoke into the receiver. When he hung up, he said an ambulance was on its way and passed us through.

"You can see, I'm very busy," he added officiously.

The staff scurried by, one and two at a time. Like all hospitals at the peak of the war, San Diego General was understaffed. When I could corner a nurse, I pestered her about Dominique's condition. The information was scant at best. She'd been sedated in the emergency room. The bleeding had slowed. She was waiting for a doctor. I pressed the nurse for more information and got nothing.

The clock ticked off an hour as I thumbed through the pages of a *Saturday Evening Post*. When I could sit no longer, I began pacing. Another hour ticked off before I walked to the desk nurse to ask for directions to a pay phone. A doctor was conferring with the desk nurse, their heads leaned close, their voices hushed. The nurse saw me and nudged the doctor, who nodded to me and left without speaking.

"Where may I find a pay phone?"

The nurse directed me down a far corridor to the lobby. Then as I turned to go on my way, she asked, "Will you be long?"

"Why?"

"The doctor will probably want to talk to you."

"About Dominique?"

"He'll tell you."

"Is she okay?"

"You'll have to discuss that with him."

"Can't you tell me?"

"Please, make your phone call and come back."

"Tell me something, anything. How is she?"

"The doctor will talk to you, but only if you're a relative. Are you?"

"I'm a . . ." I started to say friend, but quickly said, "cousin."

I dialed the operator and asked her to make a collect call to Los Angeles. She requested the number and name of the party. I regretted it as soon as I said, "Anselmo Stillman, but

I don't know the number. Please, it's an emergency. The call is collect." I gave her my name.

The wait seemed endless, but a minute or so later Doreen answered, and the operator asked if Mr. Stillman would take the call. "He's not home," Doreen said, "but I will."

"Your party is on the line. Go ahead."

I apologized and explained why I was calling. I said only that Dominique had fallen sick, was in San Diego General, and the staff wouldn't offer information on her condition. Doreen offered to help and asked that I repeat the name of the hospital. She seemed pleased to offer help.

"Don't worry about Dominique. Take care of yourself," she said and hung up.

I returned to the ward where the doctor waited, beside him a uniformed policeman. The doctor motioned for me to sit and introduced the officer as Andy. In a manner of a tone suggesting disinterest, the cop said, "I have a question or two to ask."

"Okay, what?"

"Your name?"

"Eve Halvers."

He wrote that down. "Miss or Mrs.?"

"Miss."

"And you're a friend of the patient?"

"Yes. Well, a cousin."

"Okay, Miss Halvers, I won't beat around. Your friend's, I mean, cousin's medical condition was reported as an abortion, not a miscarriage. Abortion being against the law in California, she's in trouble. And you may be in trouble as well."

"Me? Why?"

"I didn't say you *are*, just that you may be. Did she have an abortion?"

They hovered over me. I took a breath and released it. "She did."

"Were you with her?"

I nodded.

"Did you perform the. . . ."

"We went to Tijuana. I went along in case something like this happened. And it has."

"Are you aware that's conspiracy?"

I had only a vague notion of what a conspiracy was. "What?"

"I thought you were going through the motions, Andy," the doctor said.

"I got to make a report, Doc, like you," the cop said. He looked down and asked, "Was one of the men who brought her the baby's father?"

"The Marines? No, they just were there. They came to our aid."

"Why'd they take off in such a hurry?"

"They were in a hurry to get wherever they. . . . I don't know."

"Mexico's off limits. But everyone kind of overlooks that." He glanced at the doctor, then back at me. "It's against the law to aid anyone having an abortion."

"If you're going to arrest me. It doesn't matter." I looked at the doctor. "Before I'm dragged out of here, please tell me how Dominique's doing?"

The doctor looked at the policeman who nodded. "She's stable right now, but weak. I'm sorry. I'm obligated to report something like this, just as I'm obligated to report a bullet wound."

The officer thanked the doctor and said that he'd done the right thing. Then he sat beside me. "I have to write a report. Nothing will come of it. The doctor said your friend needs blood."

I looked at the doctor. "How much? How bad."

"We stopped the bleeding, but she lost a lot. Blood's scarce."

"I'll give some," I said. "Take mine."

"We need her type. Type B-positive."

The cop jotted something in his notebook, faced the doctor, and said, "I've got too much blood myself, and I know others pretty much the same. Where's a phone?"

"I'll set it up with the lab," the doctor said. He offered his hand to me. "Sorry."

"We're not criminals, doctor. We're just people, just . . ." I stood tall . . . "women."

"I know," he said. "We'll get your friend through this."

Just then the big Marine ambled down the corridor. He hesitated momentarily when he saw the policeman but came on just the same. Hands in the pockets of his trousers, he rocked back and forth bashfully on his heels. "Came to find out how she's doing."

"Hope you're not AWOL," the cop said.

"No, sir. On a three-day pass. We're good for another day."

The officer smiled. "I could ask for your papers."

"Yes, sir."

"But I won't. You want to give some Marine blood for a good cause?"

The Marine seemed puzzled.

"She needs type B," I said.

"B-positive," the doctor said.

The Marine glanced down the corridor and said he'd be back in a jiffy.

A half hour later he returned with his friends and a dozen sailors and Marines he'd gathered up from somewhere nearby.

He said his name was Maxwell Jepson. He told the others to introduce themselves. They sat down with the cop and two officers who'd also come to give blood. There weren't enough chairs for all of them. Some sat on the floor in clusters, speaking softly and joking with one another. More cops arrived to donate blood. As news of the group of donors spread around the hospital, nurses and attendants came by with coffee, tea, and cookies. Some came just to offer their thanks. Two off-duty nurses sat and became part of the group.

When the doctor treating Dominique pushed through the door and saw how the numbers had multiplied, he shook his head and said the lab might not be able to accommodate so many. Then the elevator door opened and a nurse stepped out. She approached the doctor and pulled him aside. The doctor nodded and thanked her. When she left, he faced the volunteers.

"Around sixty sailors are in the lobby waiting to give blood. I sent her to get more help."

"Doc," one of the Marines said, "we're here to save some gal. Is someone going to take my blood, or do I have to cut myself open?"

"No need of that, young man," the doctor said. "We'll take all you want to give."

Later, as a nurse marched them down the corridor to the lab, a sailor anointed my head with his cap and said I was the prettiest blood donor he'd ever seen. On the other side of the double doors the hallway was packed with more young men and three women in uniform eager to donate blood. At the far end of the hall a half dozen women from the Red Cross were setting up tables and chairs to accommodate the many volunteers.

I was overwhelmed. I thought of the boys I'd danced with at the armory, and my irritation with the few with clumsy feet and errant hands. It occurred to me that my brothers would be among them if they weren't overseas. I told the men as they gave their names to a woman in a Red Cross uniform that if they ever came to the Harbor District, my friends and I would dance with them until the YMCA shut down. By then Maxwell was rolling up his sleeve. He winked at me.

In the aftermath Maxwell and his friends sat beside me. I learned that he'd been a mill worker in Oregon and was a veteran of Guadalcanal. He'd been wounded in New Georgia in the Solomons, then sent stateside to recover, promoted to the rank of sergeant, and had been training recruits for five months. He fired a few questions at me about Dominique. After what I'd been through with the officer, I was too exhausted to answer questions. I told him that he should come back and visit Dominique in the hospital and ask her any questions had about her. He thought a moment and asked if she was happily married.

"She's not married," I said.

He seemed at a loss to respond, then said, "Can I come see you in Los Angeles?"

"Sure. Thanks for everything. It's Lucien's Bootery just off Harbor Boulevard."

I returned to the visitor's room and took a seat. A nurse handed me a blanket and told me to lie down if I wished. Sometime past midnight a hand nudged me. Selmo and Doreen sat on either side of me. They helped me gently to my feet and walked me out of the hospital.

# -21-

A CHITTERING PIGEON AWAKENED ME. I rubbed my eyes and sat upright and looked out from my room on the seventh story of the Grant Hotel. My head ached. I vaguely remembered walking into the room the night before and Doreen spreading the drapes and saying the sunlight would wake me in the morning. After that she'd stood silhouetted in front of the moonlit window lost in thought. Exhausted from the day, I'd drifted off.

I stretched and walked to the window. The pigeon was perched on the ledge. I tapped the pane. The blank stare the bird gave me in a way reminded me of Mr. Tinkler. It flew off and I closed the drapes, returned to the brass bed, and sank into the soft mattress. For a time, I stared at the ceiling but soon got out of the bed and opened the overnight bag Doreen had brought. Inside I found toiletries, a clean slip, brassiere, and panties.

I wrapped my hair in towel, sat on the edge of the bathtub and filled it. The steam rising from the tub brought a sense of life to me. Having grown up where a galvanized tub with water heated on the stove was our only bath, I considered a bathtub a luxury and intended to soak away the previous day's stress. Before I could step into the bath, the telephone rang. I caught it on the fifth ring.

"I hope I didn't wake you," Doreen said.

"No. A pigeon did."

Doreen relayed that to Selmo, then said, "Well, how are you?"

"Did I thank you? I don't remember. I didn't know who else to call."

"You called the only people you could. Don't mention it again. I hung something up for you in the closet. When you're dressed, come join us for breakfast."

"That's kind of you." I said goodbye, hung up, went to the closet, and found she'd left me a yellow dress. I held it in front of a mirror to check the fit. She did have good taste. I took a quick bath, then dressed and hurried out.

As I seated myself at their table, Selmo said, "We took the liberty of ordering for you."

"You'll like the food," Doreen said. "Isn't the weather in San Diego optimum?" She smiled at Selmo. "We don't come here often enough."

"Yes," Selmo said. "We took a train. Couldn't drive here at night with headlights off."

Flabbergasted, I said, "Why?"

They exchanged looks. Selmo said, "Why what?"

"Why all this? Why'd you come? You could've said no. It wasn't your responsibility."

Doreen said, "You asked for help. So, what exactly happened with your friend?"

They sat waiting. I knew that no matter how I colored events, it would sound bad. I decided to lie. "We were in Mexico. It was hot. She collapsed. Heatstroke I think."

Doreen offered me a patient smile. "It's nice that you want to be loyal."

"What?"

She gave me a patient smile and said, "She had an abortion."

Blood rushed to my cheeks. In the silence that followed I could hear my mother chastising me for lying. Thankfully, the meal came—bacon, scrambled eggs, and toast. Doreen and Selmo picked up their forks and began to eat. I stared at my plate.

"You should eat, Eve," Doreen said.

I couldn't look at her. I shook my head. "I lied to you. I'm sorry."

"To protect your friend," she said. "Loyalty's a good quality, don't you think, dear."

Selmo cleared his throat. "Yes. According to the doctor our Eve was a hero or a saint. The hospital was almost out of whole blood. You and the Marines replenished it. And a fresh supply went to the Red Cross." He held up a slice of bacon. "Let's eat."

"Yes, let's," Doreen said.

She gave me that same cool smile. "What's better for a bad night than a good breakfast?"

They seemed content that the matter was resolved. But, despite their dismissing my lie, I felt guilty. Perhaps, I thought, this is how people of good breeding behave, much like those sophisticates portrayed in Hollywood films did.

# -22-

A WOMAN ROVER FROM THE night crew temporarily took over Dominique's role. While she was on the mend, word circulated in the factory that Dominique had been hospitalized following an abortion. The girls on my crew were curious, especially Tiff, who tried to pry information from me. I offered no details, just that Dominique had been hospitalized. All the same, the story, in varying versions, began circulating around the factory floor. When asked, I refused to talk about it until Bea, one of the Black Rosies, cornered me.

"Eve, girl. Don't you let those tongue waggers get you down."

"I don't know what you're talking about."

"Honey, I'm talking about talk." She took both of my hands in hers and rubbed them. "It ain't your mistake. You're a country gal, like me, right. I would'a done the same. Right or wrong 'cause if you hadn't been there. Well, Dom's alive ain't she. What you did is love her, nothin' more." She dropped my hands and wrapped me in a tight embrace.

"Thank you," I said as she released me. "I needed to hear that."

"You get yourself right with H.T., hear?"

"What?"

"He's feeling blues and not singin' them. I think it's you

can lift them from him." She smiled and swung about, leaving me perplexed.

I worked my shift and kept mostly to myself. After work I went straight to the apartment where I fed and watched over Dominique. Women, even those on other crews, brought me baskets of vegetables from their Victory Gardens and offered kind words for me to pass on to Dominique. Some of the women among the tanners baked sweet breads for me to take home.

I spoke to Selmo in passing. He didn't bring up the weekend, but twice he stopped me to say that Doreen wanted me over for dinner once Dominique was "up and about." His inviting me began preying on my thoughts. I'd left San Diego with the impression they'd come because they wanted me obligated to them. What did I have to offer that they didn't already have? The more I pondered the situation, the more it shaped out like a Hollywood film muddled up with corny dialogue and stiff acting.

Except for her sniffling when she saw a bird sitting on a branch outside and later a wilted flower lying in the garden, Dominique seemed improved. Then one morning I brought her a glass of fresh milk and she bawled as she sipped on it. The worst of her tears came when she looked out the bathroom window and saw a baby stroller abandoned in the alley behind the apartment building. I hurried to her bed and she sobbed into her pillow as I stroked her hair.

"I'm sorry," she said. "Look what I brought on you. I'm nothing but a burden. I wish I were like you."

"How's that?"

"You don't cry. Look what it does to me."

One evening Dominique and I were listening to war news on the radio when suddenly she was cheered by the news of an Allied victory in southern France. She stood up straight and said, "Let's take a walk before dinner. I've been lying around too long."

Though pale, she seemed otherwise fine as we stepped outside. She looked toward the sky, sighed as she grabbed the rail, and began the descent. A breeze blew in from the channel. We paused by the garden. I'd come to appreciate how Mr. Tinkler attended to the garden. Someday, I thought, I'll have a garden like this one and cut flowers to wear in my hair.

"Dom," I said, "I'm tempted to break a bud off and put it in my hair."

"Don't even think about it," she said.

"Tinkler is probably spying on us right now."

Over the weeks I'd come to recognize his peculiar behavior, especially his peering out from his cracked blinds as we passed by. Coming home from an evening out, I'd once seen him lurking in the shadows of the trees. When I'd called out hello, he'd retreated deeper into the shadows. One morning I'd spread the curtains and locked eyes with him. He wiped the window with his shirt sleeve, shrugged, and walked away.

"Maybe he's a German agent. Tinkler sounds German," I said, offering her an arm.

She smiled and shook my arm off. "I can walk on my own."

We strolled east on Alma Street. Behind us the sun was bleeding into the ocean. Our shadows moved before us, long and distorted. We didn't talk until we neared 20th Street. We stopped and gazed at the harbor where the sun cast the water in purple tones and pelicans circled and suddenly splashed into the waves.

Dominique licked her lips. "I'm going back to work in the morning. Who all knows?"

"Do you think I would ever . . .?"

"No. But gossip is a pastime for the women and most of them don't like me."

"Why do you say that?"

"Eve, it doesn't matter." She sighed. "I pretended for a while that I loved him. Even thought about keeping the baby. Know why I didn't?"

"You don't have to tell me."

"I want to. I know I'm vain. But that's only part of me. I didn't want to hurt my mother and father or my son or you. I need to grow up. I'm not a girl. You're so much more mature than me and you're years younger."

"Not so many if I use my sister's ID."

She offered a thin smile. "You're a friend. I haven't had many. It's horrible to think what I put you through, what I put myself through. The doctor said I could have died."

"You didn't."

"But I could have. I let a weak man into my life. I'm ashamed of it. I pretended he was strong because he had money and the power to put me on a movie screen. Shame's a powerful weapon we use on ourselves. It's as powerful as pretense."

I looked at her admiringly. "You're very wise."

"Wise hell, I probably stole the lines from a movie."

"There are rumors going around about you."

"I knew there would be."

"But the girls haven't been the ones spreading them. They like you."

"They do?"

"We do. And so do the others. They gave us vegetables."

We watched the sun drop into the Pacific, then strolled back to the apartment. She stopped at the garden wall and plucked a flower and handed it to me. "It's all I have to give."

"Tinkler will shoot us," I said.

"We can always find another apartment."

"In Los Angeles? Not with our luck."

# -23-

I'D NOT FORGOTTEN THE EVENTS that followed my going to the blues club. I'd written about them in my journal, mostly dismissing them as big-city life experiences. That evening at the end of the shift, Selmo shuffled me inside his office and shut the door behind him. All that was on my mind was meeting Dominique. Two men waiting in the office stood up. I didn't recognize the one who stood at the desk until he removed his hat. Then I remembered Detective Sharkey. He introduced the second cop as Detective Sergeant Lester, then told me to have a seat. Though there were empty chairs, neither officer sat. Sharkey said the interview wasn't merely a routine follow-up.

"I want you to understand the case we're working on is serious. Sergeant Lester's from metro homicide. And that gun you claim not to have seen anyone drop killed a man. He was shot in the head six months ago." He formed a V with his forefinger and thumb, placed the fingertip to his temple, and lowered his thumb.

Following what happened to Dominique, I'd all but put the night at Pork Skins—all but my confused thoughts about H.T.—out of my head. Now the night revived itself in ugly detail: Cornell's foul breath, the panic as patrons tried to leave, the indignities of being handcuffed and accused of being a prostitute, and the VD test. I pictured Cornell slipping the gun out and wiping it off on the tail of his suit jacket. My mouth went dry. I gripped the arm of the chair and gazed dumbly at the door. It seemed to slowly move away.

"Are you okay?" Sergeant Lister asked. "Do you want to change your story now?"

I blinked. Change, I thought. I looked at him. He had soft brown eyes, kind eyes, and a fatherly manner. His question began to sink in. Sure, change. Change everything, vanish into obscurity. What would my talking change? I took a slow breath, released my grip on the chair, and held my hand to my throat.

"Howard Thomas Elders works here too," Sergeant Lister said. "He your boyfriend?"

I shook my head. "A friend. A good friend. We work together. Why?"

"So, you would lie to protect him?" Lister asked.

"No."

"Did Howard Thomas drop the gun?"

I shook my head, and as soon as I did, I realized I'd been tricked.

"So, you did see who dropped it?"

I took a breath and exhaled. "H.T. was singing. I was watching him."

"Eve," the sergeant said, "That's not answering the question. We've got a murder victim. Granted he's a nobody, someone who probably owed a debt or got in Tomato Man's way, but he deserved to live. You wouldn't want to protect a cold-blooded killer, would you?"

I shook my head.

"H.T.'s got a history with the law, but I'm not out to hurt him or you. I couldn't care less if he sends you flowers and serenades you at your window. What I want is the name of the one who dropped that gun. You know his name, don't you?"

I looked off. I'd seen detectives in movies. Didn't they check the gun for fingerprints? But what did I know about fingerprints, or guns for that matter?

Both cops, standing closer now, towering over me. Detective Sharkey pressed his hard stare on me and nudged Sergeant Lister. "We're up against a nigger-lover here. She's willing to go to jail for one. Isn't that sweet?"

I matched his stare. "You're being ugly. That's a terrible word to use."

"Wake up, young lady," Lister said. "The world's the world. If necessary, we'll book you for obstruction of justice and hold you as a material witness."

Through the milky glass door I saw the obscured shape of someone seated in the outer office.

"I wouldn't want to see you in trouble. Besides, the DA won't want a reluctant witness, so for now I won't book you. Keep in mind that whoever had that gun killed a man."

"May I go?"

The cops exchanged looks. Sergeant Lister nodded. "But think about this conversation." He wrote a phone number on the back of his card and handed it to me. "Call that number or the one on the back. It's my home. I only give it out if I think the person will need my help."

That said, the sergeant walked to the door and opened it. H.T. sat waiting his turn. It reasoned that the cops would go hard on him, and I felt obligated to somehow relay to him that my silence was assured. He stared at the floor. Before I could say or signal anything, the sergeant called H.T. into the room. In passing by, he avoided eye contact with me. The office door shut. As I descended the stairs, I felt a pinch at the base of my neck.

When the cops left for the day, Selmo led them outside,

then came to my station and said, "I'll call my attorney. He'll handle matters for you."

"I'm sorry you were dragged in. You don't have to do that."

"Doreen wouldn't have it any other way."

Since the night of the raid, H.T. had avoided me. That upset me because what occurred in the club wasn't due to anything he'd done. News that he and I had been interviewed by cops had already spread through the factory, whispered hearsay linking us in romantic ways. Oddly discomforting was the fact that the more distant he became, the more I found myself thinking about him and attracted to him. I'd go out of my way to find an opportunity to hear him play his harmonica or pass by and say hello on my way to the fire escape. Now, dragged into a murder investigation as I was, I wondered if that would further distance him. At noon break I intercepted him near the loading dock. He lowered his head to turn away.

"Don't treat me that way, Howard Thomas. I don't deserve it."

He looked up and down the hall, then took my arm and pulled me through the swinging doors to the loading platform. "They told me not to talk about this with you."

"But they didn't tell me not to talk to you."

"You're not me. They'll charge me with contributing to the delinquency of a minor."

"I'm almost twenty and I'm a woman. I'm not a minor or a child. I want you to know I didn't tell them anything."

"Makes no difference." His nostrils flared. "Selmo asked if I needed a lawyer. You think I should I get one?"

I shrugged. "Not because of anything I said."

He thought a moment and said, "He says he'll hire me one if I stay away from you."

"Is that what you want? To stay away from me?"

Someone's footsteps approached the loading room doors. H.T. backed away from me as the doors opened. Gretchen stepped out.

She looked at H.T., then me, and said, "We've been looking for you, Eve. We're having lunch on the fire escape. We're celebrating Dominique's return. Tiff made cupcakes."

I nodded. "I'll be along."

"Oh, okay," she said knowingly. "How're you, H.T.?"

"Mighty fine, Missy," he said.

"That's good." She wheeled about and passed through the swinging doors.

"Will you be all right?" I asked.

"Cornell ain't no one to mess with, but I'll be okay all the same. Why?"

I shook my head. "I'm just concerned. Thinking about you is all. Truth be told, I have been doing just that."

"Think about this. When you left that office, did Selmo ask if you needed a lawyer?"

"No. But he did offer later."

"Well, I guess there's no need in anyone being concerned. See what I mean?"

"No."

He walked to the swinging door and held it open. "Your friends are waiting on you."

The following day the five of us sat on the platform exchanging small talk. Nothing was mentioned of my being summoned to Selmo's office, but the visit with the cops was a shadow hanging over our conversation. Others might have suspected something. Only Dominique knew what had happened that night, all but my seeing Cornell with the gun.

Tiff set her sandwich aside and said, "I ever mention Emory?"

"Who?" Mitzi asked.

"What kind of name is Emory?" Gretchen teased.

"It sounds like a name with money," Mitzi said.

"No," Dominique said. "You haven't told us."

"She knows she hasn't told anyone," Mitzi said. "But she wants to."

Tiff lowered her head. "Don't make fun of me."

Dominique looked around. "Who's making fun? No one's making fun. Tell us."

The unease that had drifted among us seemed to evaporate. Tiff looked from face to face until she got a nod from each of us.

Gretchen said, "Is Emory the real reason you made cupcakes?"

"No. They're for Dominique," Tiff said. "Emory's a sailor. Yes, I know better than to get involved, but honestly, he's very nice. He's younger, twenty-seven to be exact. He has red hair, which I didn't care for, but that's shallow. And look at me. I'm fat and thirty-four."

Gretchen said, "Don't say that and don't think of yourself that way. Haven't we all learned to think of ourselves better than what's been projected on us for generations? Aren't we productive? Aren't we valuable for many reasons? Is Eleanor Roosevelt beautiful? No. But we look at her in newsreels and listen to what she has to say. We're better than just pretty. Better than. . . ." She saw the expressions on our faces. "Oh, hell, I'm sorry. But you know I'm right. And you'll know it even better when this damn war is over."

We sat in silence for a moment, some of us eating, some staring at ships in the harbor.

Breaking the spell, Mitzi said, "Tiff, I didn't say anything, but I saw you with him outside the Y. You sneak."

"We went to the movies is all . . . and a picnic. One dinner. Okay, two dinners. He kissed me after the second one. I mean, you know, a real kiss."

A kiss, I thought, seemed too innocent. I felt an urge to say that a love life seemed almost trivial, that a man had killed a man, and now I was involved in something I should not be. But saying that would've been selfish and cruel. Tiff, after all, was the most vulnerable among us.

"Didn't we have a pact? We can dance with them, but nothing more," Mitzi said. "Eve? Why are you so quiet?"

Saving me from having to answer, Tiff said, "You're my friends. I wanted you to know, but I wanted to be certain myself first. Is it okay for me to be happy? Please, understand. You may remember him, the redheaded sailor I met when we went to Santa Monica Ballroom. He can dance like Fred Astair. Well, almost."

"Oh, God. She's gone. In love. Just like a movie," Mitzi said. "Isn't it, Dominique?"

"Like one, but I hope better."

"Well, make sure he uses a rubber," Gretchen said bringing matters down to earth.

We stared at Gretchen as if she'd turned a hose on us. To hint at sexual desire was acceptable, even invited, but talking openly about sexual matters was viewed as crass. We fell silent again and, in that moment, I saw the hypocrisy. We were sexual. We had desires we'd been trained to suppress. I started to speak, but Dominique spoke up first. "Gretchen didn't mean anything," she said. "She's right. Look what happened to me."

Gretchen turned to Dominique. "I'm sorry. I didn't mean that, Dom."

"Didn't mean what?" Tiff asked.

Dominique said, "I had an abortion. Okay. Let's don't pretend."

I wondered how they would react if I drew them a picture of how Jess grabbed me, pinned me down, and pried my knees apart. "Never mind all that," I said. "Let's just eat."

"What's wrong with you?" Gretchen asked.

"Nothing." I took out my journal and began writing about an unnamed man throwing a gun under a table. I described his cold stare as he looked at a young woman. I'd never made an entry like that before. I heard Gretchen talking but paid no attention.

"Eve?" Gretchen said.

I looked up. "What?"

"Quit writing. I mean, nothing you'd care to say?" Gretchen said.

Dominique shook her head. "Gretchen, why are you being ugly?"

"This isn't very much like a celebration," Mitzi said.

Tiff picked up her lunch pail. "I haven't done anything but be with a nice man, who had manners. You made it." As she turned toward the window, it was obvious she was crying.

We clamored to our feet to go after her. My journal slipped out of my hand and fell to the platform and hung over the edge. I scrambled to the edge to reach for it and as I did the sudden shift of weight caused the grating to sway. That was followed by a groaning sound.

"What the hell?" Dominique shouted and grabbed the rail.

The next instant the platform buckled and the rivets holding it to the frame began to snap loose. We screamed. I was nearest the ladder and managed to get a handhold on it. Mitzi, Gretchen, and Dominique, saved from tumbling into the alley by the handrail, clutched onto whatever metal they could. Warped now, the platform had come to rest at a steep angle beside the wall where it hung precariously. It seemed for the moment stable, but any sudden shift of weight might unmoor it and send us tumbling.

"Don't move," I said as calmly as possible.

I swung my left leg over the handrail and gained a foothold on a rung, enough to feel secure for the moment. It appeared that if I could pull my trailing leg over the rail, I could climb to the roof and go for help, but I saw a wire barrier, installed to discourage burglars, barred me.

I looked down. Holding on with both hands, Tiff dangled precariously from the windowsill. Gretchen was an arm's reach away from the ladder.

"If you can get to the ladder, it's safe," I said.

She untangled her legs and as she did, the platform swayed. "Oh, Jesus," she shouted.

Mitzi hollered, "Don't move, anyone, please."

Dominique clutched the bars beneath her and stared off as if in a state of disbelief.

"Okay, let's don't move," I said. "Tiff, you've got the best chance to go for help."

She'd managed to keep a grip on the sill, but lacked the strength to pull herself in. "I can't. I'm afraid," she said.

"We all are," I said. To her left a cornice could serve as a foothold. From where I clung it appeared I too could reach the window. I had the strength that she lacked and could climb inside and go for help, but I'd have to squeeze past her.

"The ledge, Tiff, if you stretch your foot up, you can get to it."

She hesitated. Below the others were barely clinging on. The platform trembled. Mitzi gasped.

"Come on, Tiff," I said. "You can climb in."

She slowly lifted her leg.

"You can do it," Mitzi said, looking up. "Please."

"A little more to your left," I said.

Tiff gained a toehold but froze and began sobbing. "I can't."

"You can. What about your sailor."

"You got it," Mitzi said. "That's our gal."

I said slowly and insistently, "Tiff, just try it."

"No." She closed her eyes.

Below the platform shifted.

"Oh, shit," Mitzi said. "We're going to die."

I caught a glimpse of the bay where the huge cargo ships looked like floating toys. The enterprise of man going about his business unconcerned, I thought, and we're about to die.

Just then H.T. peered out of the window. "You ladies got a fine mess goin'."

"Help Tiff," I said.

He reached for her. She stiffened at his touch.

He gently took her by her wrists. "Relax. Howard Thomas's got you. You'll be okay. On three. Your count." He tightened his grip.

"One," she said, "two. . . ."

She didn't get to three. Weighing at least a hundred and fifty pounds, she wasn't an easy load to lift, but he eased her up over the sill and set her down inside.

"No need crying now. You go for help," he said.

But it was obvious she wasn't because we could hear her crying inside the window.

He stuck his head out. "You gotta do somethin', Eve."

"Tell me what." I looked down and my stomach curdled. I looked back up at him.

"You trust me?"

Though terrified, I wasn't about to renounce the world. I reached out and touched the sill with my fingertips.

"No, I need you to get hold of my wrist," he said.

We strained and fumbled. I couldn't quite reach to clasp his wrist.

"Go up a rung," he said.

Using one leg, I eased up a rung, held on with one hand, and stretched my arm up. He reached down and I touched his fingertips with my free hand.

"Let go of the ladder when I say," he said.

He leaned farther out and still we could only touch our fingers. I had to take a chance and put more weight on the ladder to rise enough to grab his hand. If I failed, I'd take likely the platform and my friends down with me. Holding my breath, I nodded, rose on my toes, and let go with my left hand while reaching for him with my right hand.

He latched onto my hand with both his and said, "You gotta get off the rail."

I drew my foot off the rung and closed my eyes as I swung out below the window.

His hands straining from the effort, he kept me from falling.

"Go, gal," Gretchen hollered.

Pain shot from my shoulder up my arm. I hung suspended beneath the window by my right arm. Oddly, the sensation was at once terrifying and thrilling.

"You ain't much more than a feather," he said. "Come on."

A strange notion found seed in me, and a sense of calm took hold of the moment. He told me to reach with my other hand. I did, and he caught it in his. My knees scraped the bricks. For the first time since taking the job, I was thankful to be wearing overalls.

I kept my eyes on his as, seemingly with little effort, he pulled me steadily upward. He appeared amused by the situation. When I was level with the sill, I set my elbows on it. He let go of one wrist and hauled me inside by the straps of my overalls. I dropped to the floor beside Tiff who sat slumped against the wall, her head buried in her arms. Somehow H.T. had banged his head. He touched the spot he'd bumped. His fingers came away with blood.

He wiped it on his britches and said, "Get gone. Find Selmo to call for help."

I sprang to my feet and ran to the stairs, hollering for help as I did. At the top landing I encountered Tomea and a group of women from another crew.

"We heard screams," one said.

I grabbed Tomea by her shoulders. "Where's Selmo?"

"*No se*," she said.

I brushed past her and took the steps two at a time. I passed a fire alarm without thinking to pull it. At the next landing I nearly collided with Selmo and blurted out what had happened. He continued up, paused at the fire alarm, and pulled the lever. I followed.

We reached the top floor. The hall was pandemonium. A half dozen women blocked our path. They hollered to overcome the sound of the alarm. Tomea sat beside Tiff, comforting her. Some of the women were kneeled in prayer. I hurried to a nearby window and tried to open it. It wouldn't budge. I slipped a tack hammer off one of the women's belts and used it to smash the panes. I chipped the shards of glass away, returned the hammer to the woman and peered out.

Selmo looked out the window overlooking the fire escape. When he stood upright again, he looked around, said something to H.T. and hurried off, only to return a few seconds later hauling a fire hose over his shoulder. He gripped the brass nozzle in both hands. They went to work immediately, H.T. helping him reel the hose until it was coiled in a pile at their feet. Then they tied the running end of the fire hose around Selmo's waist.

"Give us a hand," Selmo said.

The women nearest them seemed confused. I saw what H.T. and Selmo had in mind. By then the hall was filled with women. The tanners, seated on the floor, were praying. We had to improvise as well, that meant enlisting the women.

"You four," I said to the nearest women, "grab some of the hose and get ready to pull."

The women quickly formed a line behind H.T. Selmo climbed out the window. H.T. and the women reeled out the hose. I wove my way through the praying women back to the broken window and looked down. Selmo extended a hand to Gretchen, who shook it off. He wrapped an arm around one of hers and told her to let go of the grillwork. She shook her head.

He said, "Gretchen, we can't stay out here all day."

She nodded, then suddenly screamed, "Robert," and wrapped her arms around his neck.

He shouted, "H.T., bring us up."

I hurried to the end of the line of women holding the hose and said, "Let's go."

A slow arm's stretch at a time, they began reeling the hose in. One lost her grip and fell aside. A woman praying jumped to her feet and took the fallen woman's place in line. A few painful seconds passed, then Selmo's and Gretchen's heads came level with the sill. H.T. reached out, and his back and arms straining, he pulled Gretchen inside. He set her down on her feet and she crumbled to the floor. She didn't cry as Tiff had, just lay holding her stomach, repeating over and over, "Thank you. Thank you."

Without pause Selmo went back down, rappelling off the wall as if he'd been mountain climbing all his life. He came aside the platform an arm's length from Dominique. She nodded compliantly as he told her what to do. He navigated sideways to reach her.

Her hand clamped to the grillwork, she sat seemingly dazed with her legs bent to one side as she often did on the apartment floor.

Selmo said, "We need you, Dominique. Take my hand."

He extended his hand and clasped her wrist. She jerked hers away and gripped the rail.

I hollered, "Dominique!"

She looked up and blinked.

I blurted out, "Do what the director tells you!"

She looked down. "But I'm . . . I'm afraid." Slowly she extended a hand to take Selmo's while keeping a fierce grip on the grill with the other.

"Damn it, let go, Dominique!" I shouted.

She said, "Okay, okay," but didn't let go.

Selmo let go of her hand and thrust himself away from the wall. He landed close beside her and wrapped an arm around her waist. I closed my eyes.

The women prayed to "*Madre Dolarosa*," and I muttered a prayer of my own. I felt a hand on my shoulder and opened my eyes.

"It's okay," Gretchen said from beside me. "He's got you, Dom."

Dominique's legs wrapped around him as if the two of them were locked in a lovers' embrace, Selmo began scaling the wall. At the other end, H.T. and the women hoisted them up.

I hollered down to assure Mitzi, "Hold on. You're next."

Amazingly, she had the composure to shout back, "*This*, my friends, is not my idea of a celebration."

Selmo was again on his way down when he hollered for H.T., "Hold up."

Confused, I looked out again. In all the turmoil we'd missed the sounds and hadn't seen fire engines pull into the alley. Already a team had raised a ladder and a fireman was climbing up to Mitzi.

H.T. hoisted Selmo inside. The two of them slumped to the floor, their chests heaving. Selmo reached over and shook H.T.'s hand. The praying women hugged one another. I hurried to Dominique.

She buried her head in my shoulder and whimpered, "I told you I was afraid of heights."

Gretchen crawled over to Tiff, wrapped an arm around her, then took out a tissue and wiped her eyes. A squad of firemen charged up the stairwell and came to a halt. They looked around, sizing up the situation. One nearby asked if we were all right. Selmo said we would be in a few minutes. Another walked to the window and looked down. "You'll have to replace that escape," he said nonchalantly and motioned to the others, who formed up and filed down the stairs.

We sat for a time astonished that we all came through it safely. Selmo told the assembly that we had work to do, but we'd do it tomorrow. I crawled to where H.T. sat. Blood trickled from the cut on his forehead. I told him his head was bleeding.

He touched the cut and looked at his fingertip. "Proves what I been thinkin' all along."

"What's that?"

"You and trouble are one thing."

I leaned my head onto his shoulder. He swung his arm over my shoulders and pulled me closer. I didn't know what to say other than "Thank you."

He smiled and said, "Let's go. I got a bad wound to fix up."

The reporter from the *Los Angeles Times* insisted that having our picture in the paper would be a civic gesture, a way of giving the public heart by showing there were heroes on the home front as well as overseas. We looked at ourselves in our compact mirrors, quickly brushed our hair and applied our lipstick, and touched on some rouge. Embarrassed because of our overalls and lack of time to ready ourselves, we ladies lined up in front of H.T. and Selmo. The man behind the camera asked Mitzi and Gretchen to kneel as they were taller than Selmo.

Mitzi, who'd earlier been photographed in the arms of a fireman as he brought her down the ladder, said without thinking, "He can get his milk box."

Embarrassed for him we lowered our heads.

Selmo said, "I should've thought of that." He smiled at Mitzi and slipped on his glasses, which sat at an odd angle now. It seemed that during the commotion someone had stepped on the frame. Box in hand, he returned and stood beside H.T. The photographer held up his hat and told us to look at it. "Smile," he said. The bulb popped. I saw blue and red spots. It took a few blinks to bring the room into focus.

Dominique, who'd seemed fine up to then, gripped my arm. "I'm going to be sick," she said and proved it by throwing up on my overalls.

That afternoon I slipped off my overalls and hurried out to the alley. Two stories up the fire escape dangled against the wall.

I stepped in the alley and as I did, a man shouted, "Don't go in there."

I turned around and faced Selmo.

"It's not safe. That could come down at any time. I'll have someone take it down tomorrow."

"Okay. I was just coming to get something."

"It'll be there later."

I took a quick look up the alley but couldn't see my journal anywhere on the ground. I walked away thinking how lucky we were and that if I hadn't scrambled to keep it from falling, none of this would have happened. But it did.

# -24-

The Allies were approaching Paris. As they exchanged news about the Allied push through France, people seemed giddy. The employees at the bootery were also caught up in the fever of hope. Certainly, Germany would surrender rather than be invaded. Our forces spearheaded much of the assault leading to the liberation of Paris, yet when the moment to enter the city came, Americans were held in reserve as Free French forces under the command of Le Grande Charles, as de Gaulle had been anointed by the press, marched under the Arc de Triomphe to the wild cheers of flag waving Parisians. Recalling the blood of Americans spilled on Normandy beaches, some commentators demanded to know why Americans didn't enter the city first.

Now that the Germans were on the run, America cast its fortunes on a quick victory in Europe. Only the wait for fuel slowed the advance of American troops. As Allied soldiers trod toward the German frontier, Americans got a daily geography lesson. Hitherto unknown villages in the Italian and French countrysides became part of our vocabulary, and many of those listening to the radio pulled out maps of Europe and sat at their tables and tracked landmarks. Dominique and I were among them, mostly because Link was no doubt in the thick of it.

The week Paris was again under French control a new fire escape was installed at Lucien's. Spirits were high in the factory. Minus a fire escape, the factory had been temporarily shut down. There was scant metal available and few iron contractors with workers enough to fabricate a new escape in a short time. Selmo had appealed to politicians and bureaucrats in the city and county. Nothing came of his efforts until the newspaper story finally went nationwide and captured public attention. A follow-up story in the *L.A. Times* described how we women on the assembly line wrote notes to encourage the Marines, how we took pride in our efforts and felt our contribution overlooked, and how we'd acted bravely when the fire escape collapsed. The writer proclaimed that, like food and ammunition, boots were high on the infantry's priority list. Gretchen was quoted in the article as saying she couldn't understand "why everyone looks down on boots," a line that brought smiles to the girls faces despite the factory being shut down.

Ultimately, through the intervention of War Department officials, the factory was opened while repairs on the fire escape were being completed.

I'd bought six copies of the *L.A. Times* and cut the article out. Keeping one for myself, I sent four to mother, asking her to forward one to each of my brothers. I also sent one to Avis who wrote back that Ron Crisp from Colfax had been killed when his tank hit a mine in eastern France. Avis didn't mention my mother and Mother didn't write back. She hadn't written in weeks, so I wrote asking Avis to check on her. A letter finally arrived from Mother a day before the factory reopened. It began: "Is he your black man? I won't let your brothers know of this." I tore it up. I wanted to scream at her. Instead I sat and wrote her a brief letter:

Dear Mom,

His name's Howard Thomas. He's a fine man who helped save my friends. He reminds me in ways of my brothers, your sons. Remember, please, that we're all in this struggle together, your sons, the women in the factory, and, yes, Howard Thomas and others like him. My brothers would be proud to know him. I love you.

Sincerely,
your daughter Eve

Relieved to be back at work, we girls took our stations and adjusted our stools. Selmo entered holding his milk box overhead. He stood near the center of the factory floor and turned slowly about before he set the box down and said, "No speech." He pushed the box aside and pulled the conveyor lever.

Within the hour what started as roughed-out leather at one end of the process fell off the conveyor belt as finished boots complete with laces and a note. I found comfort in using my hands and eyes and was happy to be occupied. Otherwise, I feared I might write a second letter that I knew would sever me from my mother forever.

In all the excitement I'd never been able to offer H.T. the thanks I owed him. After the initial article had been printed, he'd shied away from us. Except for Dominique, who'd made it a point to tell me people harshly judge white women who date outside their race, none of my friends had mentioned H.T. to me. Still, I knew they speculated among themselves. That evening I initialed my time card and went to the dock intent on thanking him. The air inside was sultry so I stood outside on the bottom stair, nonchalantly resting hip against the rail as I looked at the clouds hugging the coast.

For an instant I thought I caught sight of H.T. standing in

the shadow of a brick wall at the edge of the alley. I wondered what he was up to. Then a shaft of sunlight pierced through the clouds and lit the alley. His hands in his pockets, the figure in the shadows stepped into the light and looked up the alley in my direction. Wearing gray trousers, a flower-print shirt, and a white Panama hat, he waved at me. My pulse racing, I turned to flee inside and was abruptly halted by H.T. who'd come up behind me.

"Did you see enough?" he asked in an offhanded way.

I couldn't speak, so I pointed down the alley until I gathered my wits. "You scared me."

"Sorry, missy." He said calmly.

The fact that H.T. was so composed angered me. "Eve. Call me Eve. It's my name."

"Didn't mean to get you all upset," he said.

I looked where I had last seen Cornell, but he'd vanished. Thinking I might be mistaken, I turned to H.T. for confirmation. "Was that . . .?"

"Cornell." His face expressionless, he nodded.

I said, "H.T., must you be so . . . so I don't know."

"Never mind. We got trouble."

"I didn't tell the cops anything. He's got no reason."

"You saw what you saw. That's enough."

It registered that he'd used we. "You saw it too, didn't you?"

"Don't matter. He knows where you work now. It was a fine photo of us all, wasn't it? Being a hero's not so damn fine when you look at it real close." He looked down where Cornell had been standing. "Can't play my music now. I'm not welcome at Pork Skins or Harlem's Castle or B 'n' Bs because of him. See, he's not just a pimp." He looked off. "He's a jobber for the boys who say who sings in their joints. I need my music and people who understand it."

"I'm sorry, but I didn't cause it. Neither did you."

"In your case it comes from hanging out where you've got no business."

"You're who took me there."

"Yes, I am."

We stared at one another, then I asked, "What's a jobber?"

"In Tomato Man's case, someone who brings girls into clubs." He took two steps and turned away. Over his shoulder he said, "And gets rid of problems for them."

"H.T., I came out here to say you were a hero that day and we all owe you thanks."

"Hero?" He chuckled and said, "Your friends are waitin'. You have a nice night, Eve." He motioned with his hand as if tipping a hat and backed away.

"Where're you going?"

He said without looking back, "Keep close with your friends," then retreated up the steps and turned toward the storage room inside.

My heart still beating heavily, I found the girls in the ladies change room shedding their overalls. Dominique said we should do something to celebrate, anything other than go the USO dance. Gretchen suggested a club in Torrance. As talk circled, debating where to go, my pulse slowed.

"Let's go to Tasco's," I said louder than I'd intended.

"I'm on board," Mitzi said in an even louder voice.

"What's a Tasco's?" Gretchen said. "Is that anything like a taco?"

"You'll see," Dominique said. "Let's vote. Mitzi, Eve, and I vote for Tasco's."

Like Dominique, I'd become a familiar face to Rosemarie and Sandy, but Gretchen and Tiff had never been to Tasco's and Mitzi had been only once. "You win," she said.

Dominique opened the door and stood aside. Tiff asked if we were sure the place was safe. Dominique nudged her inside. Though reluctant, Gretchen followed. The evening crowd had not yet arrived. Sandy said hello and hollered to the kitchen that the ladies had arrived, this time with friends. Rosemarie looked over the pass-through, shouted hello, and said heroes were welcome in her house. Her head disappeared into the steaming kitchen.

"It looks like the deck of an old ship," Gretchen said.

"It is," Dominique said.

"Where're the booths?" Tiff asked.

"No booths," Dominique said.

"How do we eat?" Gretchen asked.

"With fingers and toothpicks," I said. "Or spoons."

Gretchen curled her nose. We took stools at the bar and Sandy said, "First drinks for your friends are on me." He called Mitzi by name and remembered her preference was a whiskey sour. Mitzi asked us how he could remember that. Dominique said, "He never forgets."

"Well, these are the other heroes," Sandy said. "You look just like your pictures." He pointed to the wall farther down the bar where he'd hung the framed news clipping. "Pleased to meet you." He shook hands with Gretchen and Tiff.

"We aren't," Gretchen said. "Heroes I mean. H.T. and Selmo, they pulled us out."

"All of you are heroes here. Crab legs and steamed mussels?" he asked Dominique. "We got them steamed and ready."

"Yes, for five," she said.

He walked to the pass-though and hollered, "Legs and mussels for five." A basket appeared, and he carried it to the bar, set it before us, and peeled back the checkered cloth.

"Rosemarie knew you'd want bread," he said.

Tiff breathed in the fresh-baked aroma and said, "I'll never go to another bar." She asked where all the men Dominique had mentioned were. Dominique told her to be patient, that the evening was about to begin. Ten minutes passed before the crowd began to arrive, at first one and two at a time, then in packs of five and six.

In no time longshoremen and tugboat operators lined the bar, the wall, and filled most of the floor space. The Aussie with the accordion showed up and began playing "The Ballad of Sam Hall." Some men sang along. The owner's daughter Lana, her dark hair in a bun, bustled out of the kitchen. A half-Scot, half-Portuguese girl, Lana walked confidently among the men taking orders while never writing one down or missing one. Because I'd waited tables, I admired her efficiency. The men spoke to her with teasing adoration but didn't cross any lines. Sandy, a burly former tugboat captain himself, was quick to scold a foul mouth and equally quick to intercede in an argument, and Rosemarie tolerated no incivility, especially to her daughter.

Tiff and Gretchen were drawn into the ritual. Gretchen who usually monitored everything guardedly relaxed and hummed as the Aussie played. After two songs the Aussie pushed his way through the gathering, shaking hands as he progressed our way. He came to rest beside Tiff. A pink-faced man in his mid-forties, he had a weathered look to him and was balding. He winked at Tiff and told her in a deep voice the song was for her. He struck up a folk ballad. Red-cheeked but smiling, Tiff avoided eye contact with him, instead casting her gaze about the bar until he finished. He asked if we enjoyed it. We said we did, but Tiff kept her eyes on the bar top.

"Talk to him," Dominique whispered. "Tell him you liked the song."

"I can't," Tiff murmured.

He lingered by our table a moment, then strolled back to join his friends. When he left, she said, "He's too old. Besides, there's Emory."

"Tiff," Dominique said. "You're thirty-four and this is a war and . . . never mind."

Sandy set a round in front of us, saying the drinks were compliments of a gentleman.

"Which one?" Tiff asked, looking over her shoulder at the Aussie.

"Pick one," Sandy said and laughed robustly.

Gretchen smiled and, with the hint of a slur, said, "This is fun."

"Well, thank him, whoever, for us," Dominique said.

Sandy leaned over the bar and said to Tiff. "His name's Art. He wants to know yours."

Gretchen said, "Tell him her name is Tiffany and she's very shy."

I listened without comment. Tomato Man's sudden appearance stirred in the back of my mind. To my knowledge Cornell Jones had vanished and reappeared but once since that night at Pork Skins. I once thought I'd seen him near the piers. It momentarily unnerved me, but it turned out to be another man wearing a white Panama.

Dominique said, "Eve, you've barely spoken."

I pointed to my ears. "It's loud." I could hear fine but didn't want to talk.

Dominique shook her head. "Come on. What's going on? You're not you."

"I'm just tired."

She studied my face. "Suit yourself."

Following the rhythms of harbor work, the crowd vanished just as quickly as it had appeared. The bar top from one end to the other was left full of empty bottles and glasses. On his way out the Aussie paused to say goodbye. Then he rushed out.

"He's very good looking," Dominique said.

"You think so?" Tiff said.

"I think you should come back with us sometime and get a better look."

As Lana and Sandy cleared away glasses, Rosemarie shoved her way through the swinging door and sidled up to me. She leaned forward and rested her arms on the bar top.

"What's the matter, dear? You don't feel good?"

I was puzzled how Rosemarie, in all the commotion of work, could have even taken notice of me much less sensed something was wrong. "Thanks for asking, but I'm fine."

"I have some herbs. Follow me." She motioned for me to come.

I sensed it was a privilege to enter her kitchen and an insult to refuse. I followed her into the kitchen filled with the aroma of baked bread, crab legs, chowder, and spices. The kitchen's brick floor was worn to a lacquer smoothness. Pressed against one wall was a breakfast table with three high-back chairs. Rosemarie pointed to it and told me to take a seat. She went to the back and motioned someone to come inside from the alley.

H.T. entered and waited self-consciously just inside the door. Rosemarie asked if he was hungry. He thanked her and said he'd eat later.

Rosemarie said, "No you won't," and went to a vat where she ladled out a bowl of chowder. She set the bowl on a saucer and placed the bowl and a spoon on the table opposite me. She took his shirt sleeve and walked him to the chair. "Eat all of it," she said. "And you'll want this." She tossed a half loaf of bread to him. "Next time come to the front door, young man. You scared me to death until I recognized you from your newspaper picture."

She disappeared through the swinging door. Confused, I remained seated and stifled an urge to leave.

"She's a lady." H.T. broke a piece off the loaf, chewed it, and swallowed it down, then dipped the spoon in the bowl.

"Were you *following* me?"

He spooned some soup in his mouth, bit into the bread, and chewed. When he swallowed, he set his eyes on me. "He followed you ladies. I followed him."

"Cornell?" I looked at the back door and wondered if it was bolted.

H.T. said, "He's not fool enough to barge in here." He took another spoonful and swallowed it down. "This is good."

"I didn't tell the police about the gun."

He swallowed another mouthful and said, "Who said anything about a gun?"

"I said I didn't tell anyone."

"I know you didn't, but I did."

"You did?" To my knowledge no charges had been filed. Unless we talked there was nothing at stake for us whether Cornell Jones went to jail or not. "Why'd you do that?"

"Doesn't matter. All Tomato Man knows is cops are looking for him because witnesses said he had a gun. What matters tonight is you can't go straight home from here."

"I'll call the police," I said.

"He'll take off soon as he sees one and figure you ratted. He may be tryin' to scare you for now." He shook his head. "Best thing you can do is stay scared."

I wondered what Mother would say now. She'd lectured me often to stay out of trouble, by which she'd meant with boys. My guess was she'd say I asked for this by being with a black man. "What do we do?"

H.T. said, "Right now I'll finish eating. You'll watch." He grinned and dipped his spoon in the chowder. "Go make some excuse so's you and Dominique can leave. Come through the back door to the alley."

"Mitzi and the others. . . . What'll I say?"

He broke off a chunk of bread. "I can't figure everything out."

I scooted the chair back and stood. "Why did you tell the police?"

"Bein' black's not trouble enough. Guess I needed some more bother."

"What I meant to say is did you tell the police because of me?"

He held the bread in front of his mouth. "That'd be a silly reason."

"I wish you'd. . . . Never mind."

"Wish I'd what?"

"Finish eating."

I told Dominique we had to leave because I was starting my period. She turned toward the front door. I took her by the arm, said goodnight to the others, and marched her through the kitchen to the alley, which was empty. I looked around for H.T.

Dominique said, "Why are we standing in a dark alley?"

Trying to conceal my unease, I looked up and down the alley. "We're waiting for H.T."

"We're waiting in an alley for a man who on most days doesn't have the courtesy to say hello. I'm going back inside." She turned to leave.

"Don't." I grabbed her sleeve.

"Then explain."

"Okay." I let go of her sleeve. "The time I went to Pork Skins there was a police raid. I told you before that I was arrested. I saw something."

"What did you see?"

"Never mind." I realized I'd put my good friend at risk.

"Hey, down there," H.T. called from atop the flat roof of the warehouse across the alley.

"What the hell?" Dominique said. "I'm going to have a heart attack."

"I'm comin' down." H.T. leaped from the roof to a telephone pole near the side of the building and began clambering down.

"What was he doing up there?"

"Looking for Tomato Man."

"Tomato Man? Why not the Easter Bunny or the Gingerbread Man? I'm going inside."

"No. Wait." I grabbed her sleeve.

H.T. dropped to the ground the last few feet and hurried to us. "We best be leavin'."

"Not until I know what's going on," Dominique said. "And it better be good."

"Okay. We're looking out for a man who thinks we're witness against him."

As the story of that night unfolded, she listened and responded by shaking her head or nodding. I finished by saying, "I saw the gun. I wished I hadn't." I omitted the part about H.T. telling the cops he'd seen the gun. When I finished, H.T. leaned close and whispered, "You shouldn't have told her you saw the gun."

Dominique, who started the evening in lighthearted mood, delivered what sounded like lines from a script, "He'd best be a damned serious killer. I won't tolerate having my night disrupted by some petty crook."

H.T. pointed north. "Let's get you to home. Don't stop."

I told Dominique we'd have to change our route to make sure we reached home without Cornell finding out where we lived.

"Okay," Dominique said, "lights, roll the cameras."

I said, "Action."

"Who is this Cornell guy really?"

"A jobber," I said with authority.

Taking a circuitous route that would add a mile to the walk, we began the trek. On occasion I looked back to see if H.T. was following. Silent as a snowflake, at first H.T. trailed behind us a half block. Then he disappeared. I only hoped he was still looking after us if from a distance. The walk began taxing Dominique's reserves. She wasn't yet fully recovered from being hospitalized. Still, she toughed it out until near the end of the uphill climb, then she stopped, bent over, and began gasping for air.

I waited until she stood upright and asked, "Think you can go on?"

She nodded and we proceeded to Cabrillo Ave., where she again faltered. She said, "I knew these shoes didn't fit, but they looked so good."

I helped her to concrete steps that led to some apartments where we sat. She removed her high heel and looked at it sadly. "Out on the fire escape I kept thinking I was going to die and never know my son. I didn't know how much I needed. . . ." She grimaced as she slipped the shoe back on. I offered her a hand up. She shook it off. "I need to be better. I should be with Andy. Be his mother." She stood and tested the foot. "Let's. . . ."

"Shush," I said. "I heard something." It sounded as if someone was breathing at a distance, and it came from near where a honeysuckle bush fanned out over the sidewalk two buildings away. All was colorless in the moonless night and the more I stared downhill, the more objects lost their edges and the more my limbs stiffened.

Dominique took my wrist in hand. "Don't scare me. If he wanted to, wouldn't he have killed us by now?"

I kept squinting in the direction of the plant. Suddenly the leaves of the honeysuckle rustled, a cat broke out of the bush and darted across the street. My arms went limp. I took Dominique's arm, laid it across my shoulders and said, "Let's go. Lean on me."

She limped beside me all the way to the steps to the apartments where we saw the obscure figure of a man standing in the shadows of the entryway. Keeping myself between him and Dominique, I said, "Who are you?"

"It's me." H.T. stepped out. "What was that about back there? I told you not to stop."

When my heart slowed, I said, "Dominique had a blister."

"Why's everyone scaring us?" Dominique asked.

He said, "For a damned blister?"

I walked over to him and said, "You ever have one?"

"If anyone cares, I have to go to the bathroom," Dominique said.

I told Dominique go ahead. She hobbled to the entryway and looked back.

"I didn't see 'im," H.T. said. "If he don't already know where you live, you're probably okay. Don't answer your door for no one. Stay scared. My mama even heard about all this where she lives. He'll be back around. I know him."

"Know him how?"

"Prison. 'At's enough for you to know."

"Can we go?" Dominique said.

"Why are you doing this?" I asked. I realized as I waited for him to answer that what I wanted to hear was he was doing it because he felt something for me, something I dared not call love.

Before he could answer, Dominique limped over. "So, Mister H.T., I'm curious. What would you have done if he'd shown up?"

"'Scuse me?"

"What would you have done? Beat him up? I'd just like to know."

He lifted the back of his shirt, pulled out a revolver and said, "I know how to use it. Goodnight." He slipped the gun back in his belt and covered it with his shirt tail. "I'm doing this 'cause I never should a' taken you to the club." That said, he wheeled about and hurried off.

In the courtyard, the boughs of the mimosa transformed the walkway into a cavern. The only sounds came from crickets and the gurgling fountain. Dominique tapped my arm and said we'd had a hard week and it would be nice to have some flowers to liven up the apartment.

"Let's just go to bed. I could sleep the whole weekend."

"Just one or two," she said.

She pinched off a flower and held it for me to smell. In the corner of my eye, I saw a shadowy figure. A man's voice boomed out, "You two stop picking my flowers. And I don't want to see his kind here."

The crickets stopped chirping. Dominique dropped the flower. A porch light went on, then another. My hands trembling uncontrollably, I stood unable to move or speak. I heard a splattering on the flagstone. Tinkler stepped out of the bushes and said, "I won't have your men friends creeping around, especially that type. Well, what do you have to say?"

Dominique looked down at a puddle of urine spreading at her feet. "You made me pee my pants," she said. "I hope you're happy, you son-of-a-bitch."

# -25-

Following Cornell Jones's reappearance in my life, I mostly kept to myself. I cautioned Dominique that it was best she not be seen with me for a while. I hurriedly changed clothes at the end of our shift and took a circuitous route to the apartment. Every blind corner was suspect as was every passing car. The girls pleaded with me to go out with them, but I made excuses. At times I entertained the idea of leaving and returning to Palouse.

Then one weekend evening, I stood at the kitchen window, listening to the radio while watching the harbor waves shimmer in the late sun. I saw summer fading outside. I'd been too distracted to realize that the year was edging toward autumn. I thought about how rapidly the seasons shifted in the rolling hills of the Palouse and how subtle the change was here. I recalled the urge I'd felt to come here, and my thoughts crystalized on my reasons. I hadn't come here merely to escape. I'd come here to find, to experience. In that moment I felt a surge of energy. I was still young and alive. I belonged out in the world of sound and sights.

The next morning before dawn I got out of bed, had breakfast, and boiled another egg for Dominique. I woke her. "It's autumn," I said.

She squinted at me. "So?"

"Harvest time. Wouldn't you like to go pick apples off a tree?"

"Who do you think I am? Johnny Appleseed?"

"You're a hick like me. Here, have a boiled egg." I handed it to her.

"Let's get the girls and go to the park, the one they just renamed for General MacArthur."

She cracked the shell with the spoon I'd brought. "Welcome back." She took a bite and smiled. "Breakfast in bed. Hell, why not? Give Gretchen a call. She'll stir the others to life. I'll get some tea going and we'll take a blanket to sit on."

"No. There're benches," I said.

The day was warm. We went to the corner store and bought five apples and a cantaloupe that we sliced up. We took a streetcar and met the others at the edge of the park around noon. Tiff brought a basket of homemade bread and a block of cheddar cheese. We strung ourselves out on two park benches and began sharing food. When we'd eaten all the fruit and bread and cheese, we donned our hats and began walking the path around Echo Lake.

Gretchen wore a rag-and-bone floppy-brim. She was even more talkative than usual. She took her hat off and waved it at us to emphasize some point she was trying to make. Tiff, Mitzi, and Dominique wore elegant cloche hats. I wore the fedora I'd bought in March. By coincidence all of us wore stylish pleated slacks, our blouses neatly tucked at our waists. People smiled as we paraded by. Rounding the turn, Gretchen, in the lead as usual, stopped and raised an open hand.

"This, though it looks more like a pond, is the Lake of Bodies." She waved her hat in front of her breasts, put it on her head, and pulled the brim over her eyes. "Not all of them drowned. Some were brought here. Who wants to find one? Who's that brave? I have the power to part the waters."

We laughed, all but Mitzi who said, "Stop it. That's scary."

"She's joking," Dominique said.

Gretchen removed her hat and shook her hair loose. "You think I am? Test me."

I stared at the lake and thought, where would Cornell dump my body? As if she'd read my thoughts, Dominique took my arm and pulled me along. We paused on the far side of the lake. Gretchen returned her hat to her head and slung her arm over Mitzi's shoulders.

"I was joking about parting the waters," Gretchen said, lowering her arm, "but consider how different we might all think if it wasn't Moses, but a woman, say a woman named Rebecca, who'd parted the Red Sea and led *her* people out of Egypt?"

"That's crazy," Tiff said. "Rebecca is on Sunnybrook farm. Everyone knows that."

We laughed until Gretchen stopped us and said, "Didn't God work most all miracles through men? Couldn't a man sin and still be a saint? A man brought the laws of God down from a mountain peak, but a woman, to perform one of God's miracles, had to be pure. The one great Biblical miracle a woman performed she did through her womb."

Her words made the others uncomfortable, but for me it rang profound in some measure because Bible stories constructed history in ways that we came to understand the world order.

"That was really insightful," I said, "especially the parting of the Red Sea."

Gretchen's face glowed in the sun. "I know. Gals, I've decided to go to college when this war is over. I'll be the first in my family. I deserve that. No, we all deserve that."

Mitzi said, "We don't always agree, but you're right."

Dominique said, "Wouldn't it be nice to come back here

in forty or fifty years and walk and talk about what we did after the war?"

I looked at my roommate and whispered, "What's gotten into you?"

"I'm going to see my son. Soon."

I thought about college. Gretchen was right. I did deserve it. But study what?

"Let's go," Gretchen said, "We've got more lake to see. Let's go."

# -26-

By the second week of September, I'd convinced myself that Cornell's appearance in the alley was just meant to frighten me and nothing more. That Thursday I went with the girls to a USO dance, which I was told would showcase a live band playing dance music. I welcomed sore feet as a distraction from work and Cornell. As we readied ourselves, Dominique had said that she didn't want some clumsy sailor dancing on my toes, but that she should do it for those Marines and sailors who gave blood for her.

She hurried out on the floor the first time she was asked to dance. The soldier promptly smashed his shoe down on her toes. She sat grimacing until the band took a break, then she got up and served punch. While she was serving punch, the band returned, and a sailor approached her and asked her to dance.

She shook her head and said, "*No*. I need all my toes, but Eve would love to dance."

"Okay, let's cut a rug," the sailor said, offering me his forearm to take.

I glared at Dominique and laid my hand on the sailor's arm.

I danced two more dances before I rejoined the girls. Dominique asked how it went.

"I have all my toes on both feet."

Tiff stared at something across the room and said excitedly, "It's him."

I looked and saw a tall sailor crossing the room in our direction. I knew immediately who he was. A redhead with a palette of freckles on his round face, he was otherwise ordinary. As he neared, he gave Tiff a wide boyish grin and crossed his arms over his chest. Tiff hurried to him, took his hand, and pulled him over to the table.

"These are the girls I've told you about."

We introduced ourselves, then Tiff turned to him and said, "You could've let me know."

He grinned. "How? Smoke signals? I did call from a pay phone before I hitched a ride up. No one answered. Are you seeing anyone else?"

"I've got a dozen men on the string." She looked as us. "Right girls?"

Though she'd written him letters, they were often delayed by weeks or months before reaching fleet sailors. Tiff had begun expressing reservations about him. At times, when we were at Tasco's, she seemed captured by the Australian stevedore, but seeing her beside Emory, her face aglow, it was apparent the separation alone was what had caused her uncertainty.

Gretchen said, "No. She's lying. She's waited for you."

Tiff took his arm in both her hands and said, "I'm so happy you came."

"It was luck. My ship was sent back for repairs," he said. "We landed in Diego two days ago and I, well, I'm here. So how are you ladies? I've heard a lot about you."

Following the small talk, he walked Tiff out onto the dance floor where he pulled her closer than was permitted. She pressed her cheek to his chest, which also violated the protocols. He whispered in her ear, and she stepped back, took both of his hands in hers and kissed them.

Dominique said. "I smell something big going on."

Two women gathered at the far end of the table shook their fingers at the couple. One of them, Mrs. Carver who chaperoned the dances, charged out onto the dance floor. Emory saw her coming, pulled his hands back and resumed the proper dance position, but Tiff threw her arms around his neck. That stopped Mrs. Carver in her tracks.

"Guess we can figure it out," Mitzi said.

I poured us each a glass of punch, lifted mine, and said, "To them."

We watched a quick exchange between Mrs. Carver and Tiff that came to an end when Emory pulled out a ring, took Tiff's left hand, and slipped it on her ring finger.

Mitzi said, "She's too old for him. Besides, he's going off to fight like my husband."

Out on the dance floor another sailor slapped Emory on the back, shook his hand, and congratulated Tiff. A smiling Mrs. Carver retreated from the dance floor as the music stopped.

"Except for some action with Tiff," Gretchen said, "with luck he'll probably never see any. And don't judge our friend or any women based on age or weight or any of that crap. We're better than all that BS. We have. . . . Oh, I'm pontificating. Sorry. This isn't the time for it. And, yes, Mitzi, like our husbands. Remember?"

"What are you talking about?" Mitzi said. "Oh, yes, we promised not to talk about that."

"Love," Dominique said. "She's talking about love. Theirs and ours."

"Oh, Jesus." Mitzi shrugged her shoulders and raised her palms to the air. "I'm married."

"What we're really seeing is hope," Dominique said.

I pinched her arm. "Damn it. Who are you?"

"Ouch." She stiffened up and said, "I'm me again. Never mind anything I just said."

I raised my glass and said, "To hope." I set the glass down. "Let's go."

The others followed me out onto the floor. Tiff pulled me into an embrace. We girls formed a circle around the couple and locked arms. Soldiers and sailors and Marines, strangers to us and Emory, walked their partners over. The men shook Emory's hand. The women hugged Tiff. The normally stiff-backed Mrs. Carver stood on the sidelines smiling.

As the revelry withered, it felt as if a shadow had fallen over my mood. I didn't know why or what it meant at the moment, but I recalled a time watching my brothers as they tilled the potato patch out back, Link wiping sweat off his forehead and rubbing it into August's hair, and August retaliating by heaving a shovelful of dirt in Link's direction. Both gathered up clods of black dirt and threw them at one another, none of it malicious. It was, in fact, a kind of inexplicable sharing of joy that was pure.

A few feet away Dominique laughed. Nothing seemed funny. Then I realized I'd lost much since the incident at Pork Skins. Was it the arrest? Or the fear I'd felt because of Tomato Man? My neck knotted up. I pictured the dance floor at Pork Skins, then the stage. H.T.'s attention focused on the cops as they worked their way through the crowd. Did he see the gun? Was he lying to the police to protect me? I wanted to see him and ask why. No, I wanted him to hold me and reassure me. No, that wasn't it. I wanted him to make me feel the way Tiff now did. But that was impossible. That thought led me to realize what I had to do.

I took off my USO apron, stepped away from the punch bowl, and walked to the shelves behind the chaperone's table where we stored our purses. I rummaged through my purse until I found the card, then I went to the pay phone, dropped a nickel in the slot, and gave the operator the number. I let the phone ring until I was convinced Sergeant Lester wasn't in his office. The coin dropped in the tray. I turned the card over and read the number he'd scratched down on the back. I gave that number to the operator. He lifted the receiver on the second ring.

"Sergeant Lester?"

"Yes."

"This is Eve Halvers. I want to talk to you."

"Can this wait until tomorrow?"

"I'm at the YMCA on Harbor Boulevard. Can you come?"

"Twenty minutes. I'll meet you out front."

"Twenty minutes," I said. "Fine."

He took a deep breath and said, "You better not be playing games with me."

"No." I said goodbye and cradled the receiver.

I told the girls I was leaving and waited out front, nervously looking at every passing car. When he arrived, the sergeant reached across the seat and opened the door. I slid inside.

"I know a place where we can get coffee, or would you prefer something stronger?"

"Remember? I'm not old enough to drink."

"You look old enough to me. Who's going to arrest you?"

"Coffee's fine."

"Suit yourself." He put the car in gear and pulled away from the curb. "Be glad when we can use full headlights, not just the bottom half. I damn near ran over a dog the other night. I'd rather run over a man than a dog." He looked to see if I was listening. "Well, not really, unless I could choose the man I'd run over. A man like Cornell. That's what this is about, right?"

He took a cigarette pack out. "Smoke?" he asked, offering me the pack.

"Sometimes, but no thanks."

"Suit yourself." He tapped cigarette out of the pack, lit it, and puffed until the cab filled with smoke. He looked ahead at the blackened street. "Three years of blackouts. You'd think someone would figure out that, if they could, wouldn't the Japanese have bombed us by now?"

"I guess we're being safe."

"So, what pricked your conscience?" He steered the car off the boulevard onto a secondary street. "I figure it's because Cornell has been following you."

"Who said he was following me?"

"I'm not often wrong. Besides, we saw him."

I looked at his profile in the dim light and knew the truth. "You were following him?"

"Maybe. Maybe you."

"You don't have a warrant for him, do you?"

"No, but he thought we did. We were kind of waiting for you. We visited his haunts, asked questions, left the impression we were holding a murder warrant. He went into hiding till he saw your picture with Howard Elders in the newspaper. DA didn't care to pursue a case that hinges on the word of an ex-felon."

"You used me?"

"We told Howard to keep an eye out for us."

Why then had H.T. talked me out of calling the cops? All of this was confusing.

"You ever see *Casablanca*?" He blew smoke out the side of his mouth. "Never miss a Bogart movie. Way I see it, we're trapped in this together now, like Nick and the French cop. You know, a beautiful relationship?"

"That's going a bit far."

He chuckled. "A little coffee, some truth. Your life will change for the better."

"It's kind of hard to see it that way." I grinned, thinking, damned if I'm not playing a Hollywood role myself. Dominique would be proud.

He blew a stream of smoke at the windshield.

# -27-

Doreen set her wine glass aside and motioned for me to follow her through the French doors to the veranda. I didn't want to be there, but I was because I felt obligated. She and Selmo had been kind and had made no demands on me. I carried my glass with me and followed. Doreen's heels clicked on the flagstone announcing our coming as we crossed the veranda. Selmo sat watching the vestiges of the day. He looked at us over his shoulder. Doreen sat in a rattan chair next to him and motioned for me to sit beside her.

"Sunset's been spectacular."

A thin line of red lay on the horizon marking the day's end. An ocean breeze rustled the stems of a nearby bird of paradise.

"Did you enjoy dinner?" Selmo asked.

"Yes. Kind of you to invite me," I said, mimicking Doreen's manner of speech.

Selmo patted the arms of his chair and stood. "I could use a brandy. Who'll join me?"

"None for me," Doreen said.

"Eve?" He offered to take my wine glass.

I took a last sip and handed it to him. "I'm fine, thank you." I swatted at a mosquito buzzing by my ear.

"The disconcerting thing about this time of year," she said. "Bugs."

Selmo sauntered to the French doors, paused momentarily to adjust his glasses and look off at the last thread of sunset. When he closed the door, Doreen settled back in her chair. Her hair ruffled in the breeze. Her brow knotted, she gazed off and sighed.

She brushed a strand of hair aside and looked at me. "Are you in trouble?"

"Trouble? No."

"Selmo told me about detectives coming to talk to you and H.T."

It bothered me that she knew anything about my life. "Why are you bringing that up?"

The small-town girl in me believed a person's life should be private. Better to let gossips speculate than to give them fodder. I'd confided in Dominique only because she was unwittingly involved now, but since my ride with Sergeant Lester, I felt reasonably assured that the pimp or whatever sinister character he claimed title to would be soon out of my life.

Doreen said, "May we speak openly?"

I stiffened at the question. "I guess."

"If you're in any danger, it won't hurt to tell the truth. We're on your side. If you need an attorney, we'll get you one. The one we called after we bailed you out got that mess cleared up."

"That's thoughtful, but I'm fine." Why would I need an attorney? More important, why would she provide one? I gazed at the blackening horizon.

"Tell me what's going on. You're not obligated, but I'd like to know."

"Why?"

"I'll tell you later. For now, please think of me as a friend you can be honest with."

I told what needed to be said, beginning with the evening at Pork Skins and ended with Sergeant Lester's assurance that Cornell would be picked up and charged with murder. She listened without interrupting. Halfway through my story, Selmo returned and sat beside her sipping brandy. When I finished talking, they looked at one another.

He cleared his throat. "Doreen admired the way you walked up to our table that night."

"You were very thoughtful," she said. "And Selmo has taken special interest in you ever since he found out about the notes."

"Others wrote notes as well," I said. "You know that already."

"Yes, but you came to his attention."

Selmo said, "I hope they find this pimp and soon. I know a deputy chief. I can. . . ."

"Selmo, according to Eve, the police are already hard at work on it."

"But . . .," he started to protest, then surrendered. "Well, that's probably true."

As if trapped by the power of the stars, we sat staring at the night sky. Selmo held the snifter to his lips but didn't drink. I wanted to know what their real interest in me was and decided there was no tactful way to broach the matter. "Why am I here? The real reason?"

Doreen looked at him. He said, "Go ahead, tell her."

"Okay." Doreen reached over and squeezed his arm. "I'm in my thirties, healthy in every way. So's Selmo." She looked at him. "He's actually older. We have his business. My family is well off. In a time when so many are dying overseas, we were spared risk. I've got much to be grateful for. I have most everything people desire. I'm lucky, wouldn't you say?"

I nodded. "And beautiful."

"Well, thank you. This isn't easy. I told you or maybe I didn't?" She chewed at her lip thoughtfully. "What I don't have . . . what I want is a child. I can't have one, you see."

"I'm sorry."

"So am I. But Selmo can."

Selmo smiled. "You have qualities we admire."

"Qualities?"

He scratched his head. "You see our predicament."

"You're healthy," Doreen said.

"Yes, but. . . ."

"We know this is sudden," Selmo said, "but it's best to get it out in the open."

A silence followed. I stared at my hands wondering how could she assume I'd consent to it. The girl in me thought of a baby as a miracle of sorts. There was a time when I'd romanticized love and the idea of finding pleasure in the arms of a man. As I hugged my schoolbooks and walked to classes, I'd imagined meeting one who'd slowly woo me, become a caring husband. He'd undress me tenderly on our honeymoon night. With one sharp slap to my face, Jess had erased those girlish visions. The attention, the favors, and this evening added up to being another slap to the face. I couldn't imagine having a child with Selmo—or any man. He'd been kind and had helped save my friends, but intimacy with him was beyond a thought.

"You don't have to answer right now. Just think about it," he said.

Doreen reached over and took his hand. "Eve, your family isn't here. And we all need the help of others. We like you. You know that don't you?"

"I guess. Yes. I suppose." It occurred to me that I'd created this situation or added to it by calling them for help when Dominique was in the hospital.

"As far as we know, you aren't involved with anyone. Are you?"

"What? No."

"Do you have a boyfriend? Is someone interested in you?"

I thought of H.T. and his motive for lying about having seen the gun. It had to be because he was attracted to me. Though I'd denied it to Dominique, I *was* drawn to him. "No."

She released Selmo's hand and looked at me. "I told you she'd be receptive."

"Receptive?" I said.

"She hasn't agreed to anything," he said.

Feeling cornered, I blurted out, "There's a murderer looking for me."

Strangely, that seemed to hearten her. "Yes. That's right. Even more reason to consider our proposal. We have a cabin in Atascadero, on the lake. It's isolated. You'll have a nurse and a doctor when the time comes. Everything you need. I'll visit and watch your progress. We can sit on the porch and sip tea. I'll hold your hand like we're sisters. It will be. . . ."

"I'd like to go," I said.

"I know this was sudden," she said. "But . . . we've given it a lot of thought. We won't tell anyone about it or where you've gone." Looking for support, she smiled at Selmo. "See, she is listening. I told you she'd hear us out."

She'd obviously thought all this through and Selmo was just another pawn in her game. I wanted to shout, my name's Eve. It is not Hagar. I work for your husband, but I'm not a slave girl. My womb belongs to me.

Selmo held up his snifter. "Is anyone ready for some brandy now?"

"Don't go, dear," Doreen said. She leaned forward and held her hands out to me.

I shook my head. She slumped back into her seat. The

temperature had dropped. Nearby waves broke on shore. We were all taken by a need for silence. Wasn't this enough, I thought, this house near the beach, all the food one could want. Doreen crossed her arms and stared for a time at the patio floor. She seemed to realize she'd pressed her case too far too fast.

"Are you okay, Eve?" Selmo asked.

"She's fine." Doreen reached again for my hands. This time I let her take them. She squeezed lightly and let go but continued looking at me. "You like us, don't you? Hasn't Selmo been just wonderful?" She looked to him to intervene.

He seemed ill at ease as he cleared his throat. "We discussed it with our attorney. He went through the legalities and found nothing to be a barrier."

I'd been a poor judge of character. I'd viewed him as a sappy but earnest little man trying to impress others and undeserving of a beauty such as Doreen. Then he'd climbed out a window three stories up to pull the girls to safety. He was far more and far better than what I'd thought, but all the same he was under her spell.

I looked at Doreen who looked back anxiously. "You've been wonderful," I said. "But he's your husband. It doesn't fit. I mean, me and him?"

"You are an innocent." She seemed amused. "You and Selmo. I'd object to that myself. A doctor will do everything. It's all in the contract."

Contract? It had suddenly turned into a job offer. I tried to see the two of them as I had when the good life radiated around them like a halo, but I couldn't.

"Let's go in for dessert and coffee. Selmo will show you a copy. You'll see there's a comfortable amount of money."

"Money?"

"Certainly, you should be compensated," Selmo said.

I stood and looked at Selmo. "Really, I think I should go."

The two of them exchanged glances and stood.

"Stay for dessert," Doreen said. "We don't have to decide tonight. Wait here." She left and returned in about minute, in her hand my journal. She extended it to me and told me that I'd made some interesting observations over my months of employment.

"It's well written, mostly, but don't you think you're a little harsh about some people."

"I don't think so. And I don't use people's names."

"Well, Selmo brought it home sometime back and never looked at it. I did. And I knew it was yours."

That night before crossing the threshold as I left, I glimpsed my reflection in a mirror with a gilded frame. I saw a woman I recognized in every way, but I thought her a stranger because others saw her differently. I imagined my belly an ungainly mound, Doreen seated beside me anxious over every breath, checking my pulse while telling me I was doing a fine job.

# -28-

THE BATTLE OF LEYTE DRAGGED on in the Pacific Theater. In Europe, the U.S. First Army drove into Germany and battled Nazi troops on their own soil. The cost of the war in terms of American lives was going up. Two women in the bootery, Myrna Toller and Josefina Ortiz, lost husbands, infantry soldiers, one killed on an obscure atoll in the northern Philippines, the other in western France, both on the same day.

Selmo, whom I'd avoided since dinner at his house, cornered me and asked if I would spend a couple of days with Josefina. He said that like many in the bootery, she had moved to Los Angeles after war broke out and except for a young daughter, she had no family here. He said the factory had met the month's production quota and he could spare me, but I wasn't to take staying with her as an obligation. It seemed an opportune way to make amends for my earlier failure with Tomea. How could I not feel obligated?

The drive to her house was a strain on both of us. He chatted nervously about the war's progress and what the war's ending might mean for the bootery. He avoided mentioning Doreen or the topic of a baby. After three stops at the side of the road to look at a map, he turned onto a narrow street in south-central Los Angeles. Halfway down the block he pulled to a stop in front of a two-bedroom bungalow with a low-pitched roof and killed the engine. While it was in good shape, many of the neighboring houses were, by degrees, in disrepair.

I reached to pull the handle on my door, but he said, "Wait, I have something to say."

Here it comes, I thought. I knitted my fingers together and waited.

He noticed my knuckles tensing. "It's not what you think. Relax."

"Josephina doesn't have a phone. Here." He handed me a paper. "It's her neighbor's name and address. Josephina called me from there. If she falls apart, go to this woman's house and call that number right away."

Since the dinner at their house, I'd wondered where he truly stood in the strange proposal. Was he going along with it to placate Doreen or was he vested in the plan? I decided the test was to bring up her name. "Was it Doreen's idea for you to bring me here?"

"Mine," he said dismissively.

We stepped out of the car. He opened the trunk and took out a basket of food, then looked up and down the neighborhood. "Don't worry about a killer looking for you. No self-respecting murderer would come here."

"I guess that's funny."

He grinned. "Don't laugh. You'll ruin the mood. Let's go."

Josefina opened the door. A small girl with a round face peered around from behind her, then hid her face in Josefina's skirt. Josefina ran her fingers through the girl's hair.

Always energized at work, Josefina had a booming laugh and dark brown eyes that sparkled with amusement. As she looked at us, her eyes were vacant and dry. She appeared out of sorts, but not depressed as Tomea had been.

"I brought you a companion," Selmo said to her; but when she didn't respond he whispered to me, "Well, it's up to you."

She stepped aside and motioned us in. He held out the food basket for me to take, offered his condolences, and said he'd come by later or send someone to check on us. He tipped his hat and left. I watched him drive off, then set the basket aside, and stepped outside to check the surroundings as had become my habit. Once I oriented myself and saw that the street was vacant, I went back inside. She waited by the couch.

"Your daughter's pretty," I said. "How are you doing?"

She shrugged. "My girl's name is Sylvia. She's three. So, you're staying?"

"Yes, to help in any way you need. Today, tomorrow if you like. We brought food." I picked up the basket. "Or I'll stay until your relatives come."

"My relatives won't come."

I smiled at the little girl. "I'll be happy to watch her if that is what you need, Josefina."

"Fine." She picked up the basket and hooked it on her forearm. "Follow me." We walked through an open doorway to the kitchen. Two women sat at a table talking in Spanish while swirling coffee in mugs. She introduced us and placed the basket beside the sink, then sat with her friends, and the three of them carried on the conversation.

I took the girl's hand. "Let's get to be friends."

I walked Sylvia back to the front room where we sat on the couch. I looked at the walls and shelves and noticed no pictures of a man in uniform, no wedding pictures. The girl tugged at my arm. She had a moon face and almond-eyes. I talked to her. She responded by staring back while sucking her thumb.

"Are you afraid to speak?"

The girl didn't answer, just stood, and returned to her mother in the kitchen. A *Saturday Evening Post* lay on the end table. I passed time on the couch reading or answering the door as a scattering of neighbors came and went. They sat in the kitchen with Josefina and talked with her in hushed tones. By one o'clock the last visitors left, and Josefina sat alone at the table.

I warmed up a can of soup from the stock Selmo had brought along and buttered a few slices of bread. Josefina said she wasn't hungry. She watched in silence as I helped Sylvia who swallowed bread down a bite at time, then opened her mouth to receive a spoonful of soup. After feeding her, I washed the dishes and left Josefina alone to grieve. Sylvia followed me to the couch and sat on the floor at my feet as I read. In time she crawled up in my lap and fell asleep sucking her thumb.

She was still asleep when the front door opened and shut without a knock. I sprang to my feet to confront the intruder who stood in the entryway. A handsome, thin Mexican in his late thirties, he seemed surprised to see me. He held a hat in both hands and gave me an awkward smile. Sylvia sat up and yawned. When she saw him standing in the entrance, a smile spread over her face. She ran to him and hugged his leg. I realized then that Sylvia didn't react to the door's closing because she couldn't hear.

"I'm Josefina's friend," he said. "You are?"

"Eve. I work with her."

He looked anxiously in the direction of doorway to the kitchen where Josefina stood wringing her hands. She motioned for him to come to her. He patted the girl on the head, nodded to me, and excused himself. He hurried to Josefina who took his hands in hers. They spoke softly in Spanish.

"We will come back. You watch Sylvia, okay?" Josefina said.

"Okay," I said, and they walked through the kitchen and out the back door.

Nearly an hour passed before they returned. He stood awkwardly beside Josefina as she lifted Sylvia from my arms. The girl opened her eyes and then closed them again. Sylvia passed her over to the man and they exchanged whispers at the front door. He left with Sylvia.

"You could have told me your daughter is deaf."

"Does it matter?"

"Yes. When I'm caring for her."

"Come in the kitchen. I'll fix you something especial to eat. Then maybe you go?"

"That's not necessary," I said. "That's why I'm here. I can eat soup."

Josefina shook her head. "You are a guest and should be treated properly."

I sat at the table as she busied herself at the stove rolling flour tortillas.

"That man," she said, "he's been my lover for over two years. I fell in love with him. Do you understand?"

Taken aback by her startling confession, I could do nothing but nod.

"Ildefonso was the father of my child, but he didn't know her. It was hurried, the marriage, with everyone's blessing but mine. Then he left right away. I was sixteen and didn't know him. He was twenty-four, a man who'd said yes, then got in bed with me, and with one or two kisses, rolled on top and forced himself inside me. It hurt. I resented him for that. Then he left." She sprinkled water gently over the flour.

"I forgave him because he was gone and because there is this war, and I was pregnant. Julio, I met at a party the week Ildefonso left for the Army. He was kind. I knew him months before he ever touched me. It was a kiss. My lips burned with the memory of that first kiss. I felt a desire I would never have for Ildefonso.

"So, you see, we have sinned, not once, but continually. He is now like Sylvia's father to her, and he is my man. Ildefonso never saw Sylvia. I ache for his dying, but my heart isn't broken." She laid the tortillas aside and began slicing off strips of meat from a cold roast. "Sylvia cannot hear. She will never know her father. Julio makes her laugh. She can't hear his voice, but she knows what he says. She touches his throat when he talks. It makes her smile. He loves her. He loves me. I have shamed my parents. They don't talk to me." She looked at me. "I want to cry for all of this, but inside I'm happy too. Is being happy such an ugly thing?"

Hers was the kind of story that on the screen could bring tears to the audience, but she stated it so flatly that it stirred little emotion in me. I'd never experienced happiness of the kind she described, the kind lovers experience. Recently I had moments when I daydreamed about H.T. taking my hand and comforting me tenderly, but those times were brief. I'd accepted that our differences and how others might react to seeing us acted as wedges between us.

"Is it okay for me to be happy? If I were sad, would it bring Ildefonso back to life?"

"No. It wouldn't," I said, only to realize when I looked at her that she wasn't seeking a response.

Josefina cooked. We ate. Afterward she said she was glad I was there, that she wanted to tell her story to someone who didn't know her, and now she needed to be alone because she felt she could finally cry.

I returned from calling Selmo at the neighbors, and as I mounted the stoop, I noticed about a hundred feet away a Ford Deluxe Coupe parked close to the curb in the shade of the trees across the street. A man wearing a hat sat slouched behind the wheel. I couldn't distinguish his features or skin color. Pretending I hadn't noticed the car, I walked on. My hand trembled as I turned the doorknob and closed the door softly behind me.

Josefina lay curled up on the couch where she'd cried herself to sleep. I bolted the door and peered out through the blinds. The driver adjusted his position behind the steering wheel. It appeared he was watching Josefina's house. It was obvious that I couldn't stay, not just for my safety but for Josefina's. I nudged Josefina, who rolled away. I shook her shoulder.

"Wake up, Josefina."

She blinked.

I said calmly so as not to alarm her, "I know you're upset, and I don't want to further upset you. A man's outside in a car watching the house, probably because of me."

She bolted upright, wiped her eyes with the backs of her hands and looked about the room. "What? A man? What man?"

"Never mind. I'm going leave by the side door. Lock it after me and don't answer if someone knocks. Okay?"

She sniffled and went to the window to peer through the blinds. "There's one car."

"Yes, a Ford."

She slipped her fingers from the blinds. "He can see the side of the house from there. He'd see you."

"Not if I'm careful."

I turned toward the kitchen to leave, but she pointed at me and said, "Sit!"

She disappeared down the hall. I heard her in the bedroom, opening and slamming drawers. She came back holding a revolver at her side. In her hand it looked like a toy and very much like the snub-nose Cornell Jones had chucked on the floor. She sniffled and went to the side door, locked it, and returned. I stared at the gun and wondered if everyone in Los Angeles except me was armed with a pistol. "What's the gun for?"

She looked at it as if wondering how it got in her hand. "Julio got it. He said if I have to use it, shoot the son-of-a-bitch in the belly."

"This could be my imagination running away. Besides, I'm here to help *you*."

She rubbed her reddened eyes with her free hand. "I feel much better."

"I don't know about this," I said. "This isn't woman's work."

"But where's the man to do it?" She returned to the blinds and peered out.

The thought of leaving was frightening but staying was an impossible option. She was right. If a man wasn't around, it was woman's work. But it was my job, not hers.

"He's after me. Not you. If I'm gone, you'll be safe," I said.

"How? If he comes for you and you're gone, I'm here. If he comes for you and you stay, I'm here. True?"

"True."

"So, I'll go with you."

"No."

"Okay. We stay and I shoot him."

"That's a bad idea."

"We can climb out my bedroom window to the alley and hide in my neighbor's house."

"No, you go to your friend's and call the cops. I'll go on my own."

"Go where? Besides, I've got the gun." She held it up proudly.

I wished it appeared more imposing, enough to scare off

Cornell, if that was who was out there. "Do you know how to use that?"

"I was raised with many guns. My father's a *Policia* in El Paso. Stay with me."

The window had been painted shut. It took considerable effort for us to open it. Finally, the seal broke, and I lifted it up and unhooked the screen as Josefina brought a chair to the window.

"I'll hold the screen. You jump," she said, waving the gun.

I removed my heels, held them in one hand and lifted the hem of my skirt. I slipped a leg over the edge, then straddled the sill and swung my trailing leg up and over. It appeared impossible to jump out gracefully, and less so if I held onto the skirt.

"Here." I handed her my heels and jumped.

I landed successfully, only to have my skirt bunch up below my breasts and cover my head. I tugged on it, but the hem had snagged on the window latch. I called to Josefina for help, but she didn't answer. I turned around the best I could and tugged gently to free the skirt. It didn't give. I jerked on it. The hem tore, but I didn't free it.

Josefina appeared at the window and whispered, "You okay?"

"Not exactly. Where'd you go?"

"The gun had no bullets. I had to. . . ."

"My skirt's caught. Can you. . . ."

"Schuss," Josefina said. "Someone's knocking."

She tossed my heels out, then disappeared. It seemed illogical that a murderer would knock and announce himself. Abandoned and exposed from the waist down, I was left with two choices, both bad—stay where I was or take my skirt off and escape. *Barefoot, exposed from the waist down, I would die as an embarrassment to my mother*. I reached back, unzipped the skirt, and slipped it over my head. I gathered up my heels but remained barefoot in case I had to run.

Josefina's head popped out of the window. "No one's there. Here," she said and tossed me the revolver.

I fumbled it but managed to keep from dropping it. "Free my skirt," I said.

Josefina freed it and when she jumped, she landed gracefully and snatched the gun from me. "This way," she said and started for the alley.

I picked my skirt up and followed. We were a step from the alley when a man rounded the side of the house and shouted, "Stop. Both of you."

I clutched my skirt tightly and looked at Josefina who held the pistol in both hands, its barrel pointed at his mid-section.

She spat the words at him. "I will shoot you down like a *perro sucio*."

I hollered, "Don't, Josefina. It's Detective Sharkey."

The cop removed his hat and lifted both hands. "Put the gun down, lady. Please."

Josefina cut an eye in my direction. I nodded to her. "He's a cop like your father."

Slowly her arms went limp at her side. Detective Sharkey shifted his eyes from Josefina to me and then her again. I looked at my skirt bundled in my arms and was aware of my exposed legs and my panties.

He smiled. "I suppose you've got an explanation for all this, but I don't need to hear it."

"We thought you were a murderer," Josefina said.

"Don't be too disappointed," he said. "Eve, thought you'd want to know that we picked up Tomato Man. You won't be needing our company anymore. I came here to tell you."

"Your company?"

He replaced his hat. "Yeah."

"You've been watching me? How long?" I asked.

"Just long enough to catch Cornell before he caught you." He took in my bare legs, raised his eyebrows, and tipped his hat. "It's nice to see you." He strolled over to Josefina, took the revolver, and opened the cylinder to unload it. Shaking his head, he returned it to one hand, then opened her other hand, placed the bullets in her palm and closed her fingers over them. "The city will sleep better now." Smiling, he said, "Oh, I understand Spanish and I'm not a dirty dog. Well, ladies, it's been a delight." He tipped his hat politely and left.

Josefina didn't say why she wanted me to stand with her at her husband's funeral, but a week later I was at her side. As the bearers set the casket beside the grave, she explained that she couldn't have Julio with her when the casket was lowered. She owed that much to the father of her child and added that he was a brave man, if not the man she loved. Still, she wanted someone standing beside her and her daughter, someone who would not judge her. She accepted the folded flag with dignity and pressed it into her daughter's arms. Then she squeezed my hand, said her goodbyes to the stranger in the casket, and let her tears come as it was lowered, and the burial detail fired shots to salute the fallen soldier.

When we turned away from the grave, she said, "I'm glad for him that he did not know I betrayed the marriage."

# -29-

Following Cornell Jones's arrest, I returned to the life I'd enjoyed prior to the incident at Pork Skins. When H.T. saw me at work now, he smiled, called me Eve, and winked as if we shared a joke. I felt encouraged to think his "Hello, Eve" was meant as more than a considerate gesture.

Bigger issues struck the workplace. Four of the women at the factory lost husbands in a matter of days, another lost a fiancé, and two had brothers killed in action. In films we saw at theaters taken on the battlefronts all soldiers had become one face, but the grieving faces of women, their flesh-and-blood pain around us, took on individual character. Each woman carried the weight of her own unique grief. Though the war was not near ending, talk speculated over what the aftermath might bring. Gretchen cut out an article from the *L.A. Times* that claimed men returning from war would want to start families right away. Yes, tens of thousands of men would return. Many others wouldn't. Wouldn't those who'd survived need time to heal from war and get familiar with the world again? Starting a family seemed an absurd notion.

Gretchen nor Mitzi talked about their husbands or any fears they had about them. I asked Mitzi why that was.

"Superstition. I like to pretend he's not in harm's way."

"But he's a soldier."

"Eve, let's talk about something else."

After that exchange, I didn't ask Gretchen about her fears for Robert.

Among us some were less touched by the war than others. A few seemed entirely untouched by it. These thoughts weighed on my mind the Saturday morning I sat in the leather seat of Doreen's Packard Patrician as she drove the Laguna shoreline. The day was mild and the sky cloudless. The smell of salt was in the air and white foam bubbled on the beach.

She kept the conversation lighthearted, but I knew what was behind my being there. I'd declined her frequent invitations to get together as long as possible but relented at Selmo's request to "hear her out." I hoped to put it behind me at Castaways where we were bound to sight one or two celebrities.

Castaways sat on the cliffs north of Laguna. Doreen half-circled the lot and pulled into a parking space facing the ocean. She removed her scarf, loosened her hair, and threw her head back. She took in a deep breath of sea air and said, "Eve, may I ask you something?"

Blood rushed to my cheeks. "Sure, go ahead."

"Have you ever considered being a model?"

I felt relieved. "That's silly."

"You have no idea how pretty you are. Now, after lunch, and I've discussed this with Selmo, we're going to the beauty salon. Have you ever been?"

I shook my head. She reached over and took a strand of my hair. "It'll shine when we're through. I can't wait. It'll be like going with my cousin the first time we went to play grown-up."

Resisting an urge to push her hand away, I thanked her and turned the door handle. She withdrew her hand and smiled. I suspected she was exceedingly adept at getting her way.

We sat on a redwood deck that faced the sea. Again, Doreen kept the conversation light. I sipped iced water, nodded occasionally to signal I was listening, and enjoyed as best I could the sun and the breeze.

She said, "I've seen Cecil B. de Mille here on one occasion."

When I asked who he was, she laughed and asked why I had to joke all the time.

"I'm not joking."

"How sad," Doreen said, the remark obviously intended to stir a response.

"Yes," I said, though I had no idea what was sad.

She didn't elaborate, just stared at the waves until the waitress came to take our order. Doreen ordered tea for us and suggested I have a bowl of Mexican seafood chowder. When the waitress left, Doreen sighed and said that the war had changed even little things, that before the war the soup had been called Oriental seafood chowder, and sauerkraut and poached salmon had been on the menu, but now only the salmon was offered.

"I suppose after the war their chowder will be Oriental again and sauerkraut will be on the menu. What do you think?"

Much of what had once seemed important had lost its luster. "It's too hard to think of what will come after the war, not while it's still going on. Somehow it seems—I don't know. I don't have the exact word, but irreverent, I guess."

"Profane," she said. A breeze caught her hair. She brushed it back with her fingers, replaced her scarf, and rested her gaze on me. "The war's coming to an end. Selmo's friends say in less than a year. It'll be a fresh start, a new life. What happens during the war will be one life and what happens after will be another. Do you understand what I'm saying?"

"The war's not over."

"It will be. What do you intend to do then? The world is yours, you know. Oh, listen to me. You with brothers fighting overseas. Of course, that would be your first concern."

To my relief the waitress arrived with a pitcher of water, a pot of hot water, and cups. She poured the water and left. I was feeling trapped and getting edgy, but Doreen appeared calm as she dipped her tea bag in her cup and studied me.

"You have insight. I like that. I like most everything about you."

"Stop, Doreen."

"Stop?"

"Flattering me. I'm a country girl. Grandmother was half Indian and could barely read. My father was a lumberjack, a drunk who left us. You don't know me."

"You won't change my opinion by picking an argument, and I won't argue. Selmo told me how you handled yourself at the fire escape."

"You won't argue but answer this. Why me? Out of all the choices, why me?"

"You don't know?"

"Know what?"

"Except for the color of your hair and your hazel eyes, we could be sisters. Selmo told me when he put you to work how much alike we appeared. That night at the club when you came over, I didn't want to see the resemblance, but afterward I did. He told me you had brothers and a sister you listed on your application. Such a big family. I said, 'She's the one'."

So, that was it, I thought, she thinks of me as Abraham's slave girl who can give her what nature won't. I didn't have the broad knowledge of the world an educated woman did, but I knew scripture. Mom would have it no other way.

Trying to change the direction, I said, "I don't mean to be rude, but I can't discuss what you want to talk about."

"What I want is to watch a baby sleep, bathe it, hold it close. Is that too much to ask?"

"Why not adopt?"

"I want Selmo's baby. When it grows up, I want it to look like us."

"Like you and Selmo."

"Yes. After I had the hysterectomy, I went into a depression. It got worse. I had to go away. Sel was wonderful. He sent me to New York and Minneapolis. Doctors suggested someone else could bear us a child." She took a handkerchief from her purse, daubed her eyes, and looked in her compact before closing her purse. "My mascara. I'm sorry. We don't want to take any risks. There's always a risk with adoption."

But isn't risk, I thought, at the core of woman's being? I began to measure her in another way. Her looks and position were her coinage. Beyond that, there was a sadness that ran toward grief. She viewed her life as incomplete if not broken and thought a child would fix it. Her hidden sadness both touched and repelled me. For the first time I truly considered what Gretchen had said about women before the war being valued mostly for their looks. Now women wore military uniforms, worked in factories building the essentials needed to conduct war. They repaired potholes. When the war ended, would we revert to being valued merely for our looks?

She laid her hands flat on the table. "Eve, I talked with Sel. We'll change the terms of the contract. I told him two thousand was only fair."

I sat back and stared off. Two thousand dollars was an unimaginable sum. Without me agreeing, somehow, we had entered a stage wherein it seemed that only the terms were at stake. I thought of Dominique's desperation, the abortion, my sister Judith's death. Doreen's desperation was the opposite. Something else Gretchen had said many months ago came to mind, the idea of a world without men, without those complications, without the pain. I pictured myself pinned atop the hay in the feeding trough, Jess running his hand up my dress, his fingernails blackened with dirt, me scared and pushing him away, disgusted, afraid, protesting.

"Did you hear what I said, Eve?"

I looked at her. "That's a lot of money."

"You'll be well taken care of," she said.

That evening as I closed the door to the apartment, I thought about those I'd come to know who were affected by the war and how Doreen, obsessed with wanting a child, seemed unaffected by it. I decided that for some, or at least people of her class, the personal life transcends the greater grief that war causes.

# -30-

An airborne invasion of Holland, code-named Operation Market Garden, was launched amid bluster and brag because the Allies had ground the Germans to pieces in France. But soon enough the soldiers on the ground had discovered Field Marshall Montgomery's folly. The Germans in Holland were many, well-supplied, and rested. They were also defending the Rhine River, a door to the Fatherland. Link was among those dropped in by glider and parachute.

The worries over Cornell Jones behind me, I rejoined the world with a fresh worry—my brothers. Each evening, Dominique and I went to Tasco's and listened to news of the war on the radio until the shift workers arrived. The War Department downplayed losses and tactical and strategic decisions that had isolated American and British paratroopers behind German lines. Supplies and ammunition intended for the stranded soldiers had been dropped inside the German defenses. Americans were left to fight their way out. At the end of each newscast, Dominique would squeeze my hand and assure me that Link would make it through somehow.

On September 26th, the Army information service admitted that the paratroopers had been unable to link up with relief columns and were forced to retreat. I was with Dominique, seated in the kitchen at Tasco's when the news came over the radio. I closed my eyes. She took my hand and said that Link was already safe, she just knew it.

"How can you be so sure?"

"Because we're waiting for him," she said.

"We?"

"Yes, I'm finished with being discovered. And I'm not involving myself with any more losers."

I let go of her hand. "That's good."

"Yes. I've decided I'm going to be in love with Link."

I felt, for inexplicable reasons, protective of him. "You don't even know him."

We could hear the men arriving in the bar.

"Let's go. I'm hungry." She looked toward the pass-through. "It sounds crazy, but is it any crazier than what I've done in the past? Wouldn't loving a brave soldier make more sense?"

"Even if he doesn't come back?"

"Even then," Dominique said. "But he will."

"Has everybody gone harebrained? And even if Link is brave, he wouldn't admit it."

She stood and started for the bar. I got up from the table slowly. I couldn't explain it, but I didn't like the idea of her loving my brother. I was mildly perturbed that she had assumed I would approve. I grabbed her arm and held her at the doorway.

She pulled her arm away. "You don't know your own strength."

We stood facing one another. "You're kidding about my brother?"

"No."

I decided to lie rather than let a fantasy go on. "He has a girlfriend waiting for him."

"You never mentioned a girlfriend before. What's her name?"

Without giving it a thought, I blurted, "Serine."

Dominique smiled. "You don't have to protect your brother from me." She pushed the door open and motioned for me to go into the bar.

Two letters from Mother were in the mailbox when we arrived home later. I opened the first. Helen, my older sister, was expecting another baby. Mother said that when the war was over, I could start on my own family and catch up. Plenty of young men would be available if I didn't marry the black man. The idea of marrying a faceless soldier or sailor just to "catch up" with my sister was disturbing enough, but did she have to add the snide remark about H.T.?

I opened the second letter. It was from Link who wrote that he had had a short visit to Holland and picked up another souvenir, a shrapnel wound, but he couldn't say a lot about the country as he didn't get to see much of it. What he did see was flat farmland. He said he'd left a few buddies behind thanks to "some numbskull who didn't know how to plan an itinerary." He claimed he respected British soldiers, but the officers were another matter, and he couldn't fill in details because of censorship. The rest of the letter was about men in his ward, with all of them awaiting releases to return to their units. They played cards or checkers and mopped floors and polished furniture. He finished with "No one should worry about me. I have faith the war will end soon. Besides, one more wound and I'll be taken off the front lines."

I read the letter to Dominique, who cried, then cheered Link for his honesty. She said something about Link having tea with a bunch of British lords in powdered wigs who fanned the air with hankies as they sat down. I said that she'd seen too many movies.

She said, imitating a British accent, "My dear Sergeant Halvers, we must inform you that your attitude toward officers of the Crown best improve or we'll be forced to send you home."

"Stop," I said.

She went on. "Link, of course, would say, and just like Bogie, 'If it's all the same, General, I'll take my pals with me and here's mud in your eye'."

I dropped the letter on the couch. "He's alive."

"I like him," Dominique said.

We joined hands and whirled around, laughing uproariously, then threw ourselves down on the couch. She looked at the door as if it were about to open, then said she intended to go see her son and asked if I wanted to come along. I wasn't sure what to say.

"Well?"

"You haven't seen him for so long. Don't you want to see him by yourself?"

She sat upright. "I want him to meet my friend. I want my parents to meet my friend. I wrote to them about you. And I think I mentioned that your brother was a hero."

"You didn't?"

Dominique laced her fingers together and stared at them. "I did. I told them he wrote letters to me. I said that . . . oh, don't look at me like that."

Without speaking, I walked to my bedroom. I returned with two pillows and handed one to Dominique. I said, "Defend yourself," and hit her head with my pillow. We stood in the center of the room taking turns swinging the pillows, sometimes connecting, usually not. We kept it up until one pillow split a seam and spread feathers over the room. We sat on the floor and howled.

I said, "I'll be happy to meet your family."

"Can I write to Link?"

"Sure."

"I've got his address already."

"I guess there's no stopping you."

"I won't if you really don't want me to."

I wrapped an arm over her shoulder. "He'd like that."

"Good 'cause I already wrote him."

We lay on the floor for some time, staring at the ceiling and listening to music on the radio. Glen Miller's "Under the Apple Tree" played. I sat up, held the pillow, and swayed to the music. When the song ended, I reached over and turned off the radio.

"Why'd you do that?" Dominique asked.

I cleared my throat. "What would you be willing to do for two thousand dollars?"

Dominique thought for a moment before saying, "I'd kiss Himmler but not Goering. I'd swim to Catalina. I'd marry Bogart and Clark Gable, even if he has halitosis, which is true." She grinned. "I'd make those sacrifices for certain."

I enjoyed this lighthearted version of Dominique. I didn't want to think any longer about Doreen or her proposition. I looked around the room. The night seemed full of possibility. I felt mischievous, thought of the garden that Mr. Tinkler kept watch over like a death-row guard.

"Why don't we raid the garden? I saw a few roses hanging on."

"For ten grand, I'd star in a movie about my life," Dominique said, "and kiss Mickey Rooney."

"Game's over."

Dominique closed her eyes. "I hope he likes my letter."

"He will." I stood and offered her a hand up. "Let's get the last of those roses."

"Eve," she said, "I know I shouldn't write him. Understand

what I'm saying? Your brother seems so decent. I was lost after the abortion, maybe before, but the day the fire escape collapsed I thought how lucky I was to be alive, but also that I wanted . . . decency."

"Decency?"

"No fantasies, no Bogies. It's not your brother I want. It's a decent life."

"I understand. Let's get those flowers."

When I threw the door open, H.T. stood at the threshold ready to knock. I stepped back and gasped. He didn't move a muscle, just stood looking at me. Dominique stepped between us as if she were a barricade and demanded to know what he was doing there.

He looked past her. "Come to tell Eve somethin'," he said. "It's private."

"I can hear whatever it is," Dominique said.

"It's okay, H.T.," I said. "Come in."

He made no attempt to enter. "Stopped by to say I was hangin' at a club in Compton. They were thinkin' about givin' me a gig. Tomato Man came in the front door. I went out the back and got to a phone. Called Detective Sharkey."

My mouth went dry. I managed to ask how that could happen.

"Sharkey said a judge gave Tomato Man bail, five thousand cash. He's been out since yesterday."

I wondered why the police hadn't called to warn me. "Just like that?"

"Like that."

# -31-

H.T. INTERCEPTED ME AFTER I clocked in and asked me to come to the loading dock at noon. At lunch I found him seated on the concrete steps beside the loading dock, his sleeves rolled up to the elbow exposing his corded forearms, his hat propped back on his head. He opened his lunch pail and took out a sandwich wrapped in waxed paper.

"Try it. Mama made it, roast beef with horseradish," he said.

"Thanks," I said. "I brought my own."

"I got me one." He held up another. "Those sandwiches you eat aren't much for taste."

"How do you know what I eat?"

"You're a farm girl. You save pennies, probably on food."

"What makes you so smart?"

"I'm not." He laid the sandwich on my lap and looked down the alley. "Don't say thank you."

I didn't feel like arguing. "Thank you, Howard Thomas."

"You say, 'no, thank you,' then 'thank you.' Why are white people so polite? I'd like an answer to that one. Judge called me 'sir' all the time he was sentencing me."

"Should I thank you for coming by to warn me?"

"Never you mind." He reached over and touched the tip of my nose. "You're pretty."

"Don't tell me I'm pretty. Tell me I'm smart. Tell me I'm brave." I decided to ask the obvious question. "H.T., aren't you worried about Cornell?"

He brushed me off with a wave of a hand and took a drink of lemonade from his thermos. "His kind come at night and crawl under the cracks in doors. If I see him first, he'll be the one in fear. Are you scared?"

"Worried. Didn't he kill a man?"

"Killed more than one. Way I heard it, he collects debts in our community for the Dragna boys. You going to eat?"

"If you're trying to scare me, don't. I'm plenty worried."

"Eat. Beef's not rationed the way it was anymore. That don't mean it drops out of the sky."

I unwrapped the sandwich and bit into it. The beef, the first I'd tasted in a long while, was slightly pink and thinly sliced. I talked as I ate. "Why'd you hang around a guy like him?"

"Knew him from prison. Besides, you won't find a Rockefeller or a Hearst in a blues club. I sing blues. Least I did."

"Let's talk about something else."

"Women," he muttered dismissively.

"Your mother's a woman."

"Your's is a woman. Mine's a saint. Or tryin' to be."

I looked up at the edge of the roof and the new fire escape. I wondered what happened to Gulliver. H.T. asked what I was looking at.

"The sky."

"When I was," he said, "I don't know, six or seven, a teacher told us the sky was air and air was invisible." He rested his elbows on the step and leaned back. "I asked how could I know it was there if I couldn't see it. Know what she said?" He smiled. "She said it's there because you can feel the wind. I asked what about the blue. 'Illusion, Howard,' she said. 'Space provides background and molecules in the air bend light.'"

"In Palouse, the sky determined everything from the success of crops to the mood of the congregation in church."

He chuckled. "Farm girl."

He'd been distant and hard for so long; I couldn't believe how gentle he now appeared. It seemed the right moment to ask about his music. "Where'd you learn to sing?"

"Never learned the way you could say learning takes place. Mama took me to the Baptist Church. Everybody sang. I sang soprano 'til I was twelve and my voice deepened. Mr. Stillman bought me my first guitar and I used to. . . ." He fell silent as if a memory of something stole the moment.

I sensed there was another history tucked into what he had said about the guitar. By Stillman he didn't mean Selmo, but the father. I waited for him as he drank some lemonade.

"You were saying about Mr. Stillman."

"You got me to thinkin', Eve." He rested his arms on his knees. "You ever been up to the Valley?"

I swallowed. "The Valley?"

"San Fernando. Stands of melons and cantaloupe and peaches and apples. Farmers' wives and kids sell the fruit, sell lemonade so strong it'll make you pucker so bad your lips won't pop out for an hour. I was thinking Mama would like some melon and fruit, maybe strawberries."

"What's your mother's name?"

"Ruth." He looked away for a moment. "Maybe I'll borrow the truck from Selmo for a drive up. You could go with me."

"Are you asking?"

"And, if I was?"

I took a deep breath and said, "I might go."

"I guarantee it's one place you'll never see Cornell Jones."

"I guess that's a good reason to go."

"Then I'm askin'."

"Do you remember after the fire escape collapsed?"

"Sure. We were damned relieved, all of us."

"You put your arm around me and pulled me close."

He grinned. "Damned if I remember that."

"Yes, you do. And you liked it until people looked at us."

At shift's end Dominique and I had it in mind to go to Tasco's for dinner and drink. The cool evening air hit us as we stepped outside. At the base of the loading dock two Marine sergeants in uniform stood talking to H.T. The three of them looked up at us. The broad-shouldered Marine was taller than H.T. He hollered hello to me.

"Who's that?" Dominique asked.

"Holy cow." Without giving a thought to what I was doing, I charged down the steps, jumped into Maxwell's arms and grabbed his neck. He spun me around once and then lowered me to the asphalt.

"Meant to get up here much sooner," he said. "We were talking to H.T. here and waiting. He was playing his harmonica. You ever hear him play?"

I glanced at H.T., who seemed confused, and said, "Yes, he plays wonderfully."

H.T. tightened his grip on the mouth organ and said he had work to do. In fact, he'd clocked out for the day. Dominique, looking confused herself, stood atop the platform taking it all in. I took Maxwell by the hand and guided him toward her.

He smiled at her. "You look better than the last time I saw you."

"Me?"

"You wouldn't remember me, I don't guess."

"Oh, no. Don't tell me," she said.

H.T. had slipped into the shadows and was slowly rolling

down his sleeves. He seemed to be glaring at us. I shook my head. I was loathe to understand him and his moods. I turned to Dominique and said, "It's Maxwell."

"I figured it out. Nice to meet you," she said, her voice low and cool.

The Marine removed his white hat. "Nice to meet you again." He aimed a thumb in the direction of his companion. "This is my buddy Sy. He's named after Simon Peter, a prophet and a saint, but Sy's no saint and he can't see into the next hour."

Dominique said, "What brought you?"

Maxwell gazed up. "I've been meaning to come for some time, ma'am. But the Corps kept us busy training troops. I've got three days and was hoping you'd have some spare time."

"Well, I think we. . . ." She looked at me.

"No, we don't have some *spare* time," I said. "We have plenty of time."

Maxwell backed away a measured step and turned. "Eve," he said, "come meet Sy."

I smiled at Maxwell's friend, who smiled back shyly. With blue eyes and a round face, he was a smaller version of Maxwell. He had a thick muscular neck, a fair complexion, and sun-reddened cheeks. Though in his mid-twenties, he appeared almost adolescent.

"Sy, this is her. The Eve in your boots."

"I got your note, ma'am," he said. "In my last pair of boots. Sent it home to my mom."

"Eve. My name's Eve."

"Okay, Eve." He shook my hand then walked to the steps and shook Dominique's.

In the corner of my eye, I noticed H.T. slide farther away. Maxwell grabbed his friend by the shoulder and pointed to a ribbon at the top of Simon's awards. "Know what this Marine did?"

Simon waved him off. "Come on, Max. Leave it be."

"He's bashful. That's a Navy Cross on his blues. Won it. . . ."

"Don't," Simon said. "You don't win these. It wasn't a competition."

"Okay. Simon says, 'Don't talk'." Maxwell released his friend and smiled broadly. "You two have any plans?"

Dominique said, "Well, actually, we have a very busy schedule."

"Don't listen to her," I said. I caught a fleeting glimpse of H.T. rounding the alley.

Maxwell studied Dominique's face for a moment and said he didn't want to inconvenience us. It appeared momentarily that the matter had consumed itself, then Simon spoke up. "It's short notice, but maybe just a movie?"

I said, "Dominique, tell them you're kidding. You're free for the weekend."

"A major loaned us a car on the QT," Simon said, looking at me. "We don't have to take streetcars. We'll get you home early."

"That sounds good, doesn't it?" I asked.

"Really," Dominique said, "we . . . can't."

Simon, despite the rows of ribbons on his chest for bravery, seemed ready to retreat.

"Excuse us." I grabbed her arm and walked her inside the door. "Don't do this."

She bit at her lipstick. "I'm embarrassed. He probably thinks I'm. . . . He knows."

"He came to see you. He probably saved your life. Think about that."

She cranked her neck and glanced out at Maxwell. "He appears very nice."

"Yes. He's . . .," I searched for and found the right word, "decent. Like Link."

She took a deep breath and let it out. "Okay, here we go, deep water no life preserver."

When she approached Maxwell this time, she turned into the coquette version of herself and said, "My error, sir. It's next weekend we're expecting the Prince of Wales. I'm free."

Simon looked befuddled. Maxwell grinned.

I said, "Churchill the week after that. And Stalin. For bridge and crumpets."

"Stalin," Dominique said, "he eats with his fingers and wipes slobber on his sleeve."

"So does Churchill," Maxwell said. "Crumpets only."

Dominique's eyes shined. "Yes, but never soup. Stalin is a very messy man."

Selmo appeared at the back door, and seeing us with two Marines, shouted. "MacArthur did it! The Marines landed at Leyte! Our boys."

"What's wrong with him?" Simon asked.

"Everything," Dominique said. "Well, we've reason to celebrate now."

We were back home from an evening that included a fine meal and a movie when a knock sounded followed by Mr. Tinkler saying, "I know you're in there."

Dominique looked at me as if asking what to do.

I shrugged. "Your call."

She stood close to the door and asked. "What do you want?"

"To talk."

"It's late," she said. "And we're too tired."

"I know. Much too late for a Negro to show up on your

doorstep and be invited in. I saw it. Didn't I say I don't want his kind around?"

Dominique opened the door. "You've been spying on us."

He stepped back and fidgeted. "I don't spy. I was watering flowers. The ones you steal."

"Your flowers, yes."

"I saw that Negro and you were expecting him." He aimed a finger at me. "I can evict you for immoral behavior. And you live upstairs so you should show those who live downstairs consideration. That means no wild dancing."

I went to the door and nudged Dominique aside.

"Well," he said. "What do you have to say?"

I grinned at him, took the knob in hand, and slammed the door shut.

# -32-

THE DAY AFTER TINKLER'S VISIT was October 21st. I'd gone to bed both angry and anxious for the coming morning. I stayed in bed until after I heard Dominique rattling around in the kitchen. I wandered out and yawned. A picnic basket looped around her arm, she closed the refrigerator and apologized for waking me.

"Come with me. We'll spend the day at the beach with Maxwell and Simon."

"I have plans. I'm going to the San Fernando Valley for melons."

"I see. And you're going with?"

"You know."

"Be careful," she said. "We've gone through this before. Don't make a mistake."

"What kind of mistake? I'm good at making a variety of them."

"You know what I mean. While love may conquer all, it can't conquer itself—just let it take its course."

"Outside of a Hollywood film, does that even make sense? Have a nice time today."

Before she closed the door, she said, "I'm sorry. I'm quick to give advice, but terrible at following it. Have a good date."

A date? I thought. Was I going on a date? My thoughts

muddled with doubt, I dressed and bathed, then sat at the window wondering what the day might bring. I intended to tell H.T. that he need not walk off the way he had in front of Maxwell and Simon. While I found myself drawn to H.T., I was unsure of my feelings and how much my doubts were influenced by others, including my mother's. I admired him for coming to our aid the day the fire escape collapsed. I couldn't admit the coming afternoon was possibly a date. It was a drive into the countryside for the fresh air and melons and fruit. A date is a picnic or dinner and a movie, holding hands, smiling, feeling warm inside. But my anticipation told me otherwise. I'd be going out with a man, an older moody man I found attractive despite how others judged it.

I stood by the kitchen window and watched ships being towed in and out of the harbor. I marked the passage of time watching the ocean turn from blue to jade. When H.T. hadn't arrived by midmorning, I worried that he'd been in an accident. I began pacing and looking at the clock. 10:00, 10:15, 10:30. The minute hand became my master as I alternately looked from the window to the clock. At 11:00, my imagination took a dark turn. I pictured the truck smashed on the roadside, H.T. lying beside it, bleeding from a shot fired by Cornell Jones.

Maybe he forgot? I reminded myself of his sullenness and how he acted when he saw me embrace the big Marine. Maybe he was being jealous? With that thought in mind, I decided I'd been stood up and maybe it was best. I stepped outside, slammed the door shut, and hurried down the stairs on my way to nowhere in particular. I was halfway through the courtyard when Tinkler stepped out of the shadows and blocked my path.

"Stop," he said in sharp manner.

Without looking, I stormed past him, reached the sidewalk,

and headed uphill. I walked until I exhausted my frustration. I decided it was early enough for me to catch a streetcar and see a movie and have dinner at a restaurant. My legs were cramping up by the time I turned the final corner heading back to the apartment, but I felt better.

As I neared the apartment, I saw the pickup parked across the street. He was seated on the steps outside the apartments. He clambered down the stairs and intercepted me at the base.

"Carburetor cable broke," he said. "I had to find one. Ain't so easy on a Saturday. I went to two scrap yards."

I stepped around him. The hem of my skirt brushed his pant leg.

"Go ahead be mad," he said. "I came like I said."

I paused to get my keys from my purse. My fingers trembled.

"Guess it was a waste, me showin' up. Guess you can't take apologies. Guess. . . ."

"Just shut up," I said. "Do you like upsetting me?"

"Okay, missy. I'll be goin'."

I wheeled about and pointed at him. "My name is Eve. And I didn't hear any apology."

He shrugged. "We can pick up some fine cantaloupe and strawberries. I promised my mama I'd get some. It's too fine a day to sit at home."

"You can still get her some. And that's no apology. And you were rude last night."

"I told you what happened. The cable. . . . How was I rude? You think I was lyin'?" He stood his ground momentarily, then pivoted on his good leg and walked off.

He was near the fountain when Mr. Tinkler rounded the corner and stopped in his tracks. The little manager stared at H.T. as if trying to bring him into focus. Tinkler's dumbfounded expression brought a smile to my face. He muttered to himself, then cut a hazy eye at me.

He slurred out, "I ta, told you, did, didn't I? About them." He pointed at H.T.

Dominique had suspected that he was a drunk. I brushed my fingers through my hair. H.T. grinned. Redirecting my anger at Tinkler, I said, "I don't remember. Tell me again. What exactly was it?"

"Him. I, uh wah, warned you about what I sah, saw."

Sweetening the tone of my voice, I said, "It wasn't any of your business then, and it's not now."

As H.T. stepped toward the entrance, I hollered, "Where're you going?" I skipped across the courtyard and caught him by the arm. I looked back at Tinkler, who stood mute. Surprising myself, I boomed out, "Let's go, honey."

"I suh, suh, saw and won't, huh, have it," Tinkler said in his slurred speech.

When we reached the truck, I let go of H.T.'s arm, and waited for him to open my door.

He looked at me, then the door. "You like squash fresh out of the oven with butter?"

He opened my door and I swung up into the seat. "Don't think I'm not still mad."

"What the hell did he see?" H.T. asked.

"Beats me."

H.T. kept his eyes trained on the narrow lane of asphalt that sliced through the valley north of Los Angeles. I watched the landscape. The smell of freshly turned dirt and the sight of trees slanting over the roadside reminded me of home, not exactly home, but the sense of it. Eucalyptus lined the roadside. Black oak grew on distant slopes overgrown with chaparral and bunch grass. Fenced in truck farms and citrus groves lined the highway. Seeing it all transported me from the world of Cornell and cops back to a place and time of harvesting and fields being readied for new planting, a place where simple matters gave purpose to the days. I realized that I missed it all, the seasons and rainfall, erosion, and the dizzying geometry of furrowed land. Los Angeles was a place where dirt was covered over as if it were something shameful.

H.T. stopped near a fruit stand in the shade of a eucalyptus and opened my door. Two girls manned the stand, one behind boxes of fruit and rows of melons, the other a cash box. They were no more than fifteen and wore dresses made from flour sacks. H.T. asked if they had squash. The girl by the fruit boxes pointed to a stack of butternut squash.

"If you know anything 'bout them, you'll know them's good."

"Where are you from?" I asked.

"Us?" the girl asked, pointing to herself and then the other one.

"Yes," I said.

"Oklahoma. Come with our family ten years ago. Ma works for Mr. Palmer an' so do we. Pa is overseas. So's my brother Evan. Evan's a paratrooper."

H.T. carefully picked out two large squashes. He looked at them critically.

"My brother's in the Hundred and First Division," I said. "He's a paratrooper too."

The other girl said, "That's Evan's unit."

H.T. held the squash up and asked if that was the best they had. The first girl nodded, but the second called out, "No, those're the best out here that Mr. Palmer wants sold. Round back we got some you might like better."

"Jenny Lynn!" the first girl scolded.

"Aw, her brother is with ours, Marnie. We got fresh-picked strawberries there too, an' you'll want some asparagus. That come in this mornin' from the Majorcas's farm." The girl looked at me. "Most'a what's out here come in yesterday or Thursday, an' it was old then."

I said, "I wanted to get some melons. Cantaloupe or honeydew."

"'Bout a mile on up. See Brenda an' tell her Jenny Lynn said to sell the good stuff."

H.T. returned from the back with a box of squash which he set by the truck and left for more. He explained as he loaded the next box that he was buying for Selmo as well. That was how he'd gotten use of the truck.

"Another favor you owe him?" I asked.

H.T. looked up from the last crate. "Another I owe Mr. Stillman."

At dusk, after filling the truck bed with baskets of fruit and vegetables, we stopped at a small diner named Earnie's Eatery. It advertised the finest homemade food outside of grandma's house. I felt at ease with the world—no annoying Mr. Tinkler, no Cornell Jones, no assembly line. A home-cooked meal seemed an ideal way to cap off what had become a fine day.

The waitress looked up as we entered. We took seats at a table by a window. She slapped her ticket book against her hip and came our way. She asked if we were thirsty. Looking at H.T., she recommended the orange soda. He said water would do fine.

She set the glasses down and asked if we were from L.A. H.T. ignored the question and studied the menu. I told her yes, that we came looking for fruit and vegetables. I ordered the house special, homemade meatloaf with corn on the cob and whipped potatoes. She said that was the best choice. H.T.

decided at first on a country fried steak with green beans, then changed his mind and settled on meatloaf.

"Change your mind about the orange drink?" she asked.

"Don't like it," he said.

The waitress left to place our orders.

"What was that about?"

He looked in the direction of the kitchen. "Nothin' you'd understand."

The day had been pleasant. Now it appeared he was sinking into a mood. It struck me that just because I didn't use the words others attached to race, it didn't mean I wasn't poisoned by the coded messages of bigotry.

When I looked back, he was looking at me.

"What?"

"Nothing."

"Why do guys answer 'nothing' to avoid a question?"

"Why does every girl want to know what every guy's thinkin'?"

"There you go answering a question with a question."

"There you go avoidin' questions."

I smiled. So did he.

"How did we do today, loot-wise?"

"Mama'll be pleased. Did you have a good time with those Marines?"

"I guess."

Outside the window, evening crawled over the farmland and we silently watched the world going dark. The day had been wonderful, and I was sad it would soon come to an end. When the sky was almost black, the waitress came over to lower the shade by our table. Two trucks pulled in, and a moment later the door swung open. Two families spilled in, husbands and wives and seven energetic children. The children quickly settled down, and the waitress and parents exchanged small friendly talk as she pushed three tables together to accommodate them. One of the fathers nodded politely at H.T. who I sensed was turning morose.

The meatloaf was as the waitress had claimed. Sunburned and close to exhausted, I ate and disregarded H.T.'s return to somberness. Nearby the families quietly traded news of the war. They were indifferent to us with the one exception of a boy of about ten who kept turning his head in our direction. H.T., whose back was to the family, didn't notice him, but I did, and so did the boy's mother who scolded him.

"But she's with a nigger," the boy blurted out.

I flinched. H.T. looked up at the ceiling and moved a bite of meatloaf around the plate with his fork. I was amazed that H.T., the one most affected by the comment, barely reacted. The next instant there was a hard scraping of wood on wood as the boy's father, his face clenched like a fist, pushed his chair back. He circled the table. The youngster's expression changed from haughtiness to fright. The father lifted him by the collar and pulled him across the floor and out the door, the screen slamming behind them. The boy cried out, "No." The rest of the party and H.T. continued eating as the sound of the youngster's pleas for mercy grew louder.

A few minutes passed before the door opened. The father marched his son directly to our table. "Excuse me, sir," he said to H.T. "My boy's got somethin' to say."

"No need," H.T. said.

"Sir, I think there is a need." He nudged the boy forward.

The youngster's eyes were red, his cheeks wet. He swiped the back of his hand across his face and blinked. H.T. looked at the boy.

"I'm sorry, sir, for sayin' what I did."

H.T. nodded. "Okay. We're good."

The father tugged at the boy's sleeve, told him to go sit

down, and said to H.T. "Sir, I'd like to buy yours and the lady's dinner."

"Thank you, we're fine," H.T. said.

"Well, I'd like to buy it just the same. Boy's young and hears things. We're Christian people and I don't abide that kind of thinking. You'd be doing me a favor to accept the offer."

I looked up at the man and said, "That's kind of you. We accept."

The father wished us a good evening and left to join his family. H.T. glared at me. I glared back. Neither of us spoke until it was time to leave. He took out his billfold.

"Don't you dare," I whispered. "Just leave something for the waitress."

"Who're you tellin' what to do?"

"And say something pleasant on the way out. Both of you are entitled to your dignity."

He shook his head and mumbled. I watched him count out forty cents and leave it next to his plate. Even as we passed the tables, I had little certainty in what H.T. was or wasn't going to say. I elbowed him lightly and stopped so that he would have to stop as well.

He cleared his throat. "Hope you have a fine evening and try the meatloaf."

The father smiled. "That's what we came here for. And you have a pleasant drive."

Outside I waited for him to open my door. "That wasn't so terrible, was it?"

He settled in behind the wheel. "Boy will hate every black man he ever sees now." He started the engine and pulled out onto the road.

"Or grow up to be like his father," I said.

I felt a sudden kinship with the father. The one time I

heard the word said in my family was when Link referred to a redcap he'd seen at the railroad station as one. Mom smacked his face and told him, "Never say that in my house." Later she explained that people with ugly minds use that kind of language to separate us and that she and her family had more in common with coloreds, as she called black people, than her family had with the Rockefellers and Roosevelts or Mr. Overstreet the banker.

The temperature had dropped considerably. A half-moon hovered above the hills. H.T. kept an eye on the road and drove steadily at thirty-five miles an hour. The top half of the headlights being blacked out, the beams barely lit the road ahead. I rolled up my window.

"Was your father like that man?"

"No father."

"Everyone has a father. Country girls know how life is created. You had a father."

He chewed on this before he spoke. "He came and went from Mama's life when she was young. I didn't take his last name. I got her's on the birth certificate. Funny, ain't it how. . . ." He drifted off for a moment. "I'd pretend one day I'd hear a knock on the door. When I answered it, he'd be there hat in hand, head bowed, and introduce himself. You know, apologize for showin' up unexpected and explain he had to go to work in some faraway place so he could come back with his head high. Stupid, huh?" He glanced at me, then turned his eyes to the road.

At least I knew my father's name, had memories and a picture of him and the dual-bell alarm clock as proof of his existence. I felt a passageway open. "Did you picture him like that man tonight?"

He grinned. "No, I always figured he'd be a Chinaman. Truth is I wished I had a father like that man at the restaurant.

What I learned come down on my ass harder than any hundred spankings."

After that we drove in silence except for the wind whistling over the windshield.

Finally, I said, "I knew my father mostly from photos. If I saw him, I probably wouldn't recognize him. Guess he became nothing but a picture."

He asked me to light him a cigarette, which I did. He took a draw on it and cracked his wing window.

"I'm sorry about your father," I said.

"No need," he said softly. "Mr. Stillman treated me better than a father. And Mama did the best she could. No need to feel sorry for me. I don't feel sorry about it."

"Then I won't feel sorry for you either. Or myself. But I do feel sorry for my mother. She still sets a place setting at the table for my father and insists we call him Mr. Halvers."

He took a long draw on his cigarette as he considered this. "That's crazy."

"She wants us to respect him for giving us life."

I explained that my family once owned over a hundred acres that my mother inherited, but my father never farmed it and instead worked in Potlatch as a lumberjack. "When the Depression hit, logging died. My father fell behind on taxes and mortgaged the land. We lost it and he began drinking. My brother watched him walk away carrying a suitcase. No one ever heard another word from him again."

His face glowed as he drew on the cigarette. It appeared as if he'd not been listening. He sighed and rolled down his window. After he tossed the cigarette, he asked, "You hate him?"

"For what he did to Mother, maybe. Do you hate yours?"

"He's only an idea. No face in my head to hate, which doesn't mean I don't have anger. I got in a lot of fights growin' up because I didn't have a face to hate. There's a lot of hate out there and lot to hate. One fight got me in prison."

His remark and the darkened fields fostered equally dark thoughts—Jess dismissing me as a whore and a liar, claiming to people that I was after his share of a thousand acres of wheat, a hundred acres of which his father had bought at auction—my family's acreage.

I asked H.T. if he was religious.

"Black man has to be, especially one who doesn't believe in God," he said.

"That doesn't make sense."

"Heaven's a place where you know one another by voice. 'Til a black man goes there, all he's got is blues."

"I don't understand."

He chuckled. His eyes reflected the pale light and shone like coal.

"Don't make fun of me," I said. "I'm someone."

"A man's gotta grab a laugh 'cause life's all about workin' your back and waking up sore, and knowing men hold secrets in their eyes when they talk to you. It's takin' a woman and knowing it's just borrowing. It's walking in shackles and someone else has got the key. 'At's the blues. It's religion for a man who God turned his back on."

My mouth agape, I stared at his profile. "That was beautiful."

He stared ahead at the road. "Kind of like you."

My cheeks warmed. I was glad he was looking at the road and not me. "Tell the truth. You haven't been looking out for me just because you felt guilty for taking me to the club."

"Make up your own reason."

"You like me H.T. Elders. A lot."

He smiled but kept his eyes on the road.

The route seemed rougher and longer at night. The sound

of the engine and the tires whistling on asphalt was numbing. Near Pasadena a military convoy coming north forced us to the side of the road. When the road cleared, he asked if I wanted to stop somewhere.

"I'm fine," I said, though I didn't feel that way.

"We need gas. We can have coffee."

He turned in at the next truck stop, came around, and opened my door. Music came from inside, the tinny sound of a jukebox playing Tommy Dorsey. I extended my hand as I stepped out. He hesitated, then helped me down. He smelled of soap and cigarette smoke. We stood awkwardly until he wheeled about and walked to the diner door, which he opened for me.

"See, you can be a gentleman," I said.

The diner was stark, one long counter and two rows of tables on a concrete floor painted a battleship gray. Two truckers sat at the counter. A family of five was crowded into a corner booth. I walked to a table, sat, and ordered a lemonade. I stirred the ice with the straw and waited. He came through the doorway, limped over, and sat facing me.

"Tell me something."

"You're one for asking," he said.

"Stop it." I looked him squarely in the face.

He looked about the room and then back at me. "Okay, ask."

"Why didn't you. . . . When the boy said that you didn't even flinch."

He rolled up his sleeve and set his exposed arm on the tabletop. His was a worker's arm, corded with muscle and tendon and ligament. "Touch it."

Touching him now in public, even just an arm, seemed both intimate and intimidating. Other than H.T.'s wrapping an arm over me after the fire escape fiasco and giving my brothers a sisterly hug, I'd not had physical contact with a man, except of course Jess. I hesitated.

"Is there a problem?" he asked.

"No." I laid a hand on his arm. It felt hot.

"Snake sheds skin once a year," he said, "so it can grow. Skin means nothin' to a snake. But it's all important to us, ain't it?"

I looked at my pale hand on his dark skin. It seemed as if blood had risen to the surface of the skin, and I could feel it flow. He eased my hand away and rolled down the sleeve. I noticed stubble on his jaw and chin, his cheek bones, the veins in his neck.

"You're handsome," I said.

He took my hand in his and held it firmly. I liked how my hand fit in his. When he let go, he gave me a wry, knowing smile, and dropped his hand to his side. "We gotta get going."

As we crossed the floor, I paused at the jukebox and dropped in a nickel, then pressed the buttons for "Stardust."

"You gonna stay to hear it?" he asked.

I shook my head and motioned with my finger for him to follow. Outside in the moon-glazed parking lot the song was a muted refrain in the background barely audible over the sounds of cars and trucks rumbling by on the highway.

He gripped the door handle. "What would your friends say if they heard you?"

"Heard me what?"

"Say a black man was handsome?" He opened the door, but I didn't get in.

I slid my left hand up his arm and let it rest on his shoulder. "Dance with me."

He took my right hand in his and eased an arm around the small of my back. I closed my eyes, pressed my cheek to his chest and followed his lead. He hummed along with the music and danced as if the song were in his legs. I wanted the song to go on and the mood to linger into daylight, but when the music ended, he released me and stepped away.

"Mama's a Baptist," he said. "She don't approve of dancing. She'd see what we did as sin."

We gazed at each other until a truck pulled in and honked for the attendant. I looked at the rising half-moon through the boughs of a eucalyptus. I thought of Mother's letter and how I might explain this, whatever it was. She used to tell us not to load any more bricks on a board than it can support. Do not put another brick on, I thought, but the day had stirred something in me, something I knew might be difficult if not impossible to resist.

# -33-

I WAS A GIRL GOING out on a second date, this one a real date. I primped and worried and hoped he'd be on time. Then when I opened the door and saw him, for no good reason I felt doubt again. I'd witnessed him endure humiliation at the hands of the police and then again with a young boy. And with Tinkler. Though I had little faith in prayer, I offered up a silent one asking that the night pass without incident.

"You okay?" he asked as I shut the door.

"Fine."

"You want, we can forget this."

"I'm fine. Let's go." I smiled.

We stepped to the back of the line. People ahead of us glanced at us furtively. H.T., standing straight as a flagpole, placidly ignored the looks. I took my signals from him and studied posters advertising coming attractions, looked at the night sky, cars passing by, looked at anything but people's faces. I assured myself that people were simply curious. I'd have to adjust to it. Yet, when we took seats next to the aisle, I felt as if every eye was on us. I sat gripping the arm rests until H.T. slipped a hand atop mine and whispered, "Pretend we're alone."

The first of the news briefs showed MacArthur wading to shore in the Philippines, making good his promise to return to Manila. The second was a clip of French women stripped to bras and panties, their hair shorn, being herded into a building. A man grabbed one woman by her ponytail and used a knife to hack off her hair. My throat went dry as the scene faded. The announcer said that was how liberators among the French handled German collaborators.

A cartoon followed, but the image of near-naked women being herded like sheep into a sheering pen swamped my thoughts. The theater went completely dark. A lion's roar heralded the main feature. H.T. was quickly caught up in the film. It wasn't until the audience exploded in laughter at the antics on the screen that I finally relaxed.

When we stepped out of the theater, he asked, "Are you hungry?"

"Starving."

He offered a wide grin. "I know a place. White folks don't go there much, so we'll have to put up with black folks staring for a change."

I bowed my head and asked as I chuckled, "Is the food good?"

"Rub your stomach and burp good."

Just then it began to sprinkle, and we ran to the truck. My makeup was running, my hair was wet. I didn't feel up to being seen that way. Still, I was hungry, so I didn't say anything about forgetting dinner. We were on a narrow street of two- and three-story buildings, when the rain came down hard. He turned on the wipers and said even the rain wasn't going to ruin this night. At the café he parked under the sign that read "Tuesday's" and we hurried inside. All but two tables were occupied. The patrons were all black. As we crossed the floor, their eyes tracked our passage. Being in a room of strangers that might include some who knew Cornell revived my fears. Bile rose in my throat. Despite assurances from detectives that the pimp would not make bail, he had, and I was now in his backyard.

I gripped H.T.'s arm. "Is there any chance?"

"The Tomato Man? Not much chance. Let's eat."

I pretended to swallow down my fears. "Right."

The tall, slender waitress shot me a haughty look as she laid menus and a basket of corn muffins on our table. She addressed H.T. as "Blues Man" in an obvious effort to flirt. I felt a twinge of jealousy. "Doll Baby," she said holding her head back and looking at me over her nose, "you got a note from Mama says you can go out with the Blues Man?"

H.T. chuckled. "We work together, Georgia. She's here for the eats, baby."

My cheeks burned. I looked at the patrons nearby. Apparently, I'd become less of a curiosity. Most were intent on their plates. H.T. ordered for us—a large bowl of black-eyed pea soup and a plate of collard greens. Georgia took a long look at my damp hair before walking away, doing as much as physically possible to draw attention to her long legs and butt.

I said, "Why didn't she just sit in your lap?"

"Likes my singing's all."

"So, sing. There's the stage. She'll really like you then." I pointed to a corner of the room.

"Singing's not on the menu tonight. Jealous?"

"Hardly," I said.

Georgia sashayed back to the table carrying our meal on a tray she balanced overhead with one hand. She made it a point to bend over and expose her cleavage as she laid the tray down. She placed our plates in front of us, mine first. As a final touch, she laid down a plate with four corn muffins and said, "Compliments of the cook."

She smiled at H.T., darted a smirk at me, and danced off across the floor.

The soup was thick, and the greens were smothered in bacon fat. I ate ravenously, then wiped my plate with a muffin, ate that, and sat back. The crowd murmured as a large black man pushed a table in the corner against the wall and pulled up a stool. He opened a guitar case.

"We gotta go," H.T. said and laid money down for the bill.

"Why? I'd like to hear him."

"This ain't your world." He shook his head firmly. "Music starts, the crowd'll get different. Rowdy maybe. Looks tame now, but it turns fast."

The lights dimmed as he stood. He pulled my chair back for me.

"Why'd you bring me here if it's not safe?"

"To see if you'd come."

I trusted his judgment but resented that he'd asked me to come as a test.

The rain had stopped but the streets were wet. The awkwardness on the drive to the apartment was as palpable as the silence it brought on. I was grateful he hummed and didn't talk. He pulled up to the curb and said that he'd walk me to the door.

"No need," I said.

"There is."

"Why?"

"I want to, and. . . . Well, a man strolled himself into Tuesday's, a friend of the Tomato Man's. And he looked our way."

So that was why he'd hurried me out. My hands began to sweat.

"It's okay," he said. "He probably didn't see us, and you're home now."

The fountain bubbled. The courtyard was otherwise quiet. He took my hand in his as we entered. The damp flagstone glistened. Even though he held my hand gently, I could feel the strength in his hand. It gave me a sense of comfort and aroused feelings in me. As we passed through the garden, he released my hand. The roses were in the last bloom of the season, small now but still lovely. He snapped one off at the base, broke the thorns off with a thumb and held the flower up for me.

"The landlord," I said.

"Never mind him."

He stepped close enough that I could feel his body heat. He seemed taller now. I knew what was about to happen. I wanted it and I didn't because I knew it would open a gate I had never passed through. Blood roared in my temples when he placed the flower in my hands.

"I'm gonna go now," he said, but he made no effort to move.

I stepped closer. A breeze ruffled the leaves. It was cool and damp. I realized it more because of the heat we both radiated. My legs trembled in anticipation.

"Mama told me I was crazy." He stepped closer. "She says you're trouble."

I looked up provocatively, as I'd seen women in movies do. "I am. You even said so."

I was taken by a romantic impulse. "Not here. There." I led him to the fountain.

He looked at the white lilies in the moon glistened water. "They're beautiful."

It seemed peculiar coming from a man, too honest, too pure. But I knew he was affected by them the way I had been when I first saw them. "White lilies," I said.

"Yes, white lilies."

"Go ahead. Kiss me." I rose up on my toes, slipped into his arms and formed myself to him. Hoping he didn't notice my body shudder, I closed my eyes and waited. He touched his lips tentatively to mine, then abruptly let go and stepped back. His arms dangled at his sides.

"What's wrong?"

"I wasn't intending on kissin' you tonight." He hung his head. "You've seen a part or two of it, but you ain't ready for all that comes with being with me."

I realized whatever was to happen between us had to be decided in the next seconds, and I would be the one to decide it. I could say the evening had been wonderful and let matters die or tell him that he shouldn't shut me out. I took his hand.

"It's okay. It's fine. Remember the fire escape? I'm strong. I learned that I am."

"Some places I could get myself hung for this. There's something . . . something I keep to myself. Something that got me in prison."

Suddenly I had sense that we weren't alone, a thought made me shiver.

"Are you okay?" he asked.

"Cold, I guess." I held the rose to my nose, smelled it and said, "Kiss me."

H.T. said, "I was about to tell you somethin'."

"Shush." I laid a hand on his neck, pulled him close and offered him my lips. I was about to close my eyes when I saw the branches of a bush rustle. I supposed it was Tinkler watching over his precious flowers. Or it could've been my imagination, but if it weren't and he was spying on me again, I'd give him good reason to evict me. Suddenly I realized it wasn't my imagination. A figure in the shadows, his features obscured beneath a wide-brim hat, emerged, in his hand a gun.

The courtyard walls magnified the sound of the shots. I saw a muzzle flash, heard a gun blast three times. H.T. grabbed his side and slumped into my arms. His knees buckled and we fell together into the fountain. Two more shots ripped the night. As the sound of running feet passed nearby and then diminished, I lay in the shallow water clinging to H.T.

Lights came on. A door opened. A tenant hollered, "Everyone okay? Was anyone shot?"

Somehow, I still held the rose. I dropped it and freed my arm from beneath H.T. "Down here! Call an ambulance. Please. A man's been shot."

The rose bobbed on the rippling water. I tugged at H.T. He blinked and looked at me as if trying to focus. He pushed himself up on one knee, then the other, and tried to stand. He managed to get upright for a moment, then moaned and crumpled to the ground. His eyes closed. I shouted again, "Help. Someone call an ambulance."

# -34-

Perhaps it was the starkness of the walls, or the severe overhead lights, or the clock at the end of the hall that kept ticking off seconds that made me want to flee. More likely it was the sum of all of them and what happened to H.T. Everything seemed too big and I was too small for it. I couldn't flee from the night's events the way I'd fled Palouse. All that registered was that I'd witnessed a good man, a man I might have deep feelings for, shot down.

I couldn't sit another second looking at the clock. I rose from the bench and reeled down the hallway to the swinging doors. I pushed my way through them into the night and leaned against an outside wall. I thought of Avis, who'd try to make sense of all that happened, and then of H.T.'s mother, who'd shed tears, and my mother who'd wave a Bible and stand in judgment. "Shot because of you," she'd say. "I told you so." Everything told me that my mother's accusation would be a righteous one. It was my fault. He took the bullets that were intended for me. The tears came. I cupped my hands over my eyes. They smelled of his blood. Or did they? I'd washed them, not once but twice. How long, I wondered, would the smell of his blood remain imbedded in my mind, and I knew the sense of guilt would outlast any other smell.

Two nurses stepped out from a side exit and stood a few feet away. I ignored them and took in the night air. The lawn smelled damp and clean. I lowered my hands slowly to my sides and I tried to cry again, but no tears came. They lit cigarettes and their smoke drifted toward me.

I suddenly craved a cigarette. I rummaged in my purse for one with no success. Why would I expect to find one? I didn't smoke except when one was offered. I wiped my eyes on my sleeve and called to the nurses. "I was wondering if one of you might spare a cigarette. I forgot mine. I was in a hurry."

The taller one tapped a cigarette from her pack and signaled me over. She handed it to me, and I looked in my purse for matches. They watched as I fumbled through the side pockets, the cigarette dangling from my lips.

Finally, I gave up. "I'm sorry. I don't have a match either. I usually don't smoke. My roommate does. I smoke hers. You see my friend is in the . . . oh, God, listen to me."

The tall nurse struck a match. "Easy, easy. It's okay."

"Are you alright?" the other nurse asked.

"Thanks." I drew on the lit cigarette and exhaled. "My friend was shot. I was there."

"The Negro?"

I felt taken to task by the tone of her voice, but said calmly, "Yes, him."

"Is he your boyfriend?"

"We are. . . . No, he's not." My quick denial surprised me, but I had no words for what we were, and it was no one's business. It occurred that in the world we lived in anyone might make it his business.

"He came out of the operation alive," the shorter one said. "Could have been worse. He was lucky. Dr. Shore was on his way home when the ambulance pulled up."

There was a pause, during which we drew on our cigarettes.

"We came from the recovery room," the one who'd given me a smoke said. "Cops are waiting for word on him."

"You can't imagine how lucky he was," the shorter one said. "The young surgeons are overseas cutting on soldiers. Dr. Shore came out of retirement to fill the need. He's good though." She looked at her friend. "How old is Dr. Shore anyhow?"

"Says he's seventy, but it's closer to seventy-five. He's been with Sisters of Mary since I can remember. He did four hours of surgery after a full ten-hour day. Yeah, your friend's lucky."

"H.T.'s his name," I said. "Howard Thomas." We blew smoke into the night sky. Lucky? Maybe, I thought, because the hospital was so close, but how can getting shot anywhere be lucky? I shivered. If Cornell fired the shots, were they intended for me? I was the one who was saved. The true lucky one, I owed my life to H.T.

The taller nurse blew a billow of smoke at the sky and said, "It's the war."

"*What's* the war? I don't understand," I said.

"It's okay. I understand, honey."

Her tone put me on the defensive. "Understand what?"

A belt of light framed the side of her face. She was older, perhaps in her late thirties and attractive in a hardened way. She took a long draw on her cigarette and exhaled. "A colored lover. Who says we have to wait for the others?"

Both "lover" and "colored" sounded obscene coming from her. "It's not that way. It's not what you think."

"Hey, I didn't mean anything. I've been with one myself."

With one? She didn't know him, hadn't seen his efforts the day the fire escape collapsed, or heard him sing. The bullets in him had been intended for me. She couldn't see inside him or me or any of it. I crushed the cigarette underfoot. "Thanks for the cigarette."

"You're welcome," the tall one said. "Hope it helped."

Feeling anger helped settle me more than the cigarette had. I left them and went to the swinging doors. I wondered what was going on at the apartment and with the police. Had Dominique been with Maxwell and Simon, or were they in the apartment when the shooting occurred? Dominique wasn't among the tenants who'd pulled H.T. and me out of the fountain—or crowded around to see. The possibility of Tomato Man harming her was remote, but the chance that it could have happened nonetheless stirred my panic.

I hurried inside and found myself in a narrow hallway that seemed to close in on me. The walls were too white, the lights too intense. I felt myself trapped in a snow-less blizzard as one corridor intersected another and then another, the doors all locked from the other side. When I found one I could open, I pushed my way through. At the far end of a hall was a nurse's station. I hurried to the counter.

The nurse glanced up and pointed brusquely to a sign that said no visitors allowed.

I shook my head. "May I use your phone? I need to call my. . . ."

"It's for hospital use only," she said.

An orderly rolled a gurney past the station and spoke to the nurse. She gave him a room number. He wheeled the patient away. She pointed to a hall on the left and said, "There's a phone in the lobby. Go through the double doors and turn right, that'll get you there."

As I was about to reach the lobby, both doors opened. Maxwell and Simon—each dressed smartly in uniform—entered the hallway followed by Doreen, Selmo, and Dominique.

Dominique threw her arms around me. "We were looking for you. What happened?"

Before I could speak Selmo said, "Yes. Where've you been?"

Again, I couldn't answer because Doreen shook my arm and asked, "Are you okay?"

I stepped back from them, took a deep breath, and looked back and forth answering the fusillade of questions. "I think I am." "Cornell shot H.T." "It was supposed to be me." "I've been trying to find a phone." "Yes, I'm okay."

Doreen said. "We were all scared to death. How bad is H.T.?"

"Who did you say fired the shots?" Selmo said. "Can you identify him?"

Simon asked, "Are you in danger?"

I stepped back from them and leaned against a wall. Though I was thankful to see them, I was too exhausted to answer any more questions.

"Slow down, people," Maxwell said. "How're you holding up, Eve?"

"Barely," I said and looked at Dominique. "I'm glad you're okay."

Simon said, "Two cops in the lobby are looking for you."

"You look too frazzled to talk to the police," Doreen said.

Dominique stepped between me and the others and took my hand. "Let her breathe."

Doreen raised an eyebrow as if ready to protest but fell silent when Selmo raised a hand and asked. "Why was H.T. there?"

I squeezed Dominique's hand and let go. "No more questions." I clamped my palms over my ears. I took several deep breaths, then dropped my arms to my sides. I looked from face to face. "Until I came to L.A., I'd never talked to a cop. I'd never been in a hospital. All I know is two nurses told me H.T.'s going to pull through."

"Good. At least that," Doreen said. "I want you to meet someone in the lobby." She hooked my arm into hers and wheeled about.

The retinue turned as one. Selmo rushed ahead and opened the door to a waiting room where two uniformed policemen were leaning against a reception desk. One was talking on a phone as the other looked off. The switchboard operator sat in front of a panel of wires reading a paperback. Her gray coat unbuttoned and spread open, a slightly built black woman sat on a bench, a bag of knitting piled on her lap. She wore a tam, tilted to the right, covering one eyebrow. Doreen took my arm and walked me to her. The woman looked up. She appeared exhausted.

"Ruth, this is Eve. Eve, this is H.T.'s mother," Selmo said.

The woman set her knitting aside and looked up.

I extended my hand. "Nice to meet you."

She looked me up and down, shook her head, then stood slowly. "Wish't I could say the same." She held my hand as if she weren't going to let go. "I knew this'd happen, sure as you're standin' 'fore me. Tol' him nothin' good can come of it. Now he's shot."

"He'll be all right," Doreen said.

She dropped my hand and faced Doreen. "How's 'at? Can someone tell just how that's gonna be?"

"I'm sorry," I said. "If it helps, a nurse told me he's going to survive."

Ruth eased herself back onto the bench. She looked at me. Her eyes softened. "I ain't mad at you. World has its ways. Sit an' tell me what happened to my boy."

When I hesitated to sit, she patted the bench.

Before I could sit, a tall officer approached us. "Excuse me. Is one of you Eve Halvers?"

I turned to him. "I am."

He pointed to the double doors and asked me to step away with him. Selmo blocked the door. The officer stopped. Maxwell and Simon positioned themselves behind him. Selmo squared his shoulders and looked up at the policeman, who stood nearly a head taller.

The cop stifled a grin as he looked down at Selmo. "What's the problem?"

"Where are you taking her?" Selmo said.

"Are you her attorney?"

"Her employer," Selmo said. "We were talking."

"Fine, talk to her at work."

Selmo squared his shoulders. "Officer, I'm a contractor supporting the war effort. She serves an important function in my organization."

"Making bombs, I bet."

Selmo pointed at the cop's shoes. "Boots."

Grinning now, the cop said. "Boots."

"Yes, imagine fighting a war barefoot."

"And what important function does Miss Halvers perform?"

Selmo said without hesitation, "She's the Marine morale specialist."

Repeating it, like a schoolboy reciting a line, the cop said, "The Ma-rine mo-rale spe-shall-ist?"

"I stitch boot parts together," I said.

Selmo narrowed his eyes on me. "And she helps our boys' morale."

"I can vouch for that. She writes to us Marines," Maxwell said.

"Writes. I see, yeah." The officer gazed about nonchalantly. "Well, right now this broad's a witness, and some detectives want to talk to her."

Ruth looked up from the bench. "Officer, we're God-fearin' Christians. Be polite."

Selmo shrugged. "Actually, my wife and I are Jewish. God-fearing, of course."

"I don't care if you're a bunch of idol worshipers," the cop said. "The detectives want to talk to this woman, and we have things to do. Can't waste time on the bunch of you."

"They can just talk to her here," Doreen said, moving beside Selmo. "And be polite."

"And who are you?"

Doreen latched onto Selmo's arm. "I'm his wife."

"Can't the detectives come here?" Dominique asked.

The cop shook his head. "They got a guy in custody. They want her to take a look-see."

"It was dark," I said.

"They got the man shot my boy?" Ruth asked.

"I think so, ma'am."

"Is it Cornell Jones?" I asked.

"Wouldn't know, lady." He tugged on my arm, and we headed for the door.

Selmo and the Marines reluctantly stepped aside to let us pass, but as the cop started to move on, Selmo said, "Hold on. I'll take her to the precinct."

The cop said, "Dicks don't want her talking to no one."

I said, "I'm okay."

Doreen stepped up and took my other arm. "I'm riding with you."

"So am I," Dominique said.

"No one was invited," the cop said.

They formed a ring around the cop and me. The second cop, who had yet to speak, stepped into the middle of the circle and told the one who had my arm to wait. He had a boyish face and gray hair at his temples. He turned about slowly to make sure everyone paid attention.

"I'm Officer Turner. We've had a long night. We're hungry and you're tired. If we stand around bickering, we won't know who the hell they have in custody. And the doctor says the victim can't have visitors. Maybe he should rest, and so should you."

"My boy gonna be okay?" Ruth asked.

"I'm no doctor, ma'am," Officer Turner said. "The duty nurse said he was out of danger."

"I can't see him?"

"No ma'am. Not yet."

Ruth nodded. "Then I'm goin' with this girl. I wanna know who shot my boy and why."

The cop turned his attention to the younger one. "We got one big family," he said, then addressed Selmo. "Why don't you follow us to the station? Bring Miss Halvers along. That way we'll all know who the detectives arrested, and me and my partner can get a bite and some coffee. That all right with everyone?"

"Sure." Selmo turned to the others who nodded.

The cop said, "Good. We're all in agreement. You follow us, then."

"I'm too pooped to stand on my own," Ruth said, but when Dominique offered a hand, she shook it off. "Have one of them handsome boys in uniform give me hand up." She hooked her hand onto Maxwell's arm and pulled herself up. "My boy'll be fine if he just stays away from. . . . It's a crazy world, ain't it?"

"Crazy, ma'am," Maxwell said.

The sergeant at the reception desk gazed up at Officer Turner. "What'cha got, Turner?"

"The witness on that San Pedro shooting and her herd of friends, Marines, boot makers and maybe the navy and army are next," Turner said.

The sergeant told us to take a seat and made a call. A moment later, a burly detective with sleeves rolled up to the elbows came through the door. He had sharp features that belied his bulk and deep-set gray eyes that signaled that he'd suffer no foolishness. He surveyed the group, his eyes settling on Dominique first, then Doreen, and finally me.

He turned to Officer Turner. "How's it going, Matt?"

"Fine," Turner said and motioned toward me with his head. "The pretty one."

"They're all pretty," the detective said. He looked at me. "Detective Samuels, miss. We'll need a statement. Take maybe an hour. If you haven't heard yet, we've got us a suspect."

"Cornell Jones? You have him in custody?"

"Ma'am?"

"Cornell Jones, the guy who shot. . . ."

He shook his head. "No one named Jones."

I was confused. "But you said you have the guy who shot my friend."

"We got us a guy named Joseph Tinkler. You know him?"

# -35-

I SLEPT IN A SPARE bedroom at Selmo's that night. Despite Doreen's pleas for me to stay with her, I insisted on going to work the next day. Though the girls were curious and wanted details, I clammed up for fear I'd lose control. After work I changed clothes and hurried out while the others were still in the dressing room. I walked east on Harbor Boulevard and took in the salt air, hoping that solitude and movement would revive some feeling for life in me, but it did little to alleviate the feeling of guilt that pinched the back of my neck.

A group of Terminal Island workers spilled out of a ferry and began strolling along the walkway. It was reassuring to see the routine of life around me. I slipped into the throng and walked along with them, pausing to enjoy a short-lived sense of rapture when a pod of orcas began breaching the distant edge of the bay. I watched them sink from sight as the sun faded, then I started for the apartment. Two blocks into my climb I turned around. I couldn't go home, not yet and not just because the courtyard was a crime scene. I didn't want to see his blood.

Neither Dominique nor the girls had showed up when some twenty men and a woman in overalls entered Tasco's. I was nursing a third beer when to my right the woman pushed the stool aside and stood at the bar. She ordered a glass of water and a jigger of tequila and downed the tequila at once. She recovered from its bite and held the empty shot glass out.

"Barkeep, please."

Sandy filled the jigger.

"I don't drink," she said, then looked straight ahead, downed the contents, and coughed to clear her throat.

"Maybe you should try something less potent," I said.

She gulped a drink of water and ordered a third shot. I asked if she wanted to sit. She shook her head. A man touched her shoulder and said, "I was sorry to hear." She looked at him in the bar mirror, nodded, and picked up the jigger and downed the tequila.

"Are you okay?"

"No, no I'm not."

"Me either. Sandy, a shot of tequila."

Sandy squinted as he poured me a shot.

She pulled up the stool and sat. "I'm Elaine."

"Eve." I noticed her accent. "Where're you from?"

"Wichita Falls, Texas. Come here to work. No work there."

"Work?"

"Yep."

"What kind of work?"

She aimed her thumb in the general direction of the harbor. "Shipbuilding. Liberty ships."

A second man approached her, and like the other man, said he was sorry.

When he left, I asked, "What's he sorry about?"

"You gonna drink that shot?" she asked.

"I think I am."

"Chase it down with the beer."

I swallow the contents of the jigger. It burned my mouth and throat and brought something in me to life. I downed two gulps of beer and told Sandy I needed another tequila. He looked at me, shook his head, and reluctantly poured the drink.

"A man died today out there," Elaine said.

"I'm sorry." As I said it, I knew it sounded trite, nothing more than a mannered response. The jigger of tequila sat before me. I downed it. It burned a path through my throat before settling in my stomach where it seemed to glow. I ordered another and looked at Elaine.

"I'm guessing you knew him?"

"I worked beside him for two years as an electrician's helper. Yeah, I knew him. He has two kids and the meanest wife in the port. He loved her and those kids."

"Let's have another," I said.

We drank another shot apiece. She loosened up and in fits and starts told how her friend and coworker Anthony Scarafolo had died, rendering details as if she were again witnessing the circumstances of his death. She explained that when welders finish with the seals in a compartment, the compartment is flooded to check for leaks. A horn blare warns everyone before the flooding takes place. Anthony was in what she called the bottom deck wiring an aft compartment and must not have heard the horn. Elaine was at a ladder on an upper deck reeling out wire to him.

"The wire went slack. That indicated to me he was finished for the moment. Then he began tugging on the wire as if in a panic. Then that stopped suddenly. I was startled at first, then confused. What happened down there was the entire hull had been flooded. He didn't have a chance. I wasn't . . . I couldn't help."

I said, "I'm so sorry," and wrapped my arm over her shoulders.

She leaned a shoulder into me. "His wife, she loves . . .

no, loved him. She works in the cannery. He joked about her all the time being mean. What'd you say your names is?"

"Eve."

"Eve, think about it. Men dying overseas like flies, and we think we're safe. Anthony did." She wiped her eyes on her sleeves. "Don't let them see me cry. Women like me don't cry."

"I understand." I handed her my handkerchief. "You'll be fine."

"Fine? I got a husband in Europe who's going to be a stranger, and a two-year-old son, staying with a girlfriend. I'm trying like hell not to feel sorry for myself. I'll be okay. I'll feed my son and I'll go to work. But fine? I just don't know."

A shift of stevedores entered and swarmed the bar and tables. Elaine and I sat at the bar and stared at our images in the mirror. She said she'd never been drunk. I told her I'd never been drunk before, but this seemed like an appropriate time. I didn't tell her about H.T.

I woke up late the next afternoon in the apartment. My head throbbed. My eyes were crusted over. I sat up and rubbed my eyes until the room came into focus. The sight repelled me—bare walls, sun-bleached curtain blinds, water-stained ceiling. I called for Dominique, but got no response, so I threw aside the bedding and stumbled to the bathroom to vomit. All that came up was bile. I opened the blinds and discovered that I'd slept through most of the day and had missed work. Why, I wondered, hadn't Dominique awakened me?

I poured a glass of water, swallowed down two aspirins, then filled the glass again and finished that. I returned to the bathroom and studied my puffed face and red eyes in the mirror. My stomach was empty, but the thought of food revolted me. What I needed most was a slow, hot bath. I turned the faucet and watched the tub fill and steam up the room, then I dropped my robe and inched in slowly. I lay back and let the water envelop me. I saw a bruise on my knee and wondered where it had come from. Then I discovered a scrape on my elbow.

I reflected on the past days' events and decided that it mattered little that I'd missed work. At least I was alive and so was H.T., though for me, now, death seemed a better option.

I held the bar of soap to my nose and took in the scent. I tried to recall how I'd gotten home but couldn't remember. All I recalled was talking to a woman who'd lost her coworker in an accident. I lathered up the soap and thought, I have to somehow slow my world down. I promptly went to sleep.

I was still in the bathtub an hour or so later when the door opened, and Dominique called my name. Along with hers, the excited voices of Tiff, Gretchen, and Mitzi rang through the apartment. They shouted for me to come out of hiding. The water had turned cold. So, I experienced my first drunk, I thought, and hangover—and witnessed a shooting that could've killed a good man. Promising myself never again, I pulled the plug, lifted myself out of the tub, and grabbed the towel.

"In here," I shouted.

Dominique knocked. "Can I come in?"

"Hold on." It was impossible under the circumstance to preserve my dignity, but I wasn't about to surrender my modesty. I toweled off, then slipped on my robe and told her to come in.

As she opened the door, the others' conversation drifted in, talk of the shooting and H.T., and all of it came back.

Dominique said, "We decided on having a sleepover. Isn't that a swell idea? Just like young girls. Jesus, you still stink of booze."

"Still?"

"Yeah, but it's not as bad as when we brought you home."

"You brought me home?"

"We walked you. It wasn't easy. You fell a few times."

"I'm dying," I said.

"Ginger ale and chicken soup," she said.

I looked at my reflection in the mirror and my bloodshot eyes. Shameful, my mother would say. "A sleepover?" I said, "I never had one before."

"Well, tonight's it. We'll fix you up first, then eat and laugh and have a good time."

A good time? How can that be? I might recover from a hangover, but I still had to confront the events that occurred the previous days—the shooting, Tinkler, Cornell Jones, the death of a man I'd never met named Anthony Scarafolo, sad Elaine whose husband was going to return a stranger, and most of all, H.T. Ever since they'd joined up, my brothers had been at the center of my fears. Now the randomness of life seemed an equal threat.

"You're shaking," Dominique said.

"It's my fault he was shot. Mine." I looked at my hands and sat down on the toilet seat.

"It's okay. Get it out." She wrapped her arm around me. "You go ahead and cry."

"No. I won't."

Tiff knocked on the door and said, "Hey, gals, what's the hold up."

I squirmed away from Dominique. I didn't want to be babied. I wanted to be a farm girl. No, a woman like Elaine, a woman who didn't cry.

"We're coming," Dominique said. "Aren't we?"

"I wish I could cry, Dom. It's terrible. I think I love him."

Dominique stared. "Sweet Jesus, can't you wait to grow up first?"

The hangover had temporarily cured me of further self-flagellation. The headache was gone, my body was limbering up, and my stomach was settled down. Now, more than anything, what I felt was numb. I heard familiar noises coming from the courtyard, the sounds of planting season in the Palouse hills.

"What's going on outside?"

"The cops are digging up the garden."

"Why?"

"They think there's a body buried there. A woman's body."

"No. A body?"

"Yes. The detectives said Tinkler escaped from the state mental institution in Atascadero three years ago and came here. It's possible he killed his aunt and took over managing the apartment building. They have been unable to find her and believe she's in the garden."

"But why would he shoot H.T.?"

"I don't know. The cops think he was trying to kill both of you."

How, I wondered, could matters take such a terrible turn? I felt a deep sense of guilt. Who would have guessed Tinkler was capable of such an act? He was odd and cantankerous but seemed harmless. What was his motive? Did he harbor that much hatred for blacks? Or was it some other twisted notion, such as protecting his garden? Then it occurred to me that he'd shot a man I might be in love with.

# -36-

Before we were relieved by the late crews, Selmo brought his milk box out and turned off the conveyor. He cleared his throat and said, "We may not have heard of a place called the Gulf of Leyte, but we've all heard of MacArthur. He landed on shore and said, 'I have returned.' The Third Fleet engaged in a naval battle."

He didn't mention "our boys" as he usually did, just that our naval forces had defeated the Japanese. He began clapping and signaled for us to join him. All of us grinning, we clapped for a time and stopped when Selmo did. I saw tears flowing down Tiff's cheeks.

Selmo stepped down from his milk box and came to her. "Are you okay?"

"No. Emory is with the Third Fleet. I hope he wasn't. . . ."

"Emory?"

She showed him her ring.

"Congratulations," he said. "Let's go to work."

I remembered then that my brother August was also with the Third Fleet.

The following day I asked Dominique to sit at my station and excused myself from work early. I went to the hospital hoping for good news. I told the nurse at the desk of the intensive care ward that I was there to see Howard Elders. She looked me over and said, "Relatives only."

"He's my fiancé."

I saw disapproval in her expression as she pointed to a room across the hall. "Don't stay long. He's not ready for visitors."

He looked up as I entered, then turned his head away without speaking. He wore an oxygen mask, was on an IV drip and had a tube draining fluid from his chest.

I eased up to his bed. "Can you talk?"

He shook his head and his eyes drifted to the ceiling. I laid my hand atop his.

"I met your mother."

He nodded.

"I told the nurse I was your fiancée, so she'd let me see you. I want to help if you need anything?"

He blinked in response.

"It wasn't Cornell. The police say that Tinkler, the manager, shot you. They think he may have killed his aunt. She was the owner of the apartments."

H.T. whispered something I couldn't hear. I leaned closer. "What was that?"

He whispered again and it sounded like he said, "It's a mean world."

"Yes. Mean."

He licked his lips and closed his eyes. His breathing slowed and he drifted off.

Outside the room nurses and orderlies talked as they scurried up and down the hallways. I pulled the chair up next to the bed and for a time watched him sleep. Eventually exhaustion overtook me, and I fell asleep. Someone shook my shoulder in what seemed a dream—Mother waking me, telling me she needed the plate, the plate was gone. I blinked and looked up.

Ruth asked, "How long you been here?"

I couldn't answer her because the dream was still working on my mind.

"You okay, hon?"

I nodded. A large elderly man in a charcoal-gray suit and black shirt with a clerical collar stood in the doorway, in his hand a *King James Bible*. He had broad shoulders and his mahogany-colored forehead glistened under the white overhead light. He smiled gravely, which made him appear more imposing.

"I brung Reverend Pitts to pray for my boy," Ruth said, as if an explanation was needed.

H.T. still slept. I stood and found enough voice to apologize, for what, I was unsure, but it seemed an apology was called for. I stepped aside and offered her the chair. The preacher came to the foot of the bed. He was taller than H.T. and had fearsome eyes, but there was something else about him that intimidated me, something I couldn't put into words.

He glanced at me. "What's your name, child?" His gentle voice belied the intense eyes and imposing frame.

"Eve."

"Ah, the mother of us all. The seed of original sin. Are you a believer?" His eyes seemed to soften as he waited for an answer.

I let my arms hang. "Sort of."

"There is no *sort of*, child." He looked gravely at H.T. "Come Judgment Day the lukewarm will be spurned, and the righteous will leave them behind. The sinner will feed from fire the field he's harrowed or repent to find heaven's pastures. It all begins with believing."

I pursed my lips and stood mute.

"Is this the one?" he asked Ruth.

"Yes, she's the one," Ruth said.

H.T. awoke and struggled to bring the room into focus. He looked from the preacher to his mother to me.

The preacher, his stern gaze on me, said, "Sin, small or large, shall be punished."

"Excuse me. What sin?"

He merely stared.

"I should go," I said and slowly backpedaled to the door and left.

The preacher's voice trailed behind me in the hallway. Random thoughts clogged my mind as I hurried to the elevator. What fine words would my mother have for me? The field won't plow itself. What exactly did that mean? Mom's preacher told me once when I was barely seven that my sins were many. What was sin? Was a fleeting kiss a sin or something pure?

The nurse behind the ward desk asked, "Are you alright?"

Without answering, I pressed the button.

An orderly rolled an empty gurney to a stop and said, "Slowest elevators in L.A."

An exit sign above a door at the end of the hallway caught my eye. I hurried to the door and descended the stairs two at a time. In the lobby I slowed, and once outside, I rested my back against the trunk of palm tree. Angry, I caught my breath and watched people enter and leave the lobby and realized that life still pulsed around me and that I needed to somehow rekindle that sense of life inside myself.

Two days passed before I returned to the hospital after work. Again, I told the duty nurse I was H.T.'s fiancée and again I received a judgmental raising of the eyebrows.

The tubes in his chest were gone, he was no longer on

oxygen, but was still hooked up to a drip line and catheter. He lay looking at the ceiling. He turned his head to see who'd entered. I smiled. He nodded.

"How are you?"

He forced a smile. "You're the only one today who didn't come in here with a needle. They're movin' me tomorrow. A convalescent ward. Means I'm better."

But they didn't move him the next day because he had a relapse.

# -37-

SELMO APPROACHED ME AS THE crew was being relieved by the night shift and informed me that, following a second operation, H.T. had been moved to a convalescent ward. "Ruth says he's not the same. I don't know what that means, but he can see visitors. You don't have to be family."

I turned down an invitation to go to Tasco's with the girls and went to the hospital.

The ward had twelve beds, six on each side. All but three were occupied. H.T. lay in the fourth bed from the end on the right. In a bed beside his lay a middle-aged man with tissue-thin skin and a mop of unruly gray hair. They were talking. The patients watched me as I entered the aisle between the beds. The older man pointed in my direction.

"I think you got a visitor Howard," the gray-haired man said.

Though he was on the mend, H.T. was obviously weakened. With so many eyes on us I didn't kiss him as I'd intended. Instead, I took his hand and squeezed it. A patient across the aisle got out of his bed and pushed a chair next to H.T.'s bed.

"Here, sit," he said.

"This is the Eve I told you about, Harold," H.T. said.

"Nice to meet you," said the older patient. "You two have a lot to talk about. Howard, we'll talk about *Native Son* later." That said, he rolled over, his back to us.

"We talk about books we read," H.T. said.

My early impressions of H.T. came not just from his playing the harmonica, but because he always seemed to have a book in hand on his lunch breaks.

"He's a teacher," H.T. whispered.

He yawned as he asked about Lucien's. I said the girls wanted to hear about his progress.

"The police took a statement from me. It wasn't helpful." He yawned again. "I'm tired."

His eyelids drooped. I patted his hand and stood to leave.

He shook his head. "Stay a second. Did you know they wanted to move me to another location?"

"Move you? Where?"

"Hospital near downtown L.A. Selmo stopped it. A Marine colonel he knows argued with whoever's in charge here and said I was a critical employee in the defense industry. Know what that means?"

"No."

"Means we're important, this dolly pushin' man and needle drivin' lady. Sounds like a song, don't it?" He grinned broadly. "Will you get me some library books?"

That seemed an encouraging signal that he wanted to see me again. "Sure. What do you want me to find?"

He turned and looked at Harold as he said, "*Native Son.* And. . . ."

The man rolled over to face us. "*The Varieties of Religious Experience.* William James."

The titles seemed odd. I'd not heard of either book. "Okay. I'll get them."

Just then a voice boomed behind me. "If it isn't Eve vistin' our brother."

The Reverend Pitts had brought three women and a man with him. Absent was Ruth Elders. With no hesitation the group circled around the bed.

Reverend Pitts, who stood at the foot of the bed, said, "We come to offer up a prayer for our brother Howard Thomas, Miss Eve. You're welcome to join us."

The group joined hands and the woman closest to me took mine. I looked questioningly at H.T., who nodded. For too long I'd witnessed Mother's futile efforts at prayer, asking for my father's return. I'd lost faith in prayer and felt like a hypocrite as I bowed my head.

The preacher began. "Lord, we're here to beg You, in Your Mercy, to forgive our brother's sins and help him heal. Not just his body, but his soul. We pray for him also to return to Your flock. We will embrace him and give him whatever guidance he may need. May you also shower Miss Eve with mercy. This we ask in Your son's name."

They breathed out an "Amen" as one and dropped their hands to their sides.

"We come on behalf of your mother, H.T. She worries about you, the places you go to and," He looked at me. "The company you keep."

H.T. and I exchanged glances. I said, "Excuse me, I think should leave now."

"No need you leavin', Eve." The preacher flashed a smile. "You're among friends."

The woman who'd been holding my hand, reached over and patted my arm.

"Yes, I think I should go. Is there anything I can bring you, H.T.?"

He licked his lips. "Just *Native Son*. I've been meaning to read it. And the other."

The preacher raised the Bible. "Here's the only book you need, son."

I leaned over the bed and said softly. "I'll bring it. I need to talk to you."

# -38-

As I rode to the hospital, I finished part of a lengthy essay theorizing that culture serves an individual and society indirectly and not the other way. How the theory translated into reality or why the retired teacher wanted H.T. to read it, was lost on me, but I'd taken on the duty of supplying library books. The volume was *A Scientific Theory of Culture and Other Essays* by Bronislaw Malinowski. Published that spring, it had been checked out at the Los Angeles Central Library by one person—me. It was hardly what I'd pick to read while riding a streetcar ride; however, H.T. had fallen under the spell of Harold who'd taught classics at a prep school, and he'd insisted that H.T. read Malinowski.

As the streetcar neared my stop, I was happy to close the book. I tucked the book under my arm and started the uphill walk. It was dark by the time I covered the six blocks to the hospital. Cornell had been arrested on a new charge and the detectives had assured me the court wouldn't grant him bail again. Between work and my visits to the hospital I'd all but put the pimp out of mind. I hoped for a few private minutes with H.T. Too much was still left unsaid.

As did other civilian hospitals along the coast, Sisters of Mary took in soldiers recovering from battle wounds or those who needed extended care or specialty operations. The staff was taxed by the demands. On my last visit a nurse said she anticipated all the wards filling up soon because of the shortage of beds at Fort MacArthur Army Hospital. Already four convalescents in H.T.'s ward were amputees who'd lost limbs in the South Pacific. One of them, a boy named Leonard, had become a favorite. He'd lost his right arm and sight in his left eye in a battle in the Pacific. He was from Alabama, barely literate, and unabashedly blurted out in a strong southern accent whatever was on his mind.

I peered into the room. The preacher thankfully wasn't there. I didn't need more preaching. Leonard saw me and said, "Miss Eve, I'm goin' home. Least ways, that's what I'm told. A hospital nearby'll fix me up with an arty-ficial arm."

"That's good," I said, stepping in. "Your family's lucky you're going home."

He lifted his still-bandaged stub. "They can call me Private Hook."

In a weakened voice, Harold said, "Don't be morbid, Leonard." Nearing sixty, Harold was being treated for cancer and his skin had the waxy cast of a worn lampshade. He turned his head to me. "Well, hello, Eve. We heard rumors."

I smiled. "What kind?"

"That you ran off with some traveling Bible salesman."

I looked at H.T. and said, "I changed my mind. Too many handsome guys here."

A kid named Ernie said, "She belongs with us because she's obviously blind."

Harold pointed a finger at H.T. "See, that's the kind of irony we were talking about, H.T. It raises a question about what happens to the part of the brain used for vision if one can't see." He looked about at the other patients and received their silence. "Well, think about it."

"Can't I think about my girlfriend instead?" Adam, a one-legged patient, said.

"It's your brain. Use it if you can," Thomas, a sailor with one foot, injected.

Except for Harold, all were young. Though some weren't physically whole, most had kept their sense of humor. They teased one another and sometimes me and the nurses. While I'd witnessed cynicism in the ward, I'd also seen hope.

H.T. said, "You find the book?"

I handed him the book. "It kills me to let go of it. I fell in love with the guy's ideas."

H.T. placed the book under his pillow and said, "I'll read it in my sleep."

"From what I read, you sure will."

The others laughed. H.T. stood to join, but his chest began convulsing. He sat back down. The others watched. When the coughing spell ended, he pulled the book from under his pillow, opened it, and began reading.

"Glad I came to see you?" I said.

Leonard said, "Miss Eve, I told H.T. us should get together in Alabama someday and meet my family. He said I was one hell of dreamer."

"It's not a bad dream," Harold said. "We're only here because of circumstance of health, but look, we are together. If they learn to dream it, healthy people might also come together."

Leonard winked at me. "Yes, sir, you're right. Ain't a bad dream at all. I'd be proud to have H.T. and Miss Eve come to visit. What say you, Miss Eve?"

I blushed. H.T. glanced up at me and then returned to reading. Since the night of the shooting, he'd given no indication of the two of us sharing a future. Any future I saw was full of pitfalls. Still, I wondered if it were possible—if we were free of the influence of his mother, the preacher, and the staring judgments of strangers.

Leonard saw he'd embarrassed me. "Well, I ain't so sure my daddy would take to the idea. Old ideas don't die easy, you know."

Harold said, "Those aren't ideas; they're beliefs."

"They're the only ideas my family ever gave me. But no more."

Thomas, a double amputee from Nevada, said, "Let's all meet in Elko."

Ernie, the one the others called Jarhead, spoke up. "I heard it's not on the map."

Thomas said, "Eve, you know where it is, right?"

"It's in Utah," I said, knowing it was in Nevada. I looked at H.T., who was either deep into Malinowski's theory or lost in his own thoughts.

Thomas said, "Ernie, you'd like Elko. Probably like the cathouses most." He looked at me. "Excuse me, ma'am, I didn't mean to offend."

"It's okay. I like cats," I said.

The others laughed. Thomas's cheeks turned crimson. He reminded me of August. I envisioned him, his fingers cold and black from gathering coal on the railroad tracks, bringing his hard-gained treasure into the house and setting it down in front of the stove and apologizing because he couldn't find more.

The talk continued. I listened and didn't. At one point the exchanges got rowdy. The men seemed unaware of it until a nurse looked in and said, "Excuse me!" She stood in the doorway and waited until she had the men's attention. The men looked sheepishly at her.

"It's a hospital. Don't make me return with a needle and

syringe and give the bunch of you something to calm you down."

They apologized, but as soon as she left, they laughed. She stuck her head back in the doorway. "I'll gag you if I have to." She looked at me. "Keep them in line."

This time no one laughed.

H.T.'s guitar sat beside the bed. He motioned me over. "Been meaning to ask. Can you ask some of the ladies to come up for a visit?"

I tried not to look disappointed. "I'll see." I wondered how the girls would handle four amputees, a man wasting from cancer, a preacher who debates articles of faith against classical philosophy. How would they weigh that experience against a dance at the USO?

"Maybe," he said, "if one has a library card, she might get us a couple more books too."

"I'll see." I stood and asked. "Does anyone need help to write a letter?"

One of the newer arrivals held up a right hand that was missing a thumb. "Hi, I'm Ken, Kenneth." His left arm had been amputated at the shoulder. "I can kind of write, but the pens don't work so well when I do." He gave me a boyish smile.

"If the nurse can get some stationery, I'll be happy to write a letter for you."

I did. It would be the first of many I would come to write for the amputees and the blind.

# -39-

IT WAS LATE IN NOVEMBER when I climbed onto the streetcar and paid my fare. I sat worried about H.T. and why his release was continually delayed. Two women seated nearby talked about the Allies who were fighting a stalemate with the Germans in the North Apennines. The Apennines, I thought, such a beautiful name. It sounded like a place where skiers vacationed and couples honeymooned. I wondered if there would be an escape for me, for me and one for H.T. who'd suffered a spell with pneumonia. He'd been moved out of the ward for three days until able to breathe normally, then returned to his same bed. His health seemed improved, but still the doctors wouldn't release him.

In days that had lapsed since the shooting, H.T. had been central to my thoughts. I'd begun to shed my illusions about experiencing the bubbling happiness that Tiff and Emory shared. I didn't want a ring to slip onto my finger or people crowded around and congratulating us. I didn't even expect the trappings of romantic love or marriage. I only hoped to say that I was open to us becoming more than friends and having that grow into something special, that I knew what the barriers were, and that the world would judge us harshly. I would assure him I was up to it.

I stepped down from the streetcar and walked to the

hospital a little past 7:00 in the evening. The men were talking, but when I entered, the conversation ceased. They turned their attention to me for a moment and said their hellos. Reverend Pitts, a big man under normal condition, appeared even more imposing tonight owing to the black suit he wore and clerical collar that seemed too small for his thick neck. He stood beside Harold's bed.

"Let me have your hand, brother," he said.

Harold shook his head.

"What's it gonna hurt?"

I was confused. I looked to H.T. He placed a finger to his lips.

Harold surrendered a hand to Reverend Pitts, who took it in both hands, told him to close his eyes, and uttered a blessing, and placed a hand gently on the sick man's chest. "Do you feel closer, my friend?"

Harold shook his head. "Reverend, you shouldn't try to sell paintings to blind man."

On prior occasions I'd witnessed the two of them argue politely over differing religious views. Harold, a self-proclaimed agnostic and skeptic, seemed to enjoy the back and forth with the preacher. Reverend Pitts, though patient, seemed more duty bound as he spoke of God and doctrines of faith. The others occasionally took sides, but more often watched the exchanges.

"Well, the journey is longer for some than others." Reverend swung his huge frame around and came toward H.T. By then I'd delivered *The Good Earth* to him and was standing beside the bed.

The preacher took H.T.'s hands in his and said, "Have you thought about my ideas?"

"I have."

I didn't want to witness what I was sure would come about. I stood to leave.

"I'd like to include you too, Miss Eve," the preacher said.

My pulse jumped. "I had a rough day. I should go."

"Surely you're not leaving because of me."

"No. I have to go." I turned to leave.

H.T. said, "Wait for me."

As I waited in the hallway, I heard the preacher say, "Let her go, brother." H.T stepped out of the ward. Making small talk, he asked how work was going.

"Selmo has a new man working the dock. Otherwise, it's the same. Are you coming back soon?"

He stared off as if he didn't hear the question. His eyes seemed clearer somehow, and he appeared younger and eager for something. "What are you mad at?" he asked.

It seemed a strange question. "I'm not."

"I know about being mad. You're mad about something. You don't like Reverend Pitts. Don't you believe?"

"I don't talk about my beliefs. I've been waiting to talk with you alone. I was. . . ."

He shook his head. "He's pushing me hard to sing in his choir and join the God fearing."

"Is that what you want?"

"Want?" He pursed his lips and scratched his chin. "In that pond, I didn't think about dying. I thought, what if I can't sing again? I want to sing, but not to build a bridge to heaven. The blues is about carrying a cross, not singing to one. Me getting shot was like building a stronger bridge to songs I want to sing."

"I've wanted to tell you that I'm sorry. It was my fault. I realized it even more when I found out it was Tinkler who shot you. He did it because of me."

"No, he did it because of hate. Hate. The world's full of it. The Japanese hate Americans. We hate them. The Germans hate the Russians and us. There will always be hate, especially for a man like me."

"Like you?"

He lifted his sleeve and exposed his forearm. "Hate for this color."

He pulled his sleeve down and smiled. "Music, words, and not guns are the answer to hate. The blues is about love and pain. Never hate."

I touched my palm to his cheek. "You've changed."

"Harold's dyin', but still reaching out for life. I never had a father, and he never had a son. In there I found the man I'd always wanted as a father. He needs me to look out for him after he leaves here." He took my hand. "That's the blues."

He aimed a thumb at the door. "In here I met these good men. I'm not mad about being shot or being cut in prison. Not seeing what those boys . . . men went through, what they gave. I've sung for them. Harold says I'm obligated to sing to tell their story. Said that could be my payment. It makes sense here." He pointed to his heart.

I resisted an urge to touch his cheek again. "Next time I come I'd like to hear you sing."

"I might be out soon. If you'd invite some of the ladies, it might help those guys, especially Ernie and that kid Jerry, who never talks."

"I asked the girls. No one showed much enthusiasm. But I'll come and help write letters."

"Thanks for coming and bringing the book. All the books."

"You're welcome."

The preacher poked his head into the hallway.

I squeezed H.T.'s hand, said "Goodnight," and headed for the staircase with the feeling that H.T. had, in his way, said farewell to me.

Reverend Pitts called my name as I neared the door leading to the staircase. I ignored him, opened the door, and let it shut behind me. I reminded myself that women like me don't cry. I stepped down on the first flight successfully, my knees trembled, and they didn't stop trembling until I reached the sidewalk.

# -40-

MITZI AND DOMINIQUE DECIDED THE three of us should spend Sunday afternoon at the park before we went to the hospital. We packed a picnic and brought a blanket. The day was pleasant, a bit hazy, but fine enough for a stroll. We rode a merry-go-round and swung on the swings. At noon we spread the blanket on the lawn and opened our lunches.

"I wish I could come here every day," Mitzi said.

"You can, but you'd probably starve without work," Dominique said.

"Makes me wonder what kind of freedom my husband and the others are fighting for," Mitzi said.

We looked at her in amazement. "What?" Dominique asked.

She pointed around the park. "I mean, are they defending the freedom to enjoy this?"

Ducks and geese bobbed on the manmade lake. A man in a small boat rowed a woman around the island in the center. The woman broke off a piece of bread and held it to his mouth. On the other side of the lake, four ladies, looking much like figures in an Impressionist painting, walked the shoreline. Elderly and elegantly dressed in ankle-length skirts, they twirled parasols and chatted. As they came toward our side, they seemed to float atop the walkway.

I pointed to them. "They look like they stepped out of a book of tomorrow's promises."

"Oh, Jesus. Eve, the poet!" Dominique said. "They're four old ladies who poisoned their lover after they discovered he'd been bedding each of them to get their money."

Mitzi said, "They're just four nice old women, like we'll be someday."

"Speak for yourself. I'm not getting older," Dominique said. "And I hope I'm not nice."

"You will be, Dominique. Despite yourself," I said.

A short silence followed as we watched the women pass by.

"Is this a good idea?" Mitzi asked.

"Is what a good idea?" I asked.

"Going to the hospital. I've never been around men without legs or arms," she said.

Dominique grinned. "You've been around men without brains. If that doesn't make you act strange, you'll be okay with a missing arm."

I watched the ladies with the parasols progress toward a flotilla of ducks on the pond. "Let's come back in fifty years dressed like them and walk the shore. Wouldn't it be great?"

"Hard to imagine, isn't it?" Mitzi said. "Us that old. What do you do then?"

Dominique laughed. "What are we doing right now?"

"Can I have my husband back first? And daughter? Have my family together? Or do I just work and get old and dress funny forty years from now?" Mitzi said. "Even if this war has strengthened people's resolve and brought us together, it's cost us dearly. One sad reason I rarely mention my husband and daughter is that they've become strangers."

"Eve, a poet. Now Mitzi, a philosopher," Dominique said. "But I do understand, Mitzi. My son's a stranger. Let's go and not worry about forty years from now. Let's enjoy the day."

We walked the path around the lake. I paused to check the heel of my shoe. By chance, I looked toward the benches and the sycamores between the lake and the avenue. A lone figure caught my eye, a dark-skinned man wearing a fedora. He seemed to have been looking in my direction. He immediately walked off. I called out to Mitzi and Dominique, told them to look, but neither saw him, nor did I again.

Whatever reservations Mitzi had about our visiting the ward vanished when we entered. I introduced each of them to the patients and my friends shook each man's hand. Leonard offered both his good hand and his stub to Mitzi and said, "Take your pick." The room fell into laughter. The ward nurse stuck her head in the doorway and told us to hold the noise down.

Over the next hour Dominique and Mitzi took turns sitting beside beds. They played a game of rummy with one patient, checkers with another, and helped one compose a letter to his family. The men, relaxed as they were, smiled and talked openly about missing family and friends and the men they'd served with. They described their hometowns, their girlfriends, or wives, even their pets. What they didn't discuss was war experiences. By the time we'd exhausted the hour the men seemed more whole than broken.

His guitar strung over his shoulder, H.T., who'd been discharged, limped into the room. When he saw the girls with me, he motioned me out into the hallway.

I stepped out. "You're getting around just fine."

"Fine. I was down in a ward playing for some folks. Thanks for bringing the ladies."

"You're welcome. Are you going to sing?"

"What would you like to hear?"

"Your voice."

# -41-

NOVEMBER CAME AND, WITH IT, Roosevelt's reelection, the sweep through France and Belgium by Allied Forces, and the lopsided naval victory by Americans in the Gulf of Leyte. All had raised everyone's spirits. Now, weeks before Christmas, the Allies were pushing Germans back, though cold weather had slowed the armored units as they neared the Rhineland. The momentum and God, as the Reverend Pitts proclaimed during one of my hospital visits, were on the Allies' side.

All of L.A. seemed in a holiday mood, but hanging over my season were Doreen's proposition and Dominique's advice to forget H.T. What mostly occupied my thoughts was the fact that Cornell had somehow been granted bail and was again on the streets.

H.T. had long since been released from the hospital, but he didn't return to work at Lucien's. The girls speculated on why he wasn't at work, but it remained a mystery to them and me as well. I asked Selmo about it, but all he would say was that H.T. had a job when he was ready to come to work. I continued to visit the men in the convalescent ward and write letters for them. Some of those I'd come to know left. Fresh ones replaced them. In addition to writing their letters, I began writing in my journal, sometimes documenting what they told me, other times what I imagined they hadn't told me. I didn't know at the time that I was experimenting with fiction.

H.T. visited on weekday afternoons when I couldn't be there. The ward nurse told me he brought his guitar and harmonica and spent his time playing for patients. He even entertained the nurses and doctors in the cafeteria. She said that he had a rich voice and a kindly manner, and he was welcomed wherever he went in the hospital as a kind of hero.

As the holidays neared, Dominique asked for a week's vacation to spend with her son. The Friday before she left, she toted a shopping bag and a dwarf Christmas tree into the apartment. By then we'd more than adjusted to the idea of living above "the crime scene." Standing upright the tree barely came to my waist. We propped it up in front of the window, popped popcorn. We strung puffs of corn together and laid them over the boughs. She opened the shopping bag and took out a bottle of Cabernet Sauvignon. We uncorked it, sat on the floor, and sipped it out of teacups instead of glasses.

Decorating the pathetic tree had done little to raise my spirits. I took a sip of wine and said, "This doesn't feel like Christmas."

"No? I'll fix that." She got up and tuned the radio to a station playing Christmas music. When she sat back down, she fidgeted about as "Oh, Holy Night" played. When the song finished, she picked up the bottle and gulped down what remained of the wine.

"The music isn't fixing it," I said.

"I know. I want to spend Christmas with you, Eve, but I'm going to my parents. I need to. I feel bad leaving you here."

I'd been expecting it. "I know. That's probably the best Christmas present you could get."

"Silent Night" began playing over the radio and Dominique sang along. After it finished, she said, "When I heard that the first time, I heard 'round yon virgin' as 'Round John Virgin'. Isn't that funny? I mean, strange?"

"No. I heard it the same way. You drank all the wine."

"Yes, I did. I'm sorry."

Thinking that doing so might get me in the spirit of Christmas, I'd gone on a spending spree buying presents—a crystal seagull for Mitzi, an ice-cream maker for Tiff, an onyx ashtray for Gretchen, and a silk scarf for Dominique. I found a shawl for Mother, a lampshade for my sister Helen, and a porcelain doll for Avis that I'd sent off before the first of December. The last gift I intended to purchase was a hat for H.T.

"Wait here." I went to my bedroom where I got Dominique's gift from under the bed. I'd not wrapped the presents yet. She was sitting cross-legged in front of the tree when I returned. I sat the box on her lap. "Merry Christmas."

She looked up, blinked, and looked at the box as if deciding what to do.

"Open it," I said.

"I can't. It's not Christmas and I didn't get you anything. There's nothing under the tree. The presents I bought are for my boy." She bowed her head. "I'm trying to buy my way back into his life. I'm as pathetic as the tree."

I sat beside her, took the box, and opened it. She watched the silk scarf come out. I folded it in a triangle, placed it on her head and tied the ends in a bow under her chin.

She touched it. "It's beautiful."

"On you, yes. You'll be back before Christmas, and we'll open another bottle of wine."

Early the next morning Tiff came by with a box of homemade cookies for me to take to the ward. She walked Dominique and me to the streetcar terminal and waited beside us until our streetcar arrived. Dominique and I said our goodbyes at

Union Station, then I went downtown to buy a hat for H.T. I intended to leave it for him at the hospital.

An hour later I mounted the streetcar and swung into a seat. I set the box containing the hat beside me. The streetcar pulled away from the curb, and as it did a woman across the aisle commented about the wonderful weather.

"But no white Christmas here," she said.

It seemed to me Angelinos were obsessed with their mild weather. "No. Not here," I said.

Some men nearby speculated on the progress of war.

"We'll have 'em licked by New Year's," a man said.

Slapping his thigh, another said, "That'd bring out the champagne."

"If the damned Germans left any for us to drink," a third one said.

Outside the streetcar people in casual dress strolled the sidewalks. In ways I too was now an Angelino, privileged with good weather and spare money, but I wasn't in the state of mind to enjoy any of it. I'd once hoped to leave the snow and cold behind, but without those and the smell of wood burning in a fireplace the season seemed hollow. The California Christmas dream existed in window dressings. I longed for a moment with my mother and brothers, listening to lively exchanges as a log glowed on the fireplace.

The streetcar stopped a block short of my destination. A woman across the aisle swung out of her seat. "My street," she said. "Merry Christmas," the first stranger to say it.

"And to you." I gathered up my packages and readied myself for my stop.

Along the walk to the hospital, I shifted my load back and forth, trying to balance it and keep my purse strap on my shoulder. When I reached the hospital, I crossed the lobby, and rather than wait for the sluggish elevator, I turned to the first door on the right to take the stairs. My mind on what I'd do in the ward, I started up. At the second landing a man in a white orderly's tunic and trousers sat on the stairs, smoking. Except to notice he appeared to be black, I paid no attention. He stubbed out the cigarette and stood when I rounded the rail.

I said, "Hello," and moved to the right to pass by his outstretched legs.

He sprang to his feet and blocked my path. "Remember me?"

Before I could answer, Cornell clamped a hand over my mouth, locked the other around my throat, and dug his thumb into the soft center of my throat. The cookies and hat box fell to the stairs. I clenched my hand and struck a blow that glanced off his forehead.

"Ain't nothin', girl." He pressed me into the wall, leaned his weight against me and sunk his thumbs into the hollow of my throat. The pain made my legs buckle. In my desperation I managed to summon enough strength to rake my fingernails down the side of his face.

"White bitch," he muttered.

He let go with one hand and slapped my face. The blow snapped my head back. He immediately placed both hands on my throat again and pressed his weight into me. I clawed at his face and drew blood. Then a ringing sound erupted in my head, and I lost all strength and surrendered to what seemed inevitable. My body went limp. The stairwell blurred. The world seemed liquid. I felt his hands ease their grip on my throat.

He whispered, "Quiet, bitch." He lifted me from the rail and braced me against the wall.

The ringing in my ears ceased, replaced by a whistling that resounded in my clouded mind.

Cornell gripped a clump of my hair in one hand and pressed his forearm into my chin. "Don't say nothin', bitch." His foul breath wrapped around my face.

Weakened and disoriented, I gasped in some air. It felt like sandpaper going down my windpipe, but it restored me enough that I regained my senses. The whistling wasn't in my head, and it was getting closer as the footsteps from above neared. I recognized the whistler's song.

As the last note of "Amazing Grace" ended a voice said, "Hello."

Cornell pinned me to the rail with one arm and reached for something under his hospital jacket. Despite his forearm pressing on my chest, I could breathe, and with each breath the stairwell came into better focus. A glossy black shoe appeared on the turn above us. Then, his knuckles protruding like rivets, Reverend Pitt's large hand slid down the rail.

He saw me pinned against the wall. "What's going on here?"

Cornell said, "Me an' my woman's havin' a talk. Go on an' mind your own self."

"I'll just do that." The preacher advanced as if to round the stairs.

"Easy, friend," Cornell said and turned to watch the preacher pass by.

Cornell loosened his hold enough that it allowed me to collapse to my knees. I quickly removed one heel and when he reached to pull me up, I swung the shoe heel first and it struck the bridge of his nose. I saw in his free hand what he had reached for earlier.

"He's got a gun!"

Before he could raise it, I wrapped my arms around his forearm and bit the hand holding the pistol. He stumbled as he tried to free his hand, but I continued biting even as both men plunged to the floor. I heard the sharp report of the revolver going off beside my head. I felt the sting of gun powder. After that everything became opaque.

As the stairwell gradually came into focus, I found myself on my back, my ears ringing. The air in the cramped space smelled of gunpowder and singed hair. I needed to relieve my bladder.

"Eve, it's okay," the preacher said. "I need you to . . . Eve! Pay attention."

I rolled onto my hands and knees, spat blood on the stairwell floor and mumbled, "No, no." Touching my hand gently to my forehead, I slowly sat up. I felt a knot, but I wasn't bleeding. The Reverend Pitts had the pimp pinned to the floor on his back. Rubbing the knuckles on his right hand, he sat astraddle Cornell. He flicked his fingers as if they'd gone to sleep, then picked up the revolver and shoved it into his belt.

"Is he dead?" I asked.

He stood and looked down at Cornell. "Should be if anyone should."

Cornell moaned and opened his eyes. "What the. . . .?" he said and tried to rise.

The preacher straddled him again, gripped Cornell's collar and, with a kind of calm efficiency, smashed a fist into his jaw. Cornell's head bounced off the concrete. Reverend Pitts gripped the collar again and cocked his fist ready to strike, but there was no need. He looked at me. "Used to be a ruffian myself. Swore off it, though. Until now." He winked. "The Lord'll forgive me this one time."

I started to thank him, but my voice had quit me. I touched my throat gingerly as the preacher stripped the white orderly jacket off the pimp and used the sleeves to bind his arms.

"You know this guy?" he asked.

I nodded, then pointed to my throat to indicate I couldn't speak.

"Go find help," he said.

I didn't move right away. The box containing H.T.'s hat caught my attention. Crushed in the struggle, it lay beside Cornell, a further desecration of Christmas. I pulled myself together and began my descent to the lobby. Before I reached the next landing, someone flung the lobby door open. Two orderlies and a nurse, apparently drawn by the sound of the gunshot, stepped in the stairwell. They seemed as startled to see me as I was grateful to see them. I pointed up the stairs and tried to speak. Nothing resembling words came out. I collapsed into the arms of one of the confused orderlies.

Along with a bruised throat, I had injuries to my shoulder and back and an abrasion on the side of my head, all superficial. The nurse who treated me seemed certain I'd suffered no concussion but said that a doctor would have to check me further. She said I was incredibly lucky and left me on the examining table.

Three detectives walked into the treatment room and began firing off questions. When it became apparent I could barely talk, one left for a time and returned with a clipboard, a notepad, and a pen. He set them beside me. Two cops left to find the preacher. The one who remained to monitor me paced nearby as I wrote my statement. I scribbled down what I recalled. His pacing distracted me and made it hard to concentrate.

In mid stride, he paused. "Assaulted in a hospital, and no doctor around to treat you. What luck!"

I looked up, nodded, and went back to writing.

He said, "I understand the preacher who was visiting a

patient chose that moment to return to his church and write a sermon. Lucky you."

I'd again lost my train of thought and remembered the cookies. I jotted down on the paper that the cookies were for men in the ward and I needed them. I held the clipboard up and motioned him over.

He read my note and said, "The paper's there for your statement."

I jabbed the pen insistently at the words.

He took the clipboard, tore off the note, and handed the board back with a fresh sheet of paper. "Just give us a statement, please."

He continued his pacing as before. I was truly tired of cops and hospitals and statements. Grudgingly, I began anew. After several trips back and forth he leaned against the wall. I came to the part in my statement where I had to explain what had happened after I bit Cornell. I couldn't say exactly. I touched my hair. It had been singed from the bullet flash. I felt a lump on the back of my head and figured I must have struck my head when I fell.

The officer noticed that I'd stopped writing and cleared his throat. I felt as if in these past months I'd met every officer on the Los Angeles Police Department and, in him, all of them were here. I glanced up to show that I was annoyed.

He held his hands out and looked at his fingernails. "How's it going?"

I shook my head and continued writing. He came to my side and looked over my shoulder. I stopped writing.

"Maybe it's me. I make people nervous, even my wife. You want me to go?"

I nodded.

"I'll be out in the hall." He went to the door and opened it. Outside Reverend Pitts was recounting to another detective what had happened. It occurred to me that I owed him a great debt. I wondered when he might call that debt in. I fumbled with the pen, scratched a sentence down, and read what I'd written. The statement didn't seem important, so I set the pad aside without finishing it.

A doctor checked my eyes with a light beam and asked a series of questions. My throat had turned a deep purple. He told me to open my mouth and lean back. As he looked down my throat, he said, "You're a lucky girl. I understand a man tried to kill you. Nothing's ruptured, but you may want to wear a scarf for a few days." He instructed me to gargle with salt water five or six times a day and informed me my throat was going be too sore and speaking would be difficult. I had to be patient. "For a while," he said, "you'll sound like Lauren Bacall."

A nurse arrived with discharge papers. She repeated that I was incredibly lucky. I balled my hands into fists and covered my face. Lucky? Was it luck that someone tried to kill me? Luck that H.T. was shot? The nurse told me I'd be okay, that I had every right to cry, that I'd endured a terrible experience. I resented her kindness. I couldn't speak and explain my outrage. I showed it by grabbing the clipboard with the unfinished statement and flung it on the floor.

Astonished, the nurse looked at me. "Now, what was that all about?"

# -42-

The Monday after the assault I sat in the police station waiting to sign a final typed copy of my statement, words on a document that spoke of events but said nothing about terror or feelings of being violated. That knowledge comes only from a victim's experience. Early in the aftermath, I was left to wonder if I'd ever again feel safe. I rationalized the encounter on the stairwell, much as I had Jess's attempt at raping me. What was its significance in a world at war, one that raged on and held my brothers at risk? But the more I considered that event and others as well I couldn't trivialize any of them—the rescue at the fire escape, the police raid, Tinkler's shooting H.T., and especially that instant when, seconds away from my last breath, I wanted only to live. I realized that there is no grand scheme because life is always tentative and precious.

Reverend Pitts sat alone at an adjacent desk reading his statement. He signed it and passed it to the detective who thanked him and returned to typing. Reverend Pitts pointed at me and said, "She's the one you should be thanking. She was very brave."

"I hear this Jones fellow killed two people you know of, probably more," Reverend Pitts said. "I might have been the third he'd killed if not for her and the Lord intervening."

The detective stopped typing and said, "Yes, she *was* brave."

I started to say I wasn't, that I'd been terrified, and it was just bad luck it happened and good luck that the preacher came along. What came from my mouth was a feeble effort at talking that sounded like gravel shaken in a tin can.

Reverend Pitts gave me a kind smile and said to the cop, "You got yourselves a bad man off the streets and she was brave, no matter how she protests otherwise."

The detective handed me the typed version of my statement. Without reading it, I signed at the bottom.

Reverend Pitts, asked, "Would you be kind enough to drive us to the hospital."

"Glad to," the young cop said.

The hospital? Us? I thought. The preacher made me uncomfortable, but I did want to get the hat I bought to H.T. It was a stroke of luck that the reverend brought up driving us there.

A few blocks away from the precinct Reverend Pitts asked if I'd mind stopping. He was hungry and knew of a place near the hospital that served strong coffee and hamburgers with fried onions. Tea and French fries seemed more suited for the moment. I tried to say, "Fine with me," but my words came out, "Fi wit me."

The reverend said, "Right. Officer, can we stop at the Bob's Big Boy?"

"Sure can. We're lucky it hasn't been forced to close," the cop said.

"Close?" the preacher said.

"Yep. Hamburger meat's getting scarcer again. I know Bob, the owner. He said he's got to close at least one of his places."

"We're all tired," Reverend Pitts said, "of shortages and rationing and war."

We pulled to a stop in front of the restaurant and the detective opened my door. He pointed to my throat. "You may have to settle for a milkshake."

We took three stools at the counter. The waitress came over with menus. She paused and stared momentarily at my bruised throat but didn't ask what had happened. The cop and Reverend Pitts both ordered burgers and French fries. I pointed to a milkshake.

"Vanilla?"

I shook my head.

She smiled. "Chocolate it is."

The detective and Reverend Pitts talked about the war and left me to my own thoughts for a time. Then the preacher turned to me. "Eve, I hear you have brothers serving overseas. I spend a portion of each day praying for our young men. What are your brothers' names? I'll offer a special prayer for them."

Link's name came out "Ink." Saying the "Hundred and First" took two tries. The one name I said clearly was Richard's. I didn't mention August because I didn't think of him as being in the service. How much at risk was a merchant marine? When I thought of my seagoing brothers, I thought of them as safe from combat.

Reverend Pitts stripped his onion off the top of the burger, slapped mustard on the meat, and held the bun close to his mouth. "Just the way I like it."

I sipped on my milkshake and studied his profile as he chewed. He was a formidable figure of a man who looked younger than his years. Though I'd witnessed his strength at work as he thrashed Cornell, I sensed that he had a gentle side.

I reached over and took one of his fries, then dipped it in catsup.

He said, "Feeling better?"

I swallowed the fry and sipped some water to clear my throat. "You said you were a ruffian?"

He looked at the cop and then back at me. "Yes, well on my way to a prison or worse. Drank and fought and blamed the world for my woes. I didn't know how to blame myself or ask for forgiveness. It's the nature of the beast, Eve." He set the hamburger down and stared thoughtfully as he chewed. He swallowed and said, "No sermon. Let's talk instead."

I wanted to save whatever voice I had. I pointed to my throat and said, "No."

"Okay. I'll talk then," he said. "Do you love that young man?"

The detective politely said, "I have to go to the restroom."

I studied the preacher's face. At the same time, he was studying mine. I thought, he's about to call in the debt. I gave a feeble nod. I realized now what I'd feared in him the first time we'd met. It wasn't his imposing size or his charismatic manner. He was a man who could smell out a person's vulnerability, target it, and make it his strength.

"You understand all the difficulties? We are weak. We succumb to sin. That's why we must. . . ."

I pointed to his clerical collar and shook my head.

"Okay, I'm preaching. Sorry." He took the final bite and cut an eye at me. "You have a fine bruise."

I turned on my stool to face him, took another French fry, and motioned for him to continue.

"Howard's daddy was a bootlegger killed in a dispute. Not an uncommon thing during Prohibition. Howard's mother, a good Christian woman, worked as a housekeeper for Lucien Stillman who developed a fondness for Howard when the boy was an adolescent. I heard he treated him in some ways better than he treated his own son. He made certain Howard studied, provided him with books, and paid for music lessons. Did you know Howard plays the piano?"

"No."

"Lucien bought him his first guitar. I don't know how. . . ." He folded his hands on the counter and stared at them for a moment. "Things come hard."

I started to say something, but a cough took my words.

His eyes narrowed on the ceiling, and he clasped his collar. "I see in H.T. what I was. I failed him. I could've helped if I'd made better choices."

With that, he had my full attention.

"Weak. Weak I was. His mother's a lovely woman. You can't know how. . . . We were young. H.T. turned away from the Lord because he figured out what went on between me and Ruth. He turned to Mr. Stillman, who became his world so to speak. Howard was sixteen when the old man suffered a heart attack. He provided for Howard and Ruth in his will, but Howard dropped out of school, shut out his mama, took his guitar, and went to canteens where he sang and got drunk and fought. Beat a man to death in a fight. That's how he went to prison."

He shook his head and took a deep breath before starting again.

"I was married when Ruth and I. . . . We sinned. I loved her, you see. I broke my sacred vows. My wife left. It was hard on all, and I brought it about. You see now, don't you? He saw it. Hypocrisy. I was the one who showed it to him. That's the history.

"Now something's happening with him. Whatever it is was recumbent. Now it's awakened, his mind and heart opening at the same time. I think it may be you, or Harold."

No, he wants to play guitar, I thought, and sing blues, just that.

The preacher smiled enigmatically as if he could read my mind. "He needs more." He took a last sip from his Coke. "H.T. has a calling, but he won't come to the Lord."

"What's that about Harold?"

"The old man was discharged a day after Howard. The hospital could do nothing more for him. Sent him home to die. He had no relatives. Howard's been with him at his house, cooking for him, bathing him, helping by giving him comfort. If it's you, you should give thought to all the circumstances. Do you understand what I'm saying?"

I leaned close so I would not strain what little voice I had and spoke clearly. "You're a good man, but it's my life and my business and H.T.'s life and his business."

"You're white. All you can do is bring him down. I'm giving you good advice. Pay heed, young woman."

I picked up a fry from his plate, dipped it in catsup and suspended it for a moment before I dropped it back on the plate. I grabbed my purse and slid off the stool. "It was your sin not mine," I managed to say in a voice surprisingly strong. "You had no business telling me about it. You saved my life and I'm grateful, but I don't owe you. And no, it's not me. You're right, H.T. has a calling."

As I neared the door, the cop returned and asked, "Where's she going?"

The preacher said, "In the wrong direction. Like too many do."

Instead of going to the hospital that day, I caught a streetcar to San Pedro.

# -43-

I SAT IN THE WAITING area watching the elevator while talking to a nurse on duty. When the door finally opened, H.T., guitar case slung over his shoulder, stepped out. He walked over. The nurse I'd been talking to said, "I told you he'd be coming." She excused herself and went to her station at the desk. H.T. took the guitar off his shoulder and sat with it propped between his knees.

"I heard all about it." He looked at my throat. "Does it hurt much?"

I studied his face, thinner now. "Probably not as bad as a bullet."

He grinned. "I talked with the detectives. Cornell ain't getting bail."

I took his hand and squeeze it. He didn't respond. I looked into his eyes and struggling to come up with conversation, said, "The men you knew are gone from the ward."

"I know." He tapped the guitar case with his free hand. "I played some for the new ones."

I let go of his hand. "I guess you're taking care of Harold now?"

"With Mama's help."

"I came to see if the patients need help with letters or anything the girls or I can bring them. And to give you this."

I pulled the box containing his hat out from under the bench. For the moment I kept my real purpose for being there unsaid.

"What's this?"

"A Christmas present. They kept it here at the hospital for me. I wanted to but didn't wrap it. Go ahead, open it."

He opened it and eased the fedora out, held it at arm's length, then put it on.

"I wanted to talk to you," I said. "But you'll be coming back to work soon. It can wait."

"Won't come back until Harold . . . until he passes. Then I don't know." He frowned. "I never should'a taken you to Pork Skins. Nothin' but bad came from it."

Yes, he'd nearly died because of me, and I could have died in part because of him, but I wasn't there to revisit all that mess. "I've accepted all that you and I . . . that . . . forget it. You had good intentions. Well, it's nice to see you, but I know you came to sing to the patients, and, besides, I can't stay long."

He tilted the hat and posed for me. "You didn't have to do this, but it's nice you did."

Hearing him call the present "nice" needled me. "It wasn't nice, H.T. It was thoughtful."

"You *were* lucky the night that crazy man started shooting. Could've been you and not me." That said, he stood and leaned against the hallway wall and held the hat admiring it.

"Maybe. I don't think it was luck. I think he aimed at you intentionally."

He sneered. "If you weren't lucky, maybe you were blessed."

"You sound like your preacher." His eyes seemed rid of the ghosts that I once thought resided in him.

He touched his own throat with the back of his hand. "It must hurt."

"Not really."

"Okay, then. You know Harold's close to leaving this hard life. Crazy as it sounds, I'm going to miss what I had in the ward when I was bed bound with him and those boys. Just like I never had a father, I didn't have brothers. They were as close as I ever came to family."

"Is that why you're caring for Harold?"

"Day we took him home, he told me more than I wanted to know about him, but he'd need to say it. He's got no family. Parents both died. He never married. Had no children. Made me realize we all got a hard road. It wasn't much good for me to go on feeling sorry for myself. I did a lotta that over the years. I should be with him right now, but he insisted I come and sing for the patients. Mama's there now fillin' in. Me singing here was his idea, but it's a good idea."

In one last effort to rekindle what was between us that moment when we stood in an embrace by the fishpond, I took his hand in both of mine. "The real reason I came wasn't the hat or to visit the ward and write letters. I came to see you and find out. You know—if."

I pressed my lips to his fingers. His expression sad, he looked at me, slowly withdrew his hand, and took a deep breath. A nurse walking in our direction waved. H.T. said hello as she neared. She excused herself for interrupting and asked if he'd be singing in the cafeteria.

"Yes, ma'am," he said.

When she stepped away, I said, "I have to go. I need rest before I go to work tomorrow, and *you*? You need to go sing in the cafeteria." Even as I said it, I knew I sounded callous, but I had found what I'd come here for. We'd lost any chance of reviving what seemed possible between us the moment before the gunshots rang out.

I turned my back to him and walked to the door leading

to the staircase. Prepared to face the dreaded stairwell, I looked back and waved goodbye, then I opened the door and planted a toe inside. I slowly walked down the dimly lit stairs to the landing. As I did, I whistled a lame version of "Amazing Grace." This time, though I had reason to, I didn't shed a single tear.

# -44-

While Los Angeles enjoyed mild weather two days before Christmas, the Rhine was freezing, winter snows blanketed the ground, and Americans were engaged with German divisions that had mounted an all-out effort to halt the Allied advance into the Fatherland. News of the battle was sketchy and cast a shadow over the otherwise festive atmosphere in the bootery, especially over me because Link's unit was bearing the brunt of the assault at a place called Bastogne.

Selmo shut down the factory at noon. The holiday party began. I sat alone with a plate of turkey and dressing balanced on my knees. Dominique, a glass of bourbon and soda in hand, threaded her way through the gathering and took a seat beside me.

"Nice party," she said. "Never a dull moment." She handed her drink to me. "Here, it'll do you good."

"Thanks." I took a drink. The bourbon burned on the way down but settled comfortably in my stomach. "What I wouldn't give for a dull moment."

"I warned you about him."

"It's not like you made great choices with men."

She ran her tongue over her lips. "Cruel, but true. You ready to talk about what happened at the hospital?"

"No." I took another sip.

"If you're going to drink it all, I'll go get another."

Out of the corner of my eye I saw Doreen walking toward us. "Oh, no. I'm not ready for this." I finished the drink and handed the glass back.

"Be brave," Dominique said. By then I'd told her all about Doreen's interest in me. She said hello to Doreen and looked at her glass. "Empty. Guess I'll get a fresh one."

"Did anyone ever tell you how much you look like Jean Harlow?" Doreen asked.

Dominique shrugged. "You're the first."

I turned away to stifle a laugh.

"Well, you certainly look like her."

Dominique excused herself.

Doreen took Dominique's seat. "I hoped to catch you. I was wondering if we might talk."

For weeks I'd managed to avoid a string of similar invitations, mostly using hospital visits as an excuse. Now, faced with the inevitable, I said, "Sure. Talk."

"You've had a trying month, Eve. Actually, more."

"Yes."

She said the war had left everyone confused, was difficult for everyone, and we often made hasty decisions. I let her talk without interrupting, waiting for the subject of bearing a child for them to come up.

"May I be blunt?"

"How blunt?"

"Blunt. Are you sleeping with H.T.?"

I looked in the direction of the table where Dominique was pouring a drink. I wanted her to come to my rescue. "You don't mean sleeping, do you?"

"Are you having intimate relations with him? Sex?"

I winced, then looked her in the eyes. "Wouldn't that be my business?"

"I told Selmo this might be the case. I said that you were too naive, that. . . ."

"I'm not sleeping with him. Or being *intimate*, but not because I wouldn't. And I'm not naive."

What I said set her back, but she cloaked her reaction with a smile. "I was wrong to pry, but I think of you as a sister. I do. I really do. What a terrible thing that shooting was! H.T.'s like family. We think the world of him. Selmo depends on him for many things, and his mother nursed Lucien up to the day he died."

"I've heard," I said.

Doreen looked confused. "His mother's Christian, goes to church all the time."

"He might give up work to play his music?"

"That's just a hobby."

"So, he's coming back to work?"

"Certainly, he is," she said confidently. "What else could he do? Would you like to come to our house for Christmas? None of my cousins will be there."

We were both distracted by Selmo who hurried down the steps. "Sorry to interrupt." he said. "Eve, someone's in the office to see you."

I thought, please, not the police again. "Who?"

"Someone with a message. I'll go with you."

Doreen started to stand, but Selmo motioned to her to stay. We walked up to the front of his office where I looked through the window. A teenage boy with a Western Union hat sat on a leather couch under the portrait of Lucien Stillman. A terrible dread engulfed me.

Selmo opened the door for me. "I'll wait here."

My heart racing, I entered.

The messenger stood and removed his hat. "Miss Eve Halvers?"

Link, I thought. "Yes."

"Telegram. Sign for it, please." He held up a pencil and a pad. "There on the line."

I wanted to refuse, run out of the room. Do anything to avoid what seemed certain. My fingers shaking, I took the pencil, signed on the line, and received the telegram. It was from my sister Helen. The messenger hesitated at the door, then wished me a good afternoon. The door closed. I ripped open the seal, read the telegram, and slumped down on the couch.

I chewed at my lipstick as I pictured Link and August, fifteen and twelve, in Mr. Sorenson's field, their wild blonde hair blowing in a breeze as they tossed hay bales onto a flatbed trailer. Whatever money the boys were paid, they brought home to the penny for Mom. They worked for less wages than other farmhands because Mr. Sorenson gave them smoked hams and bags of flour that helped sustain us through the winter.

The door opened. Selmo peered in. "Are you okay?"

I pointed to the telegram and shook my head.

"Anything I can do?"

"No."

I let the telegram slip from my fingers. Selmo crossed the room and picked it up.

He sat beside me. "May I read it?"

"I expected it to be about Link."

He read it and said, "I'm terribly sorry."

"We thought August was safe. He was named August Olaf, after my grandfather. His ship was torpedoed. There won't even be a body."

Vanished, I thought. Lost. Older than I was by two years, he lied about his age to join the Merchant Marines after Pearl Harbor was attacked. A playful, sometimes serious boy, the boy who walked me to church, who'd been my guide and protector in grammar school, who'd broken up my fights and scolded me to be a lady for our mother's sake. In the winter, alongside Richard, he'd followed Link down the railroad tracks, the three of them gathering up scraps of coal.

"I'll make arrangements for you to go home." He tucked the telegram into my hands.

I stared at it, then slowly closed my fingers over it, and wadded it up.

"Here."

Selmo gave me his handkerchief. I took it, but I didn't cry.

He walked to his desk, picked up the phone and asked the operator to ring the Union Pacific Railroad terminal.

Dominique peered through the office window. He motioned her in and pointed to the couch where I clutched the handkerchief and the wadded telegram in my trembling hands. She tried to hold me, but I squirmed away and stood with my back against the wall.

"Why?" I asked. Though it had no answer, it was the only question left to ask.

When Dominique again reached for me, I went limp in her arms.

"Go ahead, cry," she said.

I shook my head.

# -45-

After the service, Helen and her husband went home to Walla Walla. For the first time since my return, I was alone with Mother. I sat across the table from her as wood crackled in the iron stove. She'd cried briefly at the service when a petty officer dressed in Navy blues laid the folded American flag in her lap. I looked at the vacant chair at the head of the table, the place setting laid out as always for my father. Her long-braided hair was a steel gray now, and her skin a parchment yellow. I looked at her hands, gnarled from hard work and incipient arthritis. I didn't see the mother who once terrified me, but a woman ashen and worn. I wondered if it was age or grief that had taken a toll on her and decided it was both.

"Mother, would you like me to cook something?"

She kept watch on the stove as if it were the center of all truth. "If you're hungry."

"That's not what I asked."

She looked past me. "Fine."

I went to the icebox. Though the house now had electricity, mother had neither refrigerator nor indoor plumbing nor any method of heating the house save for the wood-burning stove and the stone fireplace in the living room. I stared at the icebox's meager contents—two eggs left from those I'd gathered in the morning, a quart of milk, a potato, a half loaf of bread, butter, and a tin of lard. No vegetables. No meat.

"There's no food. Mother, what have you been doing with the money we've sent you?"

"Don't lean on the door. I had that fixed last month. It's expensive to get anything fixed now. No one has the time. It's not like it was during the Depression when no one had anything and were happy to do a little chore for a few fresh eggs. The boys kept food on the table that way, didn't they? Oh, Lord. If Link were here, he'd fix it. No questions asked."

"I asked a question."

"What was that?"

"Mother, don't play dumb."

"I'm saving it for you and the boys."

"Mother, it's for you. You need food."

"I get by just fine."

We stared at one another for a moment. I took out the eggs, butter, lard, potato, and bread, retrieved an eggbeater from the knife drawer and a bowl from the pantry.

"I'm hungry, Eve. I am, but I'm used to it. It's been. . . ." She closed her eyes and sighed. "How am I going to . . .? What's it going to be like with no August? He was a good boy."

Yes, a good boy, I thought and recalled the summer before he joined the Merchant Marines, shirtless and tan, as he bucked hay for Mr. Sorenson. On the train home, surrounded by able-bodied soldiers and sailors on their way to and from war, I'd thought about the men in the ward, amputees returning to uncertain circumstances, the stares they drew, whispered comments, pity. But that was better than death. Wouldn't August give up a leg or an arm to have a life?

"Yes, he was, always," I said. "You should use the money, Mother."

"I asked him to stay, you know. I said our stock came

from farmers not sailors. We need dirt under our feet. He had no business going to sea."

For a time after that exchange the only sound came from my cooking. Mother paid me no mind. She stared at the photographs of her children that hung on the far wall. I hoped I would never carry a burden like hers. I wanted to comfort her, to cross the room and hold her, but we were not a family that let affections flow easily and I didn't see a welcome path to her.

I tapped the pan with the spatula. She looked up. "Do you have syrup and nutmeg, Mother?"

"Molasses and cinnamon." She seemed alert for the first time since I arrived. "You're making French toast, Eve?"

"Yours is best. I'll try, though."

"What happened with that Negro?"

I broke the eggs in the bowl, poured in the milk, sprinkled cinnamon over the top, and began beating the mix. "His name's H.T."

"That's not a name."

"Howard Thomas Elders," I said. "And I'm not sure what happened."

I wanted more than anything not to think about Los Angeles, my friends, or the shooting that changed events, and especially H.T. Mother needed me, needed my attention. That was what I must concentrate on. Her question took my thoughts to the shooting, to the preacher and Cornell in the stairwell, matters I could never discuss with her.

"What would your brothers say?"

"Don't, Mother. Let it sleep." I whipped the eggs and milk.

"Oh, Eve. Judith gone. Now August dead. What's next?"

We picked at our plates and ate in silence. I didn't need conversation to know what was on her mind. She was worried about Link and Richard. Then her eyes strayed to the empty plate and the vacant seat filled with the ghost of my father. Her lips quivered.

"Are you okay?" I asked.

"He's in Placerville," she said. "I found out from Adel Suggs. Helen sent a telegram to the address. He didn't. . . . He didn't even respond to hearing our babies are dead, my twins. Judith, now August. He probably didn't care. I suppose I deserve this. Maybe your father didn't desert me. Maybe I drove him away and it's God's punishment. Who am I to question God?"

I recalled something Gretchen once casually tossed out as we walked around the park in Los Angeles. "Mom, He's not punishing you and it's not a test. It's life."

"I read my scriptures. All things come from Him."

"Mom, why would God single you out to punish with all that's going on in the world?"

She looked at me, her face drawn and tired. "I can't answer that."

"Okay. Answer this: What if it had been a woman named Rebecca who parted the Red Sea and led her people out of Egypt?"

"What? That's crazy."

"Think, Mom, how that would change how we see ourselves? I mean, as women?"

"We?"

"Women, Mom. What if men weren't the center of our lives?"

"I don't know what you're getting at."

I didn't know either up to then, but it suddenly came together. "We've been brainwashed, Mom. What if the Bible had said that Adam offered the Forbidden Fruit to Eve instead of the way it was given to us in the Book? What if Eve had given up a rib to make her mate? Men wrote the book, Mom, and they lay blame on Eve so that women would appear weak and. . . ."

"Stop it," she shouted. "That's blasphemy."

"What if we quit blaming ourselves? Wouldn't that free us?"

She clasped her hands over her ears and slumped to the floor. I slid my chair back and went to her. I kneeled before her and took her in my arms. We rocked back and forth. She'd always been strong, her strength coming in part from her Scandinavian stubbornness. Though it was too often expressed in mean-spirited ways, my seeing her weakened like this cut through me almost as deeply as the loss of August. When her tears slowed, I wiped her eyes with a napkin.

I helped her to her feet and returned to my seat, where I picked up my fork and motioned for her to do likewise.

Later I heated the water and filled the bucket with dirty dishes. Mother remained in her chair, outwardly calm. As I sank my hands in the hot water, she went to the head of the table and gathered up the unused setting she'd maintained there for years. She stacked the flatware on top of the plate along with the water glass and carried them to the sink.

"Wouldn't know what to say to him if he showed up," she said. "Maybe that he'd come to the wrong house." She kissed my cheek. "I'm going to turn on the radio. I'd like some company. Maybe you're right."

I watched her lumber into the living room. A terrible thing, I thought, a woman alone at her age, but then I realized that most women her age were alone, and it seemed that was the inevitable fate for most women and had been for too long. There had to be more than widowhood awaiting us. Gretchen was right. We'd earned more—no, deserved all that had been denied us.

I joined Mother and we listened to the radio for news of Allied advance as if at any moment the broadcast would tell us Link was alive. Along with a brother, I'd lost any enthusiasm for war news. I had two more brothers at risk and I wanted them safe. The fact was that even the best news from the front lines wouldn't restore life to August or all the brothers and sons lost since Pearl Harbor. When all of this comes to an end, I thought, we women must save coming generations from more slaughter and assert the independence that we, ourselves, were gaining. I didn't want to face another telegram.

"Mother, what would you think if I said I want to go to college when the war's over?"

"What? What brought that about? What do you intend to do with a degree?"

I didn't dare tell her I wanted to write. "Maybe become president."

She smiled, and in that smile, I saw a casting aside of the grief that long haunted her eyes.

# -46-

THE OTHERS HAD PAID THEIR respects and were gone. I stood beside Avis at the cross that marked the grave that wasn't a grave because my brother's body was somewhere in the depths of the Pacific. The two of us at last alone on the family burial plot, my friend took my hand and leaned into me. We'd toughened out a day of hearing condolences from neighbors and townspeople whose next words were about the wind and cold or about Mr. Newsome's stroke or Jess Newsome's engagement to Holly Rice. I'd not cried at the service we held for August's death.

Avis took my hand and squeezed it. "Eve, you know what we always said, that angels don't cry?"

"Yes."

"Well, we were wrong. This is where angels cry."

I looked at her face. Tears flowed from her eyes. I joined her. The tears I shed weren't just tears of sorrow but of acceptance. I understood too well now the hardness life can cast upon us. I thought of my sister lying in the grave next to August's cross, her life gone at such a young age. Then I thought of my other brothers, still at risk in the war, and pictured the young men in the ward who'd lost their limbs but not their spirit. Last, I thought of H.T. off now pursuing his music. Tears allow us, I understood, to accept. Tears make us tougher for the next of the hard blows life lays on us.

I let go of Avis's hand and pulled her closer to me. "Yes, Avis, this is where angels cry."

When the tears finally subsided, I walked Avis to her truck and went to my room to lie down. I looked about the room I'd shared with Judith, and Helen until she married. In the edge of the frame on the dresser mirror was a yellowing snapshot of us children, three girls, three boys, all born in a span of eleven years. At the time it was taken I was three; all of us blonde but Judith. We may have been poor, but the deprivation we shared strengthened us and we faced the world unhumbled by our circumstances. Now we were only four, and none among us lived where our roots lay. My grandfather's toe was buried in a field now farmed by Mr. Newsome. The story of my family lived in the walls of this house and that was a story of childhood deprivation and joy. I knew as I looked at the picture I would leave here and build a life. I knew also that my heart would never leave that past we shared.

I walked to the window and looked out at the rolling land that contained some of the richest and deepest topsoil on the continent. The dark earth was blanketed with winter stubble, and the cold had stripped the recumbent fields of color save for a flat ochre. I'd seen this through the seasons as I grew up. My brothers had sweated in those fields. My father had lost all but this house and a few acres to unpaid taxes. I gazed down at the potato patch, the chicken coop, and the outhouse. All of what I saw was too familiar, too filled with memories.

Helen had indicated I should stay and live with Mother to watch over her, and though she'd never said as much, I knew my mother wanted me to stay. The signals were obvious.

She'd not replaced the dinnerware for my father at the head of the table. I saw the road that paralleled the river and cut westward through dormant wheat fields. Nearly three years before I'd walked that road, devastated. I knew one absolute truth: The rich basin could give life to anything, but my living in it would stifle and embitter me. Los Angeles was where I needed to be and where my friends were. I'd started something there and the war wasn't over. I tossed my suitcase on the bed and began packing. I felt better as I stuffed clothes in the suitcase. I left a change of clothes out, then removed the snapshot of us as children from the mirror and tucked it into a pocket in the suitcase.

I snapped the locks, tightened the belt around the suitcase, and then went next door to Mr. Wooligan's to use his phone to check the train schedule.

The sun came at a blinding angle from the south, and although it was cold, it was working weather for farmers. The sky had threatened foul weather, but it had not stormed for several days, and the road was dry and hard packed. The old Dodge pickup bounded over the rutted top and tossed me around. Avis gripped the wheel and looked ahead. I could see the strain in her face.

"It'll be fine," I said.

"I don't know."

As we rounded the top of the last incline and headed downhill, she pulled to the side of the road and took a pint bottle of cheap bourbon from the glove compartment. She took a drink and offered the bottle to me.

"We're still too young for this," I said.

"Yeah. Well, aren't we the scofflaws?"

I said, "I got drunk once," uncapped the bottle of cheap bourbon and took a deep swallow.

"Tell me, is L.A. the Emerald City?" she asked.

More, much more, I thought. "Not exactly. It's the land of the famous. Go to the right restaurant at the right time, you can see movie stars. You can dream big dreams, dream of being rich. Or if you're half wise, you can find yourself." As I spoke, I understood that I was speaking for the girls in my crew and the women and men who rode the ferries to Terminal Island.

"I hoped you'd say something like that and you'd know you belong here with us."

"Avis, I'm going to apply to universities. The war should be over soon. Go with me."

"I can't."

"Why not?"

"Because I'm going to marry Link."

"No."

"Yes. He asked me in his last letter. I said yes in my letter. I didn't tell you before because of what happened to August and your family being here and all. I've always loved him. Are you happy for me?"

"I am. Congratulations." I took another drink from the bottle and handed it to her.

"Are you really going to college?"

"Yes. I'll figure it all out. I don't need Adam's rib to come to life."

"What does that mean?"

"It means let's get on the road."

"You're crazy."

I suddenly felt wise, a woman ready for the rest of life to start.

# -47-

A TREMENDOUS AMOUNT OF WAR machinery and men were still heading to coastal ports of Oakland, San Diego, and Los Angeles. The depots where I switched trains were packed and noisy, soldiers and civilians alike hunkered down on benches waiting for passage. I wondered where all the young men—many still boys—came from. Did we have an endless supply? How many millions of Augusts and Links and Richards were left to feed to the German and Japanese war machines before victory? And victory at what price? A life here. An arm or a leg there. How many boys who'd found my notes in their boots were dead, and how many more would die? I began to wonder if it were as Mitzi once said, referring to the men? Did they love war?

In Portland, I spent most of one day watching trains pull out. I remembered that Maxwell hailed from someplace nearby and wished I had his phone number so I could call his parents and tell them what fine young men he and his friend Simon were. A soldier said that if I needed some company, the book he just finished would occupy me. He gave me a copy of *Forever Amber*. I opened it and began reading.

Across the aisle two women exchanged news about the war. It seemed the army had landed on Luzon in the Philippines and pushed the Japanese inland. I tried not to listen, but then she spoke of atrocities committed by Japanese on Americans in Bataan and how our soldiers were determined to avenge Americans killed in the Death March. The second woman, perhaps in her late fifties, nodded agreeably with everything the other said.

When the first one excused herself to leave, the older woman said, "Scandalous. Trash."

I thought she was talking about me. "Excuse me?"

She pointed to the book. "That novel. I couldn't put it down."

I missed my connection in Sacramento. The woman was right—the book was scandalous. I loved it. For a few hours I forgot H.T., my brothers, the war, and Mother. Somewhere near the end of the book, I experienced a remarkable hope that the novel in its way spoke of an impending liberation. Ahead might lie a loosening of the binds that held my generation chained to outdated conventions. I finished the book, passed it on to a sailor, and catnapped on a bench until called to board my train.

The train was less crowded than the previous ones. I stretched my legs and looked out the window. When the train got under way, I opened the bag of apples and bread Avis had given me and ate a slice of sourdough. I polished the last apple on my sleeve and ate it as I watched the drifting landscape of ribbon-like orchards, fallowed grazing land, and near-barren oak trees. I realized two things, the first being that I would tell Doreen that the war would likely leave thousands of children parentless, that she should adopt one because my womb belonged to me, and I would decide when I would have a child and with whom I'd have that child—if I ever chose to. The second thing that occurred to me was that I'd turned twenty on the trip.

# -48-

After my return, I kept my commitment to the bootery and the men in the hospital. Twice a week I'd climb the staircase and, with pen and stationery in my purse, I'd visit the wards. In time I found myself not just writing words as they dictated, but composing words for them. One patient, a kid from Tacoma named Glen Harris, whose right arm had been amputated, had little problem dictating for his parents' letter, but stumbled during the letter- to his fiancée. He stopped, looked at me, and said, "Finish it for me." I looked at his gray eyes, seemingly lost in memories, and began writing.

When I set my pen down, he said, "Read it to me."

I cleared my throat and began, "I'm coming soon. I have but one arm now to hold you, but I'll use it gently to pull you close, and when I feel your heart beating along with mine, I'll feel I'm whole, and I'll know I'm home."

He turned his head away.

I whispered the closing, "Love forever, Glen," and took a tissue from the bedside stand. I gently closed his one hand around it, gathered up my papers, then sealed the letter in its envelope, and placed it beside him. There were other wards and other men who needed a scribe.

August 15, 1945, the week after Cornell Jones's conviction

for first-degree murder and attempted murder, it was hot and humid. I'd been privileged to sit in the witness stand and tell a jury what I'd seen and experienced nearly a year before. Now that and the war were both behind me. The women were sweating when Selmo came and stepped onto the factory floor, shut down the conveyor belts, and dragged his milk box to the center of the room.

We sat hushed. Production had already been reduced by half and layoff slips with termination pay and bonus checks passed out to a few workers. Those gathered now sensed that today something else was in store. Days before, a bomb, the likes of which we'd never imagined, had been dropped on Japan. That was followed by another one, equally devastating. News of the damage was vague, but the effects had spurred optimism in a nation exhausted from war.

Selmo stood, his shoulders back, and faced us. "The Emperor of Japan has signed the documents of surrender. Japan has collapsed. Our boys are coming home."

The room burst into shouts and applause. We cried out of joy, hugged, and held hands. A few women formed a circle around Selmo and danced. Dominique and I held one another and swayed back and forth.

She said, "He'll be coming back," referring to Maxwell who'd been promoted and sent to the South Pacific a few months before. "God, what will I do?"

"You'll give him a great homecoming, but please, not on the couch," I said.

"I can't believe you said that." She smiled. "You've grown up. Yes, you have."

"You know we'll all be losing our jobs."

"So what? Bring on that big Marine. But don't let me take chances."

"That's right. You've got a son to think about."

Mitzi, Tiff, and Gretchen gathered with us. We took turns hugging one another. The last time we'd all embraced was in April when Selmo stopped the conveyors to tell us Roosevelt had died. Then we hugged in sorrow. Now it was with a sense of relief and delight. When the initial joy waned, the five of us caught our breath and looked at one another.

Tiff leaned against the motionless conveyor and sighed. "Let's go to Tasco's and celebrate with our longshoremen." She looked at Gretchen. "And longshore women."

"The word is stevedores," Gretchen said. "That takes care of the sex issue."

We agreed it was a great idea and turned to leave, but Mitzi said, "Wait, we're still working technically."

"Let me handle that." Undaunted, Gretchen walked to Selmo's milk crate and stood atop it. "May I have your attention," she shouted and repeated herself three times before the room settled to a manageable range of noise. She pointed to Selmo and said, "I think we should thank our boss for giving us the rest of the day off to celebrate Victory over Japan Day."

He looked up at her, then at us, and grinned.

We cheered.

Gretchen, rarely ever exuberant, jumped onto the floor and hurried back to us. She slapped me on the shoulder and proudly announced, "I made it an official holiday."

As we punched out, I told the others I would meet them later. Mitzi asked why.

I answered cryptically, "I have something to do."

"Like what?" Mitzi demanded.

Gretchen took Mitzi's arm and said, "Let's go before the stevedores drink the bar dry."

Dominique asked. "You okay?"

"I'm fine." She raised her eyebrows and I added, "Really," and nudged her on her way.

I'd not been to the third floor since the day that had become company lore. As I neared the window to the fire escape, a peculiar feeling crept over me. I looked around to assure myself I was alone, then I opened the window. The view was the same—the harbor, the alley with trash cans filled, the distant islands. As I had on the stairwell in the hospital, I had to face this dread. I lifted my leg over the sill and eased myself onto the platform. I rested my back against the brick wall, held the rail, and looked down. I wasn't as frightened as I thought I might be. I filled my lungs with harbor air and entered the past.

I recalled H.T. playing music below us in what seemed an infinite time ago. I knew I would be leaving, not just Lucien's but my friends and Los Angeles and sooner than I cared to. I learned much from writing letters for soldiers and sailors in the hospital and at the USO, in no small part about them. But I'd also learned that the act of writing stirred a dormant passion in me for words on the page. I took out my notebook and pencil, my constant companions, and began describing the harbor, not just it, but what it meant to me and my friends.

A few minutes into writing, I heard, "This is off limits."

Selmo's voice jolted me for an instant. I gathered my wits and turned to him. "If you wanted to scare me, you managed it very well."

He climbed onto the fire escape, stood beside me, and leaned onto the rail.

"I came up probably for the same reason," he said.

"Which is?"

"You know."

He took his glasses off, wiped the lenses on his shirt sleeve, and looked off. In the distance two merchant ships took on ballast. I looked at the back of his pale hand clutching the black rail. I couldn't resist taking hold of it and squeezing it.

"Tell me why you came up here," I said. "You don't have to be embarrassed."

"I felt," he said without looking at me, "that day I wasn't just some little man pretending to be important. I was needed. So were you and H.T. He was, well, magnificent. Funny, I was jealous of him until that day we came to help up here. It seems silly boy stuff now, that jealousy. See, he was athletic, and I wasn't."

I let go of his hand. "You were too."

"I want you to know that I did nothing to intervene between you two. That he. . . ."

"Don't," I said. "It's all for the best."

He gripped the rail and looked down. "I'm scared to death of heights." He took a deep breath, let go of the railing, and relaxed his arms. "What are you writing?"

I handed him the open notebook. He read one page, then flipped through others until he stopped at one. He read in silence, then began reading aloud. "'He mounted the stage, nearly stumbling as he did. He limped to the stool in the center, swung the guitar off his shoulder, and sat. Closed-eyed, he played a series of chords and seemed afloat as he swayed on the stool. A man in the audience hollered, "Hell, man. Can a damn fool cripple even sing the blues?" The singer looked off, strummed the guitar as if listening for a flaw, then looked out at the audience. 'A damn fool cripple can't sing nothin' but the blues.' He began his song."

He handed me the notebook. "It's good. You need to finish it."

"I was trying to write a story, but it stopped on me. It's fiction."

Selmo considered that a moment and handed me my notebook.

"When I was thirteen," he said, "and H.T. was eight or

nine my father slapped me because he heard me call H.T. a name. Instead of blaming myself for that slap, I blamed H.T. Even after my father died, I held it against H.T. Then at eighteen he killed a man defending himself in a blues bar. He just wanted to stop the man from hitting him. I failed him when he needed me."

"You don't have to tell me this."

"I have to tell someone. Doreen doesn't listen to me, and from what I just read, you have a story to finish."

"I'm sorry."

"About Doreen? Don't be. I picked her. I'm an immigrant's son. She was, I don't know, the swan. We see them on the water and they're beautiful. On land, they can be vicious. Still, my happiness is wrapped up in her and I want to be as special to her as she is to me. But I'm not."

A tugboat blared its horn as it turned toward the bay. We watched its stern sink into the water and stir foam. As the tugboat headed out, Selmo sighed.

"I didn't get him an attorney after the fight. I was ashamed of myself for not helping. I imagined my father scolding me from heaven. When three other convicts cut him and broke H.T.'s leg, I saw it as my chance. I wanted him to be grateful, to be in my debt. I paid an attorney to file an appeal."

He pondered what he'd said momentarily. "I live part of life as a lie. Maybe we all do. Truth is the good things H.T. did for me weren't because I helped. It was his own character. I was cruel to him when he was younger, told him to go find his own father and leave mine alone."

"You should put that about you and him aside," I said. "What I know is you were kind to me when I arrived here a stranger and the day this fire escape collapsed you were brave."

He grinned and pointed to the bay. "Out there. All that life. The world back to normal."

We stood in silence looking off for a time. A stream of smoke blew from the stack of a tanker far out. I stared across the channel but saw only a bare tip of land where Catalina rose.

He said, "Eve, we have one last order to fill. The Department of the Navy sent me a letter a month ago. I hate to, but I'll have to cut back. I'd like you to stay."

"We all expected it to end. Did you hear from your friend Kenji?"

"You remembered? Yes, despite being wounded twice, he's still in Europe. His unit freed a concentration camp. Seeing it sickened him and reminded him of his family being interred at the camp in Owens Valley. 'Jews shrunken from malnutrition,' he wrote, 'to sinew but without sinew.' Some could barely stand. Others couldn't hold down food. The world let it happen."

"Who knew?"

"People must have. I guess there's a lesson. Hate's out there waiting to find power and Jews aren't the only target. Maybe that's why I wanted to talk about H.T.; to say I could've done better for him."

"He said something similar about hate. Now he just wants to sing and write music and you can't make that happen for him."

"He wrote me a letter. He's picking cotton. Imagine that. If he needed work, all he had to do is come back."

I thought for a moment. H.T. had been enigmatic in ways, but I understood him well enough to be confident in saying, "He's not picking cotton. He's singing and writing songs. That's his metaphor for his music." Under my breath I muttered, "You found it, H.T."

"Did you know he could play the piano?"

"Yes, the preacher told me that once."

We watched the boats in the harbor a few more minutes before I said, "I've got to go. You're welcome to join us at Tasco's. The ladies will like that."

"If it's all the same, I'd rather watch the bay for a while. You know your jobs here depended on the government contract. You should finish that story. What do you intend to do?"

"I've applied to three universities and two state colleges."

He rubbed his forehead. "And do what?"

"Find where the wheat grows the best."

He wrinkled his brow. "What's that?"

"Nothing, Selmo. Thanks for . . . everything. I hope you convince Doreen to adopt."

I climbed inside and peered back through the window. His back to me, he held his glasses at his side and gazed off. His shoulders trembled. I couldn't be certain if he was crying or laughing. He had reason to do both, just as we all did. Having put one more fear behind me, I turned away and with a renewed sense of confidence walked into my future.

